C000135968

DEATH'S AVENGER

THE MALYKANT MYSTERIES

VOLUME 2

CHARLOTTE E. ENGLISH

Copyright © 2018 Charlotte E. English

All rights reserved.

ISBN: 9789492824059

CONTENTS

THE CORPSE THIEVES 1

THE SPIRIT OF SOLSTICE 95

THE HOUSE AT DIVORO 189

SNOWBOUND 291

THE CORPSE THIEVES

1

Master, said Ootapi one rainy afternoon. *You have been too long idle, and it sours your temper. You require an occupation.*

'Quite,' said Konrad, with a curl of his lip. 'Not nearly enough people are being murdered. It is highly inconvenient of everybody to keep breathing in this detestably *ceaseless* fashion.'

Eetapi drifted closer, her chill, incorporeal presence causing the hairs on the back of Konrad's neck to rise. Her voice whispered in his mind, in the mournful tones of funeral bells: *Shall I kill someone for you, Master?*

Konrad closed his newspaper with a snap. 'A commendable thought, dear serpent, but you overlook one or two important details. *One* being that, if I am informed ahead of time as to the identity of the culprit, the search will not occupy me for very long. *Two,* since you are possessed of neither a body nor, strictly speaking, a soul, my customary response to the crime would not be required. I am afraid the idea, meritorious as it is, will not suit our purposes today.'

Eetapi vibrated with disappointment and slunk away, coiling her ethereal serpentine body into a sulky spiral in the corner of the study. To Konrad's annoyance, he experienced a flicker of guilt.

Ootapi was in no hurry to relinquish the idea. *I will hire someone,* he decided.

'Excellent thought,' Konrad agreed.

Without telling you, Ootapi added.

'Alas, it is too late for that.'

Ootapi lapsed into silent thought, an interlude which Konrad spent in looking out of the window. The sky was full of the brooding, murderous type of clouds which threatened a dramatic flourish of snow every moment, yet succeeded in producing only a feeble drizzle of rain. The conditions reflected Konrad's mood and predicament nicely, for not only was he insufficiently productive, he felt as grey as a winter morn and twice as cold at heart.

Who would you like to die? Ootapi queried.

Konrad's lips quirked. 'Oh, who hasn't wished a speedy and painless demise upon one's fellow creatures, at one point or another? Sometimes without the *painless* part, even.' His thoughts flitted to Danil Dubin, the acknowledged admirer of his closest friend, Irinanda Falenia. The young man was harmless, for all his occupation as a trader of poisons. Mild-mannered, rather meek, a little on the feeble side. Why he should irritate Konrad so much remained firmly in question, but nonetheless: if anybody of his acquaintance were to meet a swift and untimely death, it had better be Mr. Dubin.

So lost was he in these pleasant, if guilty, reflections, it took him some time to notice that Ootapi had fallen silent, and offered no further enquiries. So uncharacteristic was this of his servant's usual persistence that he was bemused, and for a moment, concerned. Had he uttered his shameful wishes aloud?

'Ootapi?' he called.

Yes, Master.

It was inconvenient, sometimes, having invisible ghosts for assistants. 'Do not kill anyone on my behalf, if you please.'

Yes, Master.

'I think you mean *No, Master.*'

No, Master.

Was that, though, a double negative? Did they cancel each other out, and result at last in a positive? Konrad grappled with the problem for thirty seconds, and then abandoned the question in exasperation.

'You are right, serpents. I need an occupation. Perhaps I will take up a hobby.'

Ice fishing, suggested Ootapi.

'Too cold. And dull.'

Gambling! offered Eetapi, apparently recovered from her sulks.

'Too costly.'

Embroidery? said Ootapi.

Konrad thought of embroidering Dubin's name in blood red silk, the letters dripping in gore, and struck through with a shiny silver knife.

'I need a hobby,' he said again with a sigh.

Drinking! Ootapi enthused.

'You have the best ideas, Ootapi.'

It was not yet late enough in the afternoon to make drinking respectable, but the members of Konrad's favourite gentlemen's club were resistant to such mundane considerations as that. He collected his hat, his stick and his coat and went out into the rain, reflecting with pleasant anticipation upon the state of blissful, untroubled inebriation he would soon enjoy.

The clouds got their act together halfway there and produced snow, in quantity.

Perfect.

For several years, Konrad had felt nothing at all, near enough. His Master, The Malykt, had judged Konrad's tumultuous emotions obstructive to his duties as the Malykant, and had accordingly stifled them. Konrad had enjoyed — or suffered — only the barest flickers of feeling, easily missed and soon gone.

He had never fully decided whether he welcomed the interference, or lamented the loss. His role was the bringer of justice, and a harsh justice it was: The Malykt meted out only death, to those who took a life, and it was the Malykant's duty to administer that punishment. A lack of feeling permitted him to conduct the role more easily, perhaps; he was not plagued with the guilt, the horror, the fear or the revulsion that had often afflicted him before. But he ceased to feel hope or joy or love either, and the price had often seemed a high one.

Now that had all changed.

Irinanda had turned out to be a trusted servant of The Shandrigal, a being who presided over life and the living in the same way that The Malykt ruled over the dead. And by her Mistress's intervention, Konrad and his emotions had been, at long last, reunited.

It hurt.

It was hard, he thought bitterly, that when at last he became reacquainted with the business of feeling he should overwhelmingly experience those of a negative character. For every flicker of hope, he suffered a crushing weight of despair, self-reproach and terror. Well, terror at least was still familiar; his Master had, so kindly, permitted him to feel plenty of *that*, on the rare occasions He chose to show Himself. But to live with it day in, day out, was new, and when it came attendant with so many other terrible, soul-destroying feelings, Konrad frequently wondered whether he would not rather return to the blissful, relatively unfeeling state he had existed in before.

Nanda was his best recourse. The Shandrigal had sent her, he had recently learned, to keep Konrad sane. Malykants had gone mad before, their sanity and peace eroded by the horror of their daily job until their minds could take no more. Without Nanda, Konrad felt that he, too, might already have succumbed.

But she was absent from the city of Ekamet, had been for a week. She had gone with Danil Dubin to her home in Marja, a neighbouring realm, and thus was Konrad deprived of the only person he could turn to in need.

He tried not to resent her absence, for she had gone to visit her family, and he did not begrudge her the time. He tried not to resent her choice of travelling companion, either, though in that he failed. Why Dubin! Just because he, Konrad, was not likely to be given The Malykt's leave to travel — people could not be prevented from being murdered, after all, just because the Malykant was away — that did not mean she had to choose Dubin instead. Dubin! What was the man's appeal? That he was meek and dull and passive? Who wanted that in a friend?

To drink, then, he turned, knowing all the while that it was the poorest of responses but unable to think of a better. If he had descended so far into misery that he was wishing actual death upon Dubin — an unoffending soul, after all, even if Konrad despised him — then he was sorely in need of *something*. Whiskey would suffice.

When he arrived at the club, he found Nuritov already there. Inspector Alexander Nuritov was a chief detective with Ekamet's police force, and as such he was not, technically speaking, a gentleman. Such a man would not ordinarily be granted admittance to a club like Zima's, but his status with the police and his likeable personality had won him an exception. He was a popular member, friends with most of the rest. Konrad had originally met him over a glass or two of whiskey and a card game at Zima's, and the friendship had served him well since.

Nuritov did not know that the man he thought of as Konrad

Savast, idle gentleman of Ekamet, was secretly the Malykant. He thought of his friend as an amateur detective with an interest in the thornier cases that cropped up around the city. If he had noticed that Mr. Savast's interest tended exclusively towards murder cases, he had never commented on it, and his manner was always congenial.

Konrad sometimes wondered what Nuritov really thought of him.

'Savast,' said Nuritov, as Konrad approached his table. He had settled into a deep, wing-back armchair with a stack of newspapers and a pot of coffee, and readily invited Konrad to take the other chair. He made no comment when Konrad ordered whiskey, either, which was gratifying. 'What do you make of this Sokol business?'

Konrad chugged whiskey, and tried to remember whether he had heard the name Sokol recently. 'Who, or what, is that?'

Nuritov tossed him a page from his newspaper. 'Silk trader. Went mad yesterday, tried to kill a rival fabric merchant. Most out of character, by all accounts.'

Konrad scanned the report, though it had little to share beyond Nuritov's abbreviated version of the tale. Kazimir Sokol, a merchant importing silks from Kayesir, had attempted to decapitate Radinka Nartovich, a rival trader whose wares were, by some, considered superior. Nothing in the man's character or his life prior to the event had given any hint that he was of unsound mind, etc, and happily the attempt had been unsuccessful.

'Pressure can affect people in strange ways,' Konrad commented, returning the paper.

'Undoubtedly, but still, this is an unusual response to it. Ordinarily, there is *some* kind of hint beforehand, some sign that there is the potential for madness. It comes down to a question of time: not *will* the person snap but *when,* and what will prove to be the trigger? This unsuspected variety is odd.'

'Have you talked to him?' Konrad downed more whiskey, wondering vaguely why Nuritov brought the matter to his attention at all, but already feeling too mellow to care very much.

'Yes.' Nuritov put down the paper. 'Sokol claims to have no memory of the event at all. He would not believe the charges brought against him, not until we had presented him with several eye witnesses. Even now, he refuses to acknowledge responsibility and seems entirely without explanation.'

This was a little more interesting. 'Do you believe him?' Konrad asked.

Nuritov took a moment to think. 'I do,' he finally decided. 'He struck me as sincere. And distraught. He has a wife, children, whom he is genuinely anxious about, and I find it hard to believe that he would lightly risk their future over a moment's homicidal whim — if that's what it was. Furthermore, when he was told *who* he had tried to kill, he was utterly taken aback. As was Miss Nartovich, of course. It seems theirs has always been a friendly enough rivalry — no lasting ill-feeling reported on either side, whatever the papers might be implying.'

'So no motive, no prior history suggesting capability, and no memory.' Konrad set aside his glass, all thought of drink forgotten. 'A strange case, to be sure. What do you propose to do?'

Nuritov shook his head sadly. 'Alas, the fact of Sokol's attempt stands too far beyond doubt to give me much leeway. He took out a sword — an actual *sword,* Savast, not merely a long knife or some such blade — and went for Miss Nartovich with clear intent to destroy her. The fact that he had such a weapon with him strongly suggests prior intent, whatever he says to the contrary, and he was observed by half a dozen people. I have to prosecute him for attempted murder.'

The inspector's regret was clear, and Konrad could well understand his predicament. The case made no sense whatsoever. How could the police comfortably prosecute such a man for such a crime, under such strange circumstances? But how could they let it slide, either, considering that a woman had only narrowly escaped death?

'I sympathise,' Konrad murmured. 'Poor man. Poor woman, too.'

Nuritov nodded his agreement. The quality of his ensuing silence struck Konrad as too casual by half; it bristled with significance.

'What is it?' Konrad enquired. 'I take it you had a reason for mentioning the matter to me.'

'I did. I wondered if you might be disposed to assist.'

Konrad, half-slouched in his comfortable chair, sat up at this surprising response. Nuritov had been forthcoming enough before, in a few cases that Konrad had (secretly) handled, but he had always done so unofficially. And he was not in the habit of entreating Konrad's assistance. How could he be? He was the police, while Mr. Savast of Bakar House was a mere dabbler. 'What would you wish me to do?'

Konrad received in response an appraising look, and Nuritov hesitated before replying. 'I understand you might be in possession of some… unusual abilities?' he said at last. 'And perhaps some useful allies with, um, other unusual abilities.'

This brought Konrad up short. Away went his fond imaginings that Nuritov was wholly unaware of his secret life. 'I do not know what you mean,' he said at once, more by instinct than upon consideration. He was used to hiding his service to The Malykt, aware that not everyone would applaud him for it. There were those who felt that the Malykant was no better than the murderers he killed, and would not rest until he had been dispatched in similar fashion. Nuritov might never have given Konrad cause for alarm, but the prospect that he might have learned — or guessed at — Konrad's other identity sent a spasm of icy terror slicing through his guts.

'Forgive me, if I have spoken out of turn.' Nuritov sat back and took up his paper again, a picture of innocuous comfort as he sipped coffee and scanned the remaining reports. He did not look as though he were preparing to remove Konrad from this earth, and the fear lessened a little.

'Upon what information do you speak?' Konrad asked, when he had composed himself.

Nuritov glanced at Konrad, and a faint flush rose in his cheeks. 'You will believe me, I hope, when I tell you I had no intention of, um, spying upon your doings.'

Konrad raised an eyebrow.

'I have a new recruit,' Nuritov continued, looking more embarrassed than ever. 'An apprentice, of sorts, though of an unusual kind. She is a young person, only fourteen winters I believe. Um, her enthusiasm rather exceeded my expectations and she was… intrigued by you.'

'She has been following me?' Konrad's breath left him in shock, and he did not remember to breathe for half a minute.

Nuritov nodded. 'I have only just learned of this side project of hers, and of course I asked her to stop at once, but she had already uncovered too many details about your habits and, um, relayed them to me.'

'Let us be clear at once. What have you been told?'

'Sometimes you go abroad in different guise,' Nuritov said,

glancing meaningfully at the fine, gentleman's suit Konrad currently wore. 'You go out into the Bones, gather poisons. You have a hut there to which you sometimes retreat. You have a close association with Miss Irinanda Falenia, a known servant of The Shandrigal. And of course, I know myself that your interest in murder cases is more acute than might be considered ordinary for a gentleman of your position. I thought you merely interested in the puzzle, in a distant way, but you investigate much more actively than I previously realised.'

Konrad heard all this in growing dismay. How sloppy had he been! That some snippet of a girl had been tailing him about for, seemingly, *weeks* without his knowledge, had observed so much! It was small comfort to him that she had not, apparently, witnessed him actually carrying out his Master's justice, but small matter that. Nuritov was more than bright enough to put such pieces together as he had received.

He noted in passing the curious point that Nanda's association with The Shandrigal's Order was considered *known*. Konrad had not known it, not until recently, for Nanda had been very secretive. If Nuritov knew, then Konrad had been blind as well as sloppy, and for years. And he had just learned that he could develop murderous feelings towards unoffending people, too.

Today was not shaping up well.

'This apprentice,' he said, trying to ignore the sinking feeling in his stomach. 'Tell me about her.' Because the girl had not only evaded Konrad's notice; the serpents had failed to spot her, too. Watching Konrad's back was a large part of their job, and they were *good* at it.

But Nuritov had little light to shed. 'Her name is Tasha, no known family name. Orphan since early childhood. We took her in recently.'

If there was more to this Tasha than met the eye — and there had to be, Konrad was sure of that — then Nuritov knew nothing of it. 'I would like to meet her,' Konrad said.

Nuritov nodded. 'Ah… are my surmises correct?' he said, diffident but by no means willing to be put off.

Konrad was grateful that the club was so empty, and that Nuritov had chosen to sit in a secluded corner, out of earshot of the few other members in residence. Nonetheless, to admit to being the Malykant at all did not come easily to him. To do so in public went sorely against the grain.

'You understand that I cannot confirm any such surmise,' he said.

'Do you deny it?'

Konrad felt torn. Ordinarily, his policy was always one of complete secrecy. The only exception he had made was in Nanda's case, and he had lately discovered that she had known all along; indeed, his status as the Malykant was why she had entered his life at all. So in effect, he had never entrusted anybody with that secret, never thrown his fate into the hands of another person, never learned whether he could do so in safety.

Which was sad. And Nanda's point was true, and chilling: the isolation of the Malykant's life, combined with its daily horrors, had sent past incumbents quite mad.

Konrad did not wish to become one of them.

'I don't deny it,' he said, and it cost him much to speak those words. The consequences of uttering them came swiftly: a fever of doubt, the worst of premonitions, and vicious self-reproach.

But Nuritov merely nodded. 'It does explain much.' He sipped coffee, eyes wandering back to his newspaper, looking unaffected by the revelation.

Konrad sat feeling like a man awaiting his execution, but nothing came. No questions, no judgements, no reproaches. Nuritov said nothing, refraining from even looking Konrad's way. His coffee and his paper absorbed him utterly.

But it was not the avoidance of distrust, or revulsion, or reproach. The silence was peaceful, and Nuritov was as relaxed as always as he read. Konrad realised that he understood some part of the feelings Konrad was now suffering under, and probably the fears, too. He was, with the utmost sensitivity, giving Konrad time to adjust and to recover his composure.

That realisation brought another with it: Nuritov was not just an acquaintance, not merely a colleague or a fellow member of the same club. He was a friend.

And Konrad felt a rush of warmer, kinder feelings than those he had lately experienced. Since they brought with them an unfortunate moistening of his eyes, he was half inclined to wish them away again.

He took a deep breath, and when he was certain he had himself under control, he spoke up. 'In the matter of Sokol. You understand that my involvement in such cases only ever comes after someone has been… er, successful in such an endeavour. My particular arts may not be of use to you.' He was adept at an odd array of things: communing with ghosts, coaxing recently-slain corpses to talk, unlocking doors at a touch. All useful, in the usual way of things, but of little probable assistance in an attempted murder case.

Nuritov absorbed this with unruffled composure. 'Still, I would be glad if you would talk to him. I fear the truth behind Sokol's actions will prove strange indeed, and I think we are out of our depth with him.'

By *we* he presumably meant the Ekamet Police. And he had a point. Konrad had encountered many oddities during his eight or nine years as the Malykant, many of which passed the ordinary citizen of Ekamet by entirely.

And then, of course, there was Nanda. She was a Reader, which meant that she could sometimes discern thoughts, feelings, memories and such of another person, if she touched them. Absent she may be, but the day of her probable return rapidly approached. Konrad would not admit that he was counting the days — or more honestly, the hours. Entreating her assistance with Nuritov's case would give him an excuse to seek her out at his earliest opportunity, supposing he needed one.

And to extract her from Dubin's company without a moment's delay.

'I will do what I can,' Konrad promised.

He was rewarded with a smile of gratitude, and perhaps a touch of relief. 'Thank you, Savast.'

Konrad wanted to thank Nuritov, too. For accepting his secret without condemnation, and for keeping it in the future, as he felt (reasonably) certain he would. For being a friend to him, whatever his reasons might be. But he was unused to uttering such heartfelt reflections and could not find the words.

'Tasha,' he said instead. 'I would like to meet your spy.' And find out two things: how she had come to evade the notice of his serpents, and whether she was likely to prove as trustworthy as Nuritov when it came to keeping his secrets.

'I will send her to Bakar House this afternoon,' Nuritov promised.

Konrad stood, and found himself a little unsteady on his feet. 'Better make it tomorrow morning,' he suggested, frowning in irritation at his empty whiskey glass as though his inebriated state was the glass's fault.

'Morning it is.' Nuritov grinned as Konrad wandered off, and kindly made no comment upon the swaying character of his walk as he did so.

And so it was proved, that friends could be more soothing to the spirits than alcohol. How remarkable. Konrad reflected upon the merits of Nuritov and Nanda as he made his way home, and barely noticed the heavy snowfall, or the biting cold. For the first time in years, he felt warm at heart.

2

Tasha appeared a few minutes before Konrad had planned to sit down to dinner, and she did so in a more literal sense than he was fully comfortable with.

He ventured down the stairs of Bakar House, dressed for dinner, moving with more care than usual considering his inebriated state. The hall was empty, as it should be, but halfway between the bottom of the staircase and the door to the dining parlour the hallway felt significantly less empty.

Master, said Eetapi. *You are observed.*

Konrad turned. A girl stood just inside the front door, hands behind her back, waiting patiently to be noticed. She looked to be about fourteen winters old, and she was dressed in the neat, nondescript clothing one might expect of a ward of the police. Her dark hair was trimmed short, half concealed beneath a black cap. She watched Konrad with an air of composure he found a trifle unsettling in so young a person.

'You were supposed to arrive in the morning,' he admonished her.

'No time like the present,' said Tasha, with no trace of apology.

Konrad squinted in her general direction. He had not heard the door open or shut, and he ought to have done, considering he was standing barely five feet away from it. 'How did you get in?'

'Kitchen window.'

'And you contrived to travel from there to my front door without my noticing you.'

'You're drunk and complacent.'

'You mean to imply that it was easy to evade my notice.'

Tasha inclined her head.

'Fair. But my spies. They are neither drunk nor complacent, or they had better not be. How did you avoid them?'

Tasha hesitated, perhaps wondering whether or not to admit to full knowledge of the incorporeal, invisible serpent spirits who were presently engaged in wafting in lazy circles a few inches below the ceiling. But her eyes betrayed her: a quick upward glance, hastily corrected.

'So you have spirit vision,' Konrad commented. 'Are you a ghostspeaker?'

'Not exactly.'

'Then what are you?'

Tasha took a moment to consider her answer. Konrad expected a verbal response, but instead Tasha opted for the more dramatic approach of keeling over stone dead.

'Interesting,' he murmured, and allowed his own spirit vision to overlay his normal sight. His elegantly decorated hallway faded to stark black and white, and lo, she reappeared: a hazy, flickering outline of a girl traced in charcoal and snow, hovering over the corpse stretched out upon his hall floor.

I am a ghost, she said, and the words reached directly into his mind, the way his serpents' did.

Konrad's lips quirked with amusement. 'That explains a thing or two.'

Tasha drifted towards the ceiling and grabbed Ootapi's tail, then swooped after Eetapi. Konrad experienced a moment's alarm: had she any intent of harming his servants? But she dragged them both into an exuberant hug, ignoring their squirming indignation.

'They are so adorable,' she said. 'But so easy to evade. You should be more careful, snakies.'

Easy! shrilled Eetapi. *Master, we take the utmost care!*

In watching the living, Tasha agreed. *Not so much the dead. Don't you think we might be interested in the Malykant, too?*

Ootapi expressed his appreciation for Tasha's affectionate criticism (or critical affection) by unleashing a tearing hiss, and writhed violently until he unstuck himself from her embrace. *She smells odd,* he complained as he shot to the other side of the hall.

'All right, leave my poor snakies alone,' Konrad ordered. 'Let's all be corporeal again for a bit, shall we?'

Tasha regained the floor obediently enough. Her ghost vanished, and her body twitched and began, once again, to breathe.

'When you say you are a ghost,' he ventured. 'Do you mean you are *lamaeni*?'

Tasha got to her feet, and grinned. 'We were amused that it took you so long to figure us out.'

Hmm. *Lamaeni* were a kind of vampire, but not the blood-supping variety. These were dead souls, but able to reanimate their own bodies at will. Konrad had encountered them for the first time a few months previously, when he had investigated a death at the famous circus that visited Ekamet every year for the Festival of the Dead. *Lamaeni* drew upon the life energies of those around them in order to feed themselves, which was tiring for the living people involuntarily providing sustenance.

'No feeding on me,' Konrad ordered.

'Can't promise.'

Which was probably fair, for if the *lamaeni* went too long without feeding, the tenuous links between their souls and their bodies could be severed forever, and they would die.

Konrad sighed. Was his headache growing worse, or was it his imagination? 'Who sent you?'

'They made me promise not to say.' She beamed angelically and added, 'No one wishing you harm!'

'Listen here, girl,' said Konrad in a dire tone.

He was brought up short by a peal of laughter from Tasha, who said in between bouts of mirth, 'You sound just like my grandpa.'

If eight years as the Malykant followed by far too much whiskey of an afternoon were not enough to make Konrad feel about a century old, this was more than sufficient to finish the job. He glowered darkly at the still-giggling girl and tried again. '*No feeding*,' he repeated. 'And since you have been spying upon me and reporting my actions to the police, you will excuse my persistence when I ask you again: who sent you?'

But Tasha shook her head. 'Don't be worried. I've done you no harm. With your copper in on the secret, he'll be much more use to you. And he weren't too concerned at finding out the truth about you.'

Nuritov was sharp enough to have suspected before, of course;

Konrad had realised that a long time ago. Probably Tasha's news had merely confirmed his suspicions, and had come as no surprise. He felt a little shamed by her words, for he ought, perhaps, to have trusted Nuritov before, and confided in the inspector himself. It was true that the need to maintain his secrecy had placed obstacles in the way of his and Nuritov's being of full use to one another before.

He did not altogether appreciate Tasha's taking that decision out of his hands, however, and managing the business herself without reference to him. Nor did he enjoy the idea that some third party had been responsible for sending Tasha, perhaps with this very errand in mind. He was growing tired of mysterious people taking an interfering interest in his business.

'Was it my Master?' he asked. 'The Malykt?'

Tasha stared back at him, expressionless. 'No.'

'The Shandrigal again?'

'No.'

'The *lamaeni*? Myrrolena?'

'No.'

Her face did not change; not so much as a muscle moved. She was far too good. Konrad abandoned his attempts at guesswork with a sigh, and surrendered himself to fate in the same breath. 'Very well. It is hardly as though I can prevent you from trailing me around, after all. But know this: my serpents are alerted to you, and you will find them much harder to evade in the future.'

'I know,' she said cheerfully.

'If you cross me, I will burn your body.'

That gave her pause, albeit brief. 'Understood,' she said, and tipped her little black cap to him.

'Very good. Then pray go away, and leave me to enjoy my dinner and my headache in peace.'

Tasha bowed. 'Don't drink too much more. It's always best to stop while you can still walk in a straight line.' She watched his moderately unsteady progress towards the dining parlour with a critical eye for a moment, and then added, 'Almost, anyway.'

Konrad ignored that with magnificent dignity, and retired to his dinner.

The next day dawned brighter, for it was the day of Nanda's proposed return. The weather had not received the news, or perhaps it existed simply to be contrary, for it presented Ekamet with a fresh load of heavy snow. Konrad spent the morning alternately worrying about Nanda's journey through such conditions, and marvelling at himself that he was once again capable of feeling anything like anxiety.

Nanda had promised to dispatch a note to Bakar House the moment she reached home, in order to assure Konrad of her safe return. But after a few uncomfortable hours of failing to focus upon the newspapers Gorev brought and forgetting to drink his tea, he abandoned his efforts to appear composed and unconcerned and set off for Nanda's shop.

He trudged through the freezing snow with cheerful determination, much better pleased by the chilly discomfort of activity than he had been by the warmth and idleness of his parlour. His serpents sailed overhead, riding the whirling currents of the winds with unseemly shrieks of glee. He tried once to recall them to a sense of dignity but soon abandoned the project, for though Eetapi's squeals of delight threatened to split his mind in two, he so rarely saw them engaged in anything that might be called *fun* that it seemed a shame to call an end to it.

And in spite of appearances it did not interfere with the performance of their duties, for halfway to Nanda's house Ootapi announced: *Master. Tasha follows behind.*

I do not see how she would follow in front, Konrad replied.

Ootapi was briefly silent. *A fair point,* he conceded.

'Good day, Tasha!' Konrad called aloud.

He felt a flicker of amusement shiver across his mind in reply, and her light voice said: *Good morning, Malykant. I see your snakies are more alert today.*

Konrad wondered whether the serpents' noisy and obvious enjoyment of the weather might have been designed to persuade Tasha of their inattention, thus encouraging her into careless behaviour. He made a mental note not to underrate their deviousness in the future. 'To what do we owe the pleasure?' he continued. He could not sense Tasha himself, so he directed the question to the empty air, trusting that she would stay close enough to hear him even over the howling winds.

Today is a momentous day. I wanted to be around for it.

'Oh? What is supposed to happen today?'

Irinanda Falenia returns!

'That is an event of some moment to me, certainly, but I fail to see why it should prove of such absorbing interest to you.'

You will see.

Konrad did not like the mystery of this, for it seemed to him to bode ill. But he shook off such feelings. He was worried, and unused to the state. It was making him jumpy, and gloomy, and superstitious, seeing impending disaster around every corner.

'As you say,' he replied, with a mental shrug, and went on his way.

He arrived at Nanda's shop weighed down with fallen snow, and took a moment to shake out his hat and cloak. The shop — the best and most popular apothecary's establishment in Ekamet — was closed, of course, but he went around to the back door with some hopes of finding Nanda already returned.

She was not. The door was locked, no lights shone inside. Konrad weighed up his options for twenty seconds before deciding that the snow probably would not kill him, if he were to wait a little while.

Three hours later she appeared.

'You are late,' Konrad told her, his words emerging oddly through his frozen lips.

Nanda tilted her head in her characteristic expression of bemusement. She had often looked at him that way. 'What are you doing waiting outside my house? You look like you have been here for a week.'

'I have.'

'Liar.' Nanda was so swathed in layers of hat, scarf, coat and cloak that he could discern little of her face or figure, but her voice was so soothingly familiar. It warmed him to the heart, even if his body remained sadly frozen. She put down her two travelling bags by the door and unlocked it, ushering him inside first. 'Go, before you shatter to pieces.'

Konrad went. The house was as cold as the street outside, but within a few minutes Nanda had divested herself of her outdoor garments and lit the fire in her kitchen grate. She and Konrad huddled before it together, shivering in tandem.

So delighted and relieved was he to find her hale and well and returned that his wits had gone to sleep, for it was only *then* that he noticed two things.

Firstly, that Dubin had not accompanied her home. Any kind of friend *or* gentleman ought to have been eager to ensure that she reached home safely, particularly in such weather. Konrad would have done so himself. What manner of wretch was Dubin, to leave her to walk home alone?

Secondly, Nanda's demeanour was decidedly *not pleased.* But Konrad did not think it was merely the displeasure of having no attendant. In fact, she was contrary enough to resent such solicitude if it was offered. She stood in silence before the fire, with no news to share and no enquiries to make of Konrad. Her pale eyebrows were furrowed in a deep frown, and her thoughts appeared to be elsewhere.

'Are you well, Nan?' he said, some small part of his earlier worries unfurling once again.

She refocused her ice-blue eyes upon his face, vaguely, as though she had forgotten his presence. 'There was some trouble,' she replied. 'I was deciding whether or not to inform you of it.'

He blinked. 'Why would you hide it from me?'

She sighed, and ran her hands through her white-blonde hair. The gesture arrested Konrad's attention, for she was not usually prone to such fidgets. 'Because it concerns Danil, whom I am well aware you do not like.'

Danil Dubin. Konrad sighed inwardly, and put aside any fond hopes he might have been harbouring that he would not have to think about that young man again for a while. 'What has gone awry with him? He may not be a prime favourite with me, but I would not wish harm upon any friend of yours.' He spoke the words with total sincerity, only belatedly remembering that he had, only the day before, been cheerfully wishing death upon the man.

He put this inconvenient recollection firmly aside.

Nanda hesitated, her face sad and grim, and a horrible thought occurred to Konrad.

'He… is alive, yes?'

Nanda arched one brow. 'Of course.'

Konrad let out a quick sigh of relief, and mentally blessed Ootapi. The serpent had not been fool enough to carry through his cheery offer of murdering the poison trader, then; for an instant, Konrad had been heart-poundingly afraid.

But his relief was short-lived, for Nanda added: 'For now.'

'Um.' Konrad took a moment to absorb these words. 'You mean

he is alive… for now?'

'Yes. It cannot last long, I am afraid.'

'He fell ill on the road. Oh, Nanda, I am sorry.' Konrad realised, to his own surprise, that he really was sorry. For all his vicious, gloomy wishes of the day before, he did not truly feel that the man deserved to die, and Nanda's pain always cut him.

But Nanda shook her head again. Finally she turned away from the fire and set about making tea and a meal. Konrad assisted her in silence, aware that she needed to gather her thoughts.

Halfway through their silent repast, Nanda finally spoke.

'Danil killed someone.'

Konrad choked upon a mouthful of hot tea. 'I beg your pardon.'

'Danil,' Nanda repeated with slow emphasis, 'killed somebody.' She swallowed half of her tea in one go, not appearing to notice its heat, and set down her cup. 'A few hours ago. We travelled home a little early, hoping to avoid the worst of the weather, and reached the outskirts of Ekamet early this morning. But as we came through the gates, Danil saw someone he knew. A man called Kovalev. And he… snapped, somehow. He took a knife out of somewhere — and I have never before known him to carry a weapon, Konrad — and stabbed Kovalev seven times before he was hauled off him, and subdued.'

Konrad heard all this in utter disbelief, and did not interrupt.

'Kovalev died, of course, and Danil is taken into custody. But, Konrad… he cannot explain to me what he has done, or why. He doesn't appear to *know*. He talks of Kovalev as some kind of rival for a girl he once courted, and appears to hold him in contempt. But not murderous contempt! And he cannot remember having killed the man! He sees the blood on his clothes and frets, because he does not know how it came to be there, and he will not believe anybody when he is told how he came to be in police custody.'

Konrad felt colder and colder as he listened, his mind making too many chilling connections for his comfort. Between Dubin's fate and that of Sokol, for a start — no reassuring pattern, that. And Dubin's relationship to Kovalev struck him as far too similar to his own relationship to Dubin. That realisation could not enhance his tranquillity either.

Nanda applied herself to her food, and at last it struck Konrad that her composure was strained, her apparent calm only a semblance of it.

'There can be no doubt that he is guilty of the crime,' she said in a low voice.

Konrad was late to arrive at the conclusion poor Nanda had probably been tormenting herself over for hours.

Dubin had murdered someone, in plain sight of many witnesses. Whether he knew what he had done or not, whether he remembered, whether he could explain it: *he was a killer.*

And that meant it would be Konrad's unhappy duty to kill *him.*

Konrad's heart smote him at the idea, and he swallowed sudden bile. He had never imagined that his deplorable duty would someday oblige him to dispense with somebody Nanda cared for.

'Nanda,' he said. 'Nan. I promise you: I will do nothing… permanent... until we have unravelled this mystery and learned the truth of Dubin's behaviour. There is more to this story you do not yet know.'

She kept her eyes upon her food for the first part of this speech, but raised them to his face at last with the news that there was more for her to hear. 'Tell me,' she said, and he detected a flicker of hope in her eyes that had not been there before.

He related everything Nuritov had said about Sokol. She was as quick to recognise the similarities between the two cases as he, and she visibly revived with every word.

'Where is Dubin now?' Konrad asked in conclusion, filled with a restless energy to begin upon the case at once.

'The police have taken him somewhere. They said he is a danger to the public, which may very well be true, for if he could kill under such conditions once, might he not do so again? I am glad he is safely away. Oh, but Konrad, he knows his life is forfeit. He knows he waits for the Malykant. He is in a sad way.'

She did not quite meet his eyes as she said this, and Konrad realised the answer to a question that had been bothering him. Why had she not come to him right away? Why had she sent no word? If he had not been here awaiting her, he would still be oblivious to Dubin's fate — or he would have heard of it from some other source.

'You do not believe me, Nan? You think I will have Dubin dispatched by tea-time.'

Nanda sighed, and rubbed at her eyes. 'I do not know what to think. I know you would not lightly destroy anything of mine, but I am also aware that your duty is all that you live for. Can you say that you have ever hesitated to deliver The Malykt's Justice, in the past?'

Never for long, certainly. But most of the cases Konrad had lived through had been fairly clear-cut. Murders had been committed by those of questionable morals (or sanity), for reasons that clearly benefited themselves at the expense of their victims. In such cases as that, Konrad felt no compunction about ushering them out of the world. He did not have to question either his right to deliver such a punishment, or the rightness of his doing so.

But that did not mean that he killed without thought, without judgement or without consideration. At his secret heart, he was petrified of the day that he committed a mistake — killed someone who did *not* deserve that fate, whatever reason they might have to claim exoneration. He *always* took great care.

He had thought that Nanda had come to accept him fully, at long last, as her friend, irrespective of the horrific things he often had to do. That she trusted his humanity, and accepted that he was not *all* horror. But his status as the Malykant could still override any other impression he might give, it seemed, and her fear of the brutal side of his nature could still overwhelm her affection for his finer characteristics.

The realisation cost him a pang, but he set it aside. He would just have to prove himself to her again. It did not matter. If he had to prove himself worthy of her friendship a hundred times over, so be it.

'I swear,' he said to Nanda, making sure that she met his eyes. 'I will do nothing to harm Dubin until, or unless, we are both fully satisfied of his full guilt in this matter.'

She winced a little when he said *until*, and he sighed inwardly. She wanted a promise that he would never harm Dubin, but that he could not give. If the little poison trader lied, and had killed the man Kovalev in cold blood, then he merited the usual consequences. And Konrad would be forced to deliver them, however he personally felt about the matter.

He had given the best reassurance he was able to offer. All that remained was to investigate, and to fervently hope that Dubin was as essentially innocent of wrong-doing as he claimed to be.

Nanda pulled herself together, and when Konrad rose from her little kitchen table she followed suit. 'I will come with you,' she announced.

She meant to do so in order to keep an eye on him, obviously, but Konrad was happy to accept the offer. 'Have you Read Dubin yet?'

'I have not had the opportunity,' Nanda replied. 'He was kept from me, while he remained armed, and soon afterwards taken away by the police. Nobody would let me near him.'

Her tone was bitter; she obviously resented that interference. But Konrad could picture the scene all too well in his mind, and privately applauded whichever passersby had contrived to keep trusting Nanda away from an apparently mad, homicidal maniac, armed with a knife and covered in the blood of the man he had just stabbed to death in the street.

'We will do that first,' Konrad decided. 'Afterwards I would be grateful if you would do the same for Sokol. It seems likely that both speak the truth, when they claim no memory of the event: it would be odd, and too much of a coincidence, for two unconnected men to commit similar crimes almost at the same time, and both claim forgetfulness. But I would like to be certain.'

Nanda nodded once, and set about readying herself to depart. Konrad regained his own cloak and hat, his thoughts turning busily upon the conundrum.

The matter of Sokol had been in the papers, of course, but Dubin had only just returned from Marja. The chances that he had read of the case, and been motivated to mimic Sokol's response to his own crime, did not seem high. Besides, there was the apparently random nature of the meeting — happening to bump into Kovalev at the gates, just as Dubin was passing through himself, would be a difficult thing to arrange ahead of time, supposing the murder both intentional and premeditated.

But then why had the peaceful Dubin carried a knife?

The matter was complex, and Konrad blessed Nanda and her abilities now more than ever.

As they left the house, a stray thought drifted into Konrad's mind: Tasha. She had told him today would be momentous, and she could not possibly have been referring to anything other than the very problem he now faced. How had she found out about Dubin's crime before he had?

The only possible explanation was that she was watching Nanda, too — she or some colleague of hers. The thought angered him, and he made a mental note to interrogate the interfering little *lamaeni* at his earliest convenience.

3

Tasha, of course, made herself scarce just when he wanted her. That or she was ignoring his attempts at attracting her attention, which was possible. The serpents could not locate her either, and Konrad soon gave up. Tasha could wait.

He and Nanda went straight to Nuritov. Konrad judged it their best course of action; they would benefit from having the Inspector's visible presence and support if they wanted to visit the two condemned men.

Konrad also thought it high time that he introduced his two friends to one another. Being able to number his friends in the plural felt odd, but good, and he felt a need to somehow cement the agreeable situation by making them known to one another. Particularly if they were to be united, for a time, in investigating the strange cases of Sokol and Dubin.

Nuritov did not seem surprised to find Konrad at his door. Nor was he much puzzled by Nanda's presence. He ushered them both inside with his usual quiet courtesy, and made his bow to Nanda with particular friendliness. 'Miss Falenia. It is a pleasure to welcome you.'

Nanda curtseyed. 'I wish it had been possible to meet you under better circumstances.'

Nuritov's friendly smile became a frown. 'Indeed. Your friend Dubin is in a poor way, I am afraid. He will be glad to see you. And we are happy indeed to have your services. Do you know how rare Readers are?'

'I have some idea, considering that I have rarely ever encountered another.'

'Shall you mind practicing your arts upon Sokol, as well?'

'Mr. Savast and I are eager to visit both gentlemen. It seems clear that the two cases are connected.'

Nuritov glanced at Konrad, and nodded. 'I believe they must be, indeed, though it is impossible to say how. Dubin and Sokol have never encountered one another before, so I understand. You are not aware of any connections between the two?'

Nanda declined any knowledge of such, as did Konrad, and Nuritov nodded thoughtfully.

'It is well to ask the question. Never mind. Let us proceed to Dubin.'

Konrad and Nanda followed him out of his office, whereafter he led the way down a great many corridors and a few sets of staircases. Konrad judged that Dubin and Sokol were being kept somewhere far beneath the police headquarters, probably in an area designed to be far removed from other prisoners — or, indeed, their jailers.

Nuritov confirmed this surmise when he finally came to a stop. He paused before a stout door of solid oak and iron, at the end of a corridor which featured no other doors at all. He said, with an apologetic air, 'It has been necessary to confine them with the utmost security, I am afraid. Though neither appears to be harbouring any violent tendencies now, the extremity of their recent behaviour is such that we cannot take any chances.'

Nanda looked grim. Konrad felt the same as they passed through the stout door into a small sequence of cells, each one iron-barred and comfortless. Most of them were empty.

Dubin sat, alone and disconsolate, at the back of his cell. His hands were in heavy manacles. His blood-stained clothes had been exchanged for the nondescript grey of a prison uniform, and he looked unkempt. He did not look up as Nuritov stopped at his door.

'Mr. Dubin,' said Nuritov, his tone friendlier than Konrad might have expected. 'I have brought visitors.'

'I will see no one,' said Dubin.

Nuritov coughed slightly. 'One of them is Miss Falenia.'

Dubin looked up at that, though he did not seem at all delighted by the prospect of Nanda's near presence. 'No!' he cried. 'Of all people, I would least like to see *her!*' He shuddered, and corrected himself. 'Or of all people, I would least like *her* to see *me.*'

Nanda stepped forward, her face grimmer than ever. 'I saw everything, Danil, but I have come anyway. Does that not tell you that I do not condemn you?'

Dubin covered his thin face with his hands, as though he could block out the fact of Nanda's presence along with his sight of her. The gesture was childlike and oddly heartrending, and Konrad felt deeply uncomfortable. 'You should go,' said Dubin, his voice muffled behind his hands. 'Please.'

'I need to remain,' said Nanda gently. 'We are here to help you. You must permit us.'

'No one can help.' Dubin removed his hands at last, though he could not meet Nanda's gaze. He sat looking at the floor, and Konrad could not tell whether he had registered the fact that Nanda was not his only visitor. 'Do you not understand?' he continued. 'I am told there is no possible doubt. I was *seen* to kill, by many witnesses. Yourself among them! I am a murderer! And there is only one fate that awaits murderers in Ekamet.' He gave another, strong shudder. 'If I have indeed killed, then it is the fate I deserve.'

'You remember nothing?' Nanda enquired.

'Nothing,' Dubin repeated. 'I was passing through the gate with you, cold and hungry and ready to be home at last. Then I was restrained, held down by people I could not see. Everybody was upset, afraid, shouting. My clothes were bloodied. The police came and took me away, and only later, much later, did I learn why.'

Konrad's heart twisted, a feeling he deeply resented considering the object of it, but he could not help it. Poor Dubin. His confusion was palpable, and Konrad could well imagine his terror at the treatment for which he could find no explanation, and the reason for which was not made clear to him until he had had plenty of time to suffer under it. And when he was told what he had done, what then? How must that have felt?

Nanda looked ready to cry, and Konrad wanted to comfort her. But he knew she would not welcome such a gesture under the circumstances, so he held his peace.

'Danil, please give me your hand,' she said.

Dubin looked up at last, surprise making him incautious. He flinched as he met Nanda's gaze, and saw there the pain she was suffering on his account. Though perhaps the lack of condemnation gave him courage, for he swallowed and got to his feet. He wore manacles around his ankles, too, and his gait was awkward as he approached the barred door. He slipped one hand in between the bars, which Nanda immediately took.

'I do not doubt you,' she told him gravely. 'But my arts will confirm everything you have said, for the benefit of the police.'

Dubin shook his head. 'It is not the police whom I fear. It is the Malykant who now holds my fate in his hands, and can either of us suppose that any testimony in my favour will invoke mercy from him? I am a doomed man, Nan, and you waste your time.'

She did not reply. Her eyes were closed; she was lost in her perusal of Dubin's mind, gathering every possible glimpse of his recent memories, his thoughts, his impressions. Konrad knew that the art was imprecise; Dubin's mind was not fully laid open to her. She could not read his every thought, access his every memory, understand his every action. But she could reap some clues: his most powerful feelings, his most persistent memories. The memory of a recent, violent murder ought to be at the top of that list, if he held any such recollection.

The silence gave him plenty of time to reflect upon Dubin's words. The man's impression of the Malykant echoed Nanda's, though he could have no idea that he stood in the Malykant's presence at that moment. If he had, his terror would have been palpable. Konrad knew that the Malykant's public image as implacable, ruthless and unavoidable was carefully cultivated by the Order. It had to be, if his existence was to serve as a deterrent. But he recoiled from this vision of himself: heartless, without conscience or will of his own. A tool for killing, and nothing more.

Should the day ever come when his own behaviour matched and justified such an image, he hoped that somebody would be obliging enough to kill him. And that The Malykt would be merciful enough to let him die.

Nanda opened her eyes at last, though she did not release Dubin's hand. She held it still, though her intention seemed more to comfort him than to Read him, for she laced her fingers through his and held tight.

'No memory whatsoever,' she said, more to Nuritov and Konrad than to Dubin. 'The events of this morning are clear enough, but it is as though... there is a gap, where the murder should be. His mind remembers just as he has said: he got down from the stagecoach outside the gates, and came through them with me. We exchanged a few words. The next instant he remembers himself in the grip of strangers, frightened and covered in blood, but with not the smallest idea how he came to be so. It is as though everything that happened in between has been neatly sliced out.'

Confidently though she spoke, Konrad knew that her testimony alone would not be enough to save Dubin. She was an acknowledged friend of his, a close friend. She had been travelling with him when he committed the crime. No third party could possibly accept her account as unbiased.

But it meant much to Konrad. He knew she would not lie to him, not even to save Dubin. If she truly suspected that her friend had knowingly, willingly, committed such a crime, she would not try to cover for him. Her principles were too unbending for that.

It was a shame that The Malykt was unlikely to accept such an argument.

'What of the knife?' he murmured.

That brought Dubin's attention upon him at last, and the young man's face darkened. 'Savast?'

Konrad nodded politely, unsure what to say of his presence there.

Dubin did not appear to know what to say either, but his joy at seeing Konrad was not profound. He stared at Konrad's face for a time, searching, perhaps, for some clue as to his intentions in accompanying Nanda. Finding none, he looked away. 'I am glad Nan has someone with her at this time,' he muttered, a little ungraciously, but the sentiment seemed sincere.

'No memory of the knife at all,' Nanda replied, letting the brief exchange pass. 'Not a one. Judging from his memories alone, I would have said there *was* no knife.'

'In point of fact,' murmured Nuritov for Konrad's ears alone, 'Witness reports all agreed about the knife, but we never found it. Or the sword either.'

That little oddity brought a frown to Konrad's face. *Both* weapons had gone missing?

'I do not carry weapons,' said Dubin. 'Not ever. If I had ever wished to kill, I possess much more expedient means.'

This was news to Konrad. 'How so?'

Dubin looked down at the grey clothes he wore, and sighed. 'I cannot show you now, but if you inspect my old clothes — wherever they are — you will find three cloth pouches sewn into the seams. They are there for self-defence. If ever I was threatened as I went about my business, or if somebody accompanying me was in danger, they were my recourse. They each contain a virulent poison which, if thrown, will cause successively greater discomfort and inconvenience to an assailant. The first would cause partial, if significant, loss of sight. The second would burn the lungs if inhaled, leading to the kind of coughing one does not lightly suffer through. If these two proved insufficient and my need was great enough, the third would cause death.' His jaw tightened and his eyes grew wintry in expression. 'I have never had reason to even think about using that third one, but believe me: if I had wanted Kovalev dead, that is how I would have accomplished it. A knife? How clumsy, how dangerous, how unsure a weapon! It is the last thing I would have chosen.'

Konrad was surprised to hear mild, meek Danil Dubin so coolly outline his preparations for violence at need, though a small part of him was impressed. He ruthlessly suppressed that part.

The argument was persuasive. Dubin was a poison trader; what else would he choose, by way of a weapon? His story could easily be verified. Nuritov looked electrified, and would, no doubt, ensure that a search of Dubin's clothing would be conducted the moment they returned to ground level.

Where, then, had the knife come from? How had he come to be carrying it at all? How had he known to reach for it when presented with an opportunity to kill Kovalev, if he had not known that he had it, and was much more inclined to reach for his poison packets?

Konrad thought of Sokol, and the sword he had used in his attempt upon the life of Radinka Nartovich. A sword was a strange weapon for a silk merchant to carry, too.

'Dubin,' said Konrad. 'If you had to find an explanation for what has happened to you, what would you conclude?'

'There is none.' Dubin returned Konrad's stare with a look of impatient resentment.

'Think.'

Dubin withdrew to the back of his cell and sat down on the bare bench there, his manacles clanking. He sagged against the wall and stared at Konrad from beneath lowered lids. His attitude was suggestive of despair, but Konrad suspected that he was thinking deeply. Nuritov and Nanda stayed quiet, the former watching Dubin with an air of mild fascination blended with sympathy, the latter staring after him with naked concern.

'It would be difficult,' said Dubin at length.

'Undoubtedly.'

'Perepin's Arrow. It is a rare poison, usually prepared for inhalation. It is mesmeric, sometimes used in low doses as an aid to hypnosis. Combine a careful dose of that with something like amberleaf, which can cause loss of memory in sufficiently high doses…' He tailed off, shaking his head. 'It would be difficult,' he said again. 'To administer both poisons to the same target in precisely the right doses to have the desired effect, and without detection, would be virtually impossible. And then, they would not produce all of my… actions unaided. Perepin's Arrow prepares the way, but the intervention of a powerfully skilled hypnotist would still be required to implant the desired suggestions in my mind, and strongly enough to compel me to act upon them. Especially when those suggestions run so contrary to my nature.'

Too many drawbacks. Besides, why Dubin? Why Kovalev? Why would anybody go to such lengths to compel a man like Dubin to slay a rival, if the process was so delicate, so likely to result in failure? Surely there were easier ways to dispose of a Kovalev undetected. Konrad could think of three or four off the top of his head.

Still, Dubin's train of thought was interesting, and he may have hit upon some part of the truth, if not the whole. 'Is there any way to detect whether Perepin's Arrow or amberleaf have been used?' He was familiar with both poisons himself, as poison collecting was one of his stranger hobbies. But he could not pretend to equal Dubin's expertise.

'Not really. A little coughing, perhaps, in the case of the Arrow. The amberleaf is ingested. Its milder effects include confusion and dizziness, neither of which I remember experiencing. But I might, of course, have forgotten all that as well as the rest.'

Konrad looked to Nanda, wordlessly asking her the question: had Dubin been coughing?

She understood, and shook her head.

Nuritov had been silent, letting Nanda work and Konrad question. But at last he spoke up. 'Mr. Dubin. How did you know Mr. Kovalev?'

'In my youth,' replied Dubin (which struck Konrad as absurd, considering the man could not be much more than five-and-twenty), 'There was a girl. Inna. Kovalev and I both courted her for a time, though she would have neither of us. I thought him a fool and disliked him very much, of course. Since then I have occasionally passed him in the street or encountered him in a shop, or some such. We both forgot Inna long ago, I believe, and our exchanges were brief but civil enough. That is the extent of my acquaintance with him.'

A bland story. Nanda would say, later, whether or not his professed feelings about Kovalev matched anything she had drawn from his memories or thoughts. For now, he had nothing further to ask.

Neither did Nuritov or Nanda, so they soon took leave of Dubin. Nanda lingered over the task long, clearly reluctant to abandon him to the cold solitude of his cell. He was equally unhappy to see her go, and Konrad averted his eyes from their anguished leave-taking.

He waited with Nuritov a few feet away, their backs discreetly turned.

'What do you think?' murmured Nuritov.

'I think him sincere.'

Nuritov nodded agreement. 'Somehow, the notion that he could be compelled to commit such a crime against his will and without his recollection seems less far-fetched than the notion that such a man could behave so by his own will, and with so little reason.'

'I have known him some little time. I do not think he has it in him.'

Nanda joined them, her face drawn and too pale. Konrad felt an impulse to take her hand, touch her, anything that might comfort her. But having witnessed her hand-holding with Dubin the gesture struck him as misplaced, and he did nothing, only signalling sympathy with his eyes when she glanced at him.

This she ignored. 'Sokol?' she prompted.

Nuritov led the way.

Sokol proved to be a rotund man in his forties, with greying hair and the kind of face that had probably been fixed in cheerful lines until recent events. He watched his visitors' approach with anxious intensity, and hope flared in his eyes.

'Is it over?' he said. 'Am I to be freed?'

'Ah… not yet,' said Nuritov. 'This is Miss Falenia and Mr. Savast, associates with the police. They are here to assist with the investigation.'

Sokol's face fell, and he shrank away from his cell door. 'More questions! I have answered your questions, over and over, and here I still am.'

'Miss Falenia is a Reader,' said Nuritov. 'That means that she is able to access your thoughts and memories in a limited way, if permitted to touch you. She will be able to verify some parts of your story.'

This was an interesting test, for a man truly innocent ought to jump at the prospect. A guilty man would find a reason to refuse, for Nanda would surely see that he lied.

Sokol all but threw himself at the bars and thrust a hand towards Nanda. 'Read, then, and you will know I speak the truth.'

Nanda took his hand, and spent her usual minute or two in quiet concentration. When she opened her eyes, she released Sokol's hand with a reassuring smile.

'Much the same,' she said, meaning much the same as Dubin. 'He and Miss Nartovich were engaged in a civil conversation about the state of the silk markets. The next thing he remembers, he was in custody. He certainly has no memory of trying to harm Miss Nartovich. Or of any kind of weapon, knife or sword.'

'Thank you.' Sokol looked ready to cry.

Konrad hoped the poor man had not concluded that Nanda's testimony exonerated him. Many assumed that if one had no memory of an action or event, then one could not have committed or experienced it. In fact, the mind and the memory were far trickier than that, as Dubin's theory suggested. There were ways to interfere with memory. And then, the mind sometimes interfered with itself, and opted not to remember things it had far rather forget…

'You do not own a sword?' Nuritov enquired.

Sokol shook his head, growing frustrated. 'I have said this over and over. I have never owned a sword! Why would I? I am a family man, and a peaceful man. I could have no use for such a weapon. I own a small dagger, which I keep with me sometimes when I am abroad, for there are dangers on the road. That is all. I do not know how to *use* a sword.'

Which, Konrad noted, was an interesting point of potential enquiry. A sword was a specific kind of weapon. It was not like using a knife. Dubin might never have picked up a knife in his life, but a simple blade like that was not hard to employ if one's intention was merely to stab blindly at a target. A sword, though, required more precision, more skill. Particularly since the newspaper report had spoken of an attempted *decapitation.* To take someone's head off with a sword was no small task, and usually required a conveniently stationary target. Konrad assumed that Nuritov had checked into the merchant's activities already. If there was any evidence that he knew how to wield a sword, the inspector would have mentioned it.

'Did you have the dagger with you at the time?' asked Konrad.

Nuritov nodded at once, so presumably the weapon had been found among Sokol's clothing. So far, so good for the confirmation of his story.

The tale so far put him in line with Dubin. He had his own, preferred, familiar weapon to hand; why use a sword?

'And Miss Nartovich?' Konrad asked.

'An old friend. A rival, sometimes. We have disagreed on occasion, but never seriously. We have even helped each other once in a while, when one of us struggled. I would never harm her, or she me.'

Nanda nodded. 'The look on Nartovich's face, in Mr. Sokol's memory. It is of utter shock. I cannot think that she had ever anticipated such violence from him.'

That could be checked when he spoke with Miss Nartovich, but Konrad trusted Nanda's assessment.

So. Konrad was satisfied, for the present, that neither man appeared to be guilty of their crimes *in intent.* He was not altogether satisfied that lack of memory equated to lack of action, for it was distantly possible that both had repressed such horrific, violent memories. But it was a shaky surmise, and the weapons were the problem with that theory. It simply made no *sense*, that both men should choose weapons unfamiliar to them for so grave a purpose.

In Konrad's not inconsiderable experience, when a person set out to commit a murder, they typically did so with two primary aims: One, to succeed in their goal. Two, to escape without being detected or caught. Controlling the outcome of the endeavour was deeply important, and that meant sticking as much as possible to ideas and methods that made the perpetrator feel comfortable, powerful and unassailable. Picking a weapon one has no familiarity with and no affinity for was the kind of mistake made only by the stupid, and Konrad did not think either Sokol or Dubin merited that word.

So, then: something else was behind the two incidents. Or perhaps *someone*. Dubin's theory merited investigation, for if neither the silk merchant nor the poison trader had planned these murders, then who had? And if they had only been *physically* responsible for carrying them out, who had been pulling their strings?

4

The serpents had been quiet for a whole day. *Too* quiet.

They soon made up for it.

Master, shrieked Ootapi in Konrad's mind, in the very small hours of the morning. Konrad had been dreaming, splayed across his bed in sumptuous comfort. The serpent's splintered-ice voice interrupted a vision of pleasant strangeness in which he and Nanda sat on the floor of his hut-on-stilts out in the Bones, filling bottles with coloured liquids.

He opened his eyes. *What*?!

Someone is dead! carolled the snake.

You arrive bearing joyous news, as always.

Ootapi beamed in his mind, as delighted as a child given a bag of sweets. *Thank you, Master.*

Eetapi and Ootapi had yet to fully grasp the intricacies of sarcasm. Konrad did not trouble himself to explain.

What are the circumstances of this death? Given Ootapi's desperation for a nice murder case to keep Konrad occupied, he felt a faint hope that his faithful serpent may have encountered a natural death and enthusiastically exaggerated its significance. It was cold out there and warm in bed, and it could not be much past two in the morning.

Deaths! Ootapi proclaimed. *Two! Out in the Bones.*

Two people together might have come to grief out in the Bone Forest in heavy snow, but Konrad would certainly have to investigate. He heaved a great, reluctant sigh and threw off the blankets.

Butchered like pigs, added Ootapi.

All right, then. *That is not something to sound so delighted about, Ootapi,* Konrad tried, knowing it was futile.

There is so much blood! Eetapi chimed. *Pretty red snow!*

Bones! chirped Ootapi. *Bones in the Bones!*

Was it any wonder he was so often dejected, when such creatures were his regular companions? Konrad hurried to get dressed, trying unsuccessfully to ignore his ghost servants' appalling glee.

I wonder, he mused as he retrieved his waxed great-coat, *whether the Master would permit me to trade the two of you in for some less bloodthirsty alternatives?*

There followed a ringing silence.

Bloodthirsty, Ootapi finally repeated in a thoughtful tone. *Is that wrong?*

Konrad made for the door. *Never mind. We go! Keep up!*

Eetapi had not exaggerated about the blood.

The serpents led Konrad through the north gate of Ekamet and into the snow-laden Bone Forest. The bodies were not very far in, barely two minutes from the gate. They were… in a poor state.

The first was a youngish man with pale hair, the second a woman perhaps twenty years older. Their garments hinted at a life of moderate prosperity. They had probably got down from the stagecoach moments before, Konrad judged, and were on their way into the city when they were attacked.

The young man's head was half-severed, his neck split open by a sharp blade. Much of the blood that stained the surrounding snow was probably his. Both he and his companion had been stabbed repeatedly, bloodied wounds covering their torsos, limbs and even their faces.

Konrad looked at them for a long time, struggling with an uncharacteristic desire to turn away, let someone else deal with it. The two still, half-frozen bodies awoke unusual pity in him, and an even more unusual distaste. He thought he had grown used to such spectacles over the years.

He smothered such feelings with an effort, and forced himself to focus. The bodies had been there for some time, he judged, for they were severely frost-bitten and partially covered in snow. Probably a few hours, perhaps a little more. No sign remained of any other passersby; the snow had filled in any footprints their killer might have left, and Konrad saw nothing else of use or interest.

His favourite knife was tucked into his coat. He withdrew it and leant over the body nearest to him, the woman. It was his duty to take a bone of hers, usually a rib bone, with which he would mete out justice to her killer. He felt curiously reluctant to proceed. Those poor, battered folk had suffered enough such indignities, and besides… there was an odd, macabre peacefulness about their inert shapes, resting among the softly falling snow. The Bone Forest was silent, eerily so, all sound muffled by the snow, and Konrad felt that to introduce more violence to the scene would be to somehow defile it.

Such strange, twisted thoughts. He shook them off and bent to his task, setting the knife to the woman's torso.

Master.

Konrad jumped, Ootapi's voice slicing through the silence like a whipcrack. *What?*

There is a person.

Sweet Malykt, another body? Konrad did not feel he could face another such torn-up carcass. *Where?* he replied and straightened up, feeling about three centuries old.

He felt a wordless summons beckoning away to his right. He trudged that way, knife in hand, trying to steel himself for another horrific scene.

It is alive, Eetapi elaborated.

It was indeed. Konrad stopped in shock, for partially concealed behind a thin, pallid tree was a living woman dressed in a long black coat, her dark red hair wind-tossed and crusted with snow. She ought not to have been so difficult to spot, for she was almost as bloodied as the two lifeless corpses he had left behind. He instantly concluded she must be injured, and hastened forward. But no. She sat upon a fallen tree trunk, and her posture was not that of a wounded person in pain. She looked frozen, not just with cold but with shock. Her face was blank, her eyes staring at nothing.

Konrad approached cautiously. 'Hello?'

The woman did not reply. Nor did she move, or blink, and he began to wonder if she might not be dead after all.

Her heart beats, Eetapi whispered.

Konrad took note of the quantity of blood upon her clothing, and her hands, and his sense of foreboding grew.

He touched her hand, very gently. 'Hello?' he repeated. 'We are here to help.'

Her eyes moved, focused slowly upon his face. It took her some time to realise that a stranger stood before her. When the fact registered with her, she shot upright, shoving Konrad away with startling violence. Her frozen body did not respond well to the sudden movement, and she almost fell into the snow.

'Stay away!' She tried to shriek the words but they emerged from her frozen throat as a cracked whisper. She coughed, hard, stumbling backwards in a desperate attempt to put more distance between herself and Konrad.

He held up his hands, stood motionless. 'I will not harm you.'

But she shook her head, so violently her hair sent up a spray of snow. 'Shall I not harm *you*? You cannot be certain I shall not, and neither can I.'

Konrad did not move. 'Tell me what tortures you.'

She covered her face with hands bleached stark-white by the cold. 'Have you seen — did you see—'

'The bodies,' Konrad supplied, when she did not seem able to finish the sentence. 'Yes.'

'I saw them,' she gasped. 'I saw them at my own feet. And my coat, my shoes…' She kept her face averted from the garments in question, unwilling, perhaps, to face again the quantity of blood that stained them.

'You do not remember committing any violence?'

'No,' she whispered. 'They were my travelling companions. We had never before met, but we rode here together upon the stage, and talked a little along the way. I remember getting down, and agreeing to walk into Ekamet together. And then…' Her voice failed, and she covered her eyes. 'Then they were dead, and I was standing over them like *this*, and I knew that somehow I had done that to them.'

Konrad stood in a state of such wretchedness, he hardly knew how to act. The evidence was as clear to him as it was to her. Duty compelled him to extract a bone from each of the two victims and employ them in killing the distraught woman before him. The Malykt's requirements were clear cut. He had no proof of her innocence, plenty of her guilt, and only an emerging pattern of similarly strange occurrences upon which to base his utter refusal to destroy her.

Refuse he did. He could no more slay her under such circumstances than he could kill Dubin. Kovalev's bone he had dutifully taken, and it now lay wrapped in cloth in one of his pockets, ready for use. But hè could not use it until he had determined the full truth of Dubin's crime, and he could not kill this poor woman either.

Master, hissed Ootapi. *You hesitate.*

I am the judge here! he shot back, swift and vicious. *You assist me. You decide nothing for me.*

He felt Ootapi's displeasure, but he ignored it.

'What is your name?' he said to the woman, still wary of approach.

'Arina.' She whispered the word, swallowed, and fell silent without offering a family name.

It was enough for the present. 'Arina,' he repeated. 'Please, calm yourself. I will help you.'

She blinked at him, confused. 'Who are you?'

'My name is Konrad.' He did not hazard the rest. He felt a brief, fervent gratitude that she had not witnessed him wresting bones from the bodies of her slain travelling companions. 'Will you come with me?'

'The police will come. I must remain.'

Konrad had no intention of permitting her to remain. For one thing, she would freeze to death. Her lips were already tinted blue, and she no longer had the energy to shiver. She was visibly weakening.

For another, he could not bear to see a third soul condemned to the confinement of Nuritov's cells. This matter was under his jurisdiction now; if the police were inclined to resent his decision or his interference, let them resent. He did not care.

'Come with me,' he repeated. 'I will see things set to rights.'

To his relief, she followed. She could barely walk, and he was obliged to support her every step. 'What have I done?' she whispered, and she would have wept, had she tears left.

'Nothing,' said Konrad, and he believed it to be the truth. 'You have done nothing.'

He took Arina to Nanda's house, certain she would receive a welcome there, and all the care she so urgently required. His faith was not disappointed. Nanda was appalled by the story, and eager to assist one thrust into the same nightmarish condition as Dubin. Arina was swiftly plied with every source of warmth Nanda could muster, and fed, and comforted, and Konrad left the house feeling more at peace about her.

He returned immediately to the site just beyond the gates. He still had to collect a bone from each victim, which he did with as much dispatch and efficiency as possible, keeping his mind averted from the task. Then he applied himself to a full examination of the scene.

Arina had spent some hours with the two victims prior to the crime. That fact struck him as significant. Why had she not killed them in the stagecoach? She had not mentioned whether there were other passengers; perhaps there had not been an opportunity. But a theory was taking shape in his mind, and the circumstance coincided with it.

The three crimes had been committed in similar ways, and with similar weapons. Swords and knives, all vanished. Stabbing, and decapitation — or attempted decapitation, in Sokol's case. By implication, one person was behind all three events; one person with a fondness for blades. Alternatively, two people: one with a preference for swords and decapitation, one who preferred to stab and rend with a knife.

How this person, or persons, had come to dominate Sokol, Dubin and Arina into committing the crimes (and contrived to spirit away the blades afterwards) remained in question, but Konrad was more interested in the *why*. All murderers wanted to cover their tracks, but this approach was cumbersome in the extreme, and had to be far more difficult to accomplish than many another method of distancing themselves from the scene. If he could learn or guess at the *why,* Konrad felt he would soon understand the whole.

He bethought himself of one or two questions that remained unanswered. What had Radinka Nartovich seen? Of the four victims, she was the only one who remained alive to give her version of the story.

Konrad resolved upon seeing her as soon as possible.

5

The house of Radinka Nartovich was in the city's old quarter, but it was not among the crumbling, neglected buildings that lined some of the streets there. Hers was of moderate size and well maintained, its facade carved and gilded and gleaming with fresh paint. Miss Nartovich was by no means poorly off.

It also bore an air of vacancy which troubled Konrad immediately. His acute senses detected no sign that anybody had passed that way in a day or two, and the lingering silence struck him as cause for concern.

He was not surprised when no one answered the door, though he knocked a few times. Glancing around at the empty street, he proceeded quietly to the back of the house. The rear door was locked, but a touch of his Malykant's fingers soon dispensed with that obstacle, and he went inside.

Serpents, find her for me, he ordered, and Eetapi and Ootapi drifted ahead of him into the house.

Konrad prowled through the ground floor rooms, taking note of the fine furnishings and ornaments that adorned Miss Nartovich's home. There was no sign of her, but there was also no sign that anything untoward had befallen her.

When his serpents reported a similar state upstairs, Konrad breathed a little easier. Hopefully she was well, then, but where was she? He performed a quick search of the upper floors himself, hopeful of some sign as to her whereabouts, but came up with nothing.

He regained the street in some frustration, irritated with himself for failing to gain access to her before. It was probably irrational of him to imagine that she held some vital piece of information, something which would elucidate everything.

He stood on the street for a few moments, unsure what to do next. He had dispatched a note to Nuritov, requesting more information as to Sokol's and Nartovich's whereabouts during his attempt upon her life; an answer had not yet come. What more could he do?

His senses prickled.

A presence, Eetapi announced.

Yes, he snapped back. *Thank you.*

Better late than never, she hissed primly.

Somebody was watching Konrad, but he did not feel under threat from the waiting presence.

'Tasha?' he said aloud. 'Do come out.'

She did not appear, but her voice spoke from nearby. 'It is not poison.'

'What is not poison.'

'The source of these crimes you are investigating. Dubin's theory is interesting, but it is wrong.'

Konrad turned in a circle, trying to spot the girl, but flurries of late afternoon snow obscured any glimpse of her. 'All right. Will you tell me how you know this?'

'I know where Radinka Nartovich is.'

'Wonderful.'

'Some of her, anyway.'

Konrad's heart sank. 'She is dead, then.'

'Not exactly.' Tasha paused, perhaps thinking. 'She is sort of alive.'

'If you could contrive to make better sense, I would appreciate it.'

Tasha appeared at last, her black cap and dark clothes materialising out of the snow a few feet away from Konrad. 'It's hard, when I don't know what's going on myself. But I saw her leave the house, early this morning.'

'Tell me everything,' Konrad ordered.

Tasha nodded. 'She came out without a coat or anything, and I thought she would come right back. But she didn't, so I followed a few minutes later. She went into a shop in the Darks and didn't come out. There's living quarters up there, so I reckon she's shacked up on the upper floors.'

Konrad frowned. The Darks was the poorest quarter of Ekamet, a winding maze of shabby streets so-named because the gas-fuelled street lamps which lit most of the city were always broken there, and no one seemed to think it worth mending them. The tall, craggy buildings leaned and loomed over the narrow streets, blocking what little light filtered down during the day. It was filthy and crumbling and rife with crime — an area Konrad avoided, as did all those of Ekamet who had any choice.

Radinka Nartovich certainly had a choice. Why would she abandon her handsome, comfortable house for premises over a shop in the Darks?

'Why do you say she is "sort of" alive?' Konrad squinted at Tasha, suspicious. She was by no means telling him everything she knew.

'Hard to explain.'

'Please make the attempt.'

Tasha sighed. 'She doesn't... feel alive, but she doesn't feel dead either. I mean, if I wanted to feed from somebody I wouldn't choose her.'

Meaning Radinka was lacking in the kind of energy a *lamaeni* would need to siphon off, in order to sustain themselves. Ordinarily that would mean she was dead, for sure, but she was oddly perambulatory for that.

Konrad opened his mouth, on the point of requesting Tasha's guidance to the shop wherein Radinka had hidden herself. But he hesitated. Something else sprang to his mind, a suggestion that had been made the last time he had encountered *lamaeni*. A possibility he had been trying not to think about.

He did not want to ask, but he had to.

'Do I?' he whispered.

'Do you what?'

Konrad cleared his throat. 'If you wanted to feed from someone, would you choose me?'

He *meant,* did he possess the living energy she would consider as food? For another *lamaeni* had claimed Konrad was not strictly alive, either; that he was more of a puppet, operated by The Malykt. That when he had died in the line of duty and been revived, he had not been brought back to *life* precisely but only some semblance of it.

It was a horrific thought, and Konrad had been dodging the idea ever since.

'I wouldn't think of feeding off my new boss,' said Tasha, with a grin.

'Of course not, but… could you? If I were not your boss.'

Tasha tilted her head at him, obviously not following his line of thought. 'Maybe.'

'Maybe? What do you mean, *maybe*?' Konrad's heart began to pound with terror, and he broke into a sweat.

But Tasha just shrugged. 'Hard to explain. Do you want to see Radinka or not?'

Konrad took a slow, deep breath and strove to pull himself together. *Maybe.* He had hazarded the question in the hope that her cheery *yes* would satisfy his doubts once and for all. Alas, the courage it had taken to ask had been poorly repaid. 'Yes,' he said shortly, and with a ruthless effort put the whole question of his own mortality out of his mind. The question of whether or not Radinka lived was more pressing.

But as he followed Tasha through the streets, the doubt lingered at the back of his mind. By the time they arrived at the shop in question, Konrad's mood was as dark as the streets around him.

It was a pawn shop, and surprisingly well kept, for the Darks. It had received a new coat of paint somewhere in the past year, and its windows were clean. A narrow alleyway ran alongside, and Tasha led Konrad just inside, and pointed at a red-painted door. 'She went in there.'

'Is she still here?'

Tasha shrugged, so Konrad sent Eetapi and Ootapi up to investigate.

One woman present, Eetapi reported. *Feels odd. Maybe dangerous.*

Konrad unlocked the red door with a touch of his fingers, and started up the narrow, steep wooden staircase that lay behind it. *Bind her then, please.*

It was one of his serpents' more terrifying abilities: to bind themselves into the body of a living person (or a recently deceased one), bending that person to their will, albeit in a limited and temporary fashion. They would hold Radinka immobile while Konrad investigated, ensuring that she did not take it into her head to attack him. Tasha's and Eetapi's vague sense of disorder left him uneasy.

He heard Tasha's footsteps behind him upon the stairs, and briefly thought of ordering her to remain behind. But he was forgetting. She was no ordinary fourteen-year-old. She was lamaeni, and as such, dangers that might threaten him could have little effect upon her.

At the top of the steps, he took care to ensure that the serpents had successfully secured Radinka before he ventured into the room beyond.

We have her! Ootapi hissed, and Konrad proceeded.

The quarters over the pawn shop consisted of one room, reasonably spacious, its walls simply white-washed and its floor bare wooden boards. Its furnishings were minimal and much worn. A bed occupied one corner, and in it lay the woman Radinka Nartovich.

Presumably. Konrad did not know her appearance. 'Is that her?' he asked of Tasha.

She nodded. 'Leastwise, that's the woman I saw leaving her house.'

Miss Nartovich was prone upon the bed and unmoving, dressed in a fine-quality gown which looked out of place in her shabby surroundings. She did not move as Konrad approached, though her eyes focused upon him. Her expression chilled Konrad to the core, for she glared at him with clear murderous intent.

Then her eyes flicked to Tasha, and if anything her hatred deepened.

Let her speak, Konrad ordered his serpents.

Aloud he said, 'Miss Nartovich. I am an associate of the Ekamet Police, and I wish to ask you a few questions.'

Radinka's lip curled. 'Little *spy,*' she spat, her gaze fixing again upon Tasha.

Konrad blinked. Radinka Nartovich appeared to be, perhaps, in her late thirties, and she was a fairly handsome woman. But the voice that emerged from her graceful throat was far deeper than Konrad might have expected, and harsh in character. The contrast was jarring.

'Boss,' said Tasha, and he thought he detected a hint of nervousness. 'Something ain't right. I would say she's lamaeni, only she's… broken.'

'Broken how?'

Tasha merely shook her head, and backed away. Her composure

had deserted her all at once, which prompted a deepening of Konrad's unease.

He looked more carefully at the prone woman, the beginnings of a theory forming in his mind. She fought the grip of his serpents, and she was strong; he would have to move quickly. 'I have already addressed you as Miss Nartovich. What is your first name?'

The woman snarled something incomprehensible.

'Try again,' Konrad ordered.

She did not try to speak further, but strained against the paralysing influence of Eetapi and Ootapi. Futilely, for the present, but Konrad feared they could not hold much longer.

'You do not know, do you?' he said. 'And I do not think it is because you have forgotten. It is because this body *does not belong to you.*'

The body of Radinka Nartovich thrashed upon the bed, but Konrad was now certain that somebody else looked out through her stolen eyes. 'Tasha,' he barked. 'What becomes of a lamaeni whose body is destroyed while their spirit is elsewhere?'

'The link is severed,' she whispered. 'They… I don't know. No one knows. We say that The Malykt has mercy upon them and takes them up, but there is no way to be sure.'

'Perhaps He does, sometimes. Not always. This one is a stray, I think.' Konrad lifted his stick and set its base against the thrashing woman's torso, holding her pinned. 'Having lost your body, you went shopping for another, did you not? And you found one. Miss Nartovich did *not* survive the attempt upon her life. It merely looked as though she did. You borrowed the limbs of Kazimir Sokol, who happened to be standing by, and slew Nartovich. You achieved this by much the same means that my serpents are holding you now.'

And they still held, though Konrad could sense their strain. It was beginning to hurt them, and he could not expect them to bear it much longer.

Master, Ootapi gasped. *We weaken.*

Konrad was not surprised to see a sword flicker into being in Radinka Nartovich's hand. It was not a fully solid weapon, but it could pass for metal if not closely inspected. Such a blade could wreak damage enough, wielded by a determined lamaeni.

Well, that explained the disappearing weapons.

'Time to go,' Konrad barked. Tasha was already running for the door. He followed, backing his way to the stairs with his eyes upon the still recumbent form of Radinka Nartovich until he reached the door. Then he turned, and fled.

Once he and Tasha were safely away, he sent a parting order to his serpents. *Release her. Or him.*

With which words he hastened on, intent upon putting the Darks behind him as swiftly as possible. The two serpents soon caught up, ragged and spent, and Eetapi's voice chimed dolefully in his mind.

I do not like lamaeni.

'I am not fond of them either,' he agreed. He eyed Tasha, who kept pace with his longer stride with remarkable ease. Her fear was gone, though she had yet to fully recover her composure. 'Present company excepted, possibly.'

Possibly. Tasha had not given him reason to distrust her, but it struck him as a mighty coincidence that a lamaeni should appear in his life just at a time when others were creating the kind of havoc he had to deal with. 'Tasha. You knew something of this beforehand, did you not?'

'No!'

'Then how did you happen to appear just at this time?'

'No one sent me,' Tasha said reluctantly. 'You caused a lot of havoc at the Circus. Some of it good, some of it bad. Things got… uncomfortable for me there, and I thought it was time to move on.'

'So you came looking for me.'

'Yes. The way you handled Myrrolena, and Alad… it was masterful.'

'I did have help,' Konrad murmured, feeling absurdly flattered anyway. The Malykt had actually handled Myrrolena, the former Ringmistress.

'Whatever. You're interesting, and if anybody can keep them off me, it's you.'

'But you informed on me to the police.'

Tasha shrugged. 'Just helping you out.'

'You have a funny way of helping.'

'As long as it works.'

Konrad found that hard to answer, for as much as he did not like having decisions taken out of his hands, Tasha's interference had indeed helped. Instead of engaging further with this thorny topic, he said: 'Do lamaeni often go dangerously maverick like this?'

'I never heard of it before.'

They were some distance from the Darks, by now. The shabbiness and filth had given way to well-swept streets and sparkling shop-fronts, and Konrad slowed his pace. 'So we have a couple of dispossessed lamaeni wandering around house-hunting, so to speak,' he said to Tasha. 'Who are they? How did they come to lose their bodies? And why is it that our knife-wielder is still looking? That one has killed three that we know of, and availed themselves of none of the corpses.'

'It seems odd to me. I mean, I never heard of anyone shacking up in a random corpse, either. It shouldn't be possible. If it was, we would do it all the time. It makes no sense.'

Interesting point. The prevalence of victims who had *not* got up again and wandered off suggested that Tasha was right — whoever had killed them had not been able to repurpose their slain corpses.

But Konrad was not disposed to doubt his theory. He felt certain that Radinka Nartovich was Radinka Nartovich no more, and he had Tasha's testimony in support of the idea that whoever occupied that body now was lamaeni. And she ought to know.

Little spy.

'She spoke as if she knows you,' Konrad observed. 'And hates you.'

Tasha gave a crooked little smile. 'It is possible. There ain't all that many lamaeni about, all told.'

'Any idea who we might be dealing with?'

'I'll look into it.'

Tasha might prove very useful indeed, at least for this case. 'I wonder why they thought it would work,' he mused. 'If it's never been heard of before.'

'And why did it work with Radinka, and not the others?'

Also a good question. 'Suppose there was something different about her.'

'There was.'

Konrad did not immediately realise that it was not Tasha who had spoken those two words, for the voice was light and female and not dissimilar to hers.

'We got company,' said Tasha, with unseemly cheer considering that the street was empty save for their two selves.

Serpents?

Dead lady incoming, Eetapi confirmed.

Minus body, Ootapi clarified.

In a flash, Konrad reached for his spirit vision and let it take over his regular sight. The colour bled out of his world, and the shops and houses around him and turned to stark, hazy black and white.

A ghost hovered directly behind Tasha. The figure was vaguely female, though too indistinct for Konrad to discern much detail.

'Radinka?' he guessed.

'Correct,' she said. 'Any chance you'll help me to get my body back?'

'Why haven't you…' Konrad began, but then the pieces came together. 'More lamaeni.'

He got the impression that Radinka smiled, a little. 'We are not all bad, I assure you.'

A strange vision passed through his mind, of the unknown lamaeni walking off with Radinka's body as though he had stolen her coat. Bizarre, bizarre. 'Why don't you tell us what happened?'

Radinka gave a gusty, ethereal sigh. 'I was in the Blue Rose Coffee House, talking with Kaz. Kazimir that is, Kazimir Sokol. I felt someone else come in, someone like *me,* in spirit form. Then Kaz went nuts, came at me with a sword and tried to cut off my head. I dodged that, but I think it was just a distraction, because he got me with slash to the belly and a psychic punch the likes of which I have never felt before. Knocked me clean out. When I came to I was like this, and my body was walking itself out the door. I've been following myself around ever since, looking for a chance to evict the bastard, but I can't match whatever it was he did to me.'

'Because you aren't possessing,' said Tasha.

'Excuse me?'

'We ain't exactly at our best in spirit-shape, right? If we were, why strive to maintain a link to our physical selves at all? It's exhausting and inconvenient. But a spirit without a body is only *half.* When those two things work in concert, everything we do is stronger. So, our mystery man probably couldn't chuck you out by himself either. That's why he grabbed Sokol, and used *him* to weaken and distract you until he could hustle you out. Mortals are pretty feeble really, not that hard to overpower for a little while. It's not the same as the link between a spirit and its *own* body — or a lamaeni vessel. But it's a lot better than nothing.'

Konrad looked sharply at Tasha, impressed. The girl had a quick mind.

'So I need to possess some hapless bystander, stick holes in my body until it weakens, and then try to batter my way back into my own head.' Radinka said all this in a flat tone, deeply unimpressed at the prospect. 'You do know what's happened to poor Kaz, I suppose?'

'Don't worry,' Konrad said absently. 'I will make sure he is fully exonerated.'

'Great, but I'm still not doing it.'

'We will work it out,' said Tasha.

'The other one,' said Konrad. 'We'll call him Knife. Or her, whatever. Sword figured out that a lamaeni target works, but Knife apparently hasn't.'

'Wrong.'

Konrad eyed Tasha in irritation. 'What do you mean, *wrong*?'

'Knife knows that he needs to find a lamaeni host. He must do. No one would be stupid enough to imagine that any old corpse would work.'

'But he's been possessing living, mortal people.'

'Yes… and vacating them again soon afterwards. I can't really explain to you what it's like to be squashed into someone else's living body, alongside someone else's living soul. It isn't what they need, or want.'

'So kill the living soul, keep the body. Come to think of it, I've no idea why he didn't do that to begin with. Why not just keep Sokol's corpse, instead of bothering with Radinka?'

'Because then it's a *corpse*. It's dead, not undead. Lamaeni are something else.'

'You mean… all the people Knife killed were lamaeni.'

'Have to have been. He just wasn't strong enough, or quick enough, to take control the way Sword did.'

'So why weren't they home? Those two victims of Arina's looked stone dead to me.'

'Knife probably managed to dislodge them, but he either failed to anchor himself in the bodies afterwards, or they fought him off in spirit-form.'

'And then they declined to reclaim their own bodies afterwards.'

'Gravely wounded. Would you want to get straight back into a body with sixteen stab wounds?'

'Fair point.'

'It takes a lot of extra energy to heal a body that's separated from its spirit. They'll do it, given time and access to enough nice, lively people.'

'Bad planning on Knife's part. If they couldn't reclaim their own bodies for a while, surely he couldn't seize them either.'

'Maybe that's what went wrong. Knife broke his prospective hosts too successfully. I don't get the impression he's thinking too clearly here.'

Konrad thought with dismay of the rib he had taken from Kovalev's corpse. In his own defence, the man had looked more than dead enough at the time. 'I wonder if any of them have got up and started wandering around, yet. That should entertain Nuritov.'

Tasha grinned. 'Better find out. It might be interesting to talk to them.'

Radinka interjected. 'Do you have any idea how cold it is with no body?'

'I cannot say I have ever mislaid mine,' Konrad replied.

'Think yourself lucky. I *really* want mine back.'

'Stick with us,' Tasha said cheerfully. 'We'll find a way.'

Konrad wondered when he and Tasha had become *us,* and moreover when the two of them had become so formidable a team that she could make promises with such unassailable confidence. 'We will try,' he corrected.

'How feeble.'

'How realistic.'

Tasha snickered. 'What aspect of your life is ever *realistic*?'

The wretched girl had a point, but Konrad was disinclined to admit it. 'Let's go see Nuritov,' he suggested. 'He might release Sokol and Dubin already. And we can find out whether any of our supposed murder victims have woken up yet.'

'Solid plan,' said Tasha.

Konrad looked at Radinka. 'Coming along?'

Radinka drifted in his general direction, shrugging wispily. 'I seem to have an opening in my schedule.'

So Konrad made his way back to police headquarters, accompanied by two lamaeni — one corporeally equipped, one rather less so — and two dead animal spirits, his inside coat pocket heavy with a rib bone its original owner probably wanted back. Realistic? Not so much.

6

'Nuritov,' said Konrad, upon finding himself restored to the inspector's presence. 'Have you happened to find any of your corpses unusually ambulatory?'

Nuritov had barely glanced up as Konrad came into his office, absorbed by some stultifying-looking stack of documents upon his desk. At these words, his head came up and he blinked at Konrad with myopic confusion. 'Ambulatory?'

'I realise the circumstance would be somewhat out of the ordinary.'

Nuritov's gaze travelled to Tasha, who responded with a casual wave. 'Not to my knowledge,' he murmured, taking the question with admirable composure. 'Ought they to be?'

'That depends on where they have been stashed, and how far away from living organisms that might be.'

'Oh.' Nuritov blinked.

It took a few minutes for Konrad to relay all that had occurred, and to explain Tasha's presence. He concluded by introducing Radinka, which was difficult considering her presently incurable ethereality and Nuritov's lack of spirit vision.

'Inspector,' she said, apparently out of thin air. 'A pleasure.'

Nuritov's composure, though impressive, was not fully up to the demands of the case. 'I see,' he said faintly, and fell silent, his eyes very wide.

Konrad judged it best not to draw his attention to the two serpents, who were presently engaged in inspecting the contents of his desk. 'I probably ought to offer Kovalev the return of his rib,' he remarked. 'If he is accessible?'

'And if you should happen to have a few colleagues handy that you don't much like?' Tasha put in. 'He will be needing food.'

Nuritov blanched at that, and repeated in a still fainter voice, 'Food?'

'In a manner of speaking,' Konrad said, with a scowl for Tasha. 'Lamaeni do not eat people, they just absorb animating energy. It does little harm.'

'*Little* harm.' Nuritov appeared to be recovering his equanimity, and fixed Konrad with a stern look. 'How much is *little*?'

'They might feel weary for a day or two.'

'Oh!' Nuritov brightened at once. 'Bykov, then, and Loronin.'

Konrad wondered about Nuritov's sudden cheer — at least, until Bykov and Loronin arrived. The former proved to be a young recruit, the kind that walked with a swagger and could not stop recounting his own merits in a manner designed to appear humble. Loronin was cursed with a pedantic air and a patronising manner, even when addressing Nuritov, his superior.

'Excellent,' Konrad approved.

Nuritov grinned. 'Gentlemen, there is some slight irregularity with some aspects of my current case, and we are bidden for the morgue.'

'The morgue?' repeated Loronin, recoiling. 'But why?'

'Will it be dangerous, sir?' said Bykov.

'Could be,' Nuritov said gravely, ignoring Loronin's question. 'That's why I need men with me that I can trust.'

Bykov swelled, and gave a crisp nod. 'I'm with you, sir!'

'Excellent,' murmured Nuritov.

'Dangerous?' repeated Loronin. 'It's a morgue. How can it be dangerous?'

'Most things stay dead when they have been killed,' Konrad offered. He uttered the word *most* with a slight emphasis.

Loronin turned paler, and tried to cover his obvious discomfort with some bluster about the enduring mythological concept of *undeath* and its essential unreliability in fact, a monologue which nobody much attended to.

Konrad enjoyed the short journey to The Malykt's Temple very much. He derived enormous satisfaction from observing the preparations of Bykov to meet any conceivable danger with staggering force, in the fullest confidence of the inevitability of his victory. He was similarly entertained by Loronin's attempts to demonstrate a knowledge he did not possess, and by his own adeptness in ignoring the other man's endeavours to discover just *who Konrad was* and why a top-hatted member of the gentry was disposed to assist with a police investigation.

Radinka amused herself by walking directly beside Loronin and periodically touching his hand, a gesture he could not feel but could, on some level, *sense,* for he jumped each time and began to stutter. The serpents improved upon this game by occasionally kidnapping Loronin's hat and whisking it away up the street, only to return it into his waiting hands moments later. And Tasha got on everybody's nerves by whistling popular tunes decidedly off-key, accompanied by an infuriating grin and an aggravatingly insouciant manner.

Konrad felt he had rarely enjoyed an outing more.

By the time they arrived at the morgue, Loronin was half out of his wits with fright; Bykov was ready to take on a small army by himself, should it prove necessary; Radinka had progressed to shadowing Nuritov, watching his every movement with a speculative, vaguely predatory interest; Tasha had abandoned whistling in favour of singing slightly bawdy circus tunes; and the serpents had decided they liked Loronin's hat and were going to keep it, in spite of his obvious dismay. Konrad began to feel a little pity for Loronin, for his worst crime was only foolishness after all. But when the silly man insisted upon preceding Konrad into The Malykt's Temple, with insufferable pomposity and a look of clear disdain, Konrad's pity melted away.

The morgue was, as ever, cold and empty. Very empty.

'Well,' said Nuritov, extracting his pipe from his pocket and absently lighting it. 'They *were* here.'

'Who were here, sir?' said Bykov.

'The corpses.'

'Body snatching,' said Loronin, with a sad shake of his head. 'Lamentable. The Malykt's Order should be able to manage better security.'

This slur upon his Order did not endear the man to Konrad.

'Maybe they're still here!' hissed Bykov, and readied himself for imminent combat.

'Thank goodness,' whispered a soft voice, which clearly belonged to no one of their party.

Loronin jumped, and instantly began haranguing Bykov for *playing pranks,* and outlining the duty he owed to his elders.

Konrad drifted around the corner. Just out of sight of Loronin, a group of three pasty-looking people huddled in a miserable, shivering cluster. They were all blood-stained, and visibly weak upon their feet. But they smiled, their eyes closed in deep appreciation for something or other.

Three lamaeni, feeding.

'Afternoon tea,' said Konrad. 'Delivered to your door.'

Kovalev opened his eyes, and lifted an eyebrow at Konrad. 'Ah. The bone thief.'

Konrad bowed. 'I do apologise. No doubt you can divine the reason for my disgraceful conduct.'

'Mm.' Kovalev looked Konrad over, expressionless. 'I would like it back.'

This request Konrad was more than happy to fulfil. He tossed back the rib bone, glad to have it out of his possession. 'If you could manage to keep that to yourself,' he ventured.

'Secrets are a lamaeni's bread and butter,' said Kovalev.

Konrad looked to the other two, Arina's victims. They were all three beginning to look healthier. Many of the wounds they had suffered were already healed; had been before they had retrieved their bodies, no doubt. To Konrad's fascination, the rest were closing up as he watched.

The others had joined him by this time. Bykov was clearly torn between a desire to prove his might by way of an instant attack, and confusion at the unthreatening picture the three made. Loronin merely looked appalled.

'Radinka,' said Kovalev. 'You weren't so lucky.'

Radinka made a disgusted noise, perfectly expressive of her feelings.

'What happened?' Konrad enquired. 'In as much detail as you can, please.'

Nuritov intervened. 'Bykov, Loronin. Guard the door, please.'

A sensible move. The presence of the lamaeni in Ekamet was not common knowledge, and that secret was not one to entrust to such people as Nuritov's despised colleagues. At the door, they would be out of hearing but not out of the lamaeni's reach.

The three were probably drawing upon Konrad and Nuritov as well, of course, but Konrad did not mind. On the contrary, he hoped he was every bit as delicious — and therefore, every bit as *alive* — as Nuritov. The inspector did not seem to mind being sustenance, either. Three fewer corpses to deal with was well worth the loss of a little energy.

Bykov and Loronin went away — the former protesting vehemently, the latter not at all — and Kovalev began. 'Favin,' he growled. 'An old… friend. Must've been following me, and my wits were asleep, I didn't notice. I stopped to talk to Dubin, Favin shoved him aside like he was nothing, took him up like some kind of puppet and Dubin came at me with those damned knives. Knocked me about pretty badly. I saw him off in the end, but he'd torn up my body so much, there was nothing I could do with it right away.' He eyed Nuritov with distaste. 'Then your lot stuck me down here, where there's hardly any food. Not my best week.'

'Sorry about that,' muttered Nuritov.

Konrad looked to the other two, both of whom stood a little way behind Kovalev. They appeared shy, or perhaps just uncertain.

'Our story is much the same,' said one, the younger man. 'Mother and I were travelling into Ekamet. We wanted to wait for Myrrolen's Circus. When we alighted from the coach, a woman we had talked to along the way produced knives from nowhere and attacked us. Almost hacked my head off, and stuck so many holes in poor mother…' He paused, and swallowed.

Konrad sympathised. The fact that all three had survived an attack which had previously appeared as the slaughter of innocents was so positive an outcome, it was easy to lose sight of the extreme trauma of the experience for *them.* How must it feel, to suffer those kinds of wounds while unable to die? To be, eventually, expelled from your own body, able to do nothing but watch as it bleeds out before you? Kovalev appeared to have taken it in stride, but the other two looked shaken and sick. The young man's mother still seemed unable to speak.

'Did you know him?' Konrad asked. 'This Favin?'

The man shook his head, and so did his mother.

'What about Sword? The one who slew Radinka.'

'I never saw him,' said Kovalev. 'But Favin was always as thick as thieves with his brother, Lazan. Whatever befell the one probably befell the other.'

So Knife and Sword were Favin and Lazan. 'How did you repel Lazan?' Konrad asked.

'Pure bloody-minded stubbornness.'

'While I applaud you for that, I was hoping for something a little more concrete.'

Kovalev shrugged. 'I don't know. We had a battle of wills, and I won.'

Konrad looked to Kovalev's companions, neither of whom had spoken. The lady merely looked at him with wide eyes, mute. Her son shook his head, and said helplessly, 'I don't know. I… was unconscious for a time, and when I woke, he was gone.'

Nuritov had held his peace for a time, listening to the various reports in quiet thought. Now he removed his pipe from his mouth and said, 'How many more of your kind are there in Ekamet, to your knowledge?'

'When the circus isn't here?' Kovalev considered the question. 'I do not know. But we are not numerous.'

Konrad saw the direction of Nuritov's thoughts immediately. He cast an eye over the two other lamaeni, whose names he had still not learned. There might be more like these, recently arrived in Ekamet and, as yet, known to none.

'We had better keep an eye on them,' Nuritov said. 'Lazan will probably try again.'

Kovalev shrugged his big shoulders. 'Yes, at some point. These failed attempts would weaken him. He'd have to recover first.'

Konrad smiled at Tasha, who instantly grew wary.

'What do you want?' she said, and took a tiny, probably involuntary step backwards.

'How would you like to be used as bait?'

Tasha adjusted her cap. 'Of all the offers I've ever received, that might just be the worst.'

'You'll be fine. Stubborn, bloody-minded Kovalev will be there.'

Kovalev folded his arms. 'Oh, will I?'

Konrad smiled at him, too. 'Lazan still needs a nice, cosy lamaeni-corpse to warm his incorporeal bones. He can chase hitherto unharrassed ones around the city and see if any of them prove an easier target. Which he might, if he can find any. Or he can have another go at one of you three. Fancy your chances a second time around?'

Kovalev growled something. 'All right. What's your idea?'

'Collect all of you into the same place and wait for Lazan to show up. We ought to be able to deal with him.'

'So we're all bait.'

'Yes. And all helping each other not be evicted.'

The lamaeni woman did not speak, but she nodded her head in obvious agreement, and with such vehemence that Konrad was slightly taken aback. Of all the assembled lamaeni, she seemed the meekest, the most damaged, the least likely to consent to anything that could put her in harm's way. He studied her carefully, and read a burning urgency in her eyes that he had no idea how to interpret.

'Thank you,' he said, hoping she would say something, elaborate upon her decision. But she did not.

'Fine,' growled Kovalev. 'Let's get it over with.'

'Excellent plan!' said the young man with enthusiasm, though he hesitated before he spoke.

Konrad looked at Tasha, who scowled back from beneath the brim of her dark cap.

'*Fine,*' she muttered. 'But if I end up homeless, I will be moving into *your* house as a poltergeist.'

'That is fair.'

Tasha nodded once.

Radinka's voice echoed out of the air a few feet away from Konrad. 'What about me? I can scarce understand how I came to be the only one unlucky enough to fall victim to these schemes. It's embarrassing. I want my life back.'

'I hope that the same stone will kill both of our birds at once.'

It passed through Konrad's mind as he spoke that his personal involvement in this case was no longer necessary. No one had been killed. There was nothing for the Malykant to do. He felt compelled to finish it because… because he disliked leaving a job undone. Because of Tasha, whose youth and stature caused him to feel a little protective, even if her obvious toughness and wily intelligence made him feel a little foolish for it. Because lamaeni like those Arina had killed deserved to be championed, too, even if the undead were not strictly under his purview. Because of Dubin and Sokol and Arina, used and discarded like faceless tools, left for days to cope with the horrific belief that they had taken lives.

And, of course, because of Nanda.

'All right,' said the young man, a little ungraciously. 'But how do you propose to catch Lazan?'

Konrad smiled. 'I have ways.'

Those *ways* might get him into serious trouble, of course, but Konrad admitted that to no one. He settled for hoping that the confidence with which he had spoken would not embarrass him later.

Well… he admitted the risks to nobody but Nanda, anyway. After the meeting in the morgue (and Konrad privately felt that far too many of his social activities took place in rooms full of dead people), Konrad went alone to Nanda's house. He found Arina still there, looking better: cleaned of the blood she had unwittingly spilled, calmer, less frightened. She was still quiet, and perhaps shy, for she barely met Konrad's eyes as he went in, and urgently occupied herself with some activity in Nanda's tiny kitchen before he could ask her how she did.

Nanda took Konrad into her workroom, and shut the door. Weveroth, her golden-furred monkey, sat upon the table with his tail curled around his legs. He sat eerily still, only his eyes moving to track Konrad's movements around the room.

'Creepy,' Konrad murmured, staring back at the monkey wide-eyed.

'Wevey,' said Nanda with gentle reproof.

The monkey's tail flicked, a gesture Konrad interpreted as faintly disdainful. His behaviour did not alter in any other respect.

Konrad turned his back upon him.

'How is Arina?' he enquired.

'Recovering, I think, but slowly. She's in a bad way. Afraid to leave the house, or to be alone at all.'

Small wonder. An experience like hers would be hard to forget. 'I need your help with something,' he said.

'Anything,' said Nanda promptly, and with a smile of such warmth that he was taken aback. He forgot his words and merely blinked stupidly, his mouth falling open.

'You're my friend,' Nanda said, her tone making it fully clear how much of an idiot she felt him to be. Well, she wasn't wrong. 'Also, you've cleared Danil, *and* proved that nobody died by his hand at all. I could hardly be happier with you just now.'

Konrad pulled himself together. 'You're welcome,' he said. 'Though I do not think you will be so happy with me once I tell you what I need.'

Her smile faded. 'I suppose it was too much to hope that you'd come here with a simple, easy, unobjectionable request.'

Konrad shrugged apologetically. 'Mine isn't exactly a simple, easy, unobjectionable life.'

'I can't argue with that.'

Weveroth appeared to have got over whatever his objections to Konrad might have been, for he decided that Konrad's shoulder might make a more agreeable seat than the table top, and availed himself of it with a flying leap. Konrad jumped violently, and almost threw the monkey off again in his irritation. But Nanda laughed, the golden smile once more lighting her face, and Konrad judged it worthwhile to hold his peace. He even stroked the monkey's furred tail as he talked, curling the tip around his finger.

Nanda did not like Konrad's idea.

'To be clear,' she said, with a wide-eyed stare at Konrad that clearly expressed her opinion of his sanity. 'You want to lure a rogue, bodiless lamaeni out of hiding by wafting the prospect of several fresh, new, lively undead bodies under his incorporeal nose. And you propose to ensure that *you* are the only living, mortal person at hand for him to possess in order to overpower one of them.'

'Correct.'

'So that he'll obligingly possess you.'

'Yes.'

'You want him to strap on the Konrad-suit and use you to hack off a few heads.'

Konrad coughed. 'Actually, it's his brother that goes in for decapitation. Lazan likes to stick holes in people.'

Nanda responded to this enlightening comment with a flat stare.

'He won't get very far,' Konrad reassured her. 'Or, he shouldn't. I am the Malykant, I have resources at my disposal that Dubin and Sokol and Arina do not share. He won't dislodge me.'

'So you are going to use yourself as a prison. A kind of live incubation system via which to kindly escort him into your Master's care.'

'Exactly!' Konrad beamed.

'While you are awake.'

'Of course I'll be awake.'

'You don't think it will be uncomfortable to have two souls squashed into one body?'

'Probably it will.'

'Please understand that when I say *uncomfortable* I mean *searingly, appallingly, intolerably unpleasant.*'

'Oh,' Konrad faltered. 'Do you think it will be?'

'Undoubtedly.'

He sighed a little, thinking of a recent case which had involved just such a scenario. Though happily he had not been the one to endure it, then. 'Ah well. I've suffered before.'

Nanda stared. Konrad thought he saw her eye twitch. 'If you were going to share body-space with somebody else's spirit, I wish you would not choose a crazy, ruthless, homicidal lamaeni.'

'I wish that, too. Wouldn't it be nice if bright, cheerful, well-adjusted and charming people would cause a little public menace from time to time? They would be so much nicer to deal with.'

'This is not a joking matter.'

'Sorry.'

Nanda scooped Weveroth off Konrad's shoulder and clutched him close, putting her cheek to the little monkey's soft fur. 'You are hard work,' she informed Konrad.

'I know. You really should pick better friends.'

'I didn't pick you.'

'Ouch.'

Her eyes twinkled a little, and she gave the great sigh that meant capitulation. 'Very well. I know it's hopeless expecting to talk you out of it. What do you want me to do? I collect you do not wish me to be present, or I might prove an unwelcome decoy.'

'Indeed, the last thing I want is for Lazan to use you instead. I need you to be my insurance.'

'In case of what?'

'In case of failure. I *believe* I can hold my own against Lazan, but I could be wrong.'

'So if Lazan overpowers you and you pass out, the way Danil did, you want me to… somehow fix it before you have chance to stick a bunch of holes in Tasha or Kovalev.'

'Yes, please. Tasha or my serpents will know to send for you, if anything goes wrong.'

Nanda rolled her eyes. 'You credit me with near godly powers. It is flattering, to be sure, but the *pressure*.'

Konrad grinned. 'You are equal to anything, I am sure.'

'There are one or two problems with all this. Or rather, questions which have not been answered.'

'Oh?'

'For one thing, how did that nameless young man and his mother avoid being dispossessed like Radinka? Did they ever offer any explanation for that?'

'They did not know. Tasha thinks that Lazan had made too much of a mess of their bodies and could not take control of them while they were weakened to such excess.'

'Sounds plausible, but what became of him after that?'

'No idea. The two of them were unconscious, and he'd gone when they woke.'

'Curious, don't you think? And why was Lazan having so much trouble, when his brother succeeded first try?'

'I don't know that either. Favin is presumably stronger, or Radinka is very weak. Or maybe he was just lucky.'

'Maybe, maybe.' Nanda frowned. 'Something is wrong.'

Konrad smiled. 'Which part of any of this strikes you as right?'

'True. I'd ask you to be careful, but I know it would be futile.'

'I will be fine. I always am.'

Nanda eyed him with vast scepticism. 'Something like that.'

7

Luring his prey into the trap did not, in the end, prove difficult. All Konrad had to do was to ensure that they received the right rumours: word of their little trio of former victims huddled in the morgue beneath The Malykt's temple, trapped and weak and helpless, ripe for the picking. Tasha's presence could not hurt either, for a young lamaeni girl might seem a likelier target if Kovalev and the others had proved too difficult. Konrad set his serpents to this task, confident in their ability to spread the desired gossip among the spirits of the Darks.

He made certain that Nanda was stationed at the other end of the street, in case of disaster; that Nuritov received only a general outline of the plan and none of its details, so that he could not helpfully show up at the wrong moment; and that Konrad's own devotions to The Malykt should happen to keep him at the temple for many hours together. The temple never hosted many devotees when there were no funerals being held, and the Order obligingly closed it for the day in order to discourage unwanted visitors.

So it was that Konrad spent most of a day in a cold, draughty, comfortless building, alone save for a group of undead strangers in the morgue below, and with nothing to do but wonder what it would be like to be possessed by a desperate killer. *Searingly, appallingly, intolerably unpleasant.*

It was not one of his better days.

He sat for a time, and when he grew too cold he got up and walked about instead, his senses on the alert for the approach either of Favin-as-Radinka or Lazan's spirit.

Company came, in the form of Eetapi and Ootapi.

Master. We bring glad tidings! Favin comes! That was Ootapi, his voice somehow more unpleasant to listen to the more gleeful his mood.

Eetapi added, *He will be here any minute.*

Favin? Konrad replied. *Is Lazan with him?*

He is alone, said Eetapi.

Konrad sat, blinking and trying to process that news. That Favin would hear his serpents' industriously-circulated rumours was of no surprise to him, and he had fully expected that the brothers would arrive together. Favin would certainly seek to assist Lazan. But what was he doing showing up alone? He had already got what he wanted. What interest could he possibly take in the other lamaeni now?

Probably he was merely travelling ahead of his brother, and Lazan would soon arrive. That changed things a little, and Konrad made some mental adjustments to his plans.

He said nothing aloud. His hands were so cold he could barely move his fingers, and he did not fancy his chances of making himself understood if he tried to speak through his frozen lips.

You look strange, Eetapi observed.

I imagine I look like a Konrad-shaped block of ice.

Eetapi apparently found this pitiable, for she drifted over and draped herself around Konrad's neck in a gesture possibly intended to be comforting. Since it felt like an unusually persistent, icy draught wrapping itself around his throat, Konrad failed to fully appreciate it.

Minutes passed. Konrad hushed his chatty serpents and sat in silence, all his senses strained to catch the first signs of approach. He had positioned himself next to the door leading down into the morgue, so he would be close at hand the moment either Favin or Lazan made any attempt upon the gathered lamaeni.

He would not admit that the fluttering sensation he was experiencing somewhere inside was nervousness. He had not been entirely honest with Nanda, which was never advisable, but she would probably have had him committed if he had told her the true extent of his plans.

Any sign of Lazan?

Not that his serpents would know Lazan just to look at him (or his shade), but they were alert to the approach of any lamaeni in spirit form.

None, hissed Ootapi. *Favin is almost at the door.*

Konrad tensed, his confidence draining away by the second. This wasn't right. *Radinka?*

Here, she said, from somewhere behind him. *Ready.*

Konrad's Master Plan, Phase One: Permit dispossessed Radinka to utilise his own body in order to dislodge Favin from hers. This done, Radinka would take possession of her undead corpse once more and tada, problem solved. Konrad, meanwhile, would (to use Nanda's typically forthright turn of phrase) use himself as a prison (*live incubation system*) within which to store Favin's spirit until he could be dispatched to The Malykt for judgement.

Konrad's Master Plan, Phase Two: Somewhere during this process, Lazan would try to possess Konrad himself, in order to use him as a weapon against one of the other lamaeni. Instead of being used to hack holes in Kovalev or Tasha, Konrad would heroically resist Lazan's attempts to master his will and instead imprison him. After that, both brothers could be delivered to his Master at once.

Simple, no? Effective? Radinka would be restored to herself, Kovalev and the others would be delivered from the threat of renewed attack, and Tasha would be safe. The fact that Konrad would have to juggle not one but *two* invading spirits without being overcome by either was incidental. Suffering was something he could do, and he was rarely to be beaten for sheer bloody-minded stubbornness (as Nanda frequently told him).

If Lazan didn't show, well, in some ways that made it easier. He could concentrate on dealing with Favin without having to fend off Lazan at the same time.

But it didn't make sense to Konrad, and that made him nervous.

He is passing the door, reported Eetapi.

Wait... passing? Passing *the door?*

Yessss.

He isn't coming in?

He is not.

Konrad was struck briefly speechless. Just what was going on? *Keep an eye on him,* he snapped.

Yes, Master. Eetapi and Ootapi streamed away.

Radinka was nervous, too. He could feel it, a palpable, thrumming tension in the air emanating from a few feet over his left shoulder. *What's happening?* she hissed.

I have no idea, but I will find out.

Konrad took a moment to think. What could Favin be doing? Where was Lazan? It seemed that neither brother had acted upon his rumours, which was disappointing and troublesome. Perhaps Favin had discovered some other lamaeni somewhere in Ekamet, and that was where Lazan had gone. In which case, his serpents would soon discover it, but probably not in time for Konrad to do anything about it.

But if that wasn't it... then what?

He got up and made for the stairs.

Down below, he found a little knot of lamaeni lingering not far from the door. They were almost as visibly tense as Radinka.

He was immediately struck by the inescapable fact that there were only *three.* Tasha, Kovalev and the woman from the stagecoach.

'Where is your son?' Konrad said sharply.

The woman just looked at him. Her eyes were huge and frightened and Konrad began to get a very bad feeling.

'Gone,' said Kovalev. 'Hours ago.'

'Nobody thought that was worth mentioning to me?!' Konrad felt like kicking something, and took a moment to master his frustration.

'His own problem, if he gets attacked again.' Kovalev was vastly indifferent.

Konrad looked at Tasha. 'Surely it struck *you* as odd?'

Tasha shrugged, but she began to look uncertain. 'He said he'd fought off Lazan once before, he could do it again. I figured it's his choice. He was still here by *repute,* and three of us is enough to carry through the plan, right?'

Konrad took three slow, deep breaths, struggling against an impulse to tear out his own hair. When he felt he had himself under control, he pointed a finger at the woman. 'Has she spoken? At all?'

'No...' said Tasha.

'I am sorry,' Konrad apologised. 'I know it is rude to refer to you as *she,* but we still do not know your name. And that is because you are, temporarily at least, muted. Is that not the case?'

The woman swallowed, and nodded.

'Let me guess,' he sighed. 'The person wearing your son's body was not him at all.'

A shake of the head.

'Your son is travelling with you, isn't he?'

She nodded.

No wonder she was paralysed, mute and frightened. 'It can be difficult to adjust to the presence of a second soul,' he commented. 'Two souls in one body, fighting for control of the vital parts, like for example the speaking apparatus. Difficult for either of you to get a word out at all. But you'll adjust, or you would if we left you in this state.'

'So that was Lazan,' said Tasha. 'Wearing her son, as you put it.'

'I assume so.'

Tasha looked at the woman. 'And you took your son's expelled spirit into your own body? Why?'

Of course, no reply came. Konrad studied her, feeling appalled but also a little curious, for it was a fair question. Finding her body stolen, Radinka had continued on in spirit form, relatively as normal. Most lamaeni occasionally abandoned their bodies and wandered the world ghost-form. It was probably an uncomfortable experience to do it for too long, particularly under the uncertainty of wondering when, or *if,* you would ever get your body back again. But it was not in itself remarkable. What had encouraged the poor woman's son to hitch a ride with his mother? Or what had compelled *her* to absorb him, if that was what she had done?

'He was either taking refuge from some lingering threat, or you were protecting him from something,' Konrad guessed, watching the woman's face closely.

She opened her mouth, spat out a couple of malformed and incoherent syllables, and settled for a nod of the head instead.

'Does the threat persist?'

She hesitated, glanced around, and finally shook her head.

'In that case, he can come forth.'

Nothing happened. The poor woman's face contorted in clear distress, or perhaps *struggle,* but she did not manage to speak, and no spirit materialised.

'He's stuck. Or petrified. Hmm.' Konrad pondered. 'Do we have your permission, madam, to apply a little force?'

A vigorous nod of the head. She was keen to be liberated.

Konrad smiled. 'Tasha, would you be so kind?'

He did not have to explain. The girl separated from her undead body at once. Her suddenly lifeless corpse fell to the ground with an unpleasant, meaty *thud,* and her spirit materialised in the air above it.

Konrad then had the pleasure of experiencing, for the first time, how it really felt to take another's spirit into his own body. *Excruciatingly painful* did not quite cover it. Though, pain was not perhaps the right word, for it was not a physical sensation. It was more a whirl of sheer confusion and mental conflict, impossible, overwhelming. Konrad felt like seventeen people at once, and within half a minute he could barely remember his own name, let alone manage to form words. It was like being squashed into a broom cupboard with about three times as many people as the room had the capacity to accommodate, except that it was happening inside his mind, and he had not the power to leave.

And he had planned to do this with *two spirits at once*? Nanda was right. He was stark raving mad.

The ordeal did not last long. In the next instant — or so it seemed to him — it was over. The alien presence in his mind was gone, and he was himself again.

A little more time and activity had passed than he was aware of, for before him the beleaguered woman lay stretched upon the floor in an attitude of dazed, pained bewilderment, a bruise darkening upon her jaw. But her eyes had lost their frightened look, and she finally spoke an intelligible word. '*Ouch.*'

'Tasha,' Konrad said evenly. 'Did you punch her in the jaw?'

'Yes.'

'I mean, did *I* punch her in the jaw?'

'Yes.'

He winced. He was no boxer, but he was not a small man, either, and his punches carried the weight of both experience and not insignificant muscle.

Brutal though Tasha's approach was, it appeared to have worked, for she could speak again. And there, materialising in the air not far away, was the wavering and visibly enraged spirit of her son. The young man delivered himself of several expletives, uttered in a hissing, unpleasantly penetrating voice which Konrad emphatically did not appreciate. It was like the mental equivalent of having spikes driven into his skull.

'Stop,' he ordered, for it was clearly having the same effect upon Tasha and Kovalev. And Radinka, who had tired of waiting upstairs and had drifted down to investigate matters in the morgue.

The young man spat one last curse and fell silent, ending with a whispered and wearied *sorry*.

'No matter,' Konrad said, a little softened. 'Tell us what possessed you, if you will.'

An unfortunate choice of words. He meant, *what possessed you to piggy-back in your poor mother's head,* but under the circumstances, it could have been better phrased.

Besides the problem of Favin, Konrad had some other questions swirling around in his mind. Most importantly: why had Lazan lingered? Having secured his new vehicle, why had he not fled at once? In fact, why had either brother remained in Ekamet, knowing that they had the vengeful spirits of at least two evicted lamaeni to deal with? He waited, hopeful of an answer that would resolve all these questions, and permit him to come up with a new, more workable plan of action.

'He was trying to *eat me,*' said the young man, with a strong shudder.

'Eat...?' Konrad echoed faintly.

'You know how lamaeni feed, I assume? We sup on the living energy of those around us — mortals. Those who have not yet died, in any sense of the term. It's because we have ceased to produce any such energy of our own. What is to fuel us, without it? How are we to maintain the fractured link between body and soul?

'But this... *thing* they have been doing. Putting the wrong spirit into the wrong body. It is unnatural — even for us! Nobody does it, because it's an atrocity but also because it fundamentally doesn't *work*. It can't be done. Spirit wars with body every waking minute, and I do not think there are any sleeping minutes to be had, because it requires ceaseless application of the will to hold the two together. Will, and as much food as can be had.'

Tasha spoke up, her eyes very wide. 'Including other lamaeni.'

The man nodded, and shuddered again. 'It is grotesque. Cannibalism. But it's like a shot of pure power, an instant boost. Imagine if you were able to consume the... the brainpower of other living souls, to temporarily boost your own cleverness.'

'I take it the thing is more easily done, with a bodiless soul.'

'Yes. Lazan knocked me for six and then tried to devour me on the spot. Mother protected me. He was weakened enough by his efforts that we were able to fight him off... or at least to convince him that it was no easy task to take on both of us, what with having a corpse-shell to protect us. We thought he would flee, but he *stayed.* He told us he would rebuild his strength right here in the morgue, and then pick us off one by one as necessary. He said it was mighty convenient, our being all gathered here together. Laid out like a feast.'

Kovalev's eyes narrowed. 'I heard nothing of this.'

'Why would he tell you, and put you on your guard? It didn't matter with us. We knew what he was up to, and he knew we couldn't speak to tell.'

'I wonder,' Konrad mused, 'how long he expected to be able to maintain such an unlifestyle? There are not that many lamaeni around.'

'More might be made,' Tasha said. 'He might still be able to do that, even with a stolen body. If not, the two of them might have allies who are still sound.'

How repellent, and how true. Was that what the two of them were planning? Set up a nice little energy farm somewhere in Ekamet, turning mortals into lamaeni only to devour them afterwards?

Not in his city.

'Radinka,' Konrad said. 'Did Favin try any such thing with you?'

No. But if you ask me, Favin is not very clever. Brute force he's got to spare, but not so much by way of brain.

That more or less agreed with the impression Konrad had received, during his brief meeting with the man. Lazan was undoubtedly the wilier of the two, the one who would quickly cotton on to the difficulties of his new situation, and hit upon a solution. And he did not lack for strength, either. That made him far more dangerous than his brother.

'Did Lazan say where he was going?' he enquired. It was a long shot, but the man appeared to have been unusually chatty.

'No, and not a word of a clue did he give,' said the young man.

Typical. 'My serpents have followed Favin. Hopefully he is on his way to wherever Lazan has gone, and we will find them both soon. In the meantime, will the two of you please tell me your names?'

The lady introduced herself as Faina, her son as Pavel. Konrad made introductions of himself, Tasha, Kovalev and Radinka in return.

'We need to stop those two,' he said grimly. 'If I'm not much mistaken, they will soon begin manufacturing their own dinner, and it is the duty of The Malykt's Order to get in the way of that. And maybe The Shandrigal's, too. But we'll need lamaeni help. May I count on you?'

To Konrad's satisfaction, he received willing agreement from them all, even those spirit-stuck and vulnerable. The extent of the danger was obvious enough, most like. Not only were they in danger of being dined upon themselves, but the survival of their kind relied upon their existence being kept largely a secret from those they (sparingly) supped upon. Having a pair of rogue lamaeni setting up in the middle of Ekamet, turning living folk undead with or without their consent and making a banquet of them all? Such an operation couldn't possibly go unnoticed.

'Right, follow along,' Konrad said, making for the stairs back up to ground level. 'We're going to fetch Nanda.'

8

'So,' said Nanda, eyeing Konrad and his entourage from over the rim of her cup of tea. 'I take it the plan did not work out as intended.'

She was waiting in a tea house not far from The Malykt's Temple. Seated by herself at a tiny table in one corner, a pot of tea set before her and a cup in her hands, she made a fine picture of tranquillity. Weveroth sat at her elbow, nibbling upon a biscuit. Konrad took in this peaceful vision with a sense of gratitude, for some little part of his tension eased.

'Total failure,' he replied, and added with a faint smile, 'Highly unusual, I know.' He relayed the morning's events as quickly as he could, part of his mind on the alert for the return of either of his serpents. That they were taking so long about it troubled him, for it meant either that the brothers were gone far, or that something had gone wrong.

Nanda heard him out with her usual cool composure, one lifted eyebrow the only hint as to her opinion of Konrad's plan and its outcome. When he had finished, she cast a swift look over Kovalev, Tasha and Faina, and stood up. 'I had better muster my Order.'

This she apparently did by way of Weveroth, for she wrote something upon a slip of paper, handed it to the little gold-furred monkey and whispered something in his ear. Weveroth bounded straight off the table and galloped out of the tea house, followed by the variously startled and intrigued looks of the tea house's customers.

Konrad had already dispatched word to his own Order. He

needed Diana Valentina, whose calm competency rivalled Nanda's. And he needed The Shandrigal's people, too, for the lamaeni dwelt in some confused realm in between those two polar opposites of Life and Death, and he could not say whose powers were best fitted to deal with the unusual threat posed by Favin and Lazan.

Eetapi's mind touched his. She was distant still, but closing fast upon the tea room. He pictured her lithe, incorporeal serpent self, streaming through the snow-drenched skies with as much speed as she could muster.

Eetapi, what news?

They are near the north gate, Master.

They!

The brothers are reunited. They are out in the Bones, and they have taken seven people.

Living or undead?

Living, for the present. They also have one other lamaeni with them.

All of which confirmed Konrad's worst fears clearly enough.

Konrad relayed this. 'We go, now,' he concluded. 'Tasha, Kovalev, Faina. I need you to disable Favin as quickly as possible, by whatever means possible. Radinka, Pavel, I fear you are in danger if you accompany us—'

You cannot leave me behind! Radinka objected. *That's my body he's using!*

'I do not suggest it. On the contrary, I want the four of you to reclaim your body from Favin as quickly as possible. But you should not travel spirit-form.'

Everybody knew well enough what that meant. Faina agreed readily enough to be her son's protector once more, though the idea displeased them both. Konrad hoped that somebody would volunteer to host Radinka, but the silence of all three disappointed him.

'Fine, I'll do it,' said Tasha at length. 'Play nice, Radinka.'

Radinka did not enjoy the idea any more than Tasha, but she could not deny the merit of his suggestion. Konrad waited impatiently while the two of them managed the business with only a little distaste and not too much horror. Tasha concluded the process with an unpleasant groan of discomfort, and he was appalled to notice an odd change in her eyes: a dizzy duality, from which he quickly averted his gaze.

'Nan?' he said, and looked to his friend.

'I must await my people here. They will not know where to go.'

'We cannot wait.'

'I will be a few minutes behind you.'

With this, Konrad was obliged to be content — until the timely return of Weveroth, who came racing back into the tea house and hurled himself at Nanda. Nan soon had him installed as her emissary, bearing another note. Konrad instructed Eetapi to remain, too, against Diana's arrival.

Then away the party went, traversing the snow-laden streets of Ekamet with as much haste as the conditions would permit.

Favin and Lazan had established themselves not far from the site of Faina and Pavel's attack. Eetapi's instructions guided them past that very spot, though all traces of the violence had long since been buried under a fresh layer of snow. Konrad expected to find a hut, or some kind of building, but the brothers had merely corralled their captives right out in the open. Each one was lashed to a bone-white, snow-covered tree, blue with cold, some of them unconscious.

Konrad did not immediately approach, but paused a little distance away, out of sight. It was Ootapi who brought Konrad him his information, together with a mental picture of the little camp.

The seven living had already been whittled down to six, one turned lamaeni by Favin's and Lazan's ally.

'I know him,' Kovalev said with a growl, upon receiving Konrad's description of the newcomer. 'I will deal with him.' An axe appeared in his hands, a wicked, deadly weapon whose outlines flickered and wavered for a short time before it solidified — by appearance, at least, well able to inflict appalling damage.

Konrad weighed his options, deeply uneasy. He was no inconsiderable power himself, and he was aided by Nanda, Ootapi and three other lamaeni (and Radinka and Pavel, however reduced they were). But Favin and Lazan had already prevailed over the latter two, and Tasha and Faina were both hampered by their passengers.

Could they wait, until Diana and others arrived? It was risky. One of the captured living had already been turned, and was in imminent danger of further violence. The remaining six could not hope to survive long.

'We must move,' Konrad decided. 'Kovalev, please dispatch their associate. Ootapi, bind Favin as you did before, give Nanda a chance to deal with him. Tasha, Faina, we need to dispose of Lazan. Pavel, use me to attack — dislodge him if you can. Release me as soon as that's done, reclaim your body. I'll take care of Lazan after that. All clear?'

Nobody liked the plan, and Konrad could not blame them, for it was a shambles. But it was the best he could come up with, and doing nothing while the three lamaeni tore through their captives would be indefensible.

Nanda cast him a sideways look, and he waited, expecting a sarcastic comment if not an outright objection.

Instead she said: 'Thank you for not trying to coddle me.'

That required a little thought to interpret. She was right: it had cost him something to direct her Favin's way, and he had to stifle the part of himself that wanted to keep her as far from the mess as possible so she couldn't get hurt. But he knew better than to underestimate her, and he badly needed her help.

He also knew she would happily kick him somewhere painful if he tried to shield her. Deservedly.

But did she really mean what she had said? Was some part of her dismayed that he hadn't shown concern for her welfare? Was she being sarcastic?

No time to think about it now. He merely gave her a nod, which she answered with a roll of her eyes.

They approached the camp — in time to watch as one of the living, a burly man with a black beard, attacked one of the others. The former was possessed, Konrad judged, and the latter probably the newly-turned lamaeni. This confused spirit was easily dislodged, and devoured on the spot by Favin-as-Radinka. The process was conducted with a chilling efficiency, though it had one advantage: so absorbed was the group of Favin and Lazan and their unnamed associate that they did not immediately observe the assault upon their camp.

Kovalev went straight for the third lamaeni, a thin, brown-haired man of indeterminate age. He was brutal. He'd made for himself a second axe, and he wielded both with ruthless savagery. Surprise served him well. His target was intent upon another captive, presumably preparing for the process of turning the next; Kovalev felled him with one staggering blow and hacked off his head with the next.

Ootapi bound Favin, before he had any chance to react to the invasion. Favin-as-Radinka was only temporarily paralysed by surprise; he fought, and Konrad knew that Ootapi could not hold him alone for long. But Nanda was there, shimmering with that odd light she had once or twice displayed before: a mantle of The Shandrigal's power, wielded with cool expertise. Konrad did not much fancy Favin's chances.

Konrad made for the figure of Pavel, within which Lazan resided. Tasha and Faina flanked him.

'What is this?' Lazan snarled with fury, his teeth bared —

— and then he was down, Pavel's body laid out in the snow with a series of shallow knife-wounds criss-crossing his flesh. Pavel had not been gentle. The body was inert, dead, which meant that Lazan was dislodged...

Konrad sought for the spirit he knew would be nearby, hoping that Pavel would soon regain possession of his stolen body. He couldn't worry about that now. Where was Lazan?

He held great power, as the Malykant; some portion of his Master's, lent to him for the performance of his duties. Usually he kept these hidden, cloaked himself from the notice of others beneath a semblance of normality. Only in times of great need did he permit that cloak to fall away, to reveal his true nature to the world. He did so now, gathering everything that he had for the fight. He felt stronger at once, his soul blazing with The Malykt's cold, bone-chilling will.

His heightened senses alerted him: a freezing, malevolent presence nearby, lunging for him, intent upon his destruction.

Excellent.

Konrad pounced. It was not a physical attack; more of a mental one. He extended his borrowed Will like a net, gathered up the enraged spirit of Lazan, and mentally swallowed him whole.

The pain began.

If the presence of Tasha in his mind had been hard to bear, this was intolerable. Lazan was like a bundle of fireworks, tearing his mind apart, burning away his resistance and shredding his sanity. The man fought to subdue Konrad's will with the strength of desperation; even with The Malykt's power supplementing his own, Konrad was hard pressed to retain control of his wits. His awareness of the world beyond his own mind faded; there was nothing but Lazan and the paralysing pain.

Distantly, Konrad thought he heard himself screaming.

Irinanda Falenia was, ordinarily, a tolerant woman and composed, not given to outbursts of high emotion of any kind. But she had spent days tending to Arina, who would probably never recover from the appalling use that had been made of her, even if she had not actually taken any lives. The knowledge that such violence had been committed by her hand; the memory of the bloodied snow and her bloodied clothes, those inert bodies felled by the grave wounds she had inflicted; the realisation that it was *possible* for her wits to be mastered by so malevolent a soul, and that she was powerless to resist; all these things took a grave toll upon her. Nanda saw that her life, her spirit, had been crushed by all of these things, and grieved. Anger had been ignited in her heart, and she had been nursing a growing desire to hurt something.

The sight, then, of this sorry, snowy clearing and its complement of terrified captives burned through her restraint in an instant. All tolerance and forgiveness melted away, and Nanda let her fury blaze forth as she made for Favin. She'd wanted Lazan, really; wanted to wreak her revenge directly upon the one who had broken Arina, and who had probably masterminded this horrible sequence of events. But she did not doubt Konrad's ability to manage him suitably, and meanwhile... Favin would do.

Nanda opened herself to The Shandrigal, letting her mistress's power fill her to her core. It blossomed and swelled within her, fuelled by her own rage until she felt she might burst with the pressure of it. She knew she was glowing as she advanced upon Favin, Ootapi at her shoulder.

She smiled upon him. It was not a pleasant smile.

'Favin,' she greeted him. 'I am somewhat displeased with you.'

He was not given time to respond. Ootapi struck, winding itself around Favin's spirit in a paralysing grip. Radinka's stolen body stiffened and froze — for an instant. But Favin gathered himself and fought; Ootapi hissed and shrieked with effort and pain; and Nanda had no time to think.

Ideally, Favin ought to be expelled from Radinka's body and captured. His judge ought to be The Shandrigal, or perhaps The Malykt, for he and his brother had transgressed mightily against Them both. But Nanda had never been faced with such a problem before; there was no clear way to proceed, no precedent for how to prevail.

So she acted on instinct. She reached for Radinka's face and gripped it in her shimmering hands, staring into the eyes that burned with a fury almost equalling her own. Then, brutally, she took all of The Shandrigal's power that ran in her own veins and forced it upon Favin. It penetrated his skin, pore by pore, and flashed through him with the speed and ferocity of a house fire.

With an agonised shriek — a sound Nanda would cherish until the end of her days — the wayward spirit of Favin died. In fact, he *melted,* all the thoughts and energies and memories and cruelties that made up the core of his soul dissolving under her burning touch.

Nanda held on, until every last flicker of Favin had vanished and she knew she beheld naught but an emptied shell. When at last she removed her hands, the body of Radinka crumpled into the snow and lay there, seared and broken.

Ootapi? Nanda enquired, suddenly frightened that she might have burned him away, too.

But the serpent shivered to life in her awareness, cringing and shrieking, shocked and damaged but essentially whole.

You did well, she praised him.

The serpent shivered on, seemingly unable to muster a response.

Sorry, she added, regretful.

She took a breath or two to steady herself, for she, too, was shocked and shaking in the aftermath of such an effort. Then she turned, seeking Konrad.

He was locked in a similar struggle with Lazan-as-Pavel as she had just won against Favin, but she immediately received the impression that he was flagging. Perhaps Lazan really was that much stronger than his brother. Perhaps Konrad lacked the burning fury that had driven her; he was not given to rage the way she sometimes was, and he had not spent days nursing poor Arina. Perhaps it was merely that The Malykt's power was less serviceable in this endeavour than The Shandrigal's; the lamaeni were undead, and that arguably placed them outside His influence.

Whatever the reason, Konrad was losing. She could see it in the uncontrollable way his body shook, sweat pouring off him despite the freezing, falling snow that turned his black coat white.

Fear blossomed in her heart. She ran for him, hampered by her skirts and her weariness and the thick snow under her feet, too *slow*.

She reached him just as his eyes rolled back and he sagged, defeated. He turned his head to regard her, and nothing of his eyes showed but the whites.

Nanda had no warning. Konrad was Konrad no longer and he lunged for her, teeth bared. No attempt to capture or distract or disable her, this: he sought to kill. A pair of ethereal knives flashed into being in his curled fists, solidifying before her horrified eyes.

She dodged. Too slow: a knife grazed her arm, slashing through her clothes and leaving a burning, stinging wound carved into her shrinking skin.

Nanda cursed, knowing herself outmatched. She was no killer; no duty of hers carried her into harm's way, ordinarily, and she was not equipped. She carried no weapons, reliant upon The Shandrigal's might to defend herself at need. But *this* was beyond her experience, and the fact that Lazan attacked her with her dearest Konrad's hands badly unnerved her. She dodged another slash of those terrible knives, and another, gaining new cuts each time: another down her arm, a second across her back.

Panic shot through her. She fumbled for the power she had wielded so easily only moments before, but fear undid her — fear, or weariness, for she had badly spent herself in her battle against Favin.

She was going to die.

Then she was no longer alone. A chill, alien, *dead* presence slithered into her mind and bound up her will, holding her terrified mind in a ruthless grip. She flailed and struggled and screamed but to no avail: she was caught tight and held fast, and the end could only be seconds away.

She was slow to realise that the ghostly spirit with whom she was suddenly sharing quarters was no enemy.

Ootapi held her in his snakey grip, binding her up as he had bound Favin. Not just Ootapi, either: Eetapi was there beside her brother, both snakes shrieking with a splintering anger which threatened to crack her bones. They had served Konrad eight years already, and perhaps another Malykant before that. They knew what to do.

Under their direction, Nanda's body dodged and whirled far more effectively than before. More than that: she ceased to withdraw and went on the offensive, advancing upon Lazan-as-Konrad with the terrible, cold might of The Malykt's own servants strengthening her limbs. Her panic faded; she remembered herself, remembered her own strength, forgot to be deterred by the sight of Konrad's contorted face. Ootapi and Eetapi loosened their grip, and Nanda's own power revived. Her spilled blood turned black and her skin began to glow.

Konrad took a step back.

Then another woman materialised behind him, a woman with a mane of curly dark hair blowing wildly in the wind. Diana Valentina.

She was *not* happy.

'That's quite enough,' she snapped. To Nanda's horror, a glimmer of metal flashed in the wan light and Konrad screamed. Diana had buried a knife in his back, slammed the blade hilt-deep with chilling precision and a shocking ruthlessness.

Konrad dropped face-first into the snow. Blood poured from the wound in his back, turning the snow red around him. He would bleed out; he must do, for his lifeblood flowed out of him with every beat of his heart and there was so *much* of it.

Diana let go of the blade as Konrad dropped and stood watching, her face utterly cold.

It was no ordinary knife. The blade glittered with a weird light that was somehow half shadow, a glittering black fire that quickly spread to engulf Konrad's whole body. It blazed and burned and Nanda had to look away.

When the fire faded, Konrad had not been consumed, as Nanda had briefly feared. But he had not been mended, either. He lay there bleeding, far too still.

Nanda dropped to her knees beside him, heedless of the wet, cold snow that instantly soaked her clothes. When she touched Konrad, she found his body almost as cold as the air around him.

'You've killed him,' she gasped, and stared at Diana with something close to hatred.

'I had to,' replied the leader of The Malykt's Order. She looked dispassionately down at Konrad, unmoved, then bent to remove the knife. More blood gushed from the wound, but the knife was somehow pristine. 'A lamaeni gone mad is a threat that cannot be lightly dealt with, and for such a being to take control of the Malykant...'

She did not finish the sentence, but she did not have to. Nanda understood. Such a combination of powers posed so severe a threat that the utmost force was justified in its removal. Konrad was...

... something else. Not undead, though Nanda knew that he worried it was so. He was not lamaeni. But Myrrolena had been right to say that he was not alive either, not in the way that Nanda was, as he had once been. He had died in the course of his duties and been revived by his Master's will, but not quite everything had been restored to life. That was beyond the power even of The Malykt.

What that meant as far as Lazan was concerned was... difficult to say. Would Lazan have relinquished Konrad's body, once he had gained control of it? Would he have found it as habitable as the undead body of a fellow lamaeni, or as repellent as the corpse of a living man?

The former was not impossible, and such a scenario must be avoided at all costs.

But that did not lessen the tragedy of it. Nanda stared at the limp form of Konrad Savast, her dearest friend, so shocked and numb she could barely think. At last she lifted his head, very gently, and placed it into her lap, stroked his half-frozen hair. 'He will be revived, of course,' she said to Diana, hoping that her confident statement would receive an immediate confirmation.

But Diana said nothing. She met Nanda's gaze, her face expressionless.

Nanda's heart quailed.

The Shandrigal's Order arrived, or two of them. Too late to be of any use, too late to prevent Konrad's paying so high a price. Nanda ignored them, did not even look their way. She stayed with Konrad, waiting for his Master to arrive and make everything right again.

But minutes ticked past and The Malykt did not appear.

'Where is He?' Nanda said at last, looking to Diana.

Diana Valentina minutely shook her head. 'He does not always answer.'

Nanda bristled. 'He must! His servant lies dead!'

'There is always another Malykant.'

The coldness, the brutality of the statement shocked Nanda to speechlessness. She could only stare at Diana, aghast.

Diana's face softened, a fraction. 'Do not mistake me. I respect Konrad, and to an extent I am fond of him. We all are. But it does not pay to grow too attached to the Malykant. A ten-year tenure in that role is considered lengthy indeed, for they rarely last anywhere near so long.'

Konrad had served eight. Did that make him unusually senior? Was The Malykt's Order expecting him to be replaced any day now, any hour?

How did a Malykant come to relinquish the role? Did they simply resign it when they grew too tired, or jaded, to continue? Did they go mad, driven so by the brutal demands of the role? Or were they killed, and at some point simply permitted to die?

'Konrad... it is not his time,' Nanda whispered. 'He is still a fine Malykant.'

'That is not for me to decide.'

Nanda fell silent, and the minutes passed. The Malykt was not coming.

Well, then. Would she accept Konrad's passing, or not? If Diana would do nothing, what could she, Nanda, do?

Konrad had not been killed in the line of his regular duties. Not really. He had been pursuing an unusual case, and for the second time — a second case involving the lamaeni, whose peculiar nature made them an obvious part of neither The Malykt's nor The Shandrigal's sphere of influence. They were neither living nor dead. The Malykant had little obligation to deal with such as they, for he could deliver no justice.

Konrad had done it anyway. He had tirelessly pursued Favin and Lazan, even after he'd learned that they had committed no crime which qualified them for his attention. He had gone after them because they posed a threat to the living people of Ekamet — and to the undead, people like Tasha and Radinka who went about their more unusual lives in much the same way, causing no real harm.

If he was jaded by the role, corrupted, maddened, he could never have acted as he had. He would have withdrawn from the case the moment he realised it was the lamaeni again, and cared nothing for the consequences. He did not deserve to be left to die.

Nanda shut her eyes, blocking out the sight of Konrad's body and the cold, motionless figure of Diana Valentina standing over him. She found the thread of magic in her heart, the shining light which bound her soul into the service of The Shandrigal. And she *pulled.*

The Malykt might sometimes ignore the call of his followers, but The Shandrigal did not. At least, not this time. An instant, and She was there, a comforting warmth and a glow which banished even the chill of an Ekamet winter.

Irinanda, said She.

Mistress. I seek aid.

So I assume.

Nanda swallowed, her heart suddenly pounding. What if she had overstepped? The Shandrigal was no more in the habit of granting boons than The Malykt.

Too late to worry about that now. Gathering her courage, Nanda laid the matter before her mistress, striving to do justice to the sense of duty and the selflessness she believed Konrad had shown. The Shandrigal listened in silence.

When Nanda had finished, the silence continued for some time.

At length, The Shandrigal spoke again.

You know him better than others, do you not?

The question came as a surprise, and Nanda was briefly disconcerted. *Um... I believe so, yes.*

Is he, in your opinion, a worthy Malykant still?

Yes. Nanda said it unhesitatingly.

Yes? Think hard, Irinanda Falenia.

Yes.

The warmth faded all at once, and the cold bit once more into Nanda's skin. Her heart was colder still, for her mistress had made no answer, had neither granted Nanda's wish nor given explanation for denying it. Tears leaked from her eyes, and she could not bear to open them only to see poor Konrad as silent and still as ever.

Then she felt movement under her hands, and almost leapt out of her skin. Her eyes flew open.

Konrad lay inert. She must have imagined the return to life and motion, her fractured heart playing tricks on her foolish mind.

But no... there it was again. A faint spasm of the muscles, a tension that had not been there a moment ago.

'Konrad?' she murmured.

He tried to say something, but she judged that his mouth was full of snow, for it emerged too muffled for comprehension. There followed an ungraceful spitting sound as he, presumably, cleared his mouth of the obstruction.

'Nanda,' he croaked. He tried to move, to turn over, but he froze halfway through the attempt and collapsed back into the snow with a groan and a curse. 'I... hurt.'

'You've been stabbed,' she replied coolly, trying not to let her absurd jubilation show. 'Lie still. You'll be tended to shortly.'

'I *hope* so,' he said through gritted teeth. 'This is not the most comfortable I've ever been.'

'Stop whining,' snapped Nanda — glad that he was faced away from her, and could not see the tears on her cheeks. 'It could be worse. You could be dead.'

Konrad sighed deeply. 'You are such a comfort, Nan,' he muttered. 'I can always rely on you to lift my spirits.'

Nanda merely patted him on the back — taking care not to get too close to his wound, which had once again begun to bleed — and said flippantly, 'That's my job.'

9

Konrad was confined to bed for two weeks, which left him with mixed feelings. On the one hand, it was rather dull. He had books to read, but that got old fairly quickly, and he received few visitors. He suffered a great deal of pain, even with the assistance of Nanda's herbs and potions, and that was an unpleasantness he would gladly have dispensed with if he could.

On the other hand, he was warm; the luxuries of Bakar House afforded him all the blankets and pillows and roaring fires he could possibly wish for. It had to beat trekking about in the frozen Bone Forest.

And he did have some visitors. Nanda came every day, though she did not usually stay long. The serpents pestered him all day long, to the point that he began to feel he would cheerfully strangle them if they were not already dead. And Nuritov came a few times, usually in the evening on his way home. With the latter, Konrad turned over every detail of the latest case, finding Nuritov to be both interested and observant. The inspector brought him word of other cases, too, some of them recent and some old, unsolved puzzles. Konrad enjoyed these conversations hugely, as did Nuritov, and by the time Konrad had recovered enough to begin moving around again, they had settled into a routine of regular meetings.

He knew that he had been stabbed, because Nanda had said so, and because through clever, if painful, use of a mirror and a little contortion he had seen the evidence for himself. But he did not remember anything about it. How he had come to be stabbed, and by who, were mysteries to him, and Nanda refused to answer any of his questions upon the subject. He had given up eventually, though her silence worried him. If it had come about by any simple, obvious way — if Lazan had stabbed him, say — then why would she not say so? Clearly something odd had happened, something Nan feared he would not like.

Konrad wished she would just tell him. He probably worried far more about the matter in the *not* knowing, than he would have if she told him the truth — however painful a truth it might be.

But he could not convince her of that, and eventually he gave up trying, and tried to dismiss the matter from his mind.

He was tucked up in his study one day, wrapped in blankets and trying to sit in such a way as to spare his shredded back from undue pain, when Nanda arrived. She announced herself by way of a gentle tap upon the door, a sound he instantly recognised. His heart leapt, and all the minor irritation and frustration he had been feeling melted away.

'Come in!' he called, delighted.

In she came. And in came Dubin, right behind her.

Konrad's heart settled down.

'Good afternoon,' he said gravely.

'How formal,' Nanda chided him. She came forward to kiss him on the cheek, a gesture he appreciated in particular considering the presence of Dubin. But that was foolish of him.

'I'm being polite,' he informed her. 'Do have a seat, won't you both?'

Nanda chose her usual chair, rolling her eyes at him in passing. Dubin hesitated rather longer, and finally perched uncomfortably upon the edge of the seat farthest away from Konrad.

That was interesting.

'To what do I owe the pleasure?' Konrad said, his gaze fixed upon Dubin as he spoke.

Nobody said anything.

'If it is to be a silent visit, you will not mind if I return to my book? It is quite gripping.' That was a lie, for he was heartily bored with it, but they need not know that.

Nanda cleared her throat and looked meaningfully at her friend. 'Danil came to thank you.'

Konrad's brows went up. 'For what, pray?'

Nanda said nothing else, her silence clearly indicating that she would speak no more on Dubin's behalf.

'Um. For saving my life,' said Dubin at last, awkwardly, though he met Konrad's gaze squarely. 'The Malykant never came for me. Nanda says it is because you proved that I did not... act voluntarily.'

'I suppose it is,' said Konrad, trying not to visibly flinch at the mention of *the Malykant*. 'I did not do it for you, precisely, but I am glad you were spared, and you are welcome to benefit from my efforts.'

Nanda made a disapproving noise, and Konrad understood by it that she found this speech insufficiently gracious.

Well, tough. It was the best he could do. Not because he continued to feel undue resentment against Dubin; in fact, that had largely melted away. Perhaps it was because of the man's obvious wretchedness and despair, when he had languished in prison awaiting what he saw as his inevitable death. It had been a sight to evoke pity in the coldest heart.

Perhaps it was also because Konrad had found himself in a position of undeniable power with regards to Dubin; the man's life had rested in his hands, and he had realised that he had no desire whatsoever to take it. He had never truly wished death upon the poison trader, and he could never be the person to deliver such a cruel fate undeserved.

However. The entire business had left him feeling oddly ashamed of himself, his lifestyle, his job, and far too aware of how easy it might someday be to get it wrong — to destroy the wrong person. Dubin stood in representation of that, and as such, he remained an unwelcome sight to Konrad.

'I shall be leaving Ekamet soon,' Dubin said, after a short silence. 'I cannot remain. There are too many here who read of my guilt in the papers, and have no faith in my exoneration.'

This news Konrad might have welcomed, a week or two before. But to his own surprise, he did not now. 'You must not feel that way,' he said. 'Those who so readily condemn you do not deserve your consideration anyway.'

Dubin smiled faintly. 'That may be true, but my livelihood depends upon my being seen as trustworthy.'

'Has it collapsed? Have all your customers deserted you?'

Dubin exchanged an uncertain look with Nanda. 'Not all, but

many.'

'Some will return. New ones will present themselves.'

'You don't understand—'

'Don't I?' Konrad stared coldly at Dubin, taking no trouble to conceal his irritation. 'You know nothing of me. I understand that the opinions of the world must never be permitted to matter very much. People will always feel fear, and because of it they will reject those things they do not understand. People will always find something to condemn, because it makes them feel better about themselves. It makes them feel safer, and superior. You must let it go. Cling to those who trust you come what may, for their value cannot be overstated. Forget the rest.'

This speech provoked no particular response from Dubin. He blinked a few times, and found nothing to say.

'Give it some thought,' Konrad advised. 'Stay another week or two. See how it goes.'

Nanda indicated her support for this approach by directing a beamingly hopeful smile at Dubin. The effects of *that* were more significant, not at all to Konrad's surprise, and the forlorn poison trader managed a wan smile back. 'All right,' he said.

'Good,' said Konrad, tired of the subject and of Dubin in equal measure.

Dubin did not appear to require much more of Konrad's company either, for he soon took his leave. Nanda, happily, opted to stay.

'How much did you tell him?' Konrad enquired.

'About what.'

'Me. Clearly he knows that I had a lot to do with his deliverance, but does he know why?'

'Of course not. I told him you're a rich, bored eccentric with a taste for the bizarre and an obsession with solving puzzles.'

Konrad eyed her with displeasure. 'I'm torn between thanking you for keeping my deep, dark secret, and admonishing you for offering so unflattering an alternative explanation.'

'Is it unflattering? What could possibly be wrong with wealth, eccentricity and strange tastes?'

'You made me sound creepy.'

'I did, didn't I?' Nanda smiled, and examined her nails. 'But maybe you are.'

'Creepy?!'

'Mhm.' Nanda spoke the word in a dreamy tone, nodding in a way that suggested she found the idea appealing. Possibly even attractive.

She couldn't possibly. 'Stop teasing me.'

'But it is so vastly amusing.'

'Well, find something else to amuse you.'

'How about a game?'

'Such as.'

'My favourite game is called "Needle Konrad Until He Either Screams or Laughs."'

'So the sooner I consent to laugh, the less likely I am to burst with fury.'

'Exactly! You catch on fast.'

'Couldn't we play something else?'

'Such as?'

'Umm.' Good question. Konrad thought a while, but it had been so many years since he had even considered playing a game, he came up with nothing.

'We could play "Drink Tea and Engage in Banal but Soothing Small-talk,"' Nanda suggested.

Konrad smiled. 'I don't hate that idea.'

'Grand praise indeed! It shall be so.'

Konrad rang for tea, which appeared with pleasing promptitude. His cook also provided a range of biscuits and cakes, all of which were Nanda's expressed favourites. He made a note to increase the observant and helpful cook's pay.

'Of course,' Nanda said with a mouth full of cake, 'We *could* play both at once.'

'You intend to enrage me with small talk?'

'It can be perfectly infuriating.'

How true. Konrad hated "light conversation." Its desultory nature struck him as a waste of good air. 'Cold today, wasn't it?' he offered.

'Oh, positively *freezing*,' Nanda agreed, punctuating her words with an over-violent shiver. 'And the sky! I do think we shall have a great deal more snow before the morning.'

'Which would be the most shocking surprise, considering the season.'

'No sarcasm!' Nanda chided. 'That's cheating.'

Konrad grinned. 'I am a filthy cheat, so be it.'

Nanda grinned back. He expected another such sally, but instead she said: 'Are you happy being the Malykant, Konrad?'

The swift change of topic took him so much by surprise, he had to take a moment to adjust his thoughts. 'Happy?'

'Well... happy enough to continue, anyway. If you were boundingly *happy* with it I would probably recommend you for committal to a madhouse.'

'I suppose so.' He frowned. 'I have had no thoughts of resigning the post, at any rate.'

Nanda nodded. 'That is a good enough answer.'

'Good enough for what?'

She shrugged. 'Just good enough.'

How mysterious. He knew better than to ask the reason behind her questions; she would not tell him, if she did not wish to.

He thought a little more. In some ways, he would be delighted to be rid of the duties he sometimes found onerous and distasteful. Particularly now, when he no longer enjoyed the relatively blissful lack of feeling he had long benefited from, courtesy of his Master. It had grown harder to do as he had to do, and in some ways... well, sometimes he wished, a little bit, that he did not have to.

But not that much. He took satisfaction in ensuring that killers received their fair reward, and in removing such people from the streets of Ekamet, so that they could not hurt anyone else.

And besides all that, what would he *do* if he was no longer the Malykant? Where would he go? The role was his entire life.

'I'm happy to continue,' he said. 'For now. Make of that what you will.'

'It's enough,' Nanda said. She took another biscuit, bit into it with a *crunch,* and smiled at him with her mouth full of crumbs. 'Thank you.'

He blinked, puzzled, but of course she did not elaborate. 'You're welcome.'

THE SPIRIT OF SOLSTICE

1

The eve before Winter Solstice arrived; heralded, as ever, by a flurry of snow and a bone-aching chill. Konrad welcomed the joys of the season by going to bed straight after dinner — alone. He took a book, three hot bricks and a glass (or two) of brandy with him, a combination which seemed to him to encompass all a gentleman could possibly wish for on such a night.

So deliciously comfortable was he in his four-poster bed, nightcap firmly warding off those errant wisps of draught which found their way around his heavy bed curtains, that he was not best pleased to be disturbed by a frigid whisper shivering through his mind like a sudden, icy wind.

Master.

If he ignored it, would it go away? Konrad tightened his grip upon his book, slithered fractionally further beneath his blankets, and read on.

Maasssssteeeer!

'Begone, foul fiend,' he muttered, without hope.

Master! Pleeeeaassssse.

Konrad sighed gustily, and closed his book. *Yes, what is it?*

We have a gift for you!

The serpents materialised before him. There were two of them, a brother and a sister (or so they had been in life): Ootapi and Eetapi, his personal plagues. Assistants, actually, bestowed upon him by The Malykt Himself. Their appointed duty was to help him with his task of delivering justice to the killers of the city of Ekamet, but they seemed to take their unofficial duty every bit as seriously — that being, to make constant nuisances of themselves.

A gift, how lovely. Konrad tried to sound as though he meant it. Really, Winter Solstice was such a trying time. Everyone expected such a total change of attitude! Cheer must abound! There must be love, joy and happiness wherever one ventured! And really, it was such an unnatural state of being. Konrad did not know anybody who managed to maintain the Solstice Spirit for the whole of the season.

Personally, he did not trouble himself to maintain it for more than a day or two. Today not being one of them.

You will love it. Eetapi's melodic, mournful voice carried a hint of smugness.

Konrad tried, briefly, to imagine what a pair of long-dead ghost snakes might decide to present him with for Solstice, but soon abandoned the effort with a shudder. Nothing he would *love,* he was fairly sure.

What has inspired this sudden fit of largesse? I do not recall your ever giving me gifts before.

Serendipity! proclaimed Ootapi.

A fortunate accident. That sounded... worse. Konrad braced himself. *You'd better tell me.*

It is a surprise! Eetapi carolled.

That was another thing about Solstice. Surprises. Who liked surprises, truly? Most of them were unpleasant. *No surprises, just tell me!*

Eetapi drifted closer to his face, until her ice-white, translucent manifestation was all that he could see. Her eyes blinked slowly. *Will you come with us, or shall we persuade you?*

That did not bode well. One of his serpents' more useful (and chilling) talents was the ability to bind the souls of others, for a time. If the person in question still lived, it had the effect of immobilising them until the serpents were pleased to release them — or until they fought their way out, which sometimes happened.

They had done it to Konrad in the past, the little dears. Once or twice, they had used it to good effect — when Konrad was about to do something oblivious and foolish, for example. Usually, though, they did it to torment him. The experience was appalling: it was like being wrapped in chains and then immersed in a frozen lake. He was not about to volunteer himself for a dose of that tonight.

It is only Solstice Eve, he tried. *Can it not wait for tomorrow?*

It will not wait, and neither will we!

Stifling a groan, he threw back his blankets and left the warmth and comfort of his bed. The cold bit into his shivering limbs as he stepped beyond the protection of the bed curtains, and his mood soured a little more. Damn the serpents. Could they not see that permitting Konrad to rest comfortably abed made for a far better Solstice gift than anything else?

How far are we going?

Not far, said Ootapi.

Probably not as far as the Bone Forest, then, in which case he would not need his most robust attire. He chose heavy black trousers and a thick cotton shirt, a woollen waistcoat to put over it, and his favourite crimson-lined winter coat. Fine black boots, a long cloak and his top hat completed the ensemble, and he was ready to depart.

Lead on, he said briefly, not troubling to disguise his lack of enthusiasm.

The serpents sailed away, and Konrad fell into step behind them. He paused only to snatch up a pair of black wool gloves on his way out of the house, and then they were away into the streets of Ekamet, exposed to all the delights of a dark night enlivened by a persistent snowfall.

It is cold, Konrad informed his detested servants, wishing that he had thought to pick up a scarf.

Try being dead, Ootapi suggested. *We do not feel the cold at all!*

A fantastic suggestion.

Ootapi, as impervious to the nuances of sarcasm as he was to the cold, rippled with pleasure.

I cannot help suspecting that our Master would be displeased, however, Konrad continued. *A dead Malykant is of little use to anybody.*

When you have finished being the Malykant, then, Ootapi amended.

We will kill you ourselves, if you like, Eetapi chimed in. *It will not hurt at all!*

If this is your idea of helping, I dread to imagine your notion of a gift.

You will love it, Eetapi promised again, and Konrad sighed.

You said it was not far? They had traversed several streets already — curiously bustling streets, considering the lateness of the hour and the season. Should not all these fine people be in somebody's home, sitting by a roaring fire and indulging in too much food? Or tucked up in bed with a book and a glass of brandy...

The serpents swerved left without warning, so rapidly that Konrad almost overshot the turn. He hastily adjusted his direction, and found himself ducking under the lintel of a shop. A liquor shop, he soon observed, which seemed to add insult to injury, for had they truly dragged their poor master away from the fine brandy he had already been enjoying in order to acquire more?

So absorbed by his grievances was he, it took a moment for him to realise that it was far too late for the shop to be open, especially at Solstice. A second look revealed that the door had been forced open.

Then the serpents began to emit an eerie, pallid glow, lighting up the dark shop, and there stretched out upon the counter was a man.

He was a decade or so Konrad's senior, as far as could be judged under such conditions: perhaps in his mid-forties, his cheeks mottled with the reddish hue of a regular drinker. He was plump and bald, dressed in a rather luxurious wine-red silk waistcoat, full-sleeved shirt and brown wool trousers.

He was also very dead, judging from the fact that half of his throat was missing.

When you spoke of a gift, Konrad said, *I did not imagine that you meant another job. This is work!*

Talk to him! Eetapi frisked about in the air over the man's rigid corpse, gambolling like a delighted child. *He is wonderful!*

She did not wait for his response. She and Ootapi instantly caught up the unravelling shreds of the man's sundered spirit and bound them back into his body. A shudder went through the corpse, and he blinked once.

Konrad stood over him, trying not to look too closely at the mess of the man's torn-out throat. 'Good evening,' he said gravely.

The dead wine merchant smiled. The movement caused his broken throat to sag horribly, leaking blood, and Konrad hastily averted his eyes. 'Evening! Come for a spot of toddy to warm up the night, have you? I've got everything you could want, sir, everything! You'll probably want the best, I should think.' The merchant folded his hands comfortably over his blood-soaked waistcoat and beamed at Konrad.

'I haven't come to make a purchase,' said Konrad, mystified. Did the man not realise he had died?

'Just as well,' said the merchant, with unimpaired cheer. 'I would have trouble assisting you like this, wouldn't I? I'd better not get up.

Ain't proper to make your acquaintance like this — ought to stand up, oughtn't I? But I'd hate to bleed on your cloak.' The man touched a finger to his torn throat. 'Has it stopped bleeding?'

'Almost,' murmured Konrad. The man was probably mad, he decided. Nobody reacted so cheerfully to their own death. 'What is your name?'

Normally he had to compel the recently deceased to speak much; they were in too much shock to co-operate without interference. But the merchant said jovially: 'Illya Vasily. Proprietor of fine wines, spirits, liquors of all kinds — the finest in Ekamet! Ask anybody!'

Konrad cleared his throat. 'And, um, Mr. Vasily... how did you come to be deceased?'

'There I can't help you.' Vasily drummed his fingers against his silk-clad belly, and hummed a few bars of a popular ditty. 'Man came in earlier tonight, just as I was about to leave. All locked up and everything. Wanted to make a last-minute purchase, he said, for a Solstice gift, and who was I to refuse? It's Solstice! So I made to get him a bottle of Kayesiri claret — that being what he'd asked for — and... now I'm as you see me.'

There were a few details missing from the story. Konrad began his questions. 'What did this man look like?'

'Couldn't tell you. He was wrapped up even tighter than you, all bundled up against the cold. Red scarf around his neck, covered half his face. All dark clothing.'

'What did he do to you?'

I don't know, sir. Can't rightly remember.'

A shame, but not unusual. It was the mind's way, sometimes, to erase from its records anything it found too shocking, too traumatic, too difficult to cope with. Violence resulting in death certainly qualified. 'How did you come to be laid out upon the bar, like this?'

'Can't tell you that, either!' Vasily smiled ruefully, and shrugged his meaty shoulders. 'I wasn't rightly aware of much until you woke me up. Good of you, by the way.' He nodded to Konrad, and — more interestingly — to the serpents who floated above. Usually they terrified people, especially the newly dead, but Vasily was as cheerfully unconcerned by their eerie, frigid presence as he was by his own demise.

'It was not done as a service to you,' Konrad felt obliged to admit. 'I am charged with finding your killer.'

'The Malykant, is it?' Vasily regarded Konrad with new interest. 'Never thought I would meet you, that's for sure! But pleasure, pleasure! Good to make your acquaintance! I hope you find him.'

'I will,' Konrad promised. *Let him go,* he ordered the serpents.

But Vasily seemed to sense that his brief revival was over, for he held up a plump hand. 'May I make a request? Seeing as it's Solstice.'

Konrad sighed inwardly. He probably wanted to be brought back to life, somehow; it wouldn't be the first time a newly expired ghost had asked for that. And it was Solstice! Of course, he would be asked such a thing on such a day, when it was especially sad to have to refuse.

'I couldn't... stay, could I?' said Vasily. 'I shan't mind being dead, but I'd rather not be parted from my shop, all the same.'

Konrad was too surprised to speak right away. Here was a new request. A ghost who wanted to remain a ghost? Who preferred to linger, sundered from his mortal body? Usually they were in a hurry to move on; to leave behind a world they could no longer share in, a world they were otherwise condemned to drift always upon the edges of, always cold, always alone.

'You do not wish for justice?' Konrad finally said.

'Yes I do! Deliver that justice, by all means, and my thanks for it! Only don't send me away!'

'I... will see what I can do.' Here was new territory; Konrad was not at all sure he could contrive to do both at once. But it was Solstice...

Illya Vasily beamed upon him. 'Talk to my cousin,' he recommended. 'I don't know why, but I feel she could probably tell you something about all of this.'

A vague and unlikely lead, but better than nothing. 'What is your cousin's name?'

'Kristina Vasily. She owns a couple of warehouses by the docks. I use her premises all the time.'

Vasily. It occurred to Konrad, belatedly, that it was a name he was not unaware of. 'Big merchant family, yours?'

'Oh, yes! Quite the network! You'll find out, I'm sure.' Vasily winked at Konrad. 'All right, I suppose my time is up, isn't it? Solstice greetings to all of you! Enjoy your fires, your dinners and above all, your wines! Enjoy them double, for me!'

The serpents released Vasily's soul, and his corpse went back to being just a corpse. Konrad regarded the inert body with regret.

Isn't he wonderful? sighed Eetapi. *No one is ever so cheerful about death!*

How did you know? He said himself, he has been insensible since the moment of his death until now.

It's the way his spirit resonates, Eetapi answered incomprehensibly. *Such merry vibrations! Never have we seen the like!*

Konrad judged it best not to enquire further. *Eetapi, let Nuritov know about this,* he instructed. *Ootapi, with me.* Inspector Nuritov would not be best pleased to be interrupted on such an evening, but somebody had to deal with poor Vasily's corpse, and that was a job for the police.

His job was a little different. Steeling himself, for he had never before had to carve open the body of so friendly and chatty a ghost, Konrad applied his knives to Illya Vasily's vacated corpse and extracted a single, thick rib bone. This he carefully wrapped, and stored inside his coat for later use.

Finding a way to dispatch Vasily's killer without also dispatching Vasily's ghost into the Malykt's care would be impossible; the two had to occur together. But he had not had the heart to admit that to Vasily.

So your idea of a Solstice gift is an unusually challenging job, with next to no leads. Konrad made for the door, donning his gloves once more.

No! Eetapi sounded disgusted with him. *A man who is not afraid of death! Who can greet his own demise with equanimity, and optimism! Is that not an example of true Solstice cheer?*

The serpents could do with an education about Solstice, Konrad thought. Somehow, he did not feel that their interpretation of Solstice Spirit was likely to be much taken up.

2

Konrad tried to convince himself that he was free to postpone the next stage of the investigation until the morning. It was Solstice Eve, after all. Not only was he entitled to revel in the joys of the season himself; those whom he needed to speak to were likely to be busy doing exactly that. Would they welcome a visit from a stranger bearing ill-news, on such a night?

He could not carry these ideas very far. For all that his fireside and his bed might beckon, a man had died tonight, and violently. Could he be certain that the person responsible had now completed their brutal errands, and had no further targets in mind? Of course he couldn't. Proceed he must.

But how? Vasily had not appeared to know of anyone who might wish him harm; he'd had no notion whatsoever as to the identity of his killer. What had he meant by pointing Konrad in his cousin's direction? He could not mean to imply that Kristina Vasily might have had something to do with his death, surely? If she had, she had not carried out the crime herself. Illya Vasily had described a man... though could he be certain of that? Yes, for the person had spoken, ordered claret. It would not be easy to mistake a woman's voice for a man's.

I wonder, thought Konrad vaguely, what became of the claret?

Warehouses by the docks. Kristina Vasily would not be at her warehouses at such a time of night, surely? She would be at home, with her family. Konrad could not follow her there. Having no official, public role as an investigator had its drawbacks; he was not part of the police force, he could not simply present himself on somebody's doorstep late at night and expect them to co-operate with him. Nor could he be the person to share the news of her cousin's death with Kristina Vasily, and therefore, how could he ask her if she knew anything about it?

He would relay this suggestion to Nuritov. The Inspector knew of Konrad's identity as the Malykant, as of recently. To Konrad's surprise, and secret pleasure, Nuritov had altogether failed to baulk at the news, or to condemn Konrad for it. Instead, he had accepted this insight into Konrad's life with a mixture of calm unflappability and characteristic curiosity. True, the fact that Konrad interested himself in murder investigations was not news to him; this was how they had become friends in the first place. But he had taken the rest well.

It was useful as well as reassuring, for now Konrad could share the burdens of his investigations more freely with Nuritov, and vice versa. It was almost like having a partner.

So, Kristina Vasily was Nuritov's territory. What did that leave for him?

Ootapi? Have you suggestions?

Yes, said the serpent promptly.

Konrad waited, but nothing followed.

Well?

The snake was behaving oddly, floating back and forth over the door of Vasily's shop like a streamer caught in the wind. Konrad watched these antics for a few moments, until Ootapi let his manifestation fade into nothing, and vanished from sight.

There is a trail, he finally reported. *A scent, a vibration.*

A what?

A disturbance in the aether. Something has torn through here...

You did not notice this on the way in? Konrad growled something inarticulate. If this "trail" had been left by the person who slew Vasily, they should have followed it at once. They might have caught up with him already!

It was not here earlier, replied Ootapi, and that brought Konrad up short.

You mean this was done while we were in the shop?

Yes.

Hm. Then it was either unrelated, or... Vasily's killer had lurked outside while Konrad was within.

Let's follow it, shall we? Lead on.

Ootapi gave a mental salute and took off, and Konrad fell into step behind, musing. This *disturbance in the aether,* what did that mean? It certainly was not usual for any killer to leave such a trail behind, or to have any such effect upon their environment. If this was the doing of Vasily's killer, he might be unaware that he was doing it at all. If he was, and he had indeed lingered outside the shop... perhaps he intended that Konrad and Ootapi should follow.

Suspicion and paranoia... Konrad was becoming far too adept at both. He dismissed the idea from his mind — mostly. It would not hurt to take some care.

Ootapi gathered speed, soaring overhead with the swiftness of a bird. Konrad hoped that the trail might lead them away from the centre of Ekamet and its busier streets, but no such luck: he was forced to push and dodge his way through crowds of smiling, red-cheeked passersby, and felt in danger of losing Ootapi any moment. The serpent was excited, deaf to Konrad's pleas to slow his pace.

'Konrad?'

The voice was familiar, and dear. Konrad stopped dead, Ootapi forgotten, for Nanda stood before him. She was wrapped in a warm blue coat, a dark scarf encircling her throat, a woollen hat covering her pale blonde hair. She held a bag bulging with parcels in one hand.

Konrad grabbed her free arm and set off once more. 'There's trouble!'

'But it's Solstice—'

'Season of Joy and Cheer, I know. But not everybody can keep it up quite *all* the time.'

'There's been a killing?'

'You don't truly believe people will refrain from hacking each other to pieces just because it's Solstice, do you?'

'I suppose not.' Nanda trotted along behind him in silence after that, leaving Konrad to wonder why he had dragged her along. Some mad impulse. Poor Nanda, he ought to let her get back to her celebrating. Just because he had to be out chasing killers all nigh—

He stopped, because a woman lay sprawled in the street and he had almost run over her. Her enthusiasm for the season had perhaps got out of hand, for she was decked in sprigs of holly and everything about her was red: her coat, her hat and shawl, her gloves, dress, shoes... and the blood that soaked the front of her clothing, from her torn-out throat down to her waist.

'Oh!' Nanda came to an abrupt halt beside him, her toes only inches from the woman's out-flung arm. She stared down at the body in wide-eyed horror, and Konrad bitterly regretted whatever whim had prompted him to bring her along.

'Sorry, Nan,' he sighed, and knelt by the woman's head. The blood still flowed; she had not been dead for long. *Ootapi, bind her up.*

Nanda collected herself and approached the crowd of horrified onlookers who were beginning to gather; Konrad heard her soothing people, asking if anyone had seen anything. His feelings turned about again, and he was glad he had her close. She was eternally reliable.

Of course, the crowd was slightly inconvenient. He couldn't very well compel a visibly slaughtered woman to start talking, not with such an audience at hand. Not if he wanted to maintain the secrecy of his position as the Malykant, anyway, and that was vital.

He would have to do it the more difficult way.

Ootapi, keep her mouth shut.

The serpent obeyed. The woman's eyes lost the staring look of death, filling with character and a semblance of life once more, and fixed upon Konrad. He gazed back, taking note of the lines about her eyes and mouth, her grey hair: she was older than Vasily, much older.

Speak, he ordered her. *Not aloud. What happened to you?*

She blinked slowly, twice, and tried to move, but Ootapi had her bound fast. *I do not understand. Is something amiss? Have I fainted?*

Konrad winced inwardly. Once in a while, he encountered someone whose death had come upon them so swiftly, so unexpectedly, they failed to realise it had happened at all. He did not relish having to break such news. He never knew how to do so gently.

You are dead, he told her.

So much for gently. Her eyes filled with tears, and a suppressed shudder racked her body.

Then, to his immense surprise, she smiled — if not with her mouth, then with her eyes. *Oh, thank goodness.* The words formed in his mind, wreathed in relief and joy.

I... I beg your pardon?

But she would not speak another word. A breath, two, and she was gone from his mind, inattentive; deaf to his pleas that she would return, tell him her name, anything.

You can let her go, Konrad said at last to Ootapi.

Konrad got to his feet, trying to ignore the stares of the people around him. He did not look as though he had any right to be taking such an interest in the corpse; he was obviously neither a doctor, nor a member of the police force. The other, obvious alternative was that he was the person who had inflicted the wound, and he could see that conclusion forming in the minds of some of those nearby. They stared in growing horror, and began to back away.

Good, let them take themselves off. They were only in the way.

He toyed with the idea of sending Ootapi to Nuritov in his sister's wake, but abandoned the thought. The news would travel by itself, and fast.

That trail, Ootapi. Does it continue?

Yes, Master.

Then we follow.

This was no time to collect a bone from her; that would have to wait. Konrad paused only to collect Nanda, who was talking to a sobbing woman a few feet away.

'We go,' he told her, voice pitched too low to be overheard. 'There may be more.'

Nanda awarded the afflicted woman a parting smile and a friendly squeeze of the arm. 'The police will be here soon,' she said. 'I am sure there is no danger now.'

Then they were away once more, leaving the dead woman prostrate in the snow behind them. 'She knows nothing,' Konrad said as they walked, Ootapi riding the winds ahead. 'Nor would she tell me her name.'

'I gleaned little from the onlookers,' Nanda admitted, pulling her cloak closer around herself as a strong gust of wind blew through the street. 'No one recognised her. Some of them described the attacker, though. A tall man in a tall hat, shrouded in a dark cloak.'

Konrad grunted, remembering the frightened, accusing stares of some of those who had been close to him. 'Are you sure they were not talking about me?'

'Possible.'

Then again, the description was not inconsistent with Vasily's recollections of his final customer, either. A tall, dark man. What a fine cliche it made.

Some ten minutes passed. Ootapi forged ahead, oblivious to the freezing wind and the driving snow. Konrad and Irinanda followed, considerably more afflicted by both. They covered a significant distance in the time, moving as fast as they could down the snow-laden streets, and Konrad began to relax. Perhaps there would be no more deaths tonight; perhaps the blood-thirst was slaked, the killing over...

The streets were growing dark, now, most of the shops closed for the night. Streetlamps shone upon shut doors and shadowed windows, and the crowds were dissipating at last. But one window up ahead glowed with the welcoming, flickering light of lit candles. The sight ought to have been inviting, but Konrad felt a sense of dread, for the door was wide open...

Sure enough, Ootapi swerved, and dived inside.

The establishment proved to be a cheese shop. Its proprietor had been prevented from closing it up, in all likelihood, by the attack that had made a bloody ruin of his throat. Unlike Vasily, he had not been laid out upon the counter. He lay in the middle of the floor, a slight man dressed in a black coat patched at the elbows. His dark hair was swept back in a shaggy mane, all askew and spattered with blood. His dark, vacant eyes stared sightlessly at the ceiling, one discoloured with a blood-red stain.

Ootapi, quickly. Bind!

The snake flew to obey, and within moments the slain man's body began to shudder. He coughed and gagged, and could not seem to stop.

Konrad realised, with shock, that the man was laughing.

'Speak,' he ordered.

The man continued to chortle, wheezing and hacking and spluttering in helpless mirth.

'Please, stop laughing,' Konrad said, aware that he sounded both plaintive and weary but unable to help it. 'We are not blessed with an abundance of time.' There was a killer tearing through the streets of Ekamet and if Konrad was to have any hope of finding him, he needed information *soon*. 'Who killed you?'

The man was giggling now, his lips spread in a rictus grin. 'Charming fellow. Dark cloak, hat, all that. Scarf over his face, couldn't see much.'

'Why do you say he was charming? I do not see the humour.'

'You w-wouldn't, would you?'

Konrad exchanged a look with Nanda. She looked as disturbed as he.

'Nan. That Reader thing you do. It doesn't work on corpses, does it?'

Her eyebrows rose. 'It... oddly enough, I have not had occasion to try it, very often.'

'Don't handle corpses much, hm?'

'Not especially often, no. It might work tonight, since he's in residence. So to speak.' Nanda knelt beside Konrad, gingerly avoiding the pool of sticky, congealing blood spread across the floor, and wrapped her fingers around the giggling man's wrist. Konrad gave her credit for doing so unflinchingly.

After only a few seconds, she released him with a gasp. 'I think his mind's slipping. There's nothing but laughter!'

'Nothing?'

'All I can discern otherwise is a lack of familiarity for this place. He isn't the proprietor.'

'What? Then where is the shopkeeper?'

Nanda shrugged.

Konrad made one last effort. He gripped the lapels of the laughing corpse's coat and tugged, forcing the man to return his gaze. 'Tell me who you are.'

An answer came, but so smothered in laughter that Konrad couldn't understand a word.

He gave up. Time pressed; their quarry was out there still, somewhere in the city, possibly slaying someone else while Konrad wasted his time trying to talk to a dead madman. *Release him,* Konrad ordered, and Ootapi shot free of the man's soul with a strangled noise of disgust.

He is mad.

We noticed that.

Out into the street they hurried, hats and hoods pulled close against the snow. But the chase ended abruptly, and in disappointment, for not twenty steps beyond the cheese shop's door, Ootapi came to a dead halt.

What is it? Konrad watched, bemused, as the serpent turned in agitated circles overhead.

The trail ends here.

Ends? Just like that?

Just like that! It is gone.

3

Konrad stood nonplussed, unsure how to proceed. How could so clear a trail vanish without trace? *You are certain?*

Ootapi did not deign to respond, but he expressed his opinion of Konrad's doubts clearly enough by way of a few disgusted flicks of his sinuous tail.

All right, I apologise.

He thought of Eetapi, and Nuritov. Had the inspector caught up yet? Perhaps he was even now attendant upon one of the earlier victims.

Konrad shared this notion with Nanda, and she, for lack of a better alternative, swiftly agreed to retrace their steps.

They found Nuritov by the side of the murdered woman. The inspector wore his usual wide-brimmed rain hat and long coat; he had a pipe in his hand, which he could not possibly hope to keep lit under such wet, windy conditions, but perhaps merely holding the familiar object was of comfort. He greeted Konrad and Nanda kindly, if a trifle abstractedly. 'Thought I might see you two turn up.'

'We were here earlier,' Konrad said.

Nuritov transferred his gaze from the dead woman's visage, to Konrad's. 'Oh?'

Konrad drew him aside, for though the inspector's men had largely dissipated the earlier crowd, there were still far too many people nearby for public conversation. In a low voice, he related all the events of the night thus far.

Nuritov's gravity deepened with the tale, especially at the news of a third victim. 'Eetapi brought me word of the wine merchant, but the cheese shop, I hadn't heard about.'

'All we know of the man is that he's not the shopkeep. No sign of him or her.'

Nuritov put his unlit pipe into his mouth and sucked upon it, his gaze distant. 'That could be suspicious.'

'Could be.'

'You don't think the shopkeep might be responsible for all this?'

Konrad shrugged. 'I can't yet say, but I... tend to doubt it. All the descriptions of the culprit point towards a large, powerful man, and we know he is capable of brutality. Those who spend their lives quietly vending produce do not often display those characteristics.'

'True.'

'Then again, sometimes they do.'

'Also true.' Nuritov fell silent again, and Konrad allowed his thoughts to wander. His steps, too; he drifted back to the side of the fallen woman, and indulged in a leisurely, more considered examination than he had previously had time for.

She looked peaceful, he thought, looking once more into her face. How often could he say that, of the bodies he tended to encounter? The victims of violent deaths, all of them; slain against their will and before their time. Except, apparently, for this one. Grateful to find herself dead, however violent the means of dispatch. How odd. He had never encountered its like.

'Who is she?' Konrad asked, wandering back to Nuritov. 'Did you find that out?'

'Mm.' Nuritov removed the pipe from his mouth, glancing at it in a vague, puzzled way. 'Her name is Albina Olga Narolina. Wife of Sergei, deceased. If she has living relations, we have not yet discovered who they are.'

'Vasily, though. The cousin. Have you spoken to her?'

'Not yet. I was waiting for you.'

'You... you were?' Konrad tried not to feel ridiculously pleased, like a girl asked to dance against all her expectations.

Nuritov's wry smile suggested that he guessed at Konrad's feelings. 'Your insights are always of interest, and frequently of use.'

'Thank you.'

'In addition to which, if I did not take you along, I would only have to fill you in later. Saves time.'

'How practical.'

Nuritov gave a tiny bow. He leaned closer and said in a much lower voice, 'I see you have not... taken anything, from the body.'

He referred, of course, to the rib bone. 'Too busy,' Konrad replied. 'I will do so later.'

'Ah. Then I may have her transferred to the morgue?'

'Please.'

Nuritov absorbed this, then looked to Nanda. Nan had declined to participate in their conversation, choosing instead to wander the environs of Mrs. Narolina's body, her watchful gaze fixed upon the crowd. 'Will Miss Falenia be joining us?'

'Yes.' He had not asked her, of course, but he intended that she should. She had once reproved him mightily for leaving her out, excluding her, keeping secrets from her. Actually, she had done so more than once. They had moved far beyond those days, now; frequently of use to one another, their lives and duties were increasingly bound up together. And he had grown to trust her. Far from wanting to keep her away, he now sought to keep her close — by any means necessary. He'd beg if he had to.

Fortunately, he was not driven to such lengths this time. Nanda serenely took it as read that she was invited along, and did not wait for anybody to assure her of it. She fell into step in between Konrad and Nuritov as they departed, and took the opportunity to say in an undertone: 'I could not read her. She is gone.'

'Thank you for trying.' Konrad was not surprised. Albina had been broadly unresponsive even when Ootapi had held fast her spirit; now that she was released, there could be little hope that Nanda's talented touch would encounter anything but dead flesh.

Kristina Vasily lived unusually close to the docks. Those who owned property typically preferred to distance themselves from the more unsavoury aspects that sometimes came with it; while owning a warehouse or two was undoubtedly advantageous for anybody with mercantile leanings, these structures were almost universally situated in the insalubrious docks area.

This did not appear to matter to Kristina. Her house was a mere three minutes' walk from the docks, situated upon a street of only modest pretensions towards gentility. Not that she herself suffered from any such shortcomings. When Nuritov, Konrad and Nanda presented themselves at her door, it was swiftly opened by a nicely-dressed manservant who did his best to repel them at once. Upon finding Inspector Nuritov most insistent, he reluctantly summoned his mistress.

Kristina Vasily did not lack for money; that much was immediately obvious. She was swathed in fine velvets and adorned with gems, though perhaps the season had something to do with her choice of attire. The noise from within the house indicated that some manner of gathering was underway.

She did not invite them inside. Looking down upon them from her admittedly impressive height — an effect exacerbated by her elevation several inches above street-level — she said in forbidding tones: 'What is it?'

'Madam,' said Nuritov politely. 'I am Inspector Nuritov, of the Ekamet Police, and—'

'I have been informed of your name,' she interrupted.

'Mm. Well, I do of course apologise for calling upon you at such a time, but I am afraid I have bad news.'

'What...what kind of bad news?'

'The worst, I'm afraid.'

Madam Vasily's gaze travelled to Konrad, to Nanda, and back to Nuritov. The prospect of ill tidings robbed her of some of her importance, and she invited them inside rather more cordially. She led them to a tiny parlour — 'I apologise, all the better rooms are in use this evening' — and waited with an air of ill-suppressed anxiety.

'Are you close to your cousin, madam?'

'Which cousin? I believe I have at least seven, at last count. First cousins, I suppose you mean?'

Nuritov hesitated. 'Ah... I speak of your cousin Illya.'

'Cheerful fellow,' said Kristina. 'Not one of the family's brightest stars, but he's done well for himself.'

He had owned a popular and apparently successful shop in an expensive part of town, and that made him only modestly successful in his cousin's eyes? The same cousin who lived a stone's throw from her warehouses on the docks? Konrad made a note to look into the Vasily family's holdings.

Nuritov began the delicate process of explaining to Kristina that her relative had been murdered. Konrad did not listen closely to the words. He watched Kristina's face, alert for any expression, any betrayed thought, that seemed out of place.

He was disappointed. She was not devastated by the news, but her indifferent attitude in speaking of Illya Vasily had prepared Konrad for that. There was no sign of satisfaction, however, nor any attempt at feigning a grief she clearly did not feel. She was shaken by the news, disturbed, but not distraught.

'We do not appear upon your doorstep by happenstance,' Nuritov ventured, once Kristina had been permitted a few minutes to accustom herself to the news. 'Illya... indicated that you may have some idea of...'

Nuritov trailed off, at a loss. And well he might, for he was trying to find a way to inform Kristina that her dead cousin had named her as a possible source of information about his murderer. Konrad's abilities in that direction were not exactly common, and few held such sway over the likes of Eetapi and Ootapi. Talking corpses were somewhat out of the ordinary.

Typically, Konrad found it best to skip over such details as *why* he had chosen to interrogate a particular person. It was always virtually impossible to explain. Nuritov was a novice at this; he would learn.

Konrad stepped forward a little. 'Madam. Do you know of anybody who might have wished your cousin ill? Anyone who might have reason to harm him?'

He asked the question without much hope of a useful response. If Illya Vasily had been the only victim, questioning the family for precisely such details would probably have been his first action. But with three victims to investigate, apparently chosen at random, he held out faint hope that Kristina would be of any use at all. With so few leads to follow, however, he had little choice but to try.

Kristina did not seem as quick to dismiss her own usefulness as he had, however. She frowned, and thought. Konrad imagined he detected a trace of concern in her eyes. 'Do you know anything about our family?' she finally asked.

'Biggest merchant family in Ekamet, no?' said Nuritov. 'Vasily? Own about a quarter of the shops in the city, sell most everything, fleets of trading vessels and caravans.'

'And warehouses,' said Kristina, with a faint smile. 'Quite.' Konrad revised his opinion of her affluence: she was probably mistress of rather more than a couple of warehouses. 'Such dominance makes enemies, of course. There are those who resent our success, who would give a great deal to see us fall.'

Undoubtedly true, but unhelpfully general. 'Do you know of anyone in particular?' Konrad prompted. 'Has anybody made threats? Perhaps especially towards your cousin?'

Kristina shook her head, impatient. 'Illya did well enough for himself, but he was no star of the Vasily clan. I do not see why anybody would target him in particular. He was revoltingly well-liked for a Vasily. If he has been killed, I would wager it is part of a broader attempt to damage us.'

Which explained her air of anxiety. Probably she was picturing a spate of such killings, and possibly attacks of other kinds.

It made for an interesting point. Konrad had no intention of revealing that others had died tonight, not unless — or until — they proved to be a part of this "Vasily clan" as well. 'Again, madam. Do you know of anyone in particular, who might have cause to wish your family harm?'

Kristina regarded him in thoughtful, worried silence for some moments, and he despaired of her ever answering his question. But at last, she spoke up. 'Iyakim.'

Konrad repeated the word to himself, but it did not resolve into anything more meaningful. 'I beg your pardon?'

'Iyakim. They are a vast trading family, from Kayesir. Our main competitors in that region, and... they have been making forays into Ekamet, this past year. Competing with us at every turn, jostling us, applying pressure, shelling out bribes, subverting our best connections. It has swiftly become... tense. If someone attacked Illya because he's Vasily, it was one of them.'

She spoke with deadly certainty, a flat hatred bleeding into every word. "Tense" would appear to be an understatement. 'That is a grave accusation, ma'am,' Konrad said quietly. 'Are you certain?'

'Certain that they're capable of it? Yes. They have used violence against us before, though they have stopped short of murder until now.'

Konrad recognised a fierce personal hatred in action, the kind that blinded a person to reason, to rationality, to evidence... everything. He might have been inclined to dismiss the idea, or at least to treat it with extreme scepticism.

Except that the Iyakim family were from *Kayesir.* What had Vasily said?

I made to get him a bottle of Kayesiri claret — that being what he'd asked for.

A tenuous link, but Konrad had learned to pay attention to every connection that offered, however distant, however faint. Illya Vasily's killer had arrived at his shop with a very particular request, and Konrad would not ignore the implications of that.

'Thank you,' Konrad said, allowing his tone to indicate that the interview was at an end.

'Do you...' Kristina hesitated, and looked pleadingly at Nuritov. Her manner could not be more different from her earlier pomposity. 'Do you think we are in danger, Inspector?'

'I hope not, ma'am, but it cannot hurt to take one or two extra precautions.' Nuritov bowed. That he did not offer any kind of protection or police support suggested to Konrad that he did not find the notion of a vendetta against the Vasily family especially compelling. But he did add: 'If you have reason to feel concern, or if you should remember anything that might be important to the case, I do invite you to come by the station.'

Kristina was forced to be contented with that. She accepted the dismissal with good grace; her family was more than wealthy enough to protect themselves, after all.

Nanda, hitherto a silent, watchful presence, now metamorphosed into a vision of warmth, kindness and sympathy. She extended a hand to Kristina in sisterly invitation, saying in her softest, most winning way, 'Such news to receive on Solstice Eve! A grave affliction for your family. I am so very sorry for your loss, my dear. I feel deeply for you.'

Privately, Konrad felt that Nan might have overdone it a little. But Kristina's eyes actually filmed with tears, and she took Nanda's hand in a trembling grip. 'Thank you,' she whispered. Her emotion was probably derived more from fear than grief, but nonetheless, Nanda achieved her object: a lingering touch, her bare fingers entwined with Kristina's for the few moments necessary to catch a glimpse of her thoughts.

Then it was over. Nanda released her victim, Nuritov and Konrad excused themselves, and soon all three were returned to the street outside. The snow had stopped at last, Konrad was pleased to note, though the wind howled on, unabashed. 'Well?' said Konrad.

'When people speak with such conviction, I sometimes wonder

whether they are affecting it. The Iyakim family look like an awfully convenient scapegoat, to me. But no! She was utterly sincere, hates them with a passion, and genuinely believes them to be responsible for Illya's death. What's more, she's now developed a certainty that the Iyakim family intend to achieve dominance by way of murder, and mean to carve their way through Vasily after Vasily until they achieve their goals. She is petrified.'

Konrad felt a stab of remorse, for she was almost certainly exaggerating the danger, and now she was condemned to spend Solstice in a fever of fright. But he could have no control over that. She had invented the threat herself; no one had suggested it to her. They had not even informed her of the other two deaths...

...which was an interesting point. 'Why didn't you ask her about the others?' he enquired of Nuritov. 'She might be able to tell us if they're connected to the family.'

'She might, but she leapt to ideas of grand danger quickly enough as it was. We have other ways to find out more about Albina Olga Narolina, and we still do not know the other gentleman's name. Speaking of which, thither we must now go. My men will, I hope, have gleaned something of use from the scene.'

Master! Ootapi's voice shattered his thoughts like an axe through glass. *You are observed!*

Konrad tensed at once, every sense alert, though he took care to give no obvious sign of it. He walked on beside Nuritov, Nanda on his other side, Nuritov's man — a bodyguard in effect, if not in name — keeping step a few paces behind. *Where? Who?*

A tall, dark man, Ootapi whispered gleefully. *He has a thick scarf around his throat. End of the street, behind you.*

Electrified, Konrad strove hard to stifle his impulse to leap into action. He wanted to chase the man down, he wanted to—

Well, and why should he not? The man was a murderer, a fugitive. Konrad had a job to do.

He whirled, and tore off down the street back towards Kristina's house. He allowed his stride to lengthen impossibly, until he was covering several yards of distance with each overlong step — another advantage of the Malykant, and one he often employed. Konrad arrived at the corner of the street in seconds, searching every shadow for the dark-cloaked man.

He is gone, hissed Ootapi.

No! He cannot be!

The serpents dutifully searched, but no sign of the watcher could they find.

Konrad took two deep breaths, until he had brought his frustration under control. *You did not imagine him, I suppose?*

I saw him, too! Eetapi chimed in with girlish glee.

Konrad sighed.

'Something the matter?' said Nuritov, as he and Nanda caught up.

'No. A false alarm.'

4

Konrad parted ways with Nuritov and Nanda soon afterwards. The inspector returned to the third crime scene, Nanda choosing to accompany him. Konrad sent Ootapi with them.

He and Eetapi went to The Malykt's temple, and the morgue that lay beneath. Albina Olga's body had arrived. She lay, cold and still, upon one of the narrow tables, laid out ready for burial.

Konrad surveyed the vacated corpse with mixed feelings. She made for a pitiful sight: by all appearances a kindly old woman, carried away with holiday spirit, a cheerful figure in her jaunty red clothes. But the ragged mess of her throat, the dried blood staining those same garments she must have donned with such joyous anticipation this morning... it was impossible to feel that her death was anything but a tragedy, whatever her own feelings about the matter might be.

'Why were you so happy?' Konrad murmured. The three of them made his job unusually difficult, tonight. Illya Vasily, and his merry refusal to be cast down by the news of his demise; Albina Olga and her relief; the unnamed man in the cheese shop, and his uncontrollable mirth. Delivering the most brutal vengeance upon foul murderers had never been *easy,* precisely, but in the usual way of things, the principles were clear-cut. Somebody lay dead, when they should be alive. Some severed, traumatised soul heaped opprobrium upon the head of their murderer, and welcomed Konrad's justice with a sense of relief. The victim was avenged, the killer was punished, and that was the end of it.

But Konrad had trouble believing that Albina Olga would feel that way. If anything, she seemed more likely to heap praise and thanks upon her murderer's head than to call for his demise. And here he stood upon the point of extracting a bone from her, obliged to perform his duty however he or Albina Olga felt about any of it.

'I wish you'd had just a few more words for me,' he sighed as he set about the unpleasant task. 'Just one more sentence, maybe two, and I might have some idea of how to proceed.'

Master, Eetapi announced from somewhere over his head, *You complain too much.*

Konrad brandished his sharp, sharp knife, stained now with Albina's blood. 'Really? I would like to see you do my job.'

Eetapi sniffed. *I would like to see you do mine.*

'I am not dead enough for your job.'

I am not self-pitying enough for yours.

'Harsh, Serpent.' Konrad stored Albina's bone with the one he had taken from Vasily. 'What happened to Solstice Spirit?'

Someone has to be honest with you, and we can no longer rely on Irinanda to perform that service.

That was true. Nanda *had* been less critical of him lately. 'Maybe she likes me, a little bit.'

The mad cannot help being so.

'Are you referring to the lady, or to your master?'

The lady. My master is not afflicted with madness, merely a lamentable fragility.

'It is sometimes known as having feelings, Eetapi. I know you are not accustomed to witnessing anything like *emotion* from me, but you will have to get used to it.'

Eetapi heaved a mournful sigh, and faded into the aether.

In spite of Eetapi's harsh words, Konrad left the temple in good spirits. He was even smiling, at least until he once more encountered the snow, the driving wind, and the impenetrable darkness of the night. The Malykt had separated Konrad from his emotions for many years, judging them obstructive to the performance of his Malykant's duties. He had recently relaxed that grip. While the effects were frequently unpleasant — Konrad knew fear, doubt, anxiety, shame and sadness every day — he would not willingly give up the beauties of it, either. Like the indescribable joy of knowing himself to be accepted, by somebody he respected and admired.

Nanda doesn't hate me!

Could anything be equal to so profound a blessing as that?

Your expectations really aren't high, are they?

'Eetapi,' he sighed. 'Go away. Come back when you have discovered the true meaning of Solstice.'

Then alas, for we must part for all of time. Farewell, Master.

'Good riddance! With friends like you, who needs the grinding misery of daily life as the Malykant?'

As I was saying about self-pity...

'I jest, serpent.'

Silence.

You made a joke?

'Yes! I, Konrad, jest sometimes!'

Master. Eetapi's mental voice vibrated with fulsome emotion. *I am proud.*

'Now you mock me.'

I do.

'I seem to remember telling you to go away.'

Or do I?!

Konrad consulted his pocket watch. The hour was much advanced: well past eleven, and midnight rapidly approached. The city was quiet; Konrad thought wistfully of the fine denizens of Ekamet, tucked up warmly at home with all their loved ones near. 'Enough. We have work to do.' He had not yet secured a bone from the body of the laughing man, and that had to be his next duty.

Yes, Master.

'We return to the cheese shop. Stay alert, Eetapi. If any trace of our killer lingers, inform me at once.'

Yes, Master.

Well. The creature may be insubordinate, insulting and totally devoid of anything describable as human feeling, but at least she was obedient. Occasionally.

Konrad found Nuritov and three officers of the police still occupying the cheese merchant's shop, together with a man he did not know. The latter resembled Illya Vasily in his rotund figure, soft features and genial demeanour. He appeared to have only just entered the shop, for his hat was still covered in melting snow. There was no sign of Nanda.

'But I do not understand!' the stranger was saying. 'Nothing is amiss, save that I must have forgotten to lock the door. Foolish of me, eh? But Solstice luck! No one has robbed me, and all seems well. I won't be so careless again, Inspector, I assure you.'

Nuritov nodded to Konrad and said in an undertone: 'Proprietor.'

'Vasily, by any chance?'

The cheese merchant took instant exception to this question. 'Vasily! No indeed! Got nothing to do with them, save that I sell some of their imports. No choice, no choice.'

'Iyakim?' Konrad hazarded.

That merely won him a puzzled frown. 'A what?'

'Never mind.' All right, so the shop had nothing to do with the Vasilys, but what about the murdered man?

Nuritov cleared his throat, and said to Konrad: 'Ah... may I talk to you for a moment?'

Konrad allowed himself to be led to the far side of the shop, away from the shop's proprietor. 'Something wrong?'

Nuritov murmured, 'This is the right place, I suppose?'

'Yes.'

'Where you found the giggling man?'

'Yes, this is the shop. Why?'

Nuritov looked around. 'Do you, ah, happen to see him anywhere?'

Konrad blinked, and focused anew upon the empty stretch of floor where the man had lain. 'He... you have not had him removed?'

'No. When we arrived, the place was as you now see it. Door open, lanterns lit, empty.'

On a long, long sigh, Konrad muttered, 'It is always so entertaining when they wander off.'

'They who?'

'The dead people.'

'Ah.'

Silence for a space, as each gentleman turned the problem over in his own mind. It was not the first time such a thing had happened; not long ago, Konrad had presided over a case wherein *all* the corpses had proved to be curiously perambulatory, on account of their being not so much dead as undead. He did not think that was the case here, but perhaps he was wrong.

'Vasily?' he enquired.

'Was where you left him. No oddness there.'

No "oddness" with Albina Olga, either.

'Ah well,' said Nuritov. 'Hard to examine a missing body.' He signalled to his men to depart.

'Nothing of note in here, I take it?' Konrad asked.

'Some blood.' The inspector indicated the cheese merchant with a nod: the man, sceptical that anything untoward had occurred in his apparently peaceful establishment, had been confronted with the blood stain upon the dark wood-panelled floor. His flow of good spirits was quite unable to withstand such a blow, and he stood regarding the evidence of violence in appalled silence.

Konrad regarded him with narrowed eyes. 'No reason to think him involved?'

'Not so far. We will keep an eye on him.' Nuritov stood with his hands in the pockets of his coat, his pipe in his mouth, deep in thought. 'Time,' he said around the stem, 'to learn more about Madam Narolina.'

Konrad nodded, but his thoughts were running along different lines. 'There is one thing the three have in common, and that is the mode of death.'

Those throat wounds were... unusual. Study them though he might, Konrad had not been able to determine how they were inflicted. They were messy, imprecise, brutal, the throat torn away as though a reaching hand had grasped the flesh and ripped it free. But that made no sense, and it certainly could not be reconciled with the vision of the dark-clad man he had received from multiple sources. What man could rip out a throat with his bare hands?

How had the laughing man's body vanished?

Why had he been so amused?

'If you can,' said Konrad, 'Find out why Albina might have wanted to die.'

'Mm.'

A young man entered the shop, his cloak emblazoned with the police insignia. He made straight for Nuritov and put a folded page of newsprint into his superior's hands. 'This the one you wanted, sir?'

Nuritov unfolded it, and nodded his approval. 'Very good. Thank you.' He handed the page to Konrad.

And there, sketched in sombre black lines, was the face of the laughing man. His grizzled features were harsh, craggy, his swept-back hair wild and unkempt. There was nothing of mirth about this portrait; his face was set in hard, angry lines.

'Is that him?' said Nuritov.

'You are a wonder,' Konrad replied. 'How did you find this?'

'The description you gave was distinctive. That's from last week.' He indicated the newspaper in Konrad's hands with a nod. 'Thought the hair seemed familiar.'

'Mm.' Konrad read the brief article through, his eyes skimming eagerly over the headline and the story that followed. 'You mean to tell me,' he said when he had finished, 'That our mirthful murder victim is also a thief.'

'That's right.'

'And he robbed... a library.'

'Mm.' Nuritov lit his pipe, and puffed thoughtfully.

'The article doesn't say who he was.'

'Fugitive. Not apprehended.'

'Or what he took.'

'A book, we may presume.'

'Yes, but it must have been a significant book. Nobody robs a library at random. For that matter, nobody robs a library! The whole point is that the books can be borrowed.'

'If one is a member, and invariably one is expected to return the volume by a specific time.'

'So he was not a member.' Konrad referred to the article again. 'The Volkov Library. I haven't heard of it.'

'It is a tiny place, devoted to myth and folklore. Not many people know of it.'

Myth and folklore? The words sparked a thought, but the idea dissipated before Konrad could take hold of it. 'Do you know which book he took?'

'No. Their librarian has yet to establish what's missing. They know that something was taken, for he was seen fleeing the building with a book in hand. But there are thousands of volumes in their keeping. It will take some time for them to discover which book it was.'

So. Their mystery man had a taste for obscure academic works, and was either unable to secure a membership to the Volkov Library, or in too much of a hurry to do so.

'You've known about this for a week, but no one has identified this man?' Konrad jabbed a finger at the scowling portrait.

'No one has come forward, or at least, not with any credible information. I suspect he had not been living in Ekamet for long.'

An outsider, a stranger, who travelled into the city in order to procure... a book of folklore, by any means necessary. Who ended up dead in a cheese merchant's shop on Solstice Eve, only a week later, and who seemed to find the whole sequence of events terribly amusing at that.

A wine merchant, also slain, with the same horrific wounds in his throat. A man who did *not* want to pass into The Malykt's care, as everyone ultimately did; who pleaded to remain with his shop, dead though he might be.

And an old woman, found alone in the snow, who was relieved and thankful to die.

'None of it makes any sense,' Konrad sighed. 'But that's normal enough.'

'Quite,' agreed Nuritov.

'It's not boring.'

'Never that.'

Nanda appeared at Konrad's elbow. He felt her warmth, discerned a trace of her familiar scent upon the air, and a knot of tension eased. 'Somebody mention a book?' she murmured.

Nuritov removed his pipe from between his lips. 'Have you found one?'

'Something of that nature.' She held out her gloved hands. Nestled in her cupped palms was the charred remnant of a slim, leather-bound volume, its pages burned to ash. Only the spine remained, and that was blackened almost beyond legibility. Unwilling to touch it, Konrad craned his neck, trying to read the obscured letters.

'It says "folk" and "of",' Nanda reported. 'That is all I could read.'

'Folkore, probably,' Konrad sighed. 'Of somewhere. Damn.'

Nuritov regarded the forlorn, blackened spine with interest. 'Why would he burn it?'

'Where did you find that, Nan?'

'Storeroom upstairs. Doesn't look like anybody uses the place much. There is a grate, dusty but otherwise clean, save for the remains of a single fire. And this.'

'I wonder if he had anywhere to stay?' Konrad mused. Finding himself regarded with puzzled curiosity by Nanda and Nuritov both, he realised his leap of intuition had not been universal. 'Well, Nuritov thinks he was not local, and consider the circumstances. Our proprietor, eager to get home for his revels, forgets to properly secure the door. But it does not seem likely that he also left lanterns alight, and a fire burning in a storeroom upstairs. Laughing man is looking for somewhere to go for the night, finds the door unlocked...'

'Possible,' said Nanda. 'But does it matter?'

'Yes, because if he lacked a residence that makes him part of the street flow. And we may be able to use that to learn more about him.' Konrad looked to Nuritov. 'Still have Tasha in your employ?'

'She's around.'

'What do lamaeni do at holidays?' Nanda murmured.

'Same things as the rest of us, probably,' said Konrad. 'I'll have to interrupt Tasha's party.'

Nuritov smiled faintly. 'She won't be happy.'

'Life is pain.'

5

Tasha presented herself at the station with decidedly ill grace. 'Yes?' she said, slouching into Nuritov's office with her cap pulled so low over her face, Konrad saw nothing but her nose and lips.

'Nice to see you again,' said Konrad.

She lifted her chin, and cast him a most unfavourable look. 'You couldn't have chosen a better time, I suppose? It had to be tonight?'

'Murderers are not usually considerate about things like holidays.'

Tasha brightened at the word "murderer", her resentment fading a little. Wretch. Lamaeni she may be, but she was only fourteen. 'You are far too young to be so bloodthirsty,' Konrad informed her.

'Oh yes? At what age did you begin?'

Nuritov intervened. 'Please try to be vaguely polite to our associates, Tasha.'

She flashed Konrad a swift grin, and doffed her cap in acknowledgement of the inspector's words. 'You have a job for me, I take it?'

'One of our victims was on the streets for a while,' said Konrad. 'We need you to find out about him.' He described the laughing man as minutely as he could, though he left out the mirthful part. Better not encourage Tasha's macabre side too much.

'Ivorak,' she said immediately.

'What?'

'That's his name. Ivorak.'

'You know him.'

Tasha took off her cap and stuffed it into her pocket, tousling her flattened hair with her fingers. 'He made himself memorable. Prowling around the city all night long, asking for *volk, volkov.* His Assevi was decent but sometimes uncertain and he spoke with a thick accent. Nobody took the trouble to understand him, so no one knew what he was after. Until he robbed that library.'

Nuritov was disapproving. 'You told me nothing of this.'

'You didn't ask,' replied Tasha with a shrug. 'And it was not relevant, before. I have no more idea than you do why he robbed the library, or which book he took. I never saw him with a book.' She paused, and added, 'Come to think of it, I haven't seen him since that robbery.'

'Apparently he found *volkov,*' Konrad said. 'Or specifically, the Volkov Library. He had no further need to go looking.'

'Maybe.' Tasha frowned, and seemed about to say something, but she changed her mind and remained silent.

'He spoke with an accent?' Konrad prompted. 'So he was foreign. Do you know where he was from?'

'I didn't recognise the accent, but I don't as a rule.'

Konrad mulled that over, but his thoughts did not carry him far. Ivorak. It was good to have a name for him besides Laughing Man, but it was of little help. And they had already known that he was interested in the Volkov Library. 'Think, Tasha. Did he ever say anything that might hint at what kind of book he was looking for?'

To his disappointment, Tasha shook her head immediately. 'He hardly said anything at all, at least in my hearing.'

Konrad sighed. 'I have a feeling that Ivorak is the key to this whole business, and it's damned thin.'

'Why, Konrad?' said Nuritov.

'Because we had three killings in quick succession and then... nothing. It's been hours. After Ivorak, it all stopped.'

'It might be a bit soon to conclude that,' Nuritov pointed out.

'Let us hope not.'

'The burned book.' Nuritov uttered only those three words, then stopped. He sat in his chair, pipe in hand, gaze fixed upon nothing.

'What of it?'

'We assumed that Ivorak burned it, but what if his killer was the one who threw it on the fire?'

'That is possible,' Konrad conceded.

'Perhaps it contained something the killer did not want Ivorak reading.'

'Something to do with folklore?' Konrad could not keep a note of scepticism out of his tone.

'Too far-fetched?' Nuritov restored his pipe to his mouth and puffed. 'Mm. Could be.'

It did seem unlikely, but Konrad tucked the thought away anyway. In his line of work, the unlikely frequently proved far more likely than he would prefer.

The remains of the book in question lay in a drawer in Nuritov's desk. Konrad wanted to take it to the Library to see if anybody recognised what was left of it; a long shot, but the attempt must be made. It would have to wait until morning, however. Nobody would be at the library tonight.

Then again, nobody would be at the library in the morning, either. It was Solstice.

Konrad heaved himself out of his chair, his limbs protesting at the effort. It was past midnight, and who knew when he would be able to go to bed. He stubbornly suppressed his weariness. 'Excuse me,' he murmured. 'I am going to break in to a library.'

'I will pretend I did not hear that,' said Nuritov.

'Good point. Perhaps one ought not to announce such intentions to the police.'

'All in a good cause.'

Konrad bowed. Tasha had turned for the door; he caught the back of her coat before she could leave. 'Tasha. You're with me.'

She sighed deeply. 'Why? Cannot you manage to get into a poorly secured building by yourself?'

'Oh, yes. But I am going to need help searching, and I can hardly ask the Inspector to come along.'

'Why not? I bet he's brilliant at trespassing, and if you get caught, who better to have along?'

Konrad ventured an enquiring glance in Nuritov's direction, but the Inspector shook his head. 'With regret, I must decline. Going a bit too far, there.'

'That's why he needs people like you and me,' Konrad said to Tasha. 'Come along. If we hurry, we might be finished by sunrise.'

Tasha slouched into the folds of her heavy dark coat, a vision of abject misery, and Konrad briefly felt guilty.

He suppressed that feeling, too. Tasha was an official police employee, albeit one they did not widely advertise. Sometimes work required sacrifices.

'Albina Olga?' he said to Nuritov on his way out of the door.

Nuritov nodded and hauled himself to his feet, with about as much enthusiasm as Konrad had shown. 'I am working on that.'

Tasha was not such congenial company as Nanda, and Konrad was ungrateful enough to wish for an exchange, as they walked to the Volkov Library in sullen silence. But Nan had left a houseful of guests behind at her home, and Konrad had not had the heart to detain her from them any longer.

'Cheer up,' he said to Tasha. 'Worse Solstices have been had.' Fittingly, a flurry of wind blew a spiral of air around his face as he spoke, and he received a mouthful of snow.

Tasha merely grunted.

'What were you doing, before?'

'Street folk were gathering at Parel's Bridge. There was wine. Vasily's gave out a couple of kegs.'

'Vasily's? You mean the wine merchant?'

'I don't know. Probably?'

How she could fail to see the connection flabbergasted Konrad — until he realised that their questions had centred around Ivorak. Had they remembered to mention Vasily at all?

'He was killed tonight,' Konrad said.

Tasha stopped. He felt her gaze on him, though he could not see her face in the darkness of the street. 'Same case?'

'Yes. Died the same way. Almost certainly the same killer.'

'Hmm.' Tasha walked on, and said nothing more.

'Were you there long? Did you see Vasily bring in the kegs?'

'No, I showed up late. I didn't see him, I just heard people repeating his name. It was impressive largesse. Good wine, not slop.'

'I take it you did not see Ivorak there, either?'

'No. But he might have been there, before I arrived.'

Konrad abandoned the questions, permitting himself a brief sigh. This particular picture was coming together fraction by fraction; pieces kept dropping into his lap but none of them seemed to fit together. If Ivorak and Vasily had both been at the Parel's Bridge gathering, what did that mean? Did it matter? Perhaps it was only a coincidence.

'Did you see an old woman dressed all in red?' he hazarded.

'No,' Tasha said sourly. 'Something else you haven't told me?'

'Third victim. Or second, in order of killing. Albina Olga Narolina.'

'I don't remember anyone like that but as I said, I was late.'

Konrad thought quickly. 'How would you like to go back after all?'

'Huh? I thought you wanted help storming the library.'

'I do, but I also want help scoping the bridge party before it's over.'

'Sounds like my kind of work!'

'I thought so. Ask around, see if Ivorak was there. If he was, I'd like to know when he left and why, if anyone knows. Same question about Vasily. And see if anybody remembers Albina being there.' The latter was improbable, for he had no reason to think that Albina Narolina was homeless. But it was worth a try.

'On it!' said Tasha enthusiastically, and darted away.

'Try not to get too drunk!' he called after her. Only belatedly did he remember that lamaeni did not precisely consume food or drink the same way he did; they dined upon the raw energies of the living. Could they get drunk on wine? She would probably be feasting upon the living guests, instead. A little sip from each of many guests would cause no harm, though he hoped there were not too many lamaeni at the bridge.

'Wouldn't dream of it!' Tasha carolled back, and he smiled.

The Volkov Library was unassuming in character. Situated on a residential street, sandwiched between rows of moderately prosperous brick houses on either side, it looked like a private dwelling itself. Only its grand stone portico hinted at its higher calling.

Konrad veered around to the rear of the building, and applied his talented Malykant's fingers to the icy-cold lock. A soft *click* sounded as the mechanism bowed to his will, and the lock sprang open. He stepped inside.

Light, please, serpents, he asked — speaking silently, just in case anybody lingered at the library. He did not think he had company. The building had a reassuring air of emptiness, a heavy silence that suggested he was as alone as he could wish.

Eetapi and Ootapi exuded their faint, horrible glow. It was pallid and sickly and quite disturbing, especially when encountered as the sole source of light in an empty, pitch-black building well after midnight. But at least he could see.

The back of the library housed a series of storerooms, Konrad soon discovered. Boxes and boxes of books, neatly labelled, lined wall after wall in chamber after chamber, and the sight made Konrad blanch. How could anybody find anything in here? He gave up after a while, and walked straight through to the main hall. This proved to be small, and not at all imposing, but its walls were lined with handsome shelves filled with dust-free, leather-bound books, as a library should be. Near the front was a desk, and inside that desk was a huge tome. Konrad hauled the massive volume out and spread it open.

What are we doing here, Master?

'We are checking the library catalogue, Ootapi.'

A short silence. *Reading a book?*

'Yes. What else does one do at a library?'

A longer silence followed. *There is nothing dead in here, is there.*

'I doubt it. Maybe a mouse or two.'

Mice. The serpent's tone was heavy with disgust. *Not a single corpse! Nothing.*

'Just books.'

Ootapi heaved a great, slithery sigh and sank a foot or two in the air, until his sinuous, incorporeal body hovered barely a few inches over Konrad's head. His eerie glow took on a dejected green colour.

'Ootapi. I cannot read if you are going to sulk right in front of my face like that.'

Good.

'Which means we will be here for much longer than necessary.'

Amid much muttering, the serpent rectified both his posture and his hue.

'Keep your brother in line, Eetapi, if you please,' sighed Konrad. 'This task is trying enough as it is.'

Yes, Master, but you should know that I hate you as well.

'Your objection is acknowledged.'

The book was truly vast, Konrad was disheartened to observe. It was two feet tall and almost the same again in width, its pages a few inches thick. What's more, there was a second, matching volume still in the desk.

His plan had been to browse the library's catalogue in hopes of matching the fragmented title against the records. He had found another stack of smaller volumes containing lists of books currently checked out; it was his hope that, by cross-referencing the two, he might be able to discover the title of the burned book, or at least to narrow it down to a list of possibilities. The Volkov Library was small and obscure; surely their catalogue could not be unmanageably huge? But he began to realise why the librarians had yet to identify the missing book, even after a week.

'Neither of you can read, I suppose?' Konrad said to the serpents.

No, they said in chorus.

'Curses.' Konrad relinquished this faint hope with a stab of regret, and settled in to read.

Much later, he had a headache, a crick in his neck, a throbbing pain in his lower back, and a short but growing list of titles which appeared to match the fragmented words gleaned from the spine of the burned book.

He was halfway through the first volume.

So long had he sat in silence, unbroken even by the complaints of the serpents, that when a voice spoke from the depths of the darkness he almost expired of fright on the spot.

'You look bored,' said Nanda.

Konrad jumped violently, and a tiny tearing sound split the silence anew. He'd ripped the page he had been in the process of turning. 'Hello, Nan,' he said weakly. 'Um, what are you... doing here...?'

'Ootapi fetched me. He said his life is in danger.'

Konrad blinked in confusion. He could barely see Nanda, as she stood beyond the pale circle of ghost-glow. 'He lied.'

'I know. He does that a lot. But he may have stumbled over more truth than he realised, for the tedium looks likely to carry you off before too much longer. What is it that you're doing?'

Konrad explained. The plan that had seemed so promising hours before now struck him as foolish in the extreme, and he fretted over how much time he had wasted on the pursuit. Two hours at least, surely?

'Madness,' Nanda said firmly, and his heart sank a little. 'What did you mean by embarking upon such a task without help? You should have called me sooner.'

'You were busy.'

'Do you have any idea what time it is? My guests left some time ago, or they are asleep.'

'You should be asleep, too.'

'So should you. What is your excuse?'

'Um. Murder and mayhem?'

'That should suffice for both of us, shouldn't it? Hand me that book.'

Nan, of course, proved to be far more skilled at the task than he. She had a way of skimming lightly over the page, her eyes gliding past title after irrelevant title and only pausing when she encountered the word *folklore*. Her pace far outstripped his, and by the time he had laboured his way to the end of the first volume, Nanda had gone through the whole of hers. Her company, too, seemed to speed the process along, for her mere presence leavened the heavy, hushed atmosphere of the deserted library, and made Konrad forget his headache and the pain in his back.

Their list, when finally compiled, consisted of more than fifty titles. Nanda immediately took up her pen again, and began skimming through that, too, crossing off title after title.

'What are you doing?'

'These do not fit. Look at the book. Not every single volume containing the word "folklore" could be a match. It has to be a short title, and "folklore" must be the first or second word — and if the second, the first word could only be something short like "the".' She crossed off a few more with thick, decisive black lines.

'You put me to shame,' Konrad said. 'I wouldn't have thought of that.'

'You probably would have, if you were not so tired, or thinking of twelve other things at once.'

Kindness in her, but Konrad knew it was not the truth. In many ways, Nanda was simply smarter than he. Particularly about anything remotely scholarly; it was not Konrad's strength.

'Nineteen left,' Nanda said when she had finished. 'Now let me at the list of checked out books.'

Once the cross-referencing was complete, Nanda presented him with a final list of only eleven titles. The other eight were listed as on loan at the time of the robbery, so they could not have been the book that Ivorak took.

Konrad browsed through them, uninspired, until he reached the title second from the end of the list.

Lost folklore of Kayesir.

'That one,' he said, indicating it with a forefinger.

Nanda's brows rose. 'Why that one?'

'Because...' Konrad sought for a way to put his vague thoughts into words. 'Because Kayesir keeps coming up. The killer asked for Kayesiri claret at Vasily's wine shop. The Vasily family's main rivals are the Kaysiri family, Iyakim. I would be willing to bet that the wine Vasily gave out to the Parel's Bridge gathering was Kayesiri, too.'

'It is a rather thin list of associations,' Nanda pointed out.

With which observation he could not argue, because she was right. But his instincts told him not to discount the links, however tenuous they appeared to be.

He put the whole list into his pocket and stood up, wincing as the cramped muscles in his neck and back stretched. 'I won't discount the rest,' he promised. 'But I think the Kayesir connection should be explored first.'

'Very well, I have no argument to make there.' Nanda smiled tiredly at him, and followed it up with a vast yawn. 'Do you suppose we have time to sleep a little?'

Konrad thought about that. 'You do,' he decided. 'And I hope you will. I want to go back to the station. Nuritov must have more information about Albina Olga by now, and Tasha may have returned with her report about Parel's Bridge.'

Nanda gave a soft, barely audible sigh, then straightened her shoulders manfully. 'You know I will not leave you to manage alone.'

'I can manage alone! I have been doing so for years.'

'Badly.'

'That's not—' Konrad broke off, sentence incomplete, for a faint sound caught his ears: the sound of a soft footfall.

Serpents! he snapped. *Who or what approaches?*

They were asleep, the slithering wretches. They came awake with a start, gabbling excuses.

Hush! Find out who brings us company!

He did not truly require their aid, for his heart and his gut told him exactly who had entered the library. The confirmation came quickly.

It is him! The man who followed us to the docks!

The killer, stalking Konrad again. And Konrad had Nanda by his side.

6

In an instant, Konrad threw off all the wards and guards he kept up day by day; the mask that hid his true nature as the Malykant, that allowed him to pass for an ordinary gentleman. He grew taller, stronger, more formidable by the second, and an icy, implacable resolve filled his heart.

He let The Malykt's chill, deathly energy fill him until he shook with it, his mind and heart focused with brutal clarity on the need — the duty — to *kill.*

Then he went after the shrouded killer.

He let his senses and his instincts take over, followed them with blind single-mindedness. The footfalls had echoed from the back of the building and thither Konrad walked, implacable and unstoppable. Eetapi and Ootapi flanked him, their glow dampened, twin terrors on the hunt.

A shadow loomed out of the near total darkness, and the serpents dived as one.

He is ours!

Konrad leapt after them, found his hands filled with the cool, snow-dampened wool of a winter coat, the scent of aromatic, unwashed man filling his nostrils. His captive thrashed, but the serpents inexorably tightened their grip until they had him bound fast. The man had only time for a few gasped syllables before he crashed to the floor like a felled tree, and lay there in stiff immobility. '*No!*' he cried. 'Please — you must—'

The words seemed odd, out of place. Not fitting for the man who had complacently hacked his way through three victims tonight.

Light him up, Konrad ordered.

Ootapi glowed with delight. *Do you mean set him on fi—*

No! Make it light in here! Illuminate him!

Oh. Crestfallen, Ootapi obeyed, and a pale light lit up the felled man's features.

'Ivorak,' said Konrad.

The man could not move, not even to nod his head. He stared back at Konrad, his eyes wide, his hair a wild mess. His coat was still stained with the blood that had gushed from his torn throat, only a few hours ago.

More lamaeni. That was Konrad's first thought, and he growled with irritation. He was running into those irksome, undead nuisances far too often of late, and he *wished* they would mind their own business and get out of his way.

But no. His sense reasserted itself, and he pushed his annoyance aside. The lamaeni were undead, but when body and soul were melded as in life, they did not look it. To look at Tasha, one would not guess that she dined not upon cheese and wine but upon life energies; that she could, at will, divide soul from body and roam Ekamet as a ghost.

Ivorak did not look nearly so dead as he ought to, considering the state in which Konrad had discovered him. But nor did he look alive. His skin had the pallor of death, the lines deepened around his eyes and mouth. His hair was rapidly turning grey. And there was an air of... of savagery about him, of wild brutality, that had nothing to do with humanity.

Ivorak stared at Konrad, breathing deeply and sharply through his nose. Reading in his eyes both horror and terror, Konrad realised belatedly that he still wore his Master's energy like a mantle. In this state, he was a study in contrasts, all death-like pallor himself and night-black shadow, his eyes blazing ice-white: a reaper, a vision of death itself come to deliver souls to his Master's care.

Konrad took a breath and let the energy fade. When the usual warm brown colour was restored to his skin, his eyes an ordinary dark once more, he quietly ordered the serpents: *Loosen up. Not too much.*

They did, and Ivorak began to shudder violently. He gasped and panted for breath, shaking like a frightened animal, and the horror in his gaze did not lessen one bit.

'Who are you?' he croaked.

That surprised Konrad, for everyone in the realm of Assevan knew of the existence of the Malykant, even if they did not know who occupied the role. He had assumed that this knowledge had travelled beyond its borders as well, but perhaps his fame was not as widespread as he imagined.

It might work to his advantage here. 'That does not matter,' he replied. Let Ivorak come up with his own theory about Konrad's identity; if he was frightened enough, hopefully he would co-operate. 'Who are you? What are you? How is it that you died tonight, and now you live?'

Ivorak shuddered harder, and icy tears crept down his cheeks. 'This,' he choked, looking with wretched horror and sadness at his trembling limbs. 'This is not living.'

'Nor is it death.' Konrad waited, inflexible.

But Ivorak's suspicion and distrust only grew. 'Are you one of *his*?' he spat.

'I do not know who you mean.'

'You know. You are. Only one of *them* could — could—'

Could what? Ivorak did not finish the sentence, for he grew wild and frenzied in his fear and began to thrash.

Hold him— Konrad warned, but he was too late. Ivorak, crazed with horror and terror, was frighteningly strong, and his sudden fight had taken the serpents by surprise. He broke free of their grip; moving faster than Konrad would have believed possible, he fled the corridor.

After him, Konrad snapped, but he knew it was hopeless. He had heard the rear door open and slam. Ivorak had vanished into the night.

Nuritov slumped in the well-worn armchair in his office, a vision of weariness to rival even the dark shadows under Nanda's eyes. It was three in the morning. Konrad and Nanda occupied other, less comfortable chairs nearby, and if Konrad's own state was anything to judge by, nobody felt like moving again for the rest of the night. A tray of tea, coffee and biscuits occupied one corner of Nuritov's desk, though where it had been spirited up from at such a time of night, Konrad could not guess.

The serpents hovered near the ceiling, livelier by far than they had any right to be.

'Albina Olga,' said Nuritov. 'Narolina by marriage, but Voronina was her birth name. She had one son, who died in infancy. No husband or children living.'

The name Voronina disappointed Konrad; he had been hoping for something else. 'No connection with the family Vasily?'

'Her mother was the daughter of Boris Belyaev, who is a cousin of the Vasily family on his mother's side. A second cousin, I believe.'

So there was a link, but a flimsy one. Was the connection strong enough to matter? He wanted to cling to the theory; it was the only one he had.

Nanda, as ever, appeared to read his thoughts. Reader she was, but Konrad felt that her abilities were not limited to the direct flashes of insight she sometimes received upon touching another's skin. She was gifted with an unusually profound intuition, too. 'It is probable that much of Ekamet can trace some part of their heritage back to the Vasily family. They are numerous, after all.'

True, true. Konrad sighed, and gave up the idea, for he could think of no reason why, of all Vasily, these two might have been singled out.

He and Nanda had already related their night's adventure, and the product of their research. Nuritov had no light to shed upon the possibility of a connection with Kayesir, and he seemed as unconvinced of its relevance as Nanda. Which left Konrad at a loss, for with his Vasily theory demolished and his hunch about Kayesir dismissed, what did that leave?

'Is Tash—' he began, but as the girl herself entered the office before he had finished enquiring after her whereabouts, he was not obliged to finish the sentence.

'I have news!' she said, beaming.

Her lethargic audience did not greet her announcement with as much enthusiasm as she was hoping, for her face fell and she sighed. 'Good work, Tasha! You're wonderful! What would we do without you?'

'Tell us the news,' said Konrad wearily, 'And we will duly decide how wonderful you are.'

She aimed a kick at his leg, stretched as it was across her path.

'Yes, your lordship. All three of them were at Parel's Bridge.'

That did interest Konrad. He sat up a little, a flicker of hope ignited. 'Go on.'

Tasha shrugged. 'That's it, really. Albina Olga was there, giving out hand-made gifts that nobody much wanted. Sweet of her, but largely useless. Ivorak was seen by a few people, prowling around and scowling and generally upsetting everyone. And Illya Vasily delivered the kegs of wine himself.'

'Were they all there at the same time?'

'I don't know. Those who linger at Parel's Bridge aren't over supplied with toys, if you follow me. Timekeeping isn't their best art.'

Konrad abandoned that line of questioning. 'What kind of wine was it?'

Tasha blinked, nonplussed. 'That is a question I did not ask.'

Ah well. Supposing she confirmed his hunch and it was Kayesiri, would that help him? Not much.

'So our killer must have been at Parel's Bridge,' he concluded. 'Early in the evening. He may have chosen his victims there, for reasons we cannot yet imagine. Perhaps he followed them, when they departed.'

'Could be.' Nuritov did not speak with conviction, but his manner was more thoughtful than dismissive. He had his pipe lit again; the aromatic smoke wreathed around his chair, mesmerising Konrad's tired mind with its gentle, hypnotic swirls. He averted his gaze.

He realised he was at a loss for a next step. Where could they now go? The Vasily connection hardly seemed worth pursuing, and he would not know how to investigate further anyway...

...no, he could. If Kristina Vasily was right, then some member of the Iyakim family was involved somewhere. That meant either that there were Iyakims living in Ekamet, or that one or more of them had recently arrived.

There was also the question of Ivorak; not merely his bizarre revival from death, but also from whence he had appeared in the first place. He was not a native of Ekamet, or even of Assevan. Konrad would have staked his best hat on the likelihood that Ivorak was Kayesiri, and that was something he might be able to find out.

And why had Ivorak returned from the dead, but Albina and Illya had not? What made Ivorak different?

'I need to go back to the docks,' he said.

'At this time of night?' Nanda cast him a worried look.

'Yes. I need to check the immigration records for anyone with the name of Ivorak, or the surname of Iyakim. I want to find out if any Iyakims have entered the city this past week or so, and where it was that Ivorak came from.'

'If they arrived by boat,' Nanda put in.

'If. But I think they did. Who travels overland through the Bone Forest in the dead of winter? And besides, I think both of them came from Kayesir. Water is by far the most efficient way to make that journey, and also the safest.'

Nanda nodded agreement, and got up from her chair with a creditable display of energy. She downed her cup of tea in one swallow, stuffed two biscuits into her mouth, and donned her coat. Unable to speak around her overlarge mouthful of confectionery, she jerked her head at the door.

'Coming,' sighed Konrad. His egress from his own armchair was considerably less energetic, and embarrassingly graceless.

'There is one more thing about Albina,' said Nuritov, which brought both Konrad and Nanda to an abrupt halt.

'Oh?'

'She was very sick. Dying. Probably she had only a few months left, at most.'

Ahhh. 'She knew it?' said Konrad.

'Oh, yes. She had been receiving regular medical care.'

'That might explain her attitude to her own death. Perhaps she had been in a lot of pain.'

'I believe she was.'

'Poor woman,' said Nanda.

'Mercies arrive in the strangest of ways,' murmured Nuritov, with an emotion which took Konrad aback. He wanted to enquire as to its source, but hesitated. The question seemed intrusive.

The moment passed. 'We go,' said Nanda. Grabbing Konrad's arm, she hauled him bodily towards the door.

'I'll be... here,' said Nuritov. 'Tasha, please go with them.'

Tasha did not even complain, which spoke eloquently of how much fun she had enjoyed at Parel's Bridge. And, probably, how much she had partaken of the bright, happy energies of those around her. 'Yes Mister Boss, sir,' she said, with only minimal cheek, and fell in step behind Konrad.

Konrad's motive in returning to the docks was actually twofold. His reasons were as he had told Nanda, in part: if there was evidence to support his hunch about Kayesir, he wanted to dig it up.

There was also the matter of Ivorak. The murdered man had tracked him to the Volkov Library, and it was probably also Ivorak who had followed him to Kristina Vasily's house. What he wanted with Konrad remained unclear, but he seemed to prefer to approach in dark, deserted places.

Well, Konrad was happy to oblige him there.

Some part of him hesitated over taking Nanda along, when he half expected trouble. But Nan had long since proved herself to be far from helpless, and he would not anger her by behaving as though she needed his protection. And the presence of Tasha soothed him. Young she might be, but she was lamaeni, and had wandered the streets of Ekamet for years. He suspected she was both more powerful and more ruthless than she appeared.

Considering that his purpose was to attract the notice of Ivorak, if he lingered near, Konrad did not trouble to employ a great deal of stealth as they approached the docks. He did not expect to encounter any other trouble, or certainly nothing they could not deal with.

'You're going the wrong way,' said Tasha, with withering disgust. 'Immigration office is this way.'

Oh. Konrad allowed himself to be led, smothering faint feelings of embarrassment.

'It's all right,' said Nanda soothingly, with another of her flashes of insight. 'No one would expect Mr. Konrad Savast to be familiar with the docks. What business do the gentry have down here?'

He could not decide whether she was being genuinely sympathetic or subtly mocking, and so vouchsafed no reply.

The office's nightly defences yielded as easily to Konrad's touch as those at the Volkov Library, and all three ventured inside. The records of passenger arrivals for the past two weeks were not difficult to find, and Konrad and Nanda fell to perusing them as quickly as possible.

'Keep watch please, Tasha,' he instructed. *You too, serpents.*

None of the three were delighted with the assignment, but none argued. Tasha slouched away to stand at the door, and the serpents trailed miserably outside.

Ivorak Nasak.

The name leapt out at Konrad, and his heart quickened with excitement. He'd been right! 'He's here,' he said to Nanda. 'Arrived almost two weeks ago, from Alakash, Kayesir.'

'I think you're onto something,' she murmured. 'Good work.'

Konrad smiled, basking in the glow of Nanda's approval. 'Iyakim, Iyakim,' he murmured, leafing through page after page. 'There has to be someone of that name here...'

But he found nothing, no passengers of that name arriving in months. 'Maybe they travel under different names,' he hazarded, without much conviction.

'Why would they do that?'

'Rivalry with Vasily, travelling incognito. I don't know.'

Nanda's look told him clearly enough how unconvinced she was; she did not need to speak. 'Ah well,' he sighed, and returned the books. 'It was worth a try.'

His other purpose in coming appeared to be useless, too, for there had been no sign either of intrusion or pursuit. Neither the serpents nor Tasha had spotted anything untoward.

Konrad decided to push his luck. As he and Nanda left the immigration office, he called loudly to the night air: 'Ivorak! Ivorak Nasak! If you are here, show yourself.'

His words echoed in the silence, but no response came.

'Ivorak!' Konrad tried, one last time.

Nothing. Wherever Ivorak was, he had no further interest in tailing Konrad.

He looked at Nanda and shrugged. 'Worth a try.'

'We'd better leave, though,' she said coolly. 'You might not have attracted Ivorak's attention, but you certainly announced our presence to anybody else who might be loitering.'

'And loiterers are, by definition, suspect,' Konrad agreed.

'Certainly those who loiter around darkened dock areas past three in the morning.'

'At Solstice.'

'At Solstice.' Konrad collected up Tasha and his serpents, and they departed with haste.

7

Nanda and Tasha were bound for Nuritov's, to report the minimal successes of the venture to the docks. Konrad, however, excused himself, for he had another errand in mind.

'I cannot take you with me,' he told the two ladies firmly.

'Why not?' Nanda spoke the words, but Tasha's belligerent posture and angry glare eloquently expressed her opposition to being left behind.

'Will it be dangerous?' said Tasha, the words dripping sarcasm.

'Not in the slightest. I go to visit a lady, without an invitation.'

That silenced them both. 'Oh,' said Nanda finally.

'And if it is rude to call upon a lady uninvited at nearly four in the morning on Solstice Eve, it must be considerably more so to bring along two other, equally uninvited guests.'

Nanda's eyes narrowed. 'What might you be doing, calling upon said lady at such an hour?'

'Asking questions.'

'And alone,' added Nanda, as if her words had not been enough in themselves to convey the direction of her thoughts.

'Asking questions,' Konrad repeated.

'I do not see why her identity must remain a secret, if all you intend to do is ask questions.'

'I want to borrow a book, too.'

Nanda's glare deepened.

'I shouldn't share everyone else's secrets as well as my — oh, forget it. It's Mrs. Halim.'

'Kavara Halim?'

'Yes, that one.'

'The Jewelled Lady?'

'The... the what?'

Nanda grinned, swift and satisfied. 'That's what they call her, outside of the gentry circles. We all know her. Very well indeed.'

Konrad folded his arms, matching her stubborn posture. 'All right, why do you non-gentry folk know Kavara Halim so well?'

'She collects secrets. Where do you think she gets most of her information?'

Interesting. 'Why The Jewelled Lady?'

Nanda shrugged. 'No idea. Probably because both she and her house are so covered with coloured shinies. It is the most easily memorable thing about her, and one that everybody who talks with her tends to recall.'

'Very well. If you will excuse me, I go to talk with the Jewelled Lady. I hope she may have some useful information for us.'

'I wish you luck in your endeavours.' Nanda made him a grave curtsey, all exaggerated formality.

Konrad returned the gesture with a bow equally as mocking, and kissed Nanda's hand. 'Thank you. I wish you the safest of travels back to Nuritov House. Do convey my warmest regards to Lord Nuritov.'

'I shall invite him to take tea with us next week.'

'Pray enquire how he enjoyed the snuff that I sent him. It is my finest mixture.'

'Of course. And the snuff box! Could anything be finer. But did it have to be diamonds, Lord Savast? And so many? Such a display could be termed vulgar, you know.'

Konrad was betrayed into a grin, and he swept Nanda another bow, this one sincere. 'I will see you soon,' he promised.

Tasha witnessed this exchange in silence, her glower gradually giving way to confusion. 'What was all that about?'

'Nothing,' said Nanda lightly. 'A little savage mockery between friends, that is all.'

'A vital component of any relationship,' Konrad added.

Tasha eyed them both, and then pointedly turned her back.

'Scorn!' said Nanda. 'And exasperation. Why, Konrad. She fits in perfectly.'

Tasha muttered something inaudible.

'What was that?' Konrad enquired.

'Nothing.'

Kavara Halim had been an acquaintance of Konrad's ever since her arrival in Ekamet, three years before. He had felt drawn to her at once, for she shared the gypsy heritage that had given the brown colour to his skin, the deep black to his hair and eyes. Such colouring was unusual in Assevan, and particularly so among the gentry. Mrs. Halim, with her grey-threaded black hair and velvet-black eyes, appeared to him as something of a kindred spirit. She was about the age his mother would have been, had she lived. Rather than suppressing her cultural roots in favour of the fashions of Ekamet high society, as many would have done in her position, Mrs. Halim had woven the two together. Konrad always enjoyed visiting her house, though he did not always approve of the company he found there. The bright silks and coloured jewels she favoured in both her dress and her decorating spoke to him, on some level he rarely communicated with.

Unfortunately, Mrs. Halim herself had proved more difficult to deal with than he had hoped. She was, indeed, a secret-keeper, as Nanda had said. Her every waking minute was devoted to collecting information, and in speaking to her, Konrad always felt wrong-footed and uncomfortably exposed. She had a way of looking at a man as though she could read all the secrets of his heart with a glance; and considering Konrad's acquaintance with such as Irinanda Falenia, he could not even discount the possibility. She might be a Reader, for all he knew. He had taken care not to let her touch him, just in case.

She had also proved to be a ghostspeaker — one who could commune with departed spirits, and even control them, to a certain extent. Another similarity with Konrad, but in this, her talents were not profound, and the use she made of her limited abilities often chilled him.

His feelings about Kavara Halim were mixed, all told, and he did not relish hazarding a visit to her under such unusual circumstances. She knew nothing of his secret duties, or so he hoped; to her, he was merely Mr. Savast of Bakar House, an idle gentleman of society. How he would explain his presence at such an hour he did not know, and the question occupied his mind all the way to her house.

Konrad still had not come up with anything by the time he arrived. He stood for a little while outside her front door, thinking, but was at last obliged to abandon the effort.

He had two choices. He could walk away, seek the information he needed somewhere else, and hazard nothing. Or he could take a risk, and... hope.

He was no more talented at hopeful optimism than Mrs. Halim was at communing with ghosts, but time pressed. All might have been quiet across the city for a few hours now, but the spate of brutal murders troubled him in ways that most such cases did not. His instincts told him to *hurry*. The same sensation affected Nuritov and Nanda, he supposed, for neither had advanced any suggestion that the case be postponed until the morning, in favour of sleep.

It would have to be risk, then.

The house was shrouded in darkness, as he had expected, and he hesitated to ring the bell. She must be asleep. But as he lingered on the doorstep, doubting, a flicker of golden light caught his eye from the storey above.

He looked again. There: the faintest glimmer, shining from in between a crack in the curtains. Someone was awake.

Serpents, see for me. Is that Kavara Halim?

They wafted through the walls like smoke, and their voices chimed in his mind a moment later. *It is she. She sits in a chair with a book, though she does not read. She stares.*

Eschewing the clamour of the bell, Konrad made use of the door knocker. *Tap tap, tap.* The sound was more than loud enough, in the deep silence of the night.

He waited.

So many minutes passed that he began to give up hope. Either she could not hear the door knocker, or she had chosen to ignore it. Should he tap again?

She is coming, whispered Ootapi.

Konrad waited, trying to ignore the nervous flutter of his heart. When the door opened, Mrs. Kavara Halim was revealed, wearing an amethyst-coloured gown and a loosely draped shawl. Her hair was unbound; of course, she had expected no further visitors tonight.

Why was she not asleep?

'Mrs. Halim,' he said softly, and bowed. 'I apologise profusely for my rudeness in calling at such an hour. Can you forgive me, and consent to grant me a few minutes of your time? It is urgent, or I would not so presume—'

'How did you know that I was awake?' she said. She spoke as softly as he had done, but a thread of steel ran through the words.

'I saw the light.'

She inclined her head and stepped back, opening the door wider to grant him entrance. Konrad followed her inside, and the door clicked softly shut behind him.

Her house was mostly in darkness. She carried a single lamp in her hand, the lantern casting a warm, flickering glow over the stairs as she led him up to her drawing-room. Konrad had been there more than once, but never at night, and never had he contrived to catch Mrs. Halim alone. The room seemed different at this hour, the bright colours muted, the shadows deeper and faintly menacing.

Konrad took the seat she indicated, and watched as she arranged herself once more in her own armchair. Her movements struck him as studied: her manner, her demeanour, was a performance. He wondered what the intended effect was supposed to be.

Kavara Halim did not speak, but merely watched him, and waited. Konrad knew she would not help him freely. He would have to offer her something, first. A secret.

Very well, then.

Eetapi, he called silently. *Ootapi. Show yourselves.*

They hesitated. *Master,* hissed Ootapi. *Are you sure?*

No, but needs must.

Gradually, Ootapi shimmered into view. He appeared directly before Mrs. Halim's face, his sinuous body shimmering eerie ice-white in the gloom of the drawing-room.

Eetapi joined him, her own manifestation threaded with glinting green.

Mrs. Halim watched this display with impassive interest, her gaze flicking from one to the other.

'Ghostspeaker,' she said at last.

Konrad inclined his head.

That cat is here again, hissed Eetapi with deep disgust. *The mad one.*

Konrad did not need to be told, for the creature had flickered into view. Whether it had been prompted to appear by the twin manifestations of the serpents, or whether its mistress had instructed it to do so, Konrad could not guess. It sat curled in Mrs. Halim's lap, and Konrad eyed the spirit with distaste, for it made a fine display of its mistress's ineptitude. The binding had been poor indeed, and the ghost was wretchedly decayed. Where his two serpents were bright, vibrant and radiating energy, the cat was a thin, feeble, pallid thing, vacant-eyed and barely visible.

Mrs. Halim's hand moved, stroking over the cat's incorporeal head as though she petted it. The cat purred, a strangely chilling sound.

'You have seen Kish before,' said Mrs. Halim.

'I have not,' Konrad replied. 'But the serpents have.'

Mrs. Halim nodded. He recognised the nod as an acknowledgement; he had paid the asking price of her attention. 'Why did you come to see me?'

'Forgive me for the personal nature of this question,' Konrad began. 'But I think you are not a native of Assevan. Is that correct?'

'It is not.'

'Oh.'

She smiled faintly, the barest upturning of her lips. 'But your instincts are not wholly misguided. I was born Assevi, but my grandfather was from Kayesir.'

Konrad leaned forward, encouraged. Now for the real reason he had come to see Mrs. Halim. Her interests were broad and varied, and they included a taste for old stories, for lost tales and myths and lore. He had lent her texts from his own library on occasion, on topics such as these. He took the charred spine of the ruined book from his pocket, and offered it to her. 'I come to consult you about this book.'

Kavara Halim gingerly took the fragile leather, and turned it over in her fingers. 'What of it?'

'Do you perchance happen to recognise it?' The question was not so far-fetched; burned though the book may be, its surviving leather was of a distinctive crimson tint, an unusual shade for a binding. And the fragment of the title may be clue enough...

Mrs. Halim was a woman who valued her heritage, and who loved stories in all their forms. If he was right — if the book was a collection of Kayesiri lore — then maybe she would know it. Maybe.

She scrutinised the book anew, paying more attention to the half-legible words than she had before. Konrad waited in hope.

'Excuse me,' she murmured and rose from her chair, the wan shade of Kish vanishing into smoke with her movement. 'One moment.' She lit a second lantern and took it with her as she left the room, leaving the first on the table at Konrad's elbow.

This was more promising than Konrad had dared hope, and he hardly dared hope now. He waited in painful suspense as minutes ticked by in darkness and silence, an insistent weariness beating at the back of his mind.

She hasn't run off, has she? Eetapi's question slithered through Konrad's thoughts like a chill breeze, and he shivered.

Why would she run off? hissed her brother. *This is her house.*

Ootapi, go and check.

You go and check!

'Silence,' muttered Konrad.

Eetapi grumbled something slithery and mutinous, but fortunately it was pitched too low for Konrad to hear. He chose to pretend that he had heard nothing at all.

Mrs. Halim came back into the room, her arrival taking Konrad by surprise, for he had heard no footfall announcing her approach. She moved silently indeed in her soft cloth slippers. She said nothing, but put a book into Konrad's hands as she passed, and returned to her chair.

Konrad's heart beat faster with hope. The volume was slim, the leather smooth beneath his fingers. He held it up to the low lamplight: crimson-red binding, deeply engraved lettering.

Lost Folklore of Kayesir.

Konrad clutched the book tighter, lest the sudden tremor in his hands cast it tumbling to the ground. 'This is more than I imagined possible,' he whispered. 'Thank you.'

He knew the question was coming, of course. 'Why do you seek this book?' said Mrs. Halim. 'And what became of the other copy?'

Konrad spent a few silent moments in thought. How much should he tell her? Hers was a sharp mind; if he tried to lie, she would soon spot the holes in his story. But how much of the truth could he afford to reveal to her?

'Did you hear of the robbery of the Volkov Library, last week?' he began.

Her eyes narrowed. 'Of course.'

'This is the book that was taken.'

'And subsequently burned.'

'Yes. It was destroyed by the man who took it, though I do not know why.'

To his surprise, Mrs. Halim shook her head, her lips tightening. 'No. Ivorak Nasak would never have burned that book.'

Konrad was too surprised to speak. He could only stare, flabbergasted.

'Yes, I knew Ivorak,' she continued, answering one of his several unspoken questions. 'He came to me in search of this book, but I did not give him my copy. He tried to take it, but found my house harder to rob than he had imagined. I did not see him again after that. When, two days later, the Volkov Library was robbed, I was not surprised to see Ivorak's face in the paper, and it was not difficult to guess which book he was looking for.'

'Did he say why he wanted the book?'

'Not in so many words. But he was afraid, and angry. He spoke of a threat, a danger thought lost but as alive as ever. I believe he expected to find some manner of evidence for it in the book.'

'He was from Kayesir,' said Konrad slowly.

Mrs. Halim merely nodded.

'You have read this book, of course.'

'Long ago. I read it afresh, after Mr. Nasak's visit.'

'Do you know what was the danger he spoke of? Is it discussed herein?'

Mrs. Halim's confidences appeared to be at an end, for she regarded Konrad narrowly and did not answer. Instead she said: 'You are most insistent upon this topic, Mr. Savast, and the significance of the unfashionable hour of your visit has not escaped me. You spoke of urgency.'

'Why was this book burned?' he countered. 'If Ivorak did not destroy it, who did?' He had not forgotten Nuritov's theory that the killer had burned it instead, but he wanted Mrs. Halim's ideas.

'Mr. Nasak was afraid,' she repeated. 'He imagined himself followed. Hunted. Whether there was any truth to his fears, I do not know.'

'He is dead.'

Konrad had hoped to surprise Mrs. Halim with so blunt a statement, to shake her impeccable composure. He succeeded, to some extent; her next words died on her lips, whatever they might have been, and her lips parted in shock. 'How did he die?' she said, so softly he could barely hear her.

'He was found with his throat torn out.'

He received the impression that *this* piece of information did not surprise her at all. Rather, it confirmed a fear; he had said exactly what she was hoping he would *not* say. Her eyes closed briefly, and she swallowed. 'Poor man,' she said at last.

Konrad did not mention the laughter. Considering the absolute lack of mirth Ivorak had displayed at the library, Konrad could not readily account for the laughter. Perhaps it had been hysteria.

Mrs. Halim watched him carefully. She appeared to sense that there was more to the story; she awaited it with, he thought, some trepidation.

'I saw his corpse,' Konrad continued. 'And I saw him once more, after that. For a dead man, he was unusually talkative.'

Konrad was certain he did not imagine the flash of fear he saw in her eyes. 'He rose?' she whispered.

'He was perambulatory, chatty. Decidedly lively, for a murdered man. And, I would say, in utter despair.'

'Where is he now?' Mrs. Halim spoke calmly, but she gripped the arms of her chair so tightly that her hands shook.

'I do not know. I encountered him at the Volkov Library; I believe he followed me there. I have not seen him since.'

Kavara Halim visibly composed herself. Kish reappeared in her lap, purring brokenly, and she lifted one hand to caress the cat's decaying, incorporeal head. 'Read that book, Mr. Savast,' she said softly. 'I direct you in particular to the sixth chapter. Read it quickly, and soon.'

'Will you not tell me what you fear?'

'The book will tell you, far better than I can.'

Konrad nodded, and rose from his chair. He bowed to Mrs. Halim, and tucked the book into his pocket. 'I will return your book,' he promised.

'I am more concerned that you should stop the... man, that pursued Ivorak Nasak. And killed him.'

Konrad regarded her thoughtfully. 'I shall do my best,' he promised, aware that in doing so he was confirming her unvoiced suspicion: Konrad Savast, of Bakar House, was no mere idle gentleman at all. 'Do you know anything else that might assist me?

Anything about Ivorak?'

'Ivorak was made prey, but he was a hunter first. He sought to prove the existence of this so-called "lost" threat, and in so doing, he drew its notice. Be very careful, Mr. Savast.'

He bowed. 'I am no prey,' he assured her, and withdrew. Mrs. Halim did not follow.

Eetapi dashed ahead of him to the door. *That was a good parting line!*

Thank you, said Konrad modestly. *It was, wasn't it?*

Ootapi's shimmering tail lashed with disapproval. *Over dramatic.*

Sweet, delicious drama, said Eetapi on a dreamy sigh.

Konrad let himself out of Mrs. Halim's house, and gently shut the door behind himself.

Immediately he encountered a problem. Snow had been falling, softly but steadily, ever since the sun had set on Solstice Eve. While he had been in Kavara Halim's house, the snowfall had become a blizzard, and a deep drift of snow was beginning to pile up around the steps.

'Great,' Konrad muttered. 'To think I could be home in bed right now, fast asleep.'

He had not gone more than three steps from the door when Tasha appeared, looming out of the snow-struck darkness so abruptly that Konrad nearly screamed. She was moving at a dead run.

'Nuritov sent me,' she panted. 'Tavern near the Darks. Two dead.'

Konrad did not need to wait for more details. Two with their throats torn out, killed while he sat chatting with Mrs. Halim. 'Which tavern?'

'Crow's Foot.'

We go, Konrad called to the serpents, and away they flew.

Cloak clutched close against the driving snow, Konrad followed as fast as he could, Tasha by his side.

8

The Crow's Foot was more improved than otherwise by the heavy snow cover, for the thick, pristine white hid the general decay of its exterior. Approaching the building at as near to a run as he could manage against the force of a driving, snow-choked wind, Konrad found his mark by way of the tavern's creaking sign, displaying a glossy black crow with only one leg.

He threw open the stout oak door and dashed inside, Tasha quick upon his heels.

The scene inside was horrific. Most of the tavern's patrons had, presumably, fled. The two remaining lay in the centre of the floor, throats torn open, their torsos soaked in crimson blood. They were both men, middle-aged: labourers, judging from their weather-roughened faces and hands.

Inspector Nuritov stood with Nanda a little ways off, some two or three of his men around him. And there was another woman, Konrad belatedly noted. She wore the same calibre of clothing as the two dead men, coarse cotton much patched up. Her face was wet with tears, and she trembled with fright. The barkeep stood behind his bar, ashen-faced.

'Revelry was going on late,' Nuritov said to Konrad in lieu of a greeting. 'The season, you know. A man came in, ordered ale, but sat a time without drinking it—'

The barkeep interrupted. 'He tried it. Took a sip an' spat it out again. My ale ain't that bad!'

Nuritov nodded acknowledgement of the interjection. 'Sat a while with his drink and then... went mad.'

'Savage, like a wild beast,' said the teary-eyed woman, and she wrung her shaking hands together as she spoke. 'Went at Yegor and tore out his throat with his hands, just like that, and then Iosif, too. And then...' She could not seem to continue, fell silent with a gulp.

'And then?' prompted Konrad, as gently as he could.

'You will think me mad,' she whispered.

'Then the gent will have to think both of us mad,' said the barkeep. 'I saw it, too. Turned into some kind of beast, he did, but it weren't no living animal. You could see right through it.'

'A wolf,' whispered the woman. 'A ghost wolf. It — it drank blood from Yegor and Iosif and then howled, the most horrible sound I ever heard. Then it ran out the door, and we never saw it again.'

'Konrad,' said Nuritov. 'It was Ivorak. The man they are speaking of was Ivorak Nasak.'

Ivorak was made prey, but he was a hunter first.

Konrad dragged the book from his pocket, fumbled through the pages. Sixth chapter, sixth chapter...

There. *Ilu-Vakatim.* Nightwolves. The chapter was short; he read it in haste, and the pieces came together at last.

'Konrad?' said Nanda, bemused. 'You are... reading?'

'It's the book,' he answered absently. 'The one that was burned.'

Nanda was at his side in an instant, demanding sight of the text. He handed it over. 'Ivorak came here hunting something,' Konrad told Nanda, Nuritov and Tasha. 'Some*one.* A person afflicted with what the Kayesiri call *the moon curse.* As the moon waxes, such a person experiences changes to their physique. Subtle at first: a lengthening and sharpening of the teeth and nails, a growing hunger that no food can satisfy. At full moon, a total transformation occurs — into a nightwolf, a ghostwolf, a feral creature with no thought for anything but to devour blood and flesh. Preferably human.

'I think that Ivorak knew such a person. He followed him here, perhaps hoping to destroy him. Instead, he was killed — and *turned.* He's a nightwolf himself, now, and out of control. That's what happened to these two men.' He stared an instant at the lifeless, bloodied shapes upon the floor, and amended his ideas a little further. 'I think he killed the others, too. Nightwolves are said to enjoy enhanced senses of all kinds, in particular to be able to discern the relative health of a living human body. Probably in order that they can choose the liveliest, healthiest targets, but I think Ivorak did the opposite. He was at Parel's Bridge, he saw Albina there. He sensed that Albina was dying; that's why he chose her, crazed for food as he was. Maybe Illya was sick, too.'

'Yegor weren't sick,' said the tearful woman. 'Iosif neither.'

'He is losing his grip on himself, I fear.' The picture they had painted of Ivorak was of a man in despair, and losing control of himself. He ought not to have come to the Crow's Foot at all, but he had, and he had left two slain men behind when he'd fled.

Konrad looked at Tasha. 'Where would Ivorak go, if he wanted to get away from people? Was there somewhere he lived, in any sense? Somewhere he felt safe?'

'I don't know! I hardly knew him!'

'It's important, Tash. Think.'

With a short sigh, Tasha tore the dark cap off her head and turned it distractedly in her hands. 'He was at Parel's Bridge so much, I wondered if he ever really left the area. If he lives anywhere, I'd bet it's somewhere near the bridge.'

'Good, Tasha. Thank you.' He looked at Nanda, who was still intent upon the book. 'Nan, I think we will need you.'

She tucked the book into a pocket of her coat, and nodded. 'I'm with you.'

Konrad raised an enquiring brow at Nuritov, who hesitated. Then he gestured with his pipe towards the door. 'Your territory, not mine. I'll clean up here.'

He was right: with no supernatural powers of any kind to draw upon, Nuritov would have little to contribute, and he would be in considerable danger. 'Wise,' Konrad said. 'I'll report soon.'

With that, he went out the door and back into the night. The blizzard had lessened somewhat, to his relief; even the heavy cloud cover had cleared in patches, revealing a glimpse of a fat, silver moon...

'We'd better run,' said Konrad. 'Will you run with me?'

They knew what he meant; they had witnessed it before. Both women nodded, and Konrad took their hands in his own.

Then he cast off his guards once more, let his mask of sober gentility fade, became the Malykant in all his terrible might. Setting his face to the frigid wind, he began to walk. His strides lengthened and lengthened, until his legs ate up an impossible stretch of ground with every step.

When he ran, he outpaced the wind.

Five in the morning, and the revelry at Parel's Bridge had finally run its course. The bridge itself was lost in shadow, but a scattering of inert figures lay prone in the snow around it, some mere inches away from falling off the bank and hitting the frozen river beyond. Breathless, Konrad ran from person to person, shaking them, brushing snow from their blue faces. They were only drunk, unconscious, not dead. He was relieved, but his relief was short-lived, for if they were not dead yet, they would die of exposure before long.

He hesitated, torn. He could not leave them, but Ivorak was a more pressing problem.

'Go,' Nanda said. 'Find Ivorak. I will deal with these, and follow soon.'

Konrad and Tasha ran on, Eetapi and Ootapi riding the swirling currents of the winds overhead. Parel's Bridge was one of the oldest in Ekamet, and it had not been well maintained. Konrad could hear its aged timbers creaking as he approached, could almost see it swaying under the onslaught of the weather. Few were fool enough to try to cross it.

'We're going over,' Konrad said to Tasha.

'In this weather! Are you crazy!' She had to shout to make herself heard over the wind.

'The river is frozen,' Konrad yelled back.

Tasha eyed the dark, looming shape of the bridge with clear misgivings. The river was wide here, and the bridge arched up high... 'It's a long drop! I may be undead but I can still *hurt*.'

'Then we will have to be intrepid, won't we?' Konrad sent the serpents on ahead, with instructions to scout for gaps, missing planks or other dangers. Then he mustered his courage — for Tasha was right, crossing such a bridge on such a night, when he could barely see two feet in front of his face, was foolhardy — and stepped onto the bridge.

The experience would not rank as one of his better decisions. The snow-laden wood was slippery, and though he clung tightly to the railing, his feet often threatened to slide out from under him and dump him into the snow. He could see very little, even with the glowing, dual presence of his serpents drifting just ahead. Tasha gamely trudged along in his wake, though he could hear her cursing in a fluid stream of vulgar language.

Halfway across, when they had inched their way almost to the apex of the bridge and it poised ready to sweep downwards to the far shore, Konrad found what they were looking for.

A little shanty-hut had been built against the side of the bridge — wrought, probably, from planks of wood taken out of the bridge structure itself. It was crude work, but it provided meagre shelter from the wind and snow. If Konrad had nowhere better to go, he supposed he, too, would find it adequate enough.

'Ivorak!' he shouted. 'Ivorak Nasak! Come out, we are here to help y—'

'GO!' The word roared forth from the darkened interior of the little shack. 'Stay away! I hurt you, I cannot help it, you must leave.'

Konrad approached the shack and stood directly outside it, his back turned to the wind. 'You won't hurt us. Tasha's dead already and it's not easy to cause me any harm. Come out.'

Whether it was the prospect of relative safety that drew Ivorak forth, or whether his curiosity was roused by the notion of Tasha's being as undead as himself, Konrad could not tell. But Ivorak Nasak crawled forth from the dubious shelter of his tiny shack, and stared up at Konrad — resplendently deadly as the Malykant — in stark terror. Eetapi and Ootapi's sickly ghost-glow dimly illuminated his face. He looked better than he had at the library: healthier, less... dead. He had fed, of course, copiously. He kept his mouth shut and his hands hidden from Konrad's sight.

'Show me,' Konrad said, quiet but firm.

'Who are you?' Ivorak whispered. He looked away from Konrad, to the dark, silent shape of Tasha just behind.

'Not one of *his*. I am the Malykant. Do you know what that means?'

In silence, Ivorak nodded. 'You here to kill me.' He withdrew his hands from their concealment, and displayed them for Konrad's scrutiny: blue with cold, sinewy, each finger tipped with a vicious claw.

'It is my duty to do so,' Konrad replied.

Ivorak bowed his head, trembling. 'Good. Do it now, please.'

'I do not want to kill you, Ivorak. I need your help. Who did this to you?'

'My... my brother.' Ivorak shook his head. 'He kill you. Even you.'

'I doubt it. I am not easy to kill.' Konrad spoke the words with confidence, and tried to expel from his mind the occasions upon which he had been slain in the course of his duty. More than once... but Ivorak did not need to know that.

'Konrad!' Nanda's voice, close by. He cursed himself, for he had not thought that she would follow, would brave the bridge alone and without the serpents' aid. He went to meet her, took her cold hands and led her to the tiny shack. He felt strengthened by Nanda's presence at his side.

'Where is your brother?' Konrad resumed.

'I know not! I follow him here, to the city. Where we come from, Kayesir, is full of *ilu-vakatim.* Too many. Harder to hide, and some people, they remember the old stories — hunt us, kill us. My brother, he go looking for new place. Assevan, say he, not many *vakatim* there. I go, take this new place, kill many. Feed much.' Ivorak's face turned grim. 'I follow him. Look for way to kill him — knives not work, water, nothing. At library they say, who are you, can't have book. I take it. Book say, silver kills *vakatim.* Where I get silver knife? Then my brother find me, with book. He know what I try to do. He kill me, he... make me like *him...* and he burn book. Say, now no one know how to kill us, and you like me now. We the same. And then he go, vanish, and I no see him since.'

'You are not the same as he,' Konrad said. He tried to speak reassuringly, but the words emerged as cold as ice. 'You were hungry. You had to feed. What did you do?'

In answer, Ivorak leaned nearer to Konrad, his eyes unfocused. 'You living,' he said. 'But not. Not sick, not well. Other. And she—' His gaze swerved to Tasha, who looked up, blinking. 'She dead, like me but not like. I see. I see sickness, health. Old woman, man with wine. Both sick, nearly dead, though he not know it. I choose them.' His head drooped, and he took a great sob. 'I have to. But the others—'

'Why did you go to the Crow's Foot?'

'I felt... right again, after old woman, and man. Felt good. Wanted ale, but when I taste, it make me sick. I stayed, should not have. Got hungry.' He began to cry in earnest, his whole body shaking. 'Kill me, then I no kill others.'

'I will not kill you,' Konrad said firmly to Ivorak. 'You have not deserved such a judgement.' Someone had to pay for the deaths of Albina Olga and Illya Vasily, and Yegor and Iosif from the Crow's Foot. But in Konrad's opinion, the responsibility for those deaths lay with Ivorak's brother; it would be *he* who would pay.

'What if he lies?' whispered Nanda, her lips so close to Konrad's ear he was certain no one but he could hear.

'Then I will kill him later,' he whispered back, with a mirthless smile. But the threat was an empty one. Ivorak's story fit his behaviour perfectly; he had neither said nor done anything to imply that he might be lying. 'Will you help him?'

'I will,' she agreed, without hesitation.

Nan was of the Shandrigal's Order, a being as devoted to life as The Malykt presided over death. Nanda's Order might find use for a person who could literally sniff out sickness, could sense death taking hold of a living person's body. And who better than they to help a beleaguered, desperate nightwolf learn to control himself? With the right help, Ivorak need never kill again.

As for penance for the damage he had already caused, the man's obvious torment was punishment enough. He had been brave beyond words, to go after his brother as he had. Many another man would have waved farewell with delight, thinking himself well rid of so dangerous a sibling. Ivorak had risked everything and lost everything. Such courage, such commitment, also fit him perfectly for the life of a Shandral.

Whether The Malykt would agree was another matter. Konrad decided to worry about that later.

He needed to explain none of this to Nanda; she reached the same conclusions as he without speech.

'What is your brother's name?' he said to Ivorak.

'Hakir,' whispered Ivorak.

Somewhere in Ekamet, Hakir Nasak prowled the night, looking for... what? He did not seem to be killing. If Ivorak had come here in pursuit of his brother, Hakir must have arrived at the same time, or even earlier — in other words, more than a week ago. Four had died since, but all four killings were committed by Ivorak; why was his brother so restrained? If he came to Assevan in search of an untapped source of food and freedom to kill at will, as Ivorak described, why had he been so quiet?

On the one hand, this boded well for Ivorak: clearly, the nightwolves *could* feed without killing, as Konrad doubted that Hakir Nasak had spent the past week or two fasting. Perhaps he was choosing to feed discreetly, so as not to draw attention to the presence of ghostwolves in Ekamet. But he had turned his brother and then let him loose, left him alone. He must have known that Ivorak, new to the state, ravenous and frightened, would be unable to help himself from killing his first victims.

So, Hakir's restraint probably had nothing to do with discretion. That suggested that his true purpose was not quite as Ivorak imagined. What might he be doing in Ekamet, if he did not come expressly in order to feed and kill at will?

My brother, he go looking for new place. Assevan, say he, not many ilu-vakatim there.

'Ivorak,' said Konrad slowly. 'In Kayesir. Do the *ilu-vakatim* have... structure? Are they loners, I mean, or do they have society, a hierarchy?'

'Some alone. Some not. Live in... um, live together. Groups.'

'Wolf packs.'

Ivorak nodded. 'Three big ones, some small.'

'Did your brother ever lead such a pack?'

'No. He try, leader almost kill him.'

Konrad sighed. His hands were so cold he could barely feel them; he dug them deep into his pockets, shivering.

'He's building a new pack,' said Tasha in awe. 'That's what he's doing here!'

'I'd say so,' Konrad agreed. 'What better way than to construct a pack from scratch, filled with people he has personally turned into *vakatim*? The only pack in Ekamet, maybe the whole of Assevan!'

'I wonder how many he's already turned?' said Nanda.

Konrad nodded grimly. 'We need to find him, and fast. Ivorak, think. Anything you can tell us will be helpful. Where would Hakir go?'

'He like good things,' said Ivorak promptly. 'Expensive things, rich people. So I come here, to this bridge. He hate... all this.' Ivorak gestured at the decaying bridge, the decrepitude of his little shack, the total lack of any kind of comfort. 'Maybe I safe here, from him.'

'Snob,' said Tasha with contempt. 'Is he rich himself?'

Ivorak nodded. 'He older than me, inherit all father's money.'

'So he's off cosying up to Ekamet's elite,' Tasha concluded. 'Konrad, you gentleman, look how useful you are! Where do the likes of you hang around?'

Konrad said nothing. He barely heard Tasha, for Ivorak's words had sparked off a series of thoughts.

At Lady Goraya's Solstice ball, ten days before: a new arrival. Sleekly handsome, his black hair oiled, dark beard perfectly trimmed. Dressed in Kayesiri silks, the man all smiles and well-bred charm. He had not been introduced as Hakir Nasak; the name he had given was...

'Vakatim,' Konrad said aloud. 'That's the name he gave.'

'What, Konrad?' said Nanda. 'Who?'

'There's a newcomer from Kayesir. He arrived a couple of weeks ago, has shown up at all the best balls since. I saw him at Zima's once or twice, too. Calls himself Mr. Vakatim, but I heard it spoken only once or twice, thought nothing of him...'

'How obvious can he be?' asked Tasha.

'There is a reason the book is called *lost* folkore of Kayesir. The nightwolves have done a fine job of talking themselves out of existence, as far as people in general are concerned. And they have never really been a part of Assevi culture. He relies on our knowing nothing of them, having no way of making that connection.'

'That's why he burned Ivorak's book,' said Nanda. 'It gives the Kayesiri name for the nightwolves, vakatim.'

'I think so,' Konrad agreed.

'And it says how to kill them,' added Tasha.

Konrad nodded. 'Silver.' He thought a moment. 'I don't know where Hakir has set up house, but it won't be hard to find out — in the morning. Which gives me a couple of hours to find a silver knife.'

'I have one,' Nanda murmured.

'You... you do?'

Nanda nodded once.

Apparently she did not wish to engage with the implied question, that being: why in the world do you have a silver knife, and what is it for? 'May I borrow it?' he said instead.

'If there is so much as a speck of blood on it when I get it back, I will have your head.'

'That's fair.'

'Then you may.'

9

Nanda's silver knife acquired, and Ivorak shepherded off into the care of The Shandrigal's Order, Konrad tried to sleep. Thoughts of the so-called Mr. Vakatim kept him awake, as exhausted as he was. The nerve of the man was incredible. He had penetrated Ekamet high society with ease, effortlessly passed himself off as a natural among the aristocracy, purporting to be a man with as much right to the drawing-rooms of Ekamet's finest as he had to breathing air. Konrad had not liked him, on the one or two occasions they had met. He had come across as cold, even calculating. But Konrad had set him down as an opportunist, a social climber, a man with an eye to his position and a desire to rise.

The truth was far worse. There could be little doubt that he intended to populate his new wolf-pack with people of refined bloodlines; an aristocracy of nightwolves taking root in the very heart of Ekamet. Hakir Nasak certainly had ambition, and more than enough nerve to act upon it.

What role he envisioned for his tormented brother in this bright new future of his, Konrad could not guess. Ivorak seemed discarded altogether, but a man with so organised a plan was unlikely to leave that kind of a loose thread dangling. Nanda had taken Ivorak away, to be tended by her Order. Konrad's strictest instructions to *take care* had gone with her, exhortations she had returned with equal force. Eetapi had also gone with her, at Konrad's insistence.

'What am I going to do with her?' Nanda had asked.

'Nothing. She's going to play lookout for you.'

'I am not in need of her assistance.'

I told you, said Eetapi.

'Take her along anyway,' he'd said, and added more tenderly, 'Please.'

Grudgingly, Nanda had relented. Konrad and Ootapi had returned to Bakar House, minus Tasha, who went first to the station to apprise Nuritov of developments. She appeared in Konrad's bedroom an hour or so later, interrupting his latest attempt to drop into an exhausted doze.

'Nuritov says hello,' she announced.

Konrad lay inert, staring at the bed curtains in despair. 'How polite of him,' he mumbled.

'He also says that Vakatim lives on Tatav Circle. Number twelve. Big place, gilding, all that.'

'I know the house.' The choice of address fitted with the profile Ivorak had made of his brother: all pomp and show. Konrad threw back the blankets and tore off his night-cap, exhausted with the effort to sleep. 'Are you up for a fight, Tash?'

'Always.'

'Me too. Forget waiting for morning. Let us go and explain one or two things to Mr. Vakatim.'

Considering the lateness of the hour, Konrad expected to find Number Twelve, Tatav Circle dark and quiet. Instead, lights blazed in most of the windows, and the sounds of music and raucous conversation were clearly audible even from the street outside.

'Mr. Vakatim likes to party,' Konrad murmured, staring up at the silhouettes of well-dressed figures passing behind the drapes that covered the house's long windows.

'Inconvenient,' Tasha observed.

Highly. Konrad thought for a moment. *Ootapi. Find Mr. Nasak, if you please. Softly, softly. We do not know what manner of help he may have.*

Ootapi did not deign to respond, and Konrad felt disgust and affront rolling off the serpent in waves as he drifted through the wall, vanishing into what was probably the house's drawing-room.

Sorry, Konrad said belatedly. *You are always careful, of course.*

It was not strictly, absolutely true, but it mollified Ootapi. The serpent's icy disdain lessened, which hopefully meant he was concentrating more on his appointed task than on his feelings about

Konrad.

While you are in there, Konrad called after him. *Take note of who you see, please, and if there are other nightwolves among the company, inform me at once.* How promptly had Nasak set about turning others to *ilu-vakatim*? His snobbishness might encourage him to take care; to be selective, elitist, and wait to act until he had forged links with the cream of Ekamet society. Or so Konrad hoped. But perhaps he would rather begin by recruiting a few lesser beings to his cause, men and women who would help him in establishing himself.

He was relieved when Ootapi reported, distantly: *No vakatim, Master.*

None? Konrad wanted reassurance.

None at all, Ootapi confirmed. *Not one.*

Oh. *Literally none?*

Yes, Master. Ootapi spoke with exaggerated patience. *Literally not a single one.*

Not even Hakir Nasak was there? Mr. Vakatim himself was absent from his own house party? Konrad stood, briefly dumbfounded.

'He is not there,' he relayed to Tasha.

'Mister Nightwolf? Huh.' Tasha surveyed the house thoughtfully, as though a closer scrutiny of its stone walls might offer some clue. 'I wonder where he is.'

'Yes,' Konrad said, a trifle testily. 'I was wondering that, myself.'

Tell me what is going on in there, Ootapi, he commanded. He needed more information, a way to picture the situation inside the house. Perhaps he would then be able to guess at Nasak's whereabouts.

Everyone is drunk, Ootapi reported. *Mixed company. No undead, no ghost presence —*

Wait. Mixed company? How so?

Gentry. Occasional aristocracy. And it is my guess that some of these are prostitutes.

Konrad blinked. Prostitutes? At snobbish Hakir Nasak's elite Solstice celebration? That did not fit with his brother's account of his tastes.

For that matter, so raucous and inebriated a party did not fit the refined picture Ivorak had painted of Hakir's preferred lifestyle, either.

Konrad felt a flicker of doubt.

Is there nobody presiding?

No. All is chaos.

'We are going in,' Konrad said to Tasha. He needed to see what was going on for himself. If he encountered anybody he knew, well, he could claim to be a late-arriving guest. But from Ootapi's account, he did not think anybody would pay him much regard.

He dutifully lifted the knocker upon the front door and rapped. It was worth keeping up appearances, if he wished to pass for a guest, but in the tumult of the party he did not think anybody would hear the knock. And so it proved, for after a minute's waiting no one came to the door.

Konrad turned the handle, and went inside. Tasha silently followed.

The scene within was as Ootapi had succinctly described: chaos. Revellers crowded every chamber, and Konrad had to force his way from room to room as he scanned the company for any sign of Hakir Nasak, for faces he knew, for anything that might assist him. But he saw little of use. Some of the guests were known to him, at least by sight, but their presence cast no light whatsoever upon the problem of Hakir Nasak. And as he pushed and shoved his way through the ground floor and then up the stairs, he had to conclude that Ootapi had been right about everything: the company was *very* mixed, and the so-called Mr. Vakatim was not there.

An unsettled feeling grew, and Konrad's thoughts began to race. His reflections were unpromising. Ivorak Nasak had given a clear picture of his brother, Hakir, but Konrad saw little that agreed with it. Hakir had certainly introduced himself to Ekamet's high society; Konrad could vouch for that, for he had encountered "Vakatim" himself. But the man who could throw such a riotous, raucous, absolutely *un*elitist Solstice party was not the would-be social leader Ivorak had described. And while Konrad had been relieved to learn that there were no nightwolves among the company, that fact, too, sat uneasily alongside everything they thought they knew about Hakir Nasak. If he had come to Ekamet in order to feed and kill as he pleased, as Ivorak had said, why had he not done so? And if he had come in order to establish his own pack, why had he not already begun? Konrad's notion that he preferred to reserve his attention for the cream of society was decidedly belied by his choice of house guests.

And where was he? Why would a man fill his house with revellers on Solstice Eve only to disappear, leaving his drunk, out-of-control guests in unsupervised possession of his property?

Konrad fought his way back out of the house and regained the street, desperate for a moment's respite from the noise and the crush. He needed to *think*.

'Konrad,' Tasha panted as she ran after him. 'What—'

'Hush,' he said softly. 'Please.'

Tasha subsided, and Konrad closed his eyes against the drifting snow. He tried to remember the man who had been introduced to him as *Mr. Vakatim,* wishing now that he had paid closer attention. He had treated the introduction with indifference, disliking the man on sight, and now he struggled to recall his face in any detail. Shiny black hair, neatly groomed beard. Fine clothes. That was all.

Oh, but Ivorak...

'You and I,' Konrad said after a while, 'have been set up.'

Tasha gave him a stare of blank incomprehension. 'What?'

Hakir Nasak. They only Ivorak's word for it that the man had ever existed — or that "Ivorak Nasak" did, either. Which persona was invented? Perhaps they both were. He and Nanda had not found Hakir Nasak's name in the immigration records, but they had not looked for it, for they had not known of the name at the time.

He could go back and look for it now, but Konrad would bet his house that the name was not there.

Because no such person as *Hakir Nasak* had entered the city lately — or ever. He conjured his memories of Hakir and Ivorak Nasak and compared the two faces, trying to see past the superficial differences — the exquisite neatness and luxuriousness of the one, the shabby, unkempt wildness of the other — and felt satisfied: they were one and the same.

'There is no brother,' Konrad told Tasha. 'Ivorak and Hakir Nasak are the same man. I do not know which of those names is his true one, if either is.'

'But...' said Tasha slowly. 'But Ivorak — the laughing man — you found him murdered!'

'I found him pretending to be murdered. I think I happened upon him at an inopportune moment, and somehow or other he got *my* measure right away. He had killed Vasily and Albina Olga, and heard — or sensed — my approach. The serpents, perhaps, gave me away. As *ilu-vakatim,* perhaps he senses spirits in ways most people do not;

and who wanders the city with a matched pair of ghost-serpents in tow? He knew he was in trouble. Those claws. He tore out his *own* throat, made me believe he was dead. After that, he followed us, Nanda and I — more than once. He wanted to know how close we were, I think, to figuring him out. He knew we were checking the immigration records. He'd used the name Ivorak Nasak when he arrived in Ekamet, and he invented a persona around it on the spot — made up a brother, too — in order to confuse us. To camouflage himself. And it worked! Oh, it worked beautifully.' Konrad felt such bitter self-reproach he could hardly breathe for the weight of it. How quick he had been to believe Ivorak's show of remorse, to sympathise with him, to find any reason whatsoever not to kill him! 'As I said, he certainly got my measure.'

Were they wrong about everything, quite? What *was* Ivorak (or Hakir) Nasak doing in Ekamet, after all? Had he come to feast, or had he come to build a kingdom? Perhaps both. Had Vasily been sick, as Ivorak had claimed? Perhaps not. Albina had probably fallen victim to simple hunger; after a week of feeding but lightly, Ivorak had been ravenous. He had killed her, followed Illya to his shop and killed him, too. But had he killed them, or turned them? Were they dead and gone, or would they revive as *ilu-vakatim*?

And there was Nuritov. *I'll clean up here,* the inspector had said, standing over the slain bodies of two labourers. Were the four victims dead, or were they... in transition?

'I think I am wrong again,' Konrad said slowly. 'He did not fabricate Ivorak in order to confuse us — couldn't have. He was giving out that name while wandering Ekamet as one of the street people. He's been playing two parts all along, and why would he do that? Why pretend to be Ivorak of the streets some of the time, and Mr. Vakatim at the top end of society the rest?'

'Same reason you do,' said Tasha promptly.

'What.'

'You pretend to be Konrad Savast, society gent, but you're also Konrad the wanderer, with that hut in the Bones and a penchant for poisons.'

'Maybe one of those is the real me,' Konrad protested, injured.

'Maybe one is the real Ivorak, too, or Hakir. Either way, by adopting two personas he has access to lots of different kinds of people. "Mr. Vakatim" couldn't walk among the street people and expect to be taken seriously, and neither could shabby Ivorak walk into the best houses in the city without being thrown straight out again.'

Hmm. 'I do it because, when I am searching for something — or someone — I can access all levels of society at need.'

'Exactly.'

'So what is he looking for?' Konrad asked the question rhetorically, not expecting a response, but Tasha immediately spoke up.

'People don't volunteer information lightly,' she said, in a conversational tone which briefly befuddled Konrad, for her choice of topic seemed a complete side-step. 'And when pressed, the stories they tell are influenced by what's on their mind at the time, even if they're making things up. So, Ivorak told you a great deal. Some of it may be discounted as manipulative, designed to bring you in line with the version of events he wanted you to believe. But he said more than he needed to. Like, he offered an explanation as to his choice of victims.'

'Illya Vasily and Albina Olga. Yes. But he wanted us to believe he had chosen them because they were sick, because he didn't want to hurt anybody. All part of his poor-Ivorak routine.'

'Why, though? With the other two, he merely said he had lost control. He could have said the same about the first two. We know nothing about the *ilu-vakatim,* we would probably have believed him. Why invent a different story for Vasily and Albina?'

'Because something about them was on his mind?'

'It's my belief he told us more truth than we might imagine right now — good liars do. The more truth to your tale, the more likely you'll be believed. But I think he told us more truth than he meant to. I think he probably did lose control at the Crow's Foot, or he was content enough to allow himself to. We know that Albina Olga was dying, and I think Illya Vasily was too, and he may have known it, even if his family did not. That's why his attitude about his death was so resigned.'

'So Ivorak did choose the first two because they were terminally ill. But why would he?'

'Think about it. You're a man with delusions of grandeur, convinced that you deserve to be of supreme importance in the world, and consumed with dissatisfaction that you aren't. So much so that, even when your leadership bid fails so badly it almost kills you, you are not deterred. You leave behind everything you know to come to a new place, where there is no competition, where you can start afresh with no real obstacles. What do you want to do next?'

'Build the greatest, the most powerful kingdom of nightwolves possible. Outdo the achievements of those who defeated and scorned you.'

'Yes — and make sure nobody can seriously challenge you again, or better yet, make sure nobody wants to. What kind of people are you going to choose? Ivorak led us to believe that "Mr. Vakatim" only wanted rich and influential people, but that seems unlikely now. He has been seeking possible recruits across all levels of society; social status has nothing to do with his selection process.'

Finally, Konrad caught her drift. 'He is choosing those who are dying, because they are about to lose *everything* and he can give it all back to them.'

'Mhm. How would you feel about the man who had given you a new life? One free of the sickness that had tormented you for months or years, which was going to kill you?'

Konrad pictured a growing army of nightwolves, all desperately grateful to Ivorak Nasak. Fanatically grateful? 'I have trouble picturing Albina Olga enjoying such an existence.'

'The plan may not work out entirely as he intends, indeed. Some would rather die, than live such a life. But such a possibility may not occur to Nasak.' She added, after a moment's thought, 'Though people can surprise...'

'The book said nothing about how a person becomes a nightwolf,' Konrad observed, with a short sigh. 'There seemed nothing amiss with Illya or Albina. They were dead, we talked to their ghosts...'

'I'm guessing it takes some time.' Tasha smiled faintly. 'It is not that easy to make a non-dead person undead, you know.'

'Time, and maybe... something else. I wonder if those corpses are still at the morgue.'

'And I wonder where Ivorak is right now.'

'He is...' Konrad's heart froze. 'He went with Nanda.' To The Shandrigal's Temple, the heart of the Order. What would he do there? At best, he would simply evade Nanda at his earliest opportunity and escape, perhaps leaving some tearful tale behind himself to explain his disappearance.

But, no. The Shandrigal's Order comprised a great many healers and doctors; one of their prime duties was to tend to the sick. And Konrad had obligingly given them Ivorak. To *help*.

He groaned. 'I've been such a fool. He wasn't following me. He was following Nanda.'

'Or both,' Tasha put in.

'And I left her with him,' Konrad continued, ignoring that. 'Think. Where would she take him?'

'To the Shandrigal's Temple?'

'At this hour?'

Tasha looked blankly at him. 'Where else, if not there?'

'You know Nanda's habit of taking in stray folk?' He did not speak lightly. She had adopted Danil Dubin, a fellow apothecary, all the more enthusiastically since his public fall from grace. And there was Arina, a woman who had become catastrophically mixed up in the same bad business, and whom Nanda had immediately taken under her wing as well. And others. There were always others.

'She took him home?'

'Of course she did,' Konrad sighed. 'She is Nanda.' He took a moment to breathe, to try to quiet the flurry of panic that overtook his heart. Nanda was not defenceless, and as dangerous as Ivorak undoubtedly was, he had no reason to want to harm her.

Even so. Nanda was alone at home with a *monster* and he, Konrad, had made it happen.

He grabbed Tasha. 'I'm going to run,' he warned.

'Go,' Tasha said.

Konrad ran.

He did not know, as he travelled, what manner of scene he might encounter when he arrived at Nanda's house. Would Ivorak maintain the facade of innocence he had adopted, so convincingly, at the bridge, or would he throw it off? Would he be brute enough, fool enough, to threaten her? Would he try to hurt her, or even turn her? Would Nanda figure him out, as Konrad finally had, or did he fool her still? As the minutes passed, his fears grew, and the visions of likely scenarios his mind helpfully provided grew more and more catastrophic.

Konrad mustered every shred of will and energy he possessed, and quickened his already flying pace.

When Nanda's modest house came into view, her shop beneath and her apartments above, he suffered a tumult of mixed feelings: part relief, part utter panic. Was she even still *alive?*

Eetapi! he bellowed the moment he was remotely within range. *Tell me all is well.*

Master? Brother? What are you doing here?

Tell me all is well, Konrad repeated.

I do not care for their choice of tea, Eetapi replied. *The aroma is offensive.*

Tea? Konrad hurtled up to Nanda's front door, all bemusement and fright, and dragged it open so forcefully he almost tore it off its hinges. He wanted to scream for Nanda, assure himself *instantly* that she was well, but some buried instinct prevented him. If Ivorak yet maintained his pretence of innocence, Konrad may not wish to instantly reveal his knowledge of the deception. And Eetapi rambled about tea...

He crossed the shop floor in three great strides, his boot-heels ringing sharply upon the hard wooden floor. The tiny door at the back divided the commercial premises from Nanda's workroom behind, and her living quarters above; he tore through it, and straight up the stairs.

The scene he encountered was the very opposite of anything he had expected. In Nanda's little parlour sat the lady herself, on one side of the worn but elegant oaken table that dominated the room. Opposite sat Ivorak, wrapped in one of Nanda's coats and with a ceramic hot brick balanced upon his lap. They were indeed partaking of tea, or at least, Nanda was. The cup before Ivorak looked untouched.

'Konrad,' said Nanda in greeting, her pale brows rising in surprise. 'I thought you gone to bed.'

'I was,' he said. He did not know what to add, so wrong-footed by the placid scene was he. Did Nanda know? She could not possibly, or she would not look nearly so relaxed. He looked hard at Ivorak, but if he expected to observe any tell-tale clue in the man's appearance, or some trace of guilt in his eyes, he was out of luck. Ivorak returned the stare with a hesitant, rather shy smile, perfectly in keeping with the character he had adopted, and Konrad could find nothing at which to object.

'We were discussing Mr. Nasak's future with the Order,' Nanda said, and got up from her chair. 'You will join us for tea, of course?

And Tasha?'

Ivorak's reaction to Tasha's appearance was the first sign of something amiss, for he watched her with the wary alertness of a cat faced with a mouse — or, perhaps, vice versa. Tasha grinned at him, and slouched down in the chair immediately adjacent. 'Tea would be nice,' she said to Nanda.

Konrad took the final unoccupied chair, bemused. Here he had run in a fit of raging fury and panic, only to engage in an odd out-of-hours tea party with the person he loved best in the world, with Nuritov's odd, undead apprentice, and with the man he had come here to kill. Nanda set a steaming cup before him, accompanying it with one of her special, warm smiles, and he only felt more confused. She looked excessively tired, and he felt smitten with remorse at having dragged her into this mess when she could have been peacefully asleep on Solstice night.

Ivorak was watching him. Konrad felt the weight of the other man's gaze, but as soon as he returned it, Ivorak returned to staring into his tea.

A show of discomfort, however subtle. Very well. He was troubled, then, by Konrad's abrupt and unannounced reappearance. Did he guess, that Konrad knew?

'What have you decided, then?' Konrad asked. 'About Mr. Nasak and the Order.'

Nanda sat down again, and took a gulp of tea. 'Mr. Nasak is eager to be of use, and I am eager to ascertain the extent of his abilities. I have hopes he will be of great assistance in determining the source of a sickness, and its extent, in ways we have yet been unable to achieve.' She smiled at Ivorak as she spoke, but there was a tension about her that Konrad did not understand. Was she aware of his deception, or was it something else?

'How generous he is with his time,' said Konrad, unsmiling, with a hard look at Ivorak.

Ivorak said nothing.

Konrad's temper began to fray. He had been up all night, dragging himself around frozen Ekamet on a night when, above all others, he — and Nanda, no doubt, too — would prefer to be comfortably at home. Ivorak had killed, deceived, lied, led him around by the nose, and now sat there looking as innocent as a summer sky. Why were they wasting still more time on this absurd pretence? Konrad decided to be more direct. 'We were unable to find your brother,' he said coldly. 'It seems he had somewhere else to be tonight, in spite of hosting a houseful of guests.'

'I not know where he is,' said Ivorak instantly. He was brazen enough to meet Konrad's gaze as he spoke, unflinching.

'But I do,' said Konrad, very softly. He held Ivorak's deceitful gaze and, slowly, smiled.

He could almost see the wheels turning in Ivorak's head. Should he try to brazen it out, deny everything, rely on Nanda's soft (sort of) heart and Konrad's rather better hidden sympathetic side to save him? Or accept that the game was up, abandon the deceit, and... and what? What would he do?

Ivorak looked from Konrad to Tasha to Nanda, the latter of whom continued to sip her tea with a show of placidity which convinced Konrad she knew everything he had guessed. She hadn't reacted at all to Konrad's revelation that he knew where Ivorak's so-called "brother" was.

Ivorak's eyes glittered, and his mouth twisted in a malicious smile. 'She is sick,' he said, indicating Nanda with a tilt of his head. 'Very sick. You do not know it, I think.'

Konrad's eyes flew to Nanda's face. 'She... she's what? Nan? Is this true?'

Nanda met his eyes only briefly and then stared into her tea, her lips forming a grim line. Oh, she looked desperately tired, but so did Konrad himself, no doubt; probably the shadows under his own eyes were a match for hers. But was she paler than usual? Was her air of weariness merely the product of a long, long night, or was it something more?

Konrad stared long, his heart sinking like a rock. 'You lie,' he snarled at Ivorak, and he hoped fiercely that it was so. Ivorak had lied about virtually everything; why not this, too?

But he knew it to be false hope. Nanda's tension was now explained. She would not meet his gaze, and she did not even try to dissemble. She merely sat, defeated, bitter, staring sightlessly into her cooling cup of tea.

Ivorak beamed at Konrad. 'You are welcome,' he said. 'I cannot tell you how delighted I am to be of use.'

Then he moved. Konrad, fixed as his attention still was upon Nanda's wan visage, realised the man's intention too late. Ivorak shot for the stairs, moving with unthinkable speed, and within seconds he was gone.

But Tasha had been ready for him. Neither so distracted as Konrad, nor so slow, she barrelled after the fugitive, supernaturally fast herself. The room emptied of them both, and Konrad still sat in his chair, flummoxed, unable to catch his breath for the sudden weight of fear.

He had time for only one last, anguished, reproachful look at Nanda, and then he, too, was gone.

Konrad reached the street several seconds behind Tasha, too late to see where she or Ivorak had gone.

Master, hissed Eetapi from somewhere overhead. *This way.*

He could not see her. The night was too dark, the full moon hidden once more behind great banks of clouds. Snow blew into his face, stinging his eyes, and the street's lamps had long since burned out.

But he could sense her: some way above his head, a few feet in front of him. *That* way. She set up a glow, exuding that faint, sickly ghost-light, making a beacon of herself.

She sped away, and he followed. Ootapi raced in from who-knew-where and fell in by his sister's side, and Konrad set off after them both, his stride lengthening to impossible speed. Buildings melted away around him as he hurtled through the streets of Ekamet, noting distantly that they were not headed for Parel's Bridge or for Tatav Circle. They were making for the west gate, and he was not surprised when his serpents led him out into the Bone Forest. Ivorak was far from the only killer to seek shelter, concealment, amongst those gnarled, craggy trees, who thought that the twisting, tangled branches and swirling snow would obstruct his pursuer.

Fool. The Malykant was at home out in the Bones; more so, in some respects, than he was among all the comforts and luxuries of Bakar House. He found a way through the maze of trees with ease, strode over the dips and hillocks and frozen marsh-puddles without missing a step. The snow he simply disregarded, for he did not precisely need his eyes, not out here. His serpents shone in the darkness ahead of him, twin wisps of deathlight half-glimpsed with every step. They shone in his mind, too, beacons to guide him safely down a death-trap of winding, treacherous pathways.

He caught up with Tasha, grabbed her in passing. 'You should not be out here alone,' he hissed.

Tasha writhed in his grip, seething. 'I may *look* like a kid, but I'm as dangerous as you are.'

'No one's as dangerous as me,' Konrad said, but the chill ebbed from his words, and he spoke them more with regret.

Tasha merely snorted. 'Anyway, I am not alone, because here *you* are. Inevitably.'

'I apologise, if my appearance disappoints you.'

'Maybe I wanted to catch the killer.' Tasha gave up fighting — realising, perhaps, that their joint progress was indeed rather faster than hers had been alone — but her annoyance did not lessen one whit.

'You will help me to catch him.' Konrad stopped speaking, for Eetapi and Ootapi had sung out in victory, their twin voices sounding like frozen bells in the darkness. *There! How he runs!*

Konrad saw him, too: a dark figure darting through the trees ahead, moving with all the speed of fury and terror but *not fast enough,* for Konrad was almost upon him.

Ivorak looked back, once, and oh, he was afraid now.

Konrad leapt, Tasha an instant after. Together they crashed into the fleeing figure of Ivorak Nasak, bringing him sharply to the hard, icy ground. Konrad felt a thrill of victory, and of malicious glee, the latter of which he tried to supress.

'Hold him a moment,' he said. He did not know if he spoke to Tasha or to his serpents, but they all obeyed, binding Nasak to immobility with their array of supernatural arts.

Konrad retrieved the bones he had harvested from Ivorak's victims, and carried about with him all the night since. They fell into his hands as he opened their bundle of cloth, stained with blood and delightfully blunt.

Also, he took up Nanda's silver knife.

'Turn him,' he whispered.

The motionless body of Ivorak Nasak flipped in the air, turning face-up. His eyes met Konrad's, full of desperate fear. His teeth were gritted, and he fought. They would not hold him long.

Konrad lunged — but too late. The human, solid figure of Ivorak Nasak shimmered and transformed, and a ghostwolf leapt away into the night. What a vision he made! Thrice the size of the living creature, all rippling ghost-light, nothing of him wan or sickly like Konrad's serpents. He shone bright and true, like the moon, and waves of fury rolled off him like mist.

But Tasha had been ready for that, too. Her body — the slim figure of the fourteen-year-old girl she appeared to be — fell lifeless into the snow with a sickening *thud,* and her lamaeni spirit-form shimmered into being beneath the trees. She was as bright and glorious to the eye as Ivorak, and she burned with an awe-inspiring strength. She shot after the fleeing nightwolf, Eetapi and Ootapi in her wake.

It did not take long. Tasha caught him in seconds, and after that... Konrad could not tell what followed. Battle raged, swift and fierce, the four spirits merging into a flurry of ghost-light so bright-burning that Konrad could barely stand to look. Rage and terror poured off them. In the two or three seconds it took Konrad to catch them, it was over. The light ebbed and faded, and Ivorak Nasak lay once more on the frozen ground, human and inert and furious.

Konrad wasted no time. He took the bones of Illya Vasily, Albina Olga, and the two labourers, and punched them through the shrinking chest of Ivorak Nasak, *one-two-three-four*, ignoring the creature's howls of fury and pain.

Then the knife, the silver knife, its blade biting deep. Only then did the light in the man's eyes die, and he lay with the stillness of death, blood seeping from the five wounds in his chest.

Konrad knelt in the snow, watching in fascinated horror as Ivorak Nasak died. He would never, ever get used to it, no matter how many he killed, nor how much they deserved to die. So profound was the alteration from *living* to *dead,* so permanent, so appalling. He did not know, would never understand, how those such as Ivorak could deal out death so freely and with such insouciance — indeed, some actively took pleasure in it. The thought made Konrad shudder with a crawling revulsion.

'He deserved it,' said Tasha.

Konrad sighed deeply, and wearily uttered: 'I know.' It didn't help all that much, and it never would.

But his duty was performed. Ivorak Nasak would kill no one else. He was dispatched into The Malykt's merciless care, there to atone for the lives he had taken, his soul irrevocably bound to the souls of those he had killed until he had done so. And they would not treat him kindly.

Nanda wanted her knife back. Konrad eyed the hilt sticking out of Ivorak's chest with misgiving. He did not want to remove it, did not want to touch the corpse again at all, if he could help it. As far out in the Bones as they were, he could and would simply leave it here, let it rot, let the crows devour its revolting flesh.

But Nanda wanted her knife back. Konrad steeled himself and wrenched the blade out of the ruined chest, averting his eyes to the sticky mess of blood. He wrapped the knife in his handkerchief, resolving to clean it later, and return it to Nanda.

Nan. Who waited at home, her terrible secret revealed against her will, waiting perhaps with dread for Konrad's return. He got to his feet slowly, wearily. 'Thank you,' he said to Tasha. 'But for you, he might have escaped.' He did not really think it was so; no one could outrun the Malykant, not for long. But it might be true, and Tasha swelled with pride to hear it.

And thank you, Konrad said to his serpents. *You have served me well.*

They were too surprised to respond, though eventually a shiver of Eetapi's approval crept down his spine. As it felt like a sliver of ice inching its way down his shrinking skin, he did not altogether appreciate it.

'Time to go home,' he said, and turned his steps back towards Ekamet. Slowly, trembling with fatigue, he made his way home, Tasha and his serpents by his side.

10

Upon arrival at Bakar House, Konrad wanted nothing more than to collapse instantly into bed. But he could not — not without first seeing Nanda. He would change his clothes, settle Tasha somewhere comfortable, and return to Nanda's shop.

But when he stepped into his hall he was met, rather to his surprise, by his butler.

Gorev bowed. 'Miss Falenia is waiting in the drawing-room, sir.'

'Ah,' he said, dripping melted snow onto the pristine tiled floor. 'Thank you.' He wanted to go in to see her at once, but a glance at his sodden, blood-stained clothes convinced him to reconsider. Nanda was wonderfully tolerant and virtually unshockable, but still, it would not be civilised to appear before her in such a state, especially if she was primly ensconced in the drawing-room. Besides which, he could not stop shivering. 'Thank you,' he said again. 'Will you find dry clothes for Tasha, Gorev? Anything warm will do. Raid my wardrobe, if you have to.'

'I am sure something can be found, sir.' Gorev had kindness enough to smile at Tasha, in spite of her bedraggled street-rat appearance. Tasha looked too bemused to know how to respond.

Gorev, of course, looked impeccably neat and exquisitely groomed, as always. It occurred to Konrad that this might be considered odd. 'Gorev. Why are you out of your bed at this hour?'

The butler gave a slight cough. 'It is rather past the seventh hour of the morning, sir.'

Ah. What a fine sight his master made, returning to his house at so late an hour, having spent all night away, his clothes torn, soaked through with melted snow and stained with blood besides. But Gorev remarked upon none of it, nor did he seem at all nonplussed. 'Shall I draw you a bath, sir?' was all the comment he had to offer.

Konrad took a moment to appreciate his blessings, Gorev's merits chief among them. 'A little later, please. I ought not to keep Miss Falenia waiting.'

'Very good, sir.'

'Serve refreshments, will you? I may be a few minutes.'

'I have already taken the liberty of serving tea to Miss Falenia, sir, together with an assortment of delectables.'

'Good man. Tash, come to the drawing-room when you're dry.'

With that, he wearily climbed the stairs and wandered into his dressing-room, grateful beyond words that he did not have to go back out into the snow tonight. His limbs were so numb with cold, his hands would barely function, and it took him much longer than usual to change his attire. But at length he was able to return downstairs, clad in fresh, deliciously dry clothing, cleaned of blood and snow, his hair brushed and warmth gradually seeping back into his frozen body.

Nanda sat before a blissfully roaring fire, and Konrad saw at once that when Gorev had described *an assortment of delectables* he had rather understated the case. The table was piled high with pies, cold meats, wedges of cheese, cakes, pastries, tartlets, fruits both fresh and dried, nuts, bonbons, and several jugs and pots containing, apparently, several varieties of beverage. There was also a gigantic teapot whose spout steamed most promisingly, and decanters containing wine, whiskey and brandy.

'Your obliging butler appears to have received the impression that I am wasting away,' Nanda informed Konrad with a suspicious narrowing of her eyes. The plate before her contained the wreckage of some few of the delicacies, and Konrad felt oddly relieved to see the evidence of her having made a respectable repast.

'I haven't said anything,' he protested. 'I only just returned home. He is merely being bountiful.'

'Then it must be that he likes me,' Nanda replied with vast satisfaction, and took another biscuit with a complacent smile.

'You are easy to like,' Konrad offered, collapsing into a chair.

'I am, quite,' Nanda agreed, and proved it by ministering to

Konrad's exhaustion with cheerful solicitude. She collected a heap of what Gorev called *delectables* upon a plate and set it before him, following it with a cup of tea, a glass of wine and a glass of whiskey. Konrad watched all this with a mixture of pleasure and concern, unwilling to admit that his eyes traced every feature of Nanda's face, alert for signs of ill health. Was it weakness that made her hands slightly tremble, or was she merely as tired as he? Did she return to her chair a little too soon? Were her legs weak, did she lose her breath and need to rest?

'I am not *dying,* Konrad,' Nanda said at last, waspish, when he continued to stare at her and ignore the feast she had painstakingly prepared.

'Sorry.' Konrad pulled himself together and attacked the food. He *was* famished, he found, once the more immediate discomfort of cold had receded, his exhaustion somewhat mitigated by the comfort of his seat. But he paused halfway through a shredded beef pie, unable to maintain the silence. 'Is that true?'

Nanda rolled her eyes. 'Would I lie?'

'If failing to tell me important things is *lying,* then yes.'

'I didn't want to tell you.'

'Why not?'

She eyed him. 'Because I knew you would fuss over me like a mother hen.'

Konrad opened his mouth to deny it, then remembered the anxious solicitude with which he had been fancying signs of weakness only moments before. It had cost him something to remain seated and let her serve him, instead of jumping up and taking the task off her.

'I am not frail,' she said firmly. 'And I don't want you clucking and flapping about me.'

Konrad sighed, and took another large bite of beef pie. He chewed slowly and swallowed, carefully gathering his thoughts. 'Will you tell me what's amiss?'

'I would rather not talk about it, today.'

That suggested she might talk of it another day, so Konrad tried to be contented with that. But it was hard. 'You aren't—'

'I am pretty certain you will die before I do,' Nanda interrupted. Her lips twitched, and she amended, 'Not that that means much. When was the last time you died, again?'

'Stop deflecting!'

'It is a fair reflection!'

'Tell me you're not fatally sick.' She was trying to defuse Konrad's concern with levity, but he would not permit it. He pinned her with a long stare, and he made no attempt to conceal his feelings: let her see the depth of his fear.

'I... hope not,' she said, softly. 'More than that, I cannot yet say.'

Konrad took a deep breath, the shivery kind that held suppressed tears somewhere behind it. He nodded, took a sip of tea and another breath. 'You'll tell me, whatever I can do.'

Nanda looked briefly forlorn, and he cursed himself for forcing the subject. But then she smiled, collected another biscuit, and bit into it with relish. 'Course I will,' she said with her mouth full. 'Can't waste the opportunity to make use of you. I'll have you waiting on me hand and foot, attendant to my every whim—'

'But *no clucking*,' Konrad agreed. 'Got it.' He flapped his arms, and was rewarded with a grin.

Tasha entered the room upon a cold draught, sighing with satisfaction.

'Shut the door!' Konrad said, shivering mightily.

'Oops.' Tasha sent the door sailing shut with a well-placed kick and then sagged into a chair. She was wearing a mismatched assortment of clothing, most of it wool, and she was pink in the cheeks.

'Enjoyed your bath?' Konrad said.

Tasha grinned. 'How can you tell?'

Konrad touched his fingers to his cheeks, and Tasha instinctively mimicked the gesture, testing the heat of her own face.

'Well, Gorev seemed eager to draw you a bath. I couldn't let it go to waste.'

'A crying shame,' Konrad agreed.

'I take it you succeeded?' Nanda said, and Konrad nodded furiously, his mouth too full of cranberry jelly tart to reply right away.

'Killed him dead,' Tasha offered. 'He sprouted like a hedgehog, bones and knives everywhere.'

Nanda winced, her eyes rolling ceilingward. 'Good. My knife?'

'I have to clean it,' Konrad said. 'And polish it and cuddle it and then I will give it back.'

'Cuddle it?'

'It's had a difficult day. It performed its terrible duty with panache, however.'

'Doubtless. It *is* mine.'

The door opened again, to Konrad's bemusement, for he had not rung for service. But in the doorway stood Inspector Nuritov, hatless and diffident and looking at Nanda.

Konrad cast a questioning look Nanda's way.

'I invited him,' she said, beaming. 'He's had a hard night, too.'

'Perfect idea,' he said, and meant it. He ought to have thought of it himself. He realised that Nuritov was awaiting *his* invitation, as host, and was quick to give it. He also realised that the sheer sumptuousness of the surroundings at Bakar House was unnerving the inspector. Konrad came from poverty; the house and all its luxuries were merely one of the trappings of his job, and its one real perk. But Nuritov couldn't possibly know that. Once suitably plied with good things, however, he began to relax.

Konrad could not, for an appalling thought occurred to him far too late and he all but leapt out of his chair. 'I forgot. The bodies — Albina and Illya — what if they aren't dead? They could turn. I have to go back.' His heart beat quick with panic, for he had left them lying unguarded in the morgue beneath The Malykt's temple. If they woke down there, alone and confused and ravenous, what harm might they do before they could be found, and stopped?

'*Konrad!*' Nanda said, and he realised she had already said his name a few times. 'Sit. Be calm. I have already taken care of it.'

Konrad blinked stupidly at her. 'What? How?'

'The possibility occurred to me, too, so I went there before I came here. The two labourers are dead, I am certain of it. The other two... I am less certain. I have had them moved to The Shandrigal's temple where they are under supervision. If they should wake, they will be tended to, and contained, and no damage will be done. Sit down again.'

Konrad sat, so overcome with admiration for her quick mind even in a state of exhaustion — and relief, that his absent-mindedness had not caused a catastrophe — that he folded limply into his chair like a bolt of cloth and lay in a fog of mixed feelings, most of them warm ones. Nanda was fortunate that she was not presently close enough to be hugged upon.

'I am eager to hear the details,' Nuritov offered.

Konrad was eager to sleep like the dead, but he owed the inspector an explanation. Before he could begin, Tasha leaned towards him.

'I am famished,' she confided.

Konrad cursed himself again, for forgetting that none of the delicacies Gorev provided could offer sustenance for a lamaeni guest. Looking at her, he saw that all the flush of colour had drained out of her cheeks; she looked wan and thin and... ravenous.

'You may take a little from me,' he whispered back. 'Just try not to send me to sleep.'

Tasha beamed at him with real gratitude, a reaction which thrilled Konrad, for it suggested that she found him perfectly edible. Or in other words, perfectly alive enough to feed upon.

'Not Nan, though,' he added, glancing at Nanda sidelong. 'She needs to conserve her strength.'

He had thought himself safe to make such a comment, for Nanda was deep in conversation with Alexander Nuritov, filling him in on all the details of the case which he had missed. But he received a swift, sharp kick to his shin, efficiently informing him as to the extent of his error.

'Ow,' he muttered.

Nanda cast him a look of withering contempt, and returned her attention to the inspector.

'When she said *no clucking and flapping,'* Konrad said to Tasha, 'she really meant it.'

A vague feeling of discomfort finally filtered through to his awareness: a protruding shape underneath his legs. He discreetly felt around beneath himself until he encountered the culprit: a small, rectangular object, very solid indeed, which he discovered to be wrapped in paper. It had a bow neatly tied around it in ribbon.

He raised an eyebrow at Nanda.

'What?' she said, all innocence.

A dangling label read: *Konrad.* He checked the reverse, but the name of the giver did not appear.

'Yours?' he asked Nanda.

'I deny all knowledge.'

'Hm.' Konrad tore off the paper, and a neat little leather-bound book fell into his hands. It was a beautiful thing, tinted dark rose-red, with glossy gilded lettering.

The title read, *The Scarlet Petticoat.*

He opened the book, and scanned the first few lines. 'This,' he said slowly, 'is a romance.'

Nanda's smile turned seraphic. 'Why, yes. Yes it is.'

His eyes narrowed.

'Are you not pleased?' said Nanda, her face falling in mock dismay. 'But I consulted Eetapi and Ootapi about your literary tastes. I was *sure* we'd got it right.'

Konrad noted the author's name, discreetly printed in small type on the inside front page: Lady Balov, who was a favourite of his. But he would rather have died than admit it, especially in such company, for Nuritov looked faintly amused and Tasha was openly grinning.

Nanda leaned towards him. 'It's new,' she whispered. 'Published last week.'

Konrad gave a tiny sigh, and hid the book away again. 'You could not have given it to me more privately?' he whispered.

'Where would be the fun in that?'

Konrad rolled his eyes, grabbed Nanda's hand, and bestowed upon it a flourishing kiss. 'Very well, then. Thank you, good lady.'

'You are *very* welcome,' she replied, beaming broadly. Then she added, in a loud whisper, 'I hope it is *steamy*.'

Too afflicted with sudden coughing to form words, Konrad could muster no reply.

THE HOUSE AT DIVORO

Starring

Konrad Savast
as
a gentleman of Ekamet
a confirmed bachelor
the Malykant
and
Diederik Nylund, a humble baker

Irinanda Falenia
as
an apothecary
a servant of The Shandrigal
a Reader of minds
and
Greta Pajari, an aristocrat

Tasha
as
an Assevan street orphan
a ward of the police
a fearsome lamaeni
and
Synnove, a divine avatar

Alexander Nuritov
as
a police inspector
a smoker of pipes
another bachelor (unconfirmed)
and
Vidar Pajari, brother of Greta

Eetapi and Ootapi
as
deadly ghost snakes
a pair of devoted siblings
master spies
and
bloodthirsty, troublesome wretches (no particular role)

as well as

sundry other persons, either of note or not

1

Three days after the end of the Solstice holiday (days which had, most blissfully, been spent tucked up in bed with a new book), Konrad stood in the hallway of Bakar House, adding the final accoutrements to his outdoor outfit in preparation for encountering the blistering cold of a mid-winter's morning. He had not left the house in days, which was good because it meant that no one in Assevan had been murdered since Solstice. It was bad because he felt as fresh as an aged pair of socks, and approximately as lively. A brisk walk out into the Bones would serve him well; it was high time he paid a visit to his beloved (if neglected) hut-on-stilts.

Hat and gloves donned, collar buttoned up over his throat, serpent-headed stick duly retrieved, Konrad made for the front door. Hand outstretched, he grasped the doorknob and yanked open the door, taking a deep breath in preparation to receive a lungful of searingly cold, exquisitely fresh air.

Nanda stood on the other side of the door.

'Nan!' said Konrad, jumping so violently he almost dropped his stick. 'How nice to—'

'Ah, excellent!' Nanda beamed delightedly. 'How prompt! I'm so pleased.'

'Prompt?' Konrad echoed in bewilderment. Nanda was not only wrapped up against the cold; she was swaddled in enough layers to encounter a winter twice as bitter. She was not well, that he knew, and he was pleased to see that she was taking care of herself. But since she had most likely taken a cab to his door, was it strictly necessary to pad herself out to quite such an advanced degree?

What's more, she was unusually well equipped for a social visit, for a pair of aged but neat travelling cases sat on either side of her booted feet, apparently just set down.

'Has Alexander arrived yet? And Tasha?' Nanda peeked past him into the house, her pale brow furrowing. 'Have you left your luggage inside? Do have Gorev bring it out. The carriage will be here any moment.'

'Tasha?' Konrad looked behind himself, as if expecting to see Tasha and the Inspector standing behind him after all — or perhaps the luggage Nanda spoke of, obligingly materialising all by itself. Nothing. 'I haven't seen th—' He began, but stopped, because here came the Inspector strolling up behind Nanda, his ward Tasha bustling along in his wake. Both were as warmly dressed as Nanda and as well prepared to travel, bearing bags and cases well swollen with supplies.

The obvious conclusion to all of these assorted hints filtered, at last, through to Konrad's sluggish brain. 'Are we going somewhere?'

Nanda merely looked at him, struck speechless, her face registering a mixture of exasperation and mild disgust with which Konrad was sadly familiar. 'Are we... you mean to tell me you did not receive my communication?'

'Was it sent by pigeon?' Konrad enquired. 'Your messenger is sadly incompetent, for I have received nothing.'

With a look of acute annoyance, Nanda withdrew a dainty pocket-watch from somewhere and consulted it. 'Then you have seven minutes to pack. Do hurry up!'

'Where are we going?'

'It's all in my note.'

'Which I have not received.'

'That can hardly be considered my fault, can it?'

'Where,' Konrad said with exaggerated patience, 'are we going?'

'A house party. In Divoro! Charming town, but quite fifty miles north at *least,* and it is perishingly cold so *do* wrap up well. And bring everything. Suitable evening attire as well, Konrad. There will be dinners.'

Konrad began to feel that he might not have left his bed after all. He had only dreamed that he had. 'A house party,' he repeated. 'In Divoro.' He looked at Nuritov and Tasha, both of whom he liked and respected but neither of whom could be described as typical guests at a house party. Nor could Nanda, in all fairness. 'Just what kind of a party is this?'

'No time for questions! I will explain in the carriage, if I must. Konrad, if you do not pack your things at once I will pack them for you.'

Konrad cast an appealing look at Inspector Nuritov, whose eyes conveyed *do not ask me I have no idea,* and an equally plaintive look at Tasha, who shrugged.

'*Konrad!*' bellowed Nanda. 'Go!'

Konrad bowed to inevitability, and went.

'It is hosted by Eino Holt,' said Nanda happily, once all four were ensconced in the promised carriage and rattling their way out of the north gate of Ekamet. 'An old friend of my mother's. Charming man, you will love him. And Kati Vinter will be there — a thousand years old if she's a day, but livelier than the four of us put together, I swear. Marko Bekk! And if we are lucky, Lilli Lahti! I have not seen her in years! I could not pass up the invitation. We are to be there for two, perhaps three days.'

None of this speech cast any light whatsoever upon Nanda's reasons for hauling Konrad along to Eino Holt's house party. Perhaps she simply wished for his company, which would be gratifying, but why had she insisted upon Alexander Nuritov's presence besides? And Tasha's? Was it merely her customary kindness of heart? They made an odd company of fellows for days of idleness at the house of an eccentric gentleman (he must be eccentric, Konrad knew; those who held house parties in isolated mansions always were, and the more eclectic the guests, the madder the host).

Konrad could not ask such an insensitive question aloud, of course, and Nanda chose to ignore his pointed questioning looks with smiling serenity. At length he abandoned the endeavour, resolved to squeeze her for information at his earliest opportunity, and devoted himself to dozing through the journey.

Only once along the way did he venture to question her, and on a different topic. He tried to sound casual as he said: 'Travelling long distances is so tiring, isn't it?'

Nanda's response was only a mildly suspicious stare.

'And staying away from home, so very—'

'Konrad.'

'Yes?'

'You are working your way around to casting aspersions upon my fitness to travel. Aren't you?'

'Well, I—'

'Am I perchance displaying an Interesting Pallor?'

'No more interesting than usua—'

'Does a sheen of perspiration glisten upon my fevered brow?'

'No no, you look perfectly—'

'I tottered into the carriage, perhaps, too weak and frail to move far unassisted.'

Konrad sighed. 'Point taken.'

Nanda directed her gaze out of the window. 'When I appear infirm or in distress, then you may assist me, and with my gratitude. Until then, please do not fuss.'

Konrad made no response, uncertain what to say. He had only recently learned of Nanda's illness, and still had no real idea as to what it consisted of. She *did* appear hale to him, but how long would that remain true?

He worried for her, but he could not express it without receiving a faceful of irritable discontent. Knowing Nanda as he did, he suspected that she resented his solicitude because she was worried for herself, too. But she would never admit it.

If all he could do was stay nearby in case she needed him, well... he could do that. If that meant suffering himself to be hauled over fifty miles or more of frozen, uneven roads to some distant town and spending days hobnobbing with strangers, so be it.

But when at last they turned in at the gate of a great house and rattled up the carriage-way, and he twisted his travel-stiff neck to look up at the place in which he would be spending the next few days of his life, he began, distantly, to reconsider.

For it was the strangest house he had ever seen, without contest. More of a castle than a house in size, it was situated atop the slope of a considerable hill, and the structure loomed over the road like some mythical beast temporarily paused. It was a mess of turrets and towers with spiralling domes and tall spires, built all out of reddish stone and painted in at least six other colours. It was the architectural dream of a madman, and Konrad felt a stirring of faint foreboding somewhere within.

But that was silly. Just because the house was strange, did not mean that anything unusual was likely to occur within. Nanda knew the owner, and at least a few of the party's projected guests. He was merely being paranoid.

2

'Interesting place,' murmured Nuritov, his gaze fixed on the peculiar house with the same wide-eyed surprise that Konrad felt himself.

'I don't want to go in it,' Tasha pronounced, and sat back with a frown.

'It is even stranger inside,' said Nanda brightly.

'Wonderful,' Konrad muttered.

'Eino bought it about two years ago,' she continued. 'It used to belong to an Assevan family, name of Vasilescu.'

'Why did they sell it?'

'They didn't.'

Konrad raised an eyebrow.

'They were all murdered, about ten years ago. The house stood empty until Eino took it on.'

This disclosure was greeted with a thunderous silence, until Nanda broke it with a peal of laughter. 'Only joking. They went bankrupt.'

Nuritov was generous enough to greet Nanda's sally with a polite chuckle, though he looked a trifle pale. Konrad merely rolled his eyes and sank back in his seat. He agreed with Tasha: he did not really want to go inside, whether or not Nanda's chilling story was true.

But he was the Malykant. If he did not shrink from facing down the vilest of murderers, he would not shrink from a mere house.

As the carriage came to a stop outside the vast, heavy wooden front door, a trio of neatly-uniformed footmen spilled forth and came to meet them. The carriage doors were opened and the luggage taken down and carried inside with impressive efficiency, and Konrad stood breathing the cold, crisp air and staring up at the house in silence. The late afternoon sun limned the turrets in wan, winter sunlight in a display of serene beauty which did... nothing whatsoever to reassure him.

Nanda swept up to the door, chin high, looking every inch a noblewoman. Konrad stumbled after her, feeling out of his depth and curiously out of place.

Master, said Eetapi in his mind, startling him, for she and her brother had maintained an unbroken silence for the past twelve hours or so.

Yes?

Pull yourself together.

Sage advice, if a trifle bluntly put. Doing his best to follow it, Konrad lifted his chin to a sharp ninety-degree angle and strode forth like the dauntless man he was.

On the other side of the enormous front door there proved to be an equally vast hallway, all tiled in coloured mosaics. In the centre of this stood a towering giant of a man with a trimmed black beard, bright black eyes and clothes as plain as the house around him was colourful.

'Our host, I presume?' murmured Konrad.

Nanda's idea of an answer was to proclaim: 'Eino!' in ringing tones, and to envelop the giant in an embrace.

Konrad stood by, observing this while trying not to seem to and wondering what one had to do to merit a hug from Nanda.

'My friends,' she said, stepping back from the giant, and made gracious introduction of Konrad, Nuritov and Tasha. Eino Holt welcomed all three with a twinkling congeniality which made Konrad feel a tiny bit better about everything.

But then Eino looked long at Konrad and said, apparently to Nanda: 'An excellent choice, my dear. He will make a fine Diederik.'

Konrad blinked. 'I beg your pardon?'

Nanda trod on his foot. 'Won't he, though? He's positively dying to get started. Aren't you, Konrad?'

'Yes...?' said Konrad.

Eino beamed hugely. 'And Vidar, lovely! Not *quite* the right colouring, but it will pass. As for your little Synnove, charming! Very clever, my dear.'

He looked from Nuritov to Tasha as he spoke, and a horrible

suspicion dawned in Konrad's mind.

Nuritov wandered closer. 'Do you have any idea what is meant by any of this?' he whispered.

Konrad gritted his teeth. 'I *believe* we are here for a theatrical party.'

Nuritov blinked and said with woolly comprehension: 'Oh.'

'A theatrical party,' said Konrad a little later, 'is a conceit sometimes adopted by the so-called elite, when they grow bored of every other conceivable leisure activity and develop a desire to torture each other instead.'

He was surrounded by several more of those conceits as he spoke, for he had been shown to a spectacularly luxurious room on the second floor by one of Eino Holt's many maids. The girl had been dressed in an immaculate, dark blue dress with a cap that covered up her hair. Konrad had passed by another two such maids on the way up the house's grand, carpeted staircases, and found he could not tell any of them apart. They appeared to be identical.

The room was large enough to accommodate at least ten people in comfort. A gigantic four-poster bed dominated the centre, draped in crimson velvet curtains, and the rest of the furniture was at least a couple of centuries old to Konrad's eye — all exquisitely well-kept, and polished to a mirror shine. The windows were fantasies: long and light, composed of hundreds of tiny panes of glass. Some of the glass was coloured, casting shimmering rainbow hues over the cool, pale marble floor of the room.

It was all spectacularly overdone.

Nuritov had been given a rather more modest chamber, in keeping with his apparent status compared to Konrad's. Absurd, considering that Konrad came from poverty; a fact of which nobody else (save Nanda) was aware, but which Konrad could not forget. The inspector had found his way to Konrad's room pretty swiftly, and now stood marvelling at the exquisite stained glass.

'So-called elite?' Nuritov echoed. He looked Konrad over with an air of faint bemusement. 'Are you not among them?'

Konrad paused to consider his reply. Once only an occasional colleague, Inspector Nuritov had graduated, by slow degrees, to something of a friend, and he was one of the very few who knew that Mr. Konrad Savast of Bakar House, gentleman of fortune, was also the Malykant. But he knew nothing of Konrad's background, and upon reflection, Konrad found that he was not yet inclined to alter that circumstance. Secrets were comfortable. Secrets were safety.

'I am,' he said. 'But I cannot altogether overlook our absurdities as a class. Theatricals! To act professionally is irrevocably lowering, and such a person could never be considered respectable. But to act out some triviality of a play in the privacy of one's own castle, that is a different matter altogether! To make a prime cake of oneself for the amusement of one's friends is in no way inappropriate.'

Nuritov sat awkwardly upon a darkwood chair which was, in all probability, worth more than his yearly salary as a police inspector. He looked like he knew it, too. In his plain, dark coat and soberly-cut waistcoat and trousers, he looked out of place in the ridiculously sumptuous room. He was a common songbird let loose in an exotic paradise.

Konrad, meanwhile, looked all too perfectly at home. *His* clothes were of exquisitely fine cloth and embroidered silk, his dark hair arranged to perfection by a valet. He felt like a painted imposter.

But such was his life, and as it held far more comforts and advantages than embarrassments or drawbacks, it behoved him to appreciate more than he condemned it. So he swallowed the rest of his complaints and said instead: 'Where have they put Tasha?'

'She has the room next to mine, but I have no idea where she has gone.'

The serpents had gone quiet again, too. This might mean they were behaving themselves impeccably, or it might mean that they had wandered off to make mischief in some other part of the castle. The latter was more likely.

Nanda had been given a room that was the equal of his own for splendour. Considering that she was only a working apothecary and not a noblewoman, that said a great deal about the heights of the esteem in which Eino Holt held her.

Konrad was not sure how to feel about that.

Nuritov wanted to say something, but apparently did not know how to begin. He opened his mouth, shifted restlessly in his seat and shut it again without uttering a syllable.

Konrad maintained his silence, and tried to look encouraging.

'Irinanda did not... happen to mention why she brought us here, did she?' Nuritov developed an apologetic look and added, 'I refer to myself of course, and Tasha. Miss Falenia needs no special reason to invite *you* to such an event, but the rest of us? I am at a loss.'

'As am I. If you are under the impression that Nanda is in the habit of confiding in me, I must relieve you of it at once. A confidence from Nanda tends to arrive with the sudden impact of a hurricane, and approximately as often.'

Nuritov accepted this with his usual placid equanimity, an attitude which Konrad sometimes envied. 'No doubt we will soon find out.'

No doubt. Nanda at her most mysterious tended to make Konrad just a trifle nervous, so he hoped he would not have to wait long.

Nor did he, in the end.

Konrad and Nuritov were not suffered long to linger above-stairs alone, for tea was served in the drawing-room. Upon presenting themselves, they discovered that the rest of the company was already collected, and a motley assortment of folk they did make. Konrad observed Holt's guests with keen interest as Nanda took it upon herself to ply him with tea, together with far more in the way of cakes and pastries than he could possibly expect to eat. He had noticed that she appeared to enjoy feeding him, and did not choose to interrupt her solicitude.

'Are you trying to fatten me?' The plate she handed to him towered with delicacies; they actually teetered, and threatened to topple onto the floor.

'Perhaps I have overdone it,' she conceded, fixing the offending plate with a swift, narrow-eyed look. She snatched it back, unloaded half of its contents and returned it to him with a dazzling smile. 'Better?'

Konrad still failed to catch a glimpse of any of the plate's fine porcelain beneath its burden of eatables, but at least the stack of pastries no longer leaned, unpromisingly, to the left. He watched surreptitiously as Nanda selected an array of sweets for herself, pleased to observe that she took plenty. 'Do you know everybody here?' he asked.

Nanda surveyed the sumptuous, velvet-furnished drawing-room and its complement of overdressed people. 'Nearly enough.'

Her tone did not suggest that she was thrilled to find herself in their company, which struck Konrad as odd considering that she had insisted upon attending the party. Perhaps he had imagined her distaste; after all, she had spoken of some of these same guests with enthusiasm, in the carriage.

Then again, perhaps he had not imagined it. Nanda began to speak, and perhaps she intended to tell him more about the people crowded into the drawing-room. The youngish woman curled up in an over-sized brocade arm chair, for one, her skin and hair as pale as Nanda's. She was dressed in faded rose-pink satin, her gown covered in cheap lace ruffles: clearly trying to make a fair show on a small budget. Konrad might have sympathised with her apparent situation, had it not been for the expression of marked sourness that twisted her handsome features into a dark scowl. Or what about the man behind her, small and trim and neat in an emerald-green velvet coat, his pale hair worn rather longer than prevailing fashions recommended? He certainly did not lack for money, or for status either, if his air of arrogance was anything to judge by. He had his back slightly turned to the rest of the room, and he supped tea from a delicate porcelain cup with the kind of greedy satisfaction that led Konrad to suspect that the contents were *not* tea at all.

But Nanda only proceeded as far as to say, in a low, confidential tone, 'Truly, they are such—' before she was interrupted. A woman stepped smartly up, her posture both commanding and demanding attention. She was tiny, the top of her head only reaching as high as Nanda's shoulder, and so ancient that Konrad could only marvel at the energy with which she moved. Her hair was a mass of thin, thready white wisps, and he could not imagine she had taken a comb to it for at least a decade. She was clad in a voluminous coat of thin, faded-blue cotton velvet, tightly buttoned up to the neck, and a pair of shabby, scuffed shoes after a fashion that had vanished about twenty years before. Not a trace of warmth did she display as she stared, hard, at Nanda.

'You are a prize fool, girl,' she said, so softly that Konrad almost failed to discern her words.

Konrad expected a display of wrath from Nanda in response to so rude a speech. But Nan sighed, took a long swallow of tea and said with rueful resignation: 'I know.'

'Do you never listen?'

'Not often, no.'

The old lady dismissed Nanda with a contemptuous flick of her cold grey eyes, and fixed her attention upon Konrad instead. She looked him over slowly, and she was utterly unimpressed. 'This is him, is it?'

'It is,' said Nanda coolly.

The woman actually rolled her eyes. Then she turned her back on them both and strode away, giving Konrad opportunity to observe that the hem of her ancient and too-long coat was a mess of rags and dirt.

'Charming,' Konrad murmured.

'Kati Vinter.'

'The lively old lady? You made her sound more... congenial, when you spoke of her before.'

'Sometimes she is.'

'What has displeased her today?'

'Why, I have.'

'I gathered that, but—'

'Ladies and gentlemen!' The booming voice could only belong to the giant, Eino Holt. It cut across the low murmur of chatter in the drawing-room with such spectacular volume that Konrad jumped, and spilled a little of the tea he had still hardly touched.

Nanda sighed, and took it off him. 'You will get used to that.'

'It is time!' continued Holt. 'We will make our way to the little theatre I have prepared for our humble theatrical, and disport ourselves among the many fine costumes I have provided for the event. They are quite wonderful! Come, I implore you, and enjoy yourselves!'

Konrad regarded him with interest. With his pale skin and black hair and eyes, the man looked Assevan. His name, though, was not of that province, and he spoke with a faint accent of a quality Konrad had not often heard before.

'Tell me about him,' Konrad whispered to Nanda, as they joined the train of people obediently drifting after Eino.

Nanda did not reply.

'Nan?'

She was staring at Eino's back, her eyes narrowed. 'I will explain later,' she muttered.

Puzzling, for there were several other, chattering people in between Nanda and Eino; the likelihood of his overhearing her remarks was slim.

Nuritov came up beside Konrad and nodded a greeting. He had

his pipe in his hand, but it was not lit. 'Odd place,' he murmured.

The inspector looked as composed as ever, but Konrad was beginning to suspect that his serenity was, sometimes, an act. When the pipe emerged but remained unlit, Alexander Nuritov was not at his ease. He clutched it a little too tightly, and did not seem to recall that its purpose was to be smoked; having it in his hand was the important part, as though it served as a kind of talisman.

'Most peculiar,' Konrad agreed. 'Where's Tasha? I have not seen her since we arrived.'

'Somewhere about the place,' Nuritov said, in so casual a tone that Konrad immediately felt suspicious.

'You know exactly where she is, do you not?'

Nuritov, surprisingly, grinned. 'Those suspicious instincts of yours have been well-honed.'

Which was not a denial. 'What is she up to?'

'Oh, just looking around.'

Konrad lowered his voice. 'Is she responsible for the disappearance of my serpents as well, by any chance?'

'I would not be surprised if the three of them should prove to be employed upon the same errand.'

'That being?'

'Reconnaissance.'

Which proved Konrad's point about the pipe: the inspector was definitely not comfortable. 'Why?' said Konrad, for discomfort did not seem to constitute reason enough to order a semi-official search of the castle.

Nuritov glanced past Konrad at Nanda. She had drifted a little away and seemed so absorbed in her scrutiny of Holt that she was clearly oblivious to their conversation.

'Suspicious you are by nature,' he said, lowering his voice still further. 'But the only person you never suspect of duplicity is that lady.'

That lady? He could not mean Nanda, surely. 'What do you mean, duplicity?'

'I mean that I remain unable to account for her most pressing invitation to myself and Tasha. Therefore, something must be afoot.'

'She is kind-hearted and sociable.'

'Insufficient. She has many friends. Why choose me? Why Tasha, with whom she is even less acquainted?'

Salient points, both. 'You are friends of mine,' Konrad tried. 'She has said lately that I should get out of the house more.' *For normal reasons,* she had added. Apparently, leaving the house in order to slay the latest murderers was not a "normal" reason.

'So we are invited on your account? That is vaguely plausible, but I still do not find it explanation enough.'

Not for nothing did one work as a police inspector, year in and year out. Konrad had to accept the justice of Nuritov's questions, and he watched Nanda with a newly troubled mind. Just what was going on here?

He sighed, for Nanda's habitual secrecy not only rivalled his own, it bordered upon the obsessive. Why could she not simply tell him what was in her mind? Was it that she still did not trust him? That thought wounded him, but he was not persuaded by it. Rather, he had sometimes felt that she enjoyed the secrecy, the mystery, the mind games. If it amused her and enlivened her life, far be it from him to condemn her for it. But sometimes, he did find it so terribly tiring.

An hour later, Konrad stood arrayed in velvet from head to toe and struggling valiantly to conceal his disgust. He had been given a kind of doublet all in crimson, hose to match, pointed leather shoes and a vast, floppy hat topped with an elegant (and sadly oversized) plume. Some hopeful, helpful soul had put a bound sheaf of paper into his hand — the script. Whoever it was had even marked his lines for him in ink as crimson as his costume.

He studied it with the bleak despair of a man learning the details of his own execution.

Around him, the theatre was all a-bustle with similar activity as the rest of Eino Holt's guests got into their own costumes, familiarised themselves with their parts and talked incessantly. The theatre was not at all humble: it was at least as bedecked in velvet as Konrad was himself, with sumptuous green drapes set up either side of a low stage. Someone had painted a jaunty scene of a prosperous Assevan town, depicted a few hundred years before, which was set up as a backdrop. There were even chairs enough set up in front for a sizeable audience, though since all of the present inhabitants of the house were expected to participate in the production, Konrad did not know who might be found to watch it. The identically-attired maids, perhaps?

Nanda came swooping up in a voluminous gown of ebony silk and a colourful woven shawl. Her hair was arranged in soft curls and covered in jewels (probably the cheap glass variety), and she wore her chin very high, notably much more pleased with her costume than Konrad was with his.

'Diederik Nylund,' Konrad intoned as she approached.

'That is to be your part, yes,' Nan agreed.

'A humble baker.'

'Most humble.'

Konrad looked down at the magnificent absurdity of his attire. 'Why,' said he with awful calm, 'am I to swagger about in this ridiculous concoction when I am but a *humble baker*? A tradesman!'

Nanda smiled in high delight. 'I believe it is a mark of respect to your rank. It would not do to put so wealthy and fashionable a gentleman in sackcloth, would it?'

'Tradesmen do not wear sackcloth.'

'I exaggerate for effect.'

'I am too high and mighty to wear, say, a simple cotton shirt?'

'Far too high, and *definitely* too mighty.'

Konrad tore off his hat, which, weighed down by its gigantic feather, threatened once again to topple to the ground. 'And you, I suppose, are the seamstress's apprentice, or perhaps a housemaid.'

Nanda swayed a little, setting the skirt of her fine silken gown a-twirl. 'No, no! I am a mere nobody, and would not merit such luxury were I not to play a high-and-mighty part. I am Greta Pajari, noblewoman.'

'You do look nice,' Konrad said grudgingly.

Nanda beamed like the sun. 'Nowhere near as lovely as you, however.'

Konrad had no answer to return save for a withering look. 'I only hope that we are to be playing minor roles, and will not be too much importuned.'

'You haven't looked at the script, have you?'

'I have.'

'Liar. We are the stars of the stage, and I hope you mean to shine very brightly, for I know I do.'

'What—'

'And what's more I expect you to be very passionate.'

Konrad blinked.

'You *are* my admirer, after all. Have you truly no idea which play we are doing? It is called *A Daubery Drama* and in it—'

'Daubery?'

'An out-dated word meaning trickery. Diederik has only to set eyes upon Greta to fall madly in love with her, and sets out to pass himself off as an aristocrat so that he may win her affection.'

'Well, that's familiar,' Konrad muttered.

One of Nanda's elegant, pale brows shot up.

Konrad coughed. 'I meant the part about passing...' He paused abruptly, and glanced about. Nobody too near. 'Er, passing oneself off as an aristocrat.'

'See, the role is perfect for you.'

'And you will have a fine time swanning about in silks with your chin in the air.'

'The *best* fun,' Nanda assured him, her smile roguish. 'Are you any good at serenading?'

'Seren... no! Not remotely!'

The smile became a frown. 'Perhaps not *quite* perfect.'

A small figure marched into Konrad's line of vision, her face a picture of utter betrayal. 'Konrad,' hissed Tasha. '*Look at this.*'

By "this" Konrad supposed she meant her own costume, and he could well understand her dismay.

'You are wearing a sheet,' he observed, at his most helpful.

'Oh, no,' Nanda disagreed, looking Tasha over with clear appreciation. She fingered the draping fabric in which the little *lamaeni* was enswathed. 'Cross-dyed silk of *the* finest quality, and all over embroidered? No mere bedsheet was ever so fine.'

Konrad opened his mouth to remark that he had seen plenty such, but decided at the last instant that he did not especially wish to be questioned as to *where*.

'It is a sheet,' Tasha said, folding her arms. Her ever-present black cap was nowhere to be seen, and someone had coaxed her short-cut dark hair into a vaguely fetching arrangement. And covered it with sparkling things, to boot.

'It is a lovely sheet,' Nanda said consolingly. 'The gods never do subscribe to mortal fashions.'

Konrad almost choked. 'She's a god?'

Tasha consulted the script that she held and quoted flatly:

'Synnove, a divine avatar.'

'Your job is to get the humble Diederik wedded to the lofty Greta,' said Nanda. 'It is True Love.'

Tasha's young face settled into an expression of such perfect incredulity that Konrad could not help laughing.

Being such a large man, Eino Holt ought not to have been able to sneak up on Konrad so undetectably as he did. His loud, deep voice spoke from directly behind, and absolutely without warning. 'She looks made for a noblewoman, does she not?'

And Nanda really did. She had the perfect posture, the gracious manner, the air of mild superiority, everything. She even had the beauty, which every noblewoman ought by duty to develop if it was at all within the bounds of possibility. But Eino Holt looked made to be an axe murderer, so what did appearances have to say about anything?

Konrad paused to reflect upon whether or not he himself looked like an axe murderer, which was more or less the truth of him (only axes had never been his weapon of choice). These disturbing and unproductive musings were interrupted, not much to his regret, by an icy whisper chiming inside his head.

Master?

Ootapi spoke so softly, Konrad almost missed his utterance altogether in the noisy theatre.

Yes, dear serpent?

There followed a short silence.

Then Ootapi said: *Dear?*

Wretched shade? Is that more to your liking?

Yes.

I spoke sarcastically, if that makes you feel better.

A great deal. Thank you, Master.

You are most welcome.

Silence again.

Was there something? Konrad prompted.

Yes, Master.

And? What was it?

Of all things the loveliest.

Specifically…?

A corpse, Master, fresh and fair.

A… oh.

He was surprised, briefly, into silence.

It is... a murdered corpse, I suppose?

Oh, yes! Quite murdered, and carefully hidden.

Murders did not typically follow the Malykant around. It was his job to follow *them.*

Konrad looked hard at Nanda. What a coincidence, that she should happen to drag the Malykant, a police inspector and his assistant along to the very house in which somebody was cheerfully doing away with somebody else...

Where is it? he enquired of Ootapi.

The pantry! The words were more sung than uttered, with an air of high glee, and Konrad sighed.

You are extraordinarily depressing to be around.

Thank you, Master!

Konrad did not find it easy to extricate himself from the theatrical proceedings. Eino Holt was bursting with an enthusiasm he seemed to expect to find reflected in every one of his guests, and was urgent to begin rehearsing scenes instantly, and without a moment's delay. Nanda appeared to be having a fine time swanning about in her gown, and was more than willing to go along with this plan. Even Nuritov, who emerged looking (to Konrad's mild irritation) every inch an aristocrat himself in his silken attire, was mildly urgent with Konrad to remain, and look over his part.

Konrad was finally obliged to be somewhat blunt, bordering even upon rude. If Nanda had brought him here *because* she somehow expected trouble (as he strongly suspected), she would have to leave him in peace so that he could go and deal with it.

'I will return,' he announced — grandly, for the dramatic nature of the proceedings seemed to require it.

And then he left.

Walking in the ridiculous shoes was no easy task, and he was not able to stride about at his usual pace. In fact, he feared he was reduced to mincing like the fop he most definitely *was not* as he made his way down tiled corridor after tiled corridor, through several false turns, and found his way at last to the kitchens (huge, scrupulously clean and well equipped) and hence to the pantry (the same). The kitchen, of course, was swarming with activity and noise, with a full complement of cooks and maids who stared at Konrad in puzzled surprise as he minced — no, *strode* — past them. All this he ignored.

The pantry, thankfully, was empty. His two serpents hovered near the stone ceiling, both invisible to the ordinary eye.

Welcome, Master, hissed Eetapi.

'Thank you. How polite. Wherein lies the unfortunate victim?'

The snakes led him deeper into the cool, dry room, past row upon row of heavy wooden shelves stacked with jars and boxes and wrapped bundles of food. At the back, a series of sturdy wooden cupboards had been built against the wall, each fitted with tightly-fitting doors.

Lockable doors.

Eetapi indicated the one tucked into the leftmost corner of the pantry. *In there.*

Of course, the cupboard was locked.

'The downside,' said Konrad conversationally to the thin air, 'of having a pair of insubstantial ghosts as assistants is that one is left with problems like these.'

It is the upside! Ootapi insisted. *For we may go where you may not.*

That is the whole point, Eetapi agreed.

'True, true,' Konrad grumbled, unconvinced. If he was not saddled with the two snakes, he would never have known about the corpse in the cupboard, let alone be forced to find a way to deal with it — starting with the simple but fiendish problem of gaining access.

It was, however, his duty.

He did not feel that he wished to announce the discovery to the household in general, not just yet. He could not openly investigate, and he did not want to put whoever was responsible for the murder on their guard. That ruled out breaking open the cupboard by force.

'Serpents, help. In your forays about the house, have you seen a housekeeper-like being?'

What is a housekeeper-like?

'Usually a female of advancing years, soberly dressed in dark gowns and carrying big bunches of things like... keys.'

Eetapi was instantly alight with enthusiasm. *I saw such a thing! It was in the hall.*

'Excellent. Then pray go and find it again, and steal its keys. Quietly. Do not let it see you.'

Will it miss its keys, all that much?

'In all likelihood, yes.'

The serpents streamed away, leaving Konrad to his own devices.

Fresh and fair, Ootapi had said, which implied that whoever was in the cupboard was not long dead. Had they been killed in that very room? Ensuring, first, that the door was properly shut, Konrad occupied himself with a thorough search of the pantry, alert for signs of unusual activity. He found none whatsoever. The stone floor was perfectly clean; no signs of bloodshed did he discover. It was dry, too, so it probably had not been cleaned that day.

Since the shelves, cupboards and other surfaces were equally spotless, Konrad judged that the killing had not taken place within.

Useful as far as it went, but it did not help him with the problem of where to look next.

The serpents reappeared as he was pondering the possibilities. He was alerted to their arrival by the sound of something metallic clattering against the outside of the door. Or, perhaps, several small somethings all in a cluster.

'Do, please, remember that not everything is as incorporeal as you are,' Konrad called, and went to open the door.

On the other side, a fat bunch of well-worn keys on a simple iron ring hung suspended in mid-air.

'Thank you,' said Konrad, and took them down.

The housekeeper did it! said Eetapi in high glee as she swooped back into the pantry.

'Oh?' Konrad closed the door again and crossed swiftly to the cupboards at the back. He could not know how long it would be before some member of the busy kitchen staff had reason to enter the room, and felt a need to hurry.

She has the key to the cupboard!

'So do I, at this moment. Does that mean I must have done it?' Konrad fitted the heavy iron key into the lock and swiftly turned it. The lock *clunked* satisfyingly.

Master, no! Eetapi was shocked. *You did not have them before!*

'My point, dear Eetapi, is simply this: if you can steal the poor housekeeper's keys, then others can, too.'

He felt her disgust. *I do not like the way she looks.*

'Oh, don't you? How does she look?'

Old.

'Ahh. Then I take it all back: she must be the culprit.'

Thank you, Master. Eetapi draped herself around his neck, like an affectionate gust of wind. A sadly frigid one, too, and he shivered.

'Away with you, please.'

Eetapi slunk away, and Konrad opened the door.

Inside, the cupboard was fitted with shelves until about halfway down. The bottommost had been removed at some time past, probably to accommodate large jars. One such, a graceless construct of stocky earthenware, still stood in one corner of the cupboard, its contents a mystery.

Next to it there lay a bulky bundle of something wrapped in white, threadbare cloth — an old sheet, perhaps, or a tablecloth.

The quantity of blood that had soaked through the fabric heralded that the serpents had not been wrong.

Konrad stared at it a moment, suffering a degree of sick foreboding that he could not comprehend. After all his years as the Malykant, how could he still feel that same dread, upon beholding the macabre — or the imminent promise of it? He had wallowed in death year in, year out; he had seen, he hoped, virtually everything of the horrific that humankind was capable of inflicting upon one another. He ought to be fully inured to it.

But the sick churning of his stomach told him he was not. He had ceased to be so aware of it, that was all, thanks to the Malykant's interference.

Sometimes he missed those halcyon days, when he had felt nothing.

Looks juicy, hissed Ootapi, and Konrad sighed.

'Someone lies dead. This is not a time for your japes.'

It is no jape, Ootapi replied, sulkily.

It does *look juicy!* Eetapi agreed.

Well enough: the serpents spoke the truth as they saw it, which was their right. It was only a pity that their little minds were so literal, and so... bloodthirsty.

Aren't you going to open it? prompted Eetapi, as though it were Konrad's birthday, and the cloth-wrapped corpse was a much wished-for gift.

'So I must,' sighed Konrad, and fell to the grim task, steeling himself against whatever he might find.

The corpse had been a man, once. His face was still intact, but the rest of him was... not. He made a strange sight, for that visage was so serene, in spite of the appalling mess someone had made of his body.

He had died in his forties, Konrad judged, or thereabouts. Weathered skin proclaimed that he had once enjoyed the outdoors a great deal, or perhaps his profession had often taken him outside. His were strong, inelegant features, and his greying hair was roughly cut.

Konrad took a swift, keen survey of the damage, grimly holding himself together by force of will alone. Both of the man's legs were missing, as was one of his arms, and the hand had been roughly hacked off the other. His torso was a mess of splintered bone and spilled blood.

Where there ought to be a heart, dead but whole, there was only a blackened, empty cavity.

Konrad wondered, distantly, what had become of the man's stolen organs and limbs.

Ohhh, this is a good one! carolled Eetapi.

'Were you not already dead, I would throttle you myself.'

Do it anyway.

'Hush.' Konrad stood very still, as a wave of nausea assaulted his own (mercifully intact) organs and, gradually, subsided. When he felt once again in control, he bent his thoughts to the question of what was to be done.

Should he announce the discovery? Perhaps, but he could not. How could he explain how he had come to find a body, inside a locked cupboard, within a room he had no business ever entering at all? Impossible. He could claim that the inspector had found the corpse; Nuritov at least could explain his right of interest in a murdered man. But he had no better reason to be poking about in the pantry than Konrad, nor any way to explain why he might have had such strong incentive to examine the contents of that cupboard as to steal the housekeeper's keys.

No. There was no way to publicise the find without revealing Konrad's secrets, and that was out of the question.

But perhaps secrecy would not be altogether a bad thing. Once a murderer learned that their crime had been discovered, they were placed upon their guard, and started taking greater pains to conceal their activities. If the man or woman responsible for this man's death imagined themselves undetected, they would be easier to investigate.

Of course, they might also imagine themselves quite free to kill again, were they disposed to.

Will we make him talk? Eetapi might be gleeful, but her brother sounded bored.

'No,' said Konrad at once. He had to pause a moment in thought, to understand the source of his own distaste for the idea. It was a common practice of his, to use the serpents to bind a murdered man's spirit back into his body for a brief time; the body could then talk, and once in a while they were able to shed significant light on the identity of their killer.

But he did not always make the attempt. If too much time passed before Konrad reached the body, the spirit had usually frayed and faded to the point that it was no longer possible to bind up its unravelling shreds. Such might be the case here.

Moreover, sometimes the prospect was simply too... horrific. It was distressing in the extreme, for a murdered man or woman to be brought back, however briefly; to discover the fact of their own death, and its appalling circumstances, and to remember how it had come to pass. This poor man had suffered to a disturbing degree, for unless Konrad misinterpreted the evidence of his own eyes, his missing limbs and hand and perhaps even his heart had been removed while he still lived.

He would not force anyone to relive such an experience as that, not for any possible advantage.

But, Master—

'No!' said Konrad again, more firmly, and Ootapi subsided into silence.

Konrad had still to perform his duty. He eyed the body in consternation. Could he remove a rib bone, without announcing his presence? He would require it, if he was to deliver the proper justice to the man's killer. But the Malykant's use of a victim's own bones was common knowledge; when a corpse was found with his chest cut open and a rib missing, it was known that the Malykant was in pursuit of the murderer. He did not wish to advertise that the Malykt's servant had already been in the house, and... might still be.

But the man's chest was such a mess, he did not think anyone would notice the interference. So he applied himself to the gruesome task of securing one of the murdered man's stoutest ribs, pleased, at least, that long experience rendered the task relatively simple to perform. This done, he wrapped the poor man back up in the cloth, as carefully and respectfully as he could, and locked the door upon him once more.

'Keep a watch on this room,' he said to his serpents. 'If anybody opens this cupboard, I must know immediately.' For the choice of hiding place puzzled him. The pantry was not often visited, but somebody came in here at least a few times a day; they must do, to retrieve some part of its contents for the preparation of meals. A body in the cupboard might escape notice for a time, if the cupboard's contents were not often accessed, but soon there would begin to be an... unpleasant aroma. Whoever had stashed the body here could only have intended it for a temporary hiding place, and must return to move it somewhere else.

Yes, Master, the serpents chorused.

'You had better return these, too.' Konrad tossed the bunch of keys up into the air, where it was caught by one or other of the snakes, he could not tell which. The keys hung there, oddly suspended.

Yes, Master, said the serpents again, and he turned to leave.

He was grateful, all of a sudden, for Nanda's foresight in bringing Nuritov and Tasha along, but he could not long entertain the idea that it had been naught but fortunate happenstance. It was time Nanda explained just what she was up to.

3

'In the pantry?' said Nanda with interest. 'Odd place to hide a body, isn't it?'

She was reclining in a blue brocade wing-back chair in her own chamber, wrapped in a purple velvet robe, and looking very queenly. She *had* been looking gloriously relaxed, too, until Konrad had arrived with his ill news. Now she looked... irritated, a feeling she was trying, unsuccessfully, to conceal.

'Rather,' Konrad agreed, with deceptive mildness. He'd taken a chair across from her and sat apparently at his ease, though he watched her closely. It was no use trying to pump Nanda for information: the more she was pestered, the more stubbornly uncommunicative she became. He would have to be wily, and patient.

But this time, Nanda surprised him. She gave a short sigh, her eyes narrowing with annoyance, and said: 'I had hoped we would be in time to prevent this.'

'Oh, did you?' said Konrad pleasantly. He wanted to add, *If you had told me of the danger right away, we might still have been.* But he did not, for such a comment could only alienate Nanda.

'I should have told you beforehand,' she said, surprising him again. 'I might have, only I thought you would not come.'

'A theatrical party in the strangest house I have ever seen, attended by a crowd of peculiar guests, and with brutal murder on the side? What could possibly have deterred me?'

She smiled, but only faintly. 'From your description, I am afraid the man in the cupboard is Alen Petranov. I believe he was invited to attend, but was not expected to arrive until tomorrow.'

'How did you—'

Nanda held up a hand, cutting him off. 'My mother.'

That did not much surprise Konrad. There was old blood in Nanda's family, old and strange, and it bestowed a range of peculiar talents. Nan herself was a Reader, and could sometimes catch a glimpse of a person's thoughts, if she came into direct contact with them. Her mother, meanwhile, was an Oracle. Her visions of the future were not usually profound or detailed, but she was sometimes gifted (or burdened) with very particular flashes of insight.

'Your mother sent you here?' Konrad was incredulous, for if the Oracle had known that this house would host so brutal a killing, why would she encourage her daughter to go anywhere near the place?

'Not exactly.' Nanda avoided his gaze, which was always a bad sign. She fidgeted in her chair, sighed deeply, and said: 'She told me on no account to accept any invitations from Eino Holt. And she gave me a general idea as to why.'

'She forbade you.'

Nanda inclined her head.

'She has *met* you before, yes?'

One of Nanda's swift, appreciative grins, and she chuckled. 'Mother she may be, but she does not appear to have developed any profound understanding of my character.'

'She ought to have known you would do exactly what you were told not to.'

'I prefer to think that I have a strong sense of duty, and could not stand idly by while such atrocities took place.'

'I am sure that's what it was.'

Nanda nodded sober agreement, and bit at one fingernail. 'We are too late, and I am sorry for it. I met Alen only once, and many years ago, but I liked him.'

Konrad tensed, awaiting further questions. He had said nothing at all about the manner of Alen's death (if it was Alen Petranov), and he did not wish to enlighten Nanda on such points of detail. Especially if she had known him.

But Nanda's thoughts turned in another direction. 'Why the pantry?'

'I was wondering the same thing. A temporary spot, most likely, so I have left the serpents standing guard.'

'But why the pantry? Was he killed in that room?'

'I do not think so.'

'Nearby, perhaps. In all probability somewhere below-stairs, for who would cart a corpse from one floor to another if all they wanted was a place to hide him for a little while?'

'Agreed.'

'In that case, what was Alen doing in the servants' quarters? He was not of the great and wealthy, but he was not a servant, either. He was a trader, I think, when I knew him. He did it the hard way, filling his packs with goods in one city and making his way to another, largely on foot. He was an old friend of Eino's.'

'Which means he will be soon missed, tomorrow, when he does not arrive. Or he ought to be.'

Nanda flashed him a narrow look. 'Ought to be?'

'If Eino does not appear concerned by Alen's absence, that must be taken as a suspicious sign.'

Nanda frowned darkly, and made no reply.

'What is it?' Konrad prompted.

'I... nothing. I am not sure, yet. I will tell you when I am.'

'Do you promise.'

With a roll of her eyes, Nanda said: 'Promise.' She surged out of her chair, energised. 'Show me the body.'

'No!'

She stopped, shocked. 'What? But I need to be involved.'

'You will be, but... not like that.'

'We are here because of me.'

'I know. And I have no intention of side-lining you, I *promise,* but you do not need to see the body.' Konrad stood up, too, and stepped in front of her, making of himself a physical barrier to emphasise his point.

Nanda stood looking up at him in dumbfounded dismay — followed by irritation. 'I have seen death before! Why must you patronise me?'

'Not like this. Nan, please trust me.'

'Why?'

Konrad took a deep breath. 'It is not a body so much as... about half a body. Approximately.'

'A... approximately?'

'There are some, um, parts missing.'

She turned pale at that, and swallowed. 'Oh.' Being Irinanda, she did not require long to recover her composure. 'I will talk to Eino,' she decided, and swept past him.

'Be careful, Nan. If Eino has anything to do with this—'

'I *know,*' she growled, and left, allowing the door to bang a little behind her.

He had been a bit patronising, he supposed. He ought to know by now: in many ways, Nan was tougher than he was.

The door opened and Nanda's head appeared around it. 'Have you told Alexander yet?'

'Alexan... oh, Nuritov. Not yet.'

Nanda's head tilted, in that way she had when she thought he was an idiot but did not quite like to say so. 'Inspector Alexander Nuritov, of the Ekamet Police. If there has been a crime, he ought to know of it.'

'Where is he?'

'I don't know. You are the detective.' Her head withdrew, and she vanished again.

Right.

First things first: Konrad rid himself of his foppish finery, and heroically resisted the temptation to throw everything into the fire.

It went against the grain with Nuritov — with *Alexander* — to hear of a crime yet refrain from investigating it.

'It is not my jurisdiction,' he said, as though attempting to convince himself of the justice of his neglect.

'No,' Konrad agreed. 'We are some way from Ekamet.'

'But we cannot leave the poor man to lie there, un... unattended to!'

'We must, for I do not see how we can remove him from the pantry without alerting the killer to our interference. And then how are we to explain? Besides, it is our best hope of catching him. Eetapi will see, if anybody tries to move the body.'

They were in some remote corner of the house which Konrad had not previously seen. It had taken him some time to track down the inspector; indeed, he had withdrawn Ootapi from guard duty at last, frustrated with the sheer size of the house and the apparent impossibility of finding one mild-mannered police inspector within it.

Nuritov proved to have taken refuge in a small parlour lit with long, many-paned glass windows, which was situated blissfully far away from the theatre and the drawing-room. It afforded a fine view over the thicket of snow-laden pine trees surrounding the castle, and boasted besides a plush-looking arm chair within which Alexander had comfortably arranged himself. He was no longer attired in his noble splendour, and looked oddly diminished because of it.

The pipe came out of a pocket, and was immediately lit. Alexander Nuritov took a long puff, and exhaled smoke with a sigh. 'I don't like it.'

'Neither do I. Do you have a better idea?'

'I do not.'

'Where is Tasha? Exploring again?'

'I believe so. She told me she would map every room in the castle by nightfall, or die trying.'

'Coming from someone who is already undead, that means little.'

'Oh, no. Tasha's stubborn, and devious. She'll carry it off. And she may return with something useful to tell us.'

Fine. So Tasha was being nosy somewhere about the place, Nan had gone after Eino Holt, and Eetapi stood guard still over the pitiful remains of Alen Petranov.

'I do not know how to proceed,' Konrad admitted. 'How do you investigate a murder while pretending to know nothing about it?'

'With difficulty.' The inspector was deep in thought, and Konrad expected something must come of it, for Alexander was a great deal cleverer than many suspected from his quiet, sometimes self-effacing ways. But a gong sounded from some distant chamber: the call to dine.

'I must see the body,' said Alexander as he rose from his chair.

Konrad's first impulse was to argue, but remembering how poorly that had gone down with Nanda, he merely nodded. 'After dinner.'

'Good. Now, I wonder how many of these fine people knew Alen Petranov.'

"After dinner" proved to be much later than Konrad had hoped, for the moment the meal came to an end, Eino Holt's enthusiasm hastened all his guests back into the theatre.

'At least *try* to sound like you mean it,' Nanda hissed, as a distracted and irritated Konrad proclaimed Diederik's frustration with his ordinary life in a fashion even he had to admit was flat. 'I told Eino you were an experienced actor! My reputation as a woman of honour is on the line here.'

'O dismal day!' stated Konrad again, through gritted teeth. 'O treacherous morn, to dawn anew upon my drudgerous life!'

Nanda sighed loudly.

'This is *terrible,*' Konrad complained in a whisper.

'Appalling play,' she agreed serenely. 'But that is no excuse.'

At least he had not been forced to don his frippery costume again, though some had chosen to sport theirs. Lilli Lahti lingered nearby — the woman in pink, who had glared so sourly at Nanda at tea earlier in the day. The ruffled gown was gone; instead she wore the plain, serviceable attire of a moderately prosperous tradeswoman, all dark blue cloth, modest skirts and thick woollen shawls. Simple garments they may be, but they were of noticeably finer quality than her own ruffled gown, and much newer, too. Perhaps that was why she had so taken to wearing her costume.

Her mood did not appear to have improved.

Konrad leaned nearer to Nanda. 'Did you not say she was an old friend of yours?' He spoke very low, and indicated Lilli with a slight inclination of his head.

'I might have.'

'You were speaking of the company in glowing terms at the time. You made them all seem excessively worth knowing.'

Nanda made a critical survey of her friend: the sour hunch of Lilli's shoulders, the fierce scowl as she flipped through her script. 'I did, didn't I?'

'You are a woman of honour, and could never have lied.'

'Never.'

Lilli looked up, glowered more deeply than ever, and turned her back upon them both.

'Best of friends,' murmured Konrad.

'Forever, and ever.'

'Is she always that way?'

Nanda hesitated before replying. 'I do not know. It is many years since last I saw her. But she was merry enough, when we were young.'

Konrad noted that. What was bothering Lilli Lahti?

He cast a glance over the rest of the theatre. Eino Holt was holding court before the raised stage, and most of his guests were gathered around him. Marko Bekk stood in an attitude of studied boredom, his dark cloak thrown dramatically over one shoulder; Kati Vinter, appropriately dressed in the sinister garb of a dark witch, absorbed whatever Eino was saying with arms folded and chin high in the air; a quiet man called Denis Druganin, garbed in an official-looking coat with the badge of some imagined public official, listened with a distracted air. Lilli Lahti drifted towards the group and stood, back resolutely turned to Nanda and Konrad.

'Now is our chance,' Konrad whispered. 'We flee!' He grabbed her hand and made for the door, expecting every moment to be detained by a good-natured shout from Eino Holt. But none came, and they were through the door and out into the cold stone passage. Nuritov, who had tidily concealed himself and Tasha behind a bookcase, followed soon after. The man was remarkably good at being unassuming and therefore going unnoticed, Konrad thought. Perhaps he should take notes.

'I liked it better in there,' Nanda complained with a dramatic shiver.

'But I need you to tell me what you learned from Mr. Holt.' Konrad marched off in the general direction of the pantry, pulling Nanda along with him.

'Nothing. I asked who else was coming and he named Alen, apparently with every expectation of seeing him arrive tomorrow.'

'No hesitation, no awkwardness?'

'None.'

So, no reason to believe that Eino was involved, at least not yet.

'Kati knows something,' said Tasha.

Konrad looked sharply at the girl. She was restored to her usual dark coat and cap, and he could see little of her face. 'Oh?'

'She is uneasy, and watches everyone.'

'She called you a fool,' Konrad said to Nanda. 'Because you came here?'

'Possibly,' Nanda allowed. 'Perhaps she has been talking to my mother, too.'

The inspector said, 'I have twice seen Marko Bekk lingering in the vicinity of the kitchens. He looked as though he would not like to be seen down there.'

'Interesting,' murmured Konrad. 'No notion what he is doing?'

'None yet.'

'I'll tail him,' Tasha offered. 'Later.'

The castle's twists and turns furnished a route to the pantry that did not require passing through the kitchen; Tasha had discovered it, and relayed it to Konrad with unflattering exasperation at his failure to find it for himself. He took that way now, circling around the noise and pungent aromas of the still-bustling kitchen and scullery.

The pantry was dark and quiet. Too dark; Konrad and Alexander both held lanterns, but even the combined glow was too weak to fully cast back the shadows. The chill of the frigid night crept into Konrad's bones, and his skin crawled at the prospect of viewing the corpse a second time, half in darkness.

He questioned the wisdom of Tasha's presence, but recalled that as a *lamaeni,* she was probably twice as terrifying as anything else in the room.

Master. The voice was Eetapi's, but in the flickering gloom, her whispered syllables were eerier than ever. *You return!*

'I am glad to find you obedient to orders, Eetapi,' he whispered. 'Ootapi, keys.'

Ootapi was quick to obey. Cold metal fell into Konrad's outstretched hand with a *clink*, and he closed his fingers around the keys. He had the cupboard door open in a trice, and gazed down into the depths with more trepidation than he cared to display.

The cupboard was empty. One sturdy earthenware jar stood in the corner, as before, but now it reigned over the interior in solitary splendour. There was no sign of the corpse.

4

Nanda peeked over his shoulder. 'I am determined not to be blocked out, Konrad.'

'There is nothing for you to be prevented from seeing,' he mumbled, dazed.

Nanda surveyed the empty cupboard in brief silence. 'Wandered off, has he?'

'It appears.'

'Why does that keep happening to you?'

'I don't know.' Konrad felt a weak-kneed desire to sit down. 'He has no... I mean, he couldn't wander off. He hasn't got any — any—' He made a vague gesture in the direction of his own legs, unable to finish the sentence.

He had presided over a string of recent cases wherein the bodies of apparently murdered people were later discovered to be everywhere but where Konrad had left them. There were a variety of explanations for this, most of which were decidedly... strange.

In this instance, Konrad held on to a faint hope that the truth was a bit more mundane.

'Someone has moved him,' said Alexander.

'But Eetapi was watching.' Konrad belatedly added, 'Weren't you, Eetapi?'

Yes, Master.

Konrad waited.

'Did you see anything relevant?' He prompted, when she did not elaborate.

No, Master. No one has come into this room today, except for a maid who was collecting food. She did not go near this cupboard.

So the corpse could not have walked off by itself, and no one had moved it, either. 'What in the world...' muttered Konrad, bemused. 'Why cannot a case be simple, for once?'

'You know you would be bored if they were,' said Nanda, unimpressed.

Konrad grunted.

Alexander had not participated in the exchange, for he was intent upon a close study of the cupboard. At length he stepped back and said softly, 'The back is loose.'

'What?' Konrad darted forward, electrified. 'Show me.'

Alexander demonstrated: a slight wobble in the back panel, as of a plank of wood poorly fitted. 'It may be possible to remove it entirely, from the back.'

'But that would place whoever removed it on the other side of this wall. Even supposing the wall itself to have been modified to permit access to the cupboard, Eetapi can see through walls. She would have noticed somebody pausing there.'

I did not, Eetapi confirmed. *No one has been there.*

An investigation ensued, which furnished the information that a storeroom lay directly behind the pantry; that the corresponding section of wall was bare and accessible; but that there was no sign that it could be opened or that the cupboard could be got into that way. Even if there was some secret to it that they had not discovered, the question of how anybody could linger in the room, so close to Eetapi, without her seeing them remained insoluble.

The matter had to be abandoned soon afterwards, for the hour grew late, and Konrad feared that some one or other of the servants would spot them if they lingered any longer.

But as he made his way back to the theatre, trailing along wearily in Nanda's wake, he received the impression that he and his friends were not the only ones with clandestine business below stairs. For a flicker of green caught Konrad's eye, whisking out of sight around a corner. He paused, hastened to catch up, and held his lantern high. But though the lamp cast a long, if faint, glow down the bare stone passage, no fleeing figure could he discern. Whoever it was — the owner of the green coat, or cloak, or gown — was gone.

The next day dawned snowy, intensely so. The world was a blur of white when Konrad shambled to the window; even the dark shapes of the craggy pine trees were obscured beneath the blinding flurry. The glass itself was coated in cracked white frost, and cold rolled off it in waves. A maid had been in to light the fire sometime before Konrad awoke, and he gravitated quickly towards its welcoming heat.

He was not given long to enjoy it.

Malykant, whispered Ootapi, when he had not done more than extend his hands towards the flames. *Eetapi sends word! The half-of-a-man is back.*

'He is wh— back? Where?'

In the cupboard.

Konrad was speechless.

He left for the pantry at a near run, hardly caring, in that moment, whether anybody saw him descending below stairs. The keys were waiting for him, hanging from nothing a few inches in front of the door. He snatched them up and dragged open the door, holding his lantern high to illuminate the interior of the cupboard.

Konrad stared for three stomach-churning seconds, and then quickly shut the door again. 'It is not the half-of-a-man.'

He felt both serpents materialise beside him, twin whorls of killing cold either side of his head. *It is not?* said Eetapi, bemused.

It's the other half! Ootapi enthused.

'No.' Konrad steeled himself, and opened up the door again. There was a body there, all right, but it was not Alen Petranov. Identifying it would be tricky, for while it retained both of its arms and hands, its head was missing. Naught but a ragged stump of a neck remained, splintered bones sticking up like broken fingers coated in dried blood.

The hands looked female, and elderly, the skin wizened and wrinkled. She — if it was a she — was wearing a shapeless black gown; Konrad could not see whether or not her legs were where they were supposed to be.

'I think it is Kati Vinter,' he said softly. The dark gown resembled the one the old lady had worn the night before, her costume as a dark witch.

He remembered what Tasha had said. *Kati knows something.*

Konrad wanted desperately to take her out of there, to restore whatever dignity he could to her poor abused body. Her torso, like

Petranov's, was a torn, ruined mess, her ribs smashed. Her heart she retained, but other organs were missing: a lung, perhaps others. He blanched and swallowed hard, wondering if she, too, had been alive when this damage was done to her.

He could not remove her. The same objections prevented him as before. But unlike Alen Petranov, he had known Kati Vinter, if only briefly. She lived for him in ways that Alen never had, and it hurt him all the more to close the cupboard door upon her and lock it.

'Eetapi,' he said, speaking very low, for there were sounds of life emanating from the kitchens: the clatter of pots and knives, the low hum of voices, as the servants prepared breakfast for the household. 'How does it come about that a second corpse should find its way into this cupboard, while you were set to guard it? You must have seen who placed her here.'

I did not see who put it there. I did not see anyone.

'Nothing at all? That cannot be, serpent. It cannot have appeared by itself.'

It. *She.* He was picking up the snakes' dispassionate language; he hoped never to develop their ice-cold attitude along with it.

I saw nothing, Eetapi insisted.

Konrad gritted his teeth upon a wave of anger, determined not to let it get the better of him. His serpents could be maddening sometimes, but they were loyal, and they were not usually careless. Their interpretations of his orders could sometimes be eccentric, but they were never outright disobedient. Eetapi had, in all likelihood, stood guard over this room all night, as he had asked of her. How, then, had it come about that she had not seen anybody put Kati Vinter's body into the cupboard? Somebody had. He refused to entertain the possibility that it had somehow materialised there all on its own.

He stood for a moment, absently jangling the keys in his hand as he thought. No, stop. They were noisy, and he could not rely on the muted cacophony of sounds from the kitchens to conceal it.

'Ootapi,' he murmured.

Yes, Malykant.

'How are you finding it so easy to keep borrowing these from the housekeeper? Does she not notice their absence?'

She sleeps much.

'Sleeps? In the day?'

She smells of drink. The serpent's tail thrashed in disapproval. *There is much snoring.*

Eino Holt kept a drunkard for a housekeeper? Excessively odd. But perhaps he did not know of her propensities.

It would be easy enough, then, for someone else to steal the keys for this cupboard. He had hoped for a clue there, but it was not to be.

'Ah, well. Take them back, please.' He handed off the keys once more, and Ootapi drifted away with them. 'Eetapi, when your brother returns please switch places with him. Ootapi shall guard, for today.'

Is it a punishment, Master? She was doleful at the prospect, but also... slightly thrilled. Her chiming tones were more funeral than ever, but her incorporeal form vibrated with the energy of anticipation.

Konrad sighed, deeply. 'No. But you will grow weary and bored if I leave you here, day after day. It is Ootapi's turn. You will return to my side.'

He departed the room immediately upon uttering these words, intent upon finding Tasha. If something was afoot that was eluding the guile even of his serpents, he was going to need better help; and who more able than a *lamaeni*?

Konrad found Tasha wandering the castle's long gallery, staring intently at each of the many aged, faded portraits that lined the walls. The vast room had an air of neglect: its tiled walls were dust-covered, their colours muted with age, the windows caked in dirt. A long, dusty-green carpet ran the length of the gallery, its edges fraying. There was little furniture in evidence: only an occasional rickety-looking wing-back chair pushed against the wall, daubed with fractured gilding.

Tasha was about halfway down the room, craning her neck to stare up at an enormous portrait of a dark-haired man wearing what looked like a silken nightcap. 'Morning,' she said, without looking at him.

'Tash, I need your help.'

That got her attention fast enough. She blinked at him, then adjusted her cap with a grin and sprawled into the nearest of the aged armchairs. Konrad winced a bit, half expecting the decayed thing to collapse even under Tasha's slight weight. But it held, merely emitting a great cloud of dust which made Konrad cough. 'What may I do for the boss?' said she.

Her tone was cheeky in the extreme, and Konrad mimed out bestowing a swift kick upon her for the impudence. Tasha only grinned wider.

He outlined the recent development and the problem of Eetapi's failed guard, all of which she listened to with quiet attention. At the end, she chewed thoughtfully upon her lip and looked him over with a critical air he did not quite like.

'The problem with you — or one of them — is a certain lack of... shall we say, practicality in your thinking? Or we could call it deviosity. Yes, let's call it that.'

'Deviosity is not a word.'

'It is now. Think. You have established that it would be possible for somebody to unlock that cupboard when they want to, and using the door would be the most obvious and convenient way to access it. Wouldn't it? Cupboards have doors for that very purpose. It is what they are for.'

Konrad's eyes narrowed. 'You border upon patronising.'

'You border upon deserving it. So the cupboard has a door, in the usual way of things, and there is a key to unlock it that (in theory) anybody could get at. That doesn't mean that the door is either the *only,* or even the most *convenient,* way of getting at the contents.'

'No, indeed,' Konrad agreed. 'The back is loose. Alexander discovered that much. But—'

'But the cupboard is backed up against a solid wall, with no apparent way to get through. So you dismissed the removable back from consideration entirely.'

'Do you know of a way to push a corpse through a stone wall?'

'No! But if the back is loose, maybe other parts of the cupboard are removable as well?'

'Like the bottom. Yes, we tested that, when the inspector found the back loose. It is solid, with no way to remove it.'

'Not from the pantry, perhaps.'

Konrad blinked.

'What if someone could get at it from the other side?' Tasha persevered. 'Maybe it is quite possible to open the bottom of the cupboard from—'

'Underneath,' said Konrad. Now that she had spelled it out, it seemed so embarrassingly obvious.

She was right, curse it. He did lack a certain something by way of obscure logic.

Tasha leapt out of her chair and stood dusting off her dark coat. 'I will investigate,' she announced.

'Thank you.'

She doffed her little cap to him. 'Go do what you do best, Sir Malykant.'

'And what is that, in your estimation?' It was probably an unwise question to ask.

'Lounge by the fire,' she said brightly. 'Eat rather a lot, and act the gent with panache. You do all three of those things extremely well.'

'Wretch.'

'Forever, for it is a sadly incurable trait.' Tasha made for the door at an insouciant saunter. 'Go and see Nanda,' she threw over her shoulder. 'You do *that* pretty well, too.'

She was gone before he could enquire into what she meant by *that*, exactly. Seeing Nanda? Talking to Nanda? Drifting around after her in fits of aching loneliness, desperate for a few words to brighten his bleak and empty day?

Probably all of the above. He heaved a weary sigh, tangled his fingers in his thick dark hair — which had not been brushed yet today, he only then recalled — and set off for his own room. First: grooming. Second: Nanda. She had planned to go after Eino Holt again, and that fact was causing him concern in the wake of Kati Vinter's murder. What if Tasha was right, and Kati had known something? What if she had been killed because of it? If Nanda was too obvious about her probing for information, she might make a target of herself, too. And if not Nanda, who else? Two victims was a problem. Two victims was a *pattern.*

Those sensations in his chest and stomach and knees: the fluttering, the tightening, the weakening, the quickening pulse of his heart. They did not grow any easier to bear. Was he cursed to suffer them forever? Would he ever cease to worry about Nanda, now that he had remembered how?

He clenched his jaw, and summoned a mental vision of himself as he had once been: cool, even cold, going about his business with bleak efficiency. Incapable of worry or fear, except when his Master appeared. Almost impervious to pain, at least of the emotional variety. Had he been a monster? Close to it, yes. But he was the

Malykant. Sometimes, he needed to be.

He fitted himself into that picture, forcing down the nausea, the dismay, and the fear. His heart rate slowed, and he breathed a little easier. The incipient trembling in his knees took itself off, and left him stronger.

Good. Now he could proceed.

5

Nuritov took the news of Kati's demise calmly.

Nanda did not.

'Kati?' she gasped.

Konrad began to wish he had chosen a better time, or better circumstances. He had found her in the theatre, rehearsing with Eino, Nuritov and and Denis Druganin. At least, ostensibly they were rehearsing; when Konrad walked in, all four had scripts gamely in hand, but the conversation appeared to be more general.

He'd purloined Nanda and Nuritov on pretence of being eager to rehearse — an attitude which endeared him to Eino on the spot — and taken them away to a quiet corner.

'I am sorry,' he whispered, panicked in the face of her white-faced shock.

Nanda collected herself. 'It is not your fault.'

'I did not know... did not realise that you were close.'

Sinking with a sigh into the nearest chair, which unfortunately was of the hardwood, uncomfortable variety, Nanda waved that away. 'We were not, exactly. But my... my mother will be unhappy.' She blinked. 'I wonder if Kati was here by her request.'

'You mean she might have forbidden you to come, but sent Kati to investigate the trouble?'

'It is possible. Kati did seem to be aware that I was not meant to be here.' Nanda took a deep breath, got up out of the chair again, and threw back her shoulders. 'Right. This has gone far enough.'

Nuritov patted her on the shoulder, a trifle awkwardly. 'We will make it right.'

'Too right we will! Where is Eino.' She made to stride off, but Konrad stopped her.

'Nan. Share the thoughts.'

Nanda's brows went up. 'Haven't I?'

'I don't believe so.'

She made an impatient gesture. 'Eino isn't being secretive, exactly, but it's been difficult to bring him around to discussing anything of use. He's so enthusiastic about this damned play. I feel certain he knows a number of things that might be relevant — whether or not he has anything to do with it himself — and I want to get back to trying to prise it out of him.'

'Maybe we could help,' suggested Nuritov.

Nanda looked him over thoughtfully. 'Maybe you could. Alexander, did you ever feel an overpowering interest in subjects like architecture? History? Strange old stories?'

'Sometimes...' said the inspector, more doubtfully than appeared to please Nanda.

'These are your new interests. Konrad, you are writing a book about ancient families, like for example the Vasilescu.'

'Writing a boo—'

'Don't argue. It is your consuming passion, but rather secretly, because you are afraid some other, eager scholar will beat you to it. Between the three of us I am sure we can squeeze something interesting out of Eino.'

Konrad's mind raced, without much effect. 'Architecture and strange old stories? What is this about?'

'This is a strange house.'

'Undoubtedly.'

'So, what in the world possessed Eino to buy it? And why has he suddenly turned all country gentleman on us, and taken to hosting theatrical house parties? How did he choose his odd assortment of guests? There is a story behind all this, and I want it.'

Konrad was given no further opportunity either to argue or to press for more detailed instructions, for she marched off towards the stage where Eino's knot of friends still stood, and Konrad and Nuritov had naught to do but fall into line behind her.

'Working with Irinanda is interesting,' offered the inspector.

'Yes, she is always like this,' Konrad replied, answering his unspoken question.

Alexander Nuritov stuck his pipe back into his mouth and took a puff. 'Hmm.'

Indeed.

Nanda directed one of her dazzling smiles at Eino and said: 'I think we should adjust the play a little. Why must my character, and Alexander's, be of a fictional Pejari family? Why cannot we be of some other extraction?'

Eino smiled indulgently down at her and rumbled: 'I take it you have some idea in mind, Miss Falenia?'

'Why not Vasilescu? What could be more ideal!'

'A wonderful idea,' said Denis, and smiled upon Nanda in a fashion which could not endear him to Konrad.

Konrad eyed him with strong displeasure. He had never taken much note of Denis Druganin before; the man was so quiet, he often went unnoticed in a room full of people. But Konrad now had occasion to note that Denis was youngish, probably around his own age; he was by no means unattractive, with his brown hair in soft waves, his deep blue eyes and engaging smile; and his deep blue coat, dark trousers and polished boots were of such a quality as to suggest that he was not too poorly off.

Sadly, it was by no means as easy to assess the merits of his character at a glance. He could be anything. A wife-beater. A murderer. Or a prince amongst men.

But Nan played up to this attention with a beaming smile by way of an answer, and a bright, almost coquettish flash of her ice-blue eyes. Konrad put this down to her eagerness to win confidences, and averted his gaze. 'So fascinating a family deserves greater consideration,' Nanda was saying. 'Especially in their own home.'

'But it is my home,' Eino objected gently.

Nanda waved that away. 'Oh, you have bought the *house,* Eino, but you are a mere newcomer yet. This place is steeped in the history of the Vasilescu, and will be for some time to come.'

There was a short silence. Eino looked inexplicably uncomfortable at this observation, though he did not volunteer any answering comment. Denis Druganin took to admiring the ceiling, as though the conversation had passed too far beyond his interest for any hope of recall. And Nanda cast Konrad a swift, meaningful glance.

Konrad realised with a flicker of panic that his cue had arrived.

But Alexander spoke first. 'Erm,' he said.

Nanda beamed encouragement.

'You were lucky to acquire such a, erm, unique building.' Apparently emboldened by this coherent string of words, he added, 'They, erm, do not come up on the market very often.'

Fortunately, Eino's enthusiasm was in such good order that he did not require much encouragement. 'There is no other house like it!' he boomed, a huge, rather self-satisfied smile wreathing his bearded face. 'A travesty, that it lay empty and unloved for so long! There is much to be done to restore all of its beauties.'

'Oh?' prompted Alexander. 'Why was it empty? I suppose it was an expensive purchase, and wealthy buyers are not easily to be found.'

Good man, thought Konrad. A little bit of flattery rarely went amiss. Eino, indeed, preened just a little at this reflection upon his financial advantages, and smiled genially upon the inspector. 'There is that,' he agreed.

'They lacked perseverance,' said Denis in his quiet way.

'Why should that be necessary?' said Nanda.

'Oh, there were two or three attempts to buy the house before Eino took it,' Denis elaborated. 'All fell through, due to one set of difficulties or another.' He glanced doubtfully at Eino, whose smiling serenity began to look fixed, and added, 'Perhaps I am misinformed.'

'You are not,' said Eino.

'How paltry!' Nanda declared. 'For I am sure it must have been the envious types who threw difficulties in the way. But no wonder you had competition.'

'I wonder,' said Konrad in a low voice, 'if there are ghosts hereabouts?'

This comment won him a sceptical look from Denis, a glow of beaming admiration from Nanda, and a startled look from Eino. 'Ghosts?' said the latter.

'Yes. Well, these old houses — ancient families — the living may depart the ancestral home, but the dead may not.'

'Forgive me,' said Denis softly, 'but there is no such thing, Mr. Savast.'

Ootapi announced his invisible presence by way of a sneeze, or perhaps it was a choked laugh. Perhaps fortunately, nobody heard him but Konrad.

Eino did not appear to share Denis's opinion. He glanced around at the theatre, as though the spirits of departed Vasilescu ancestors might descend upon him from the walls. 'I am sure they are friendly, if they are somewhere hereabouts!' he said heartily. 'I am giving the old place the care it deserves.'

'There is no telling, with the dead,' murmured Konrad. 'They may resent the house's passing out of the hands of the family at all.' He could not have said why he was goading Eino; only that the man's odd reaction to the possibility of a lingering familial presence intrigued him. 'But I have no doubt you would have seen some sign of their displeasure by now, if that were the case.'

Eino did not look reassured.

'You seem very... knowledgeable, Mr. Savast,' said Denis, and beneath the quiet courtesy of his manner there was concealed an unmistakeable note of scorn.

'I am writing a book,' Konrad returned placidly.

'About ghosts?'

'Yes. Specifically those connected to old houses like this one.'

Denis smirked. 'No doubt you will inform us, if you spot any.'

'If you wish,' said Konrad, and added with a smile, 'There *is* something of a presence, in this very theatre.'

Master! Ootapi's exclamation vibrated with outrage. *Do not reveal me!*

Peace, serpent. They are oblivious to you.

Eino looked up, again, visibly shaken, but Denis only looked bored. 'Is there,' he said flatly.

Konrad smiled.

'Come, Mr. Druganin,' said Nanda, offering the man her arm. 'We will make a tour of the house, and prove my boorish friend quite wrong about the presence of unquiet spirits.'

Boorish? Injured, Konrad watched Nanda's retreat with a sinking heart. Had he truly been rude? Was he not justified in being so, if he had? But as Nan reached the door, she looked back and smiled, and it was one of her secret smiles, full of mischief.

Oh.

The door closed behind Nanda and Denis, only to open again moments later. Lilli Lahti appeared, and made a quick survey of the room. 'I cannot find Kati,' she complained, as though it were the fault of Eino or some one or other of his guests that she could not.

Which, in all probability, it was.

'She keeps to her room,' said Eino. 'She was unwell, last evening.'

This explanation satisfied Lilli, as far as anything satisfied her; she scowled, and left.

But Konrad exchanged a look with Alexander, troubled. Was it the truth, as far as Eino knew? Kati might well have pleaded indisposition last night, and it was reasonable enough that her absence would not be remarked upon the following morning. On the other hand, was Eino covering up her disappearance as best he could, knowing she would not return? If so, it was a clumsy effort at best. There was only so long that her sustained absence would go uninvestigated, and the truth must soon come out.

Moreover, the failure of Alen Petranov to arrive over the course of the morning would raise questions, too. One way or another, the day was likely to prove interesting.

'The rumour,' said Nanda later, with a gleeful emphasis on the second word, 'is that Eino received a series of warnings about buying this place. All of which he ignored.'

She and Druganin had devoted a full hour to their fruitless ghost hunt, and reappeared only just in time to sit down to breakfast — a meal from which Kati's absence was again noted. Afterwards, Nan ambushed Konrad as he was trying to make his escape, and hauled him off to a tiny antechamber which strongly resembled a cupboard. It stank of beeswax, and something acrid.

'What kind of warnings?' he asked.

'The anonymous kind, written in crabbed script upon parchment, and all in black ink. Delivered, apparently, by crows.' She grinned. 'The tale has been embroidered in the telling, but I would not be surprised if the essential points were true enough. Eino's caginess upon the topic interests me.'

'Have you asked him about the story?'

'I have. He scoffed at the crows, probably fairly, and denied the whole. But he looked hunted as he spoke, and when I touched him I sensed a great deal of fear in his mind.'

Eino was frightened? 'So he is afraid of the idea of ghosts, and does not wish it to be known that someone hereabouts opposed his purchase of the house,' Konrad said slowly. 'I wonder what, or who, he really fears?'

Nanda had no theory to advance, for she stood in silent thought. Konrad's gaze rested absently upon her keen, ice-blue eyes; noted anew the dimple that appeared in one cheek when she smiled, or pursed her lips in thought; wandered over the pale hair in its typical state of mild disarray, a tiny face peeping out from within the tumbled blonde locks...

Wait.

A *face*?

'You brought a passenger,' Konrad observed.

Nan reached up a hand to stroke her friend's tiny nose, and the creature ventured further into view. It was a golden-furred, simian face, and familiar to Konrad, though come to think of it...

'I haven't seen Weveroth in a while.' He held out his own hand to the monkey, who roundly ignored him in favour of Nanda.

'This has only just occurred to you.' Nanda's brows snapped down in disapproval, and Konrad felt uncomfortably that Wevey was scowling at him, too.

'I, um, had other things to think about...' Nanda's frown only deepened and he abandoned his attempt at self-justification. 'Where has he been?'

'At home.'

That seemed fair enough an observation, as far as it went. And yet, Nanda's manner struck him as evasive. 'Doing what?' he prompted.

'Resting.'

'Oh no, has he been ill? Poor Weveroth.' Konrad tried again to offer greetings to the monkey, with the same result.

Nanda stared him defiantly in the eye. Were her cheeks a fraction on the pink side? 'Not ill. There was... there might have been... well the fact is that Wevey had, um, small...'

'Small...?' Konrad prompted, when her sentence trailed off unfinished.

'Creatures.'

'Wevey had small creat— oh! You mean *babies*?'

Nanda nodded. No further comment followed, but her eyebrows went up in a definite challenge.

'But that's... that means he's a she.'

'It is difficult to put anything past you.'

A comment which cut both ways, since he had never noticed the fact before. In fact, he had never given the matter any thought; he had probably referred to poor Wevey as *it* more often than was seemly. 'Er, Nan,' he ventured, when she continued to look haughty.

'Yes.'

'*You* knew that Wevey was a lady, yes?'

'Of course I did!'

Konrad folded his arms. 'Really?'

Nanda held his gaze for three seconds more, and then broke. 'How could I possibly tell?!' she protested.

'You have to look under the tail.'

'I know! Utterly impossible! The heights of rudeness, Konrad.'

Konrad began to laugh. 'It is pretty rude to get Wevey's gender wrong for years together, I'd say.'

'It is a matter of privacy! How would you like it if someone came up to you and peered into your—'

'All right,' Konrad said hastily, not at all liking the mental image Nanda was spinning.

'Exactly.' She looked triumphant.

'Are the babies here, too?'

'No, they were weaned and given to the Order before we left.'

Which gave Konrad something of a clue as to where Weveroth had come from in the first place. Tiny gold-furred monkeys were not exactly common in Assevan, and he had long wondered how Nanda came to own one. Especially as Weveroth was far too intelligent and helpful to pass as a mere ordinary creature.

He knew better than to enquire further, however, so he let it pass.

Malykant. The twin voices of his two serpents chimed in his mind at once, loud enough to rattle his teeth, and he winced.

What?

The diminutive undead requires your presence.

They had to have practiced that line, surely. *You mean Tasha, I suppose?*

The same.

They could not have practiced *that*, yet their two voices were twined still in perfect harmony. The effect was eerie beyond all reason; Konrad suffered a weird thrill combined with a shudder.

You get worse, he informed them.

We know.

Konrad took Nanda's hand and led her out of the cupboard. Or no, the antechamber. *Where is she?*

The pantry.

The said pantry seemed colder than ever when Konrad reached it, and a strong shudder on Nanda's part indicated that she felt the same way about it. Tasha sat cross-legged on the chilly floor not far from the grisly closet, her cap pulled low over her eyes. She saluted when they came in, but made no move to rise. 'Malykant,' she said perfunctorily. 'Boss lady.'

'Nan isn't your boss,' Konrad objected.

'She is everyone's boss.'

Konrad did his best to ignore the bright, smug smile Nanda directed at Tasha. 'What is it that you need?'

Tasha pointed downwards with one small, thin finger. 'There is a level beneath this one.'

'That makes sense. All such houses have cellars.'

'Yes, but this place is unusually well provided with them. There are the usual storage cellars, mostly empty, and then there is a whole complex of kitchens, sculleries, pantries. This entire floor in duplicate, only much older.'

The kitchens up here were new-looking and equipped with all the latest technology, to be sure, but if Konrad had considered the fact at all, he had simply assumed they had been lately refitted. 'What? Why were they abandoned?'

'I don't know, but the whole floor is sealed off. You can't reach it from anywhere in the house.'

'Then how did you—' Konrad stopped talking when Tasha gave him a significant look. She had gone exploring in spirit-form, of course, and drifted through the floors; that was how she had got down there. He could not follow.

Nanda spoke up. 'Why is this significant, Tasha?'

Tasha smiled upon her with benevolent approval. 'Yes. Well. There is another pantry beneath this one, with another cupboard in it that's joined on.' She pointed at the closet within which the bodies had been concealed. 'There is no floor in that part of the room. There is only a plank of wood dividing the two cupboards, and I reckon that can be removed from down below.'

Konrad's mind reeled. 'So... so it is a chute.'

That won him a smile of his own, albeit one of surprise. 'Very good. Yes, I think so.'

'That means... that means...'

Tasha eyed him with sceptical attention. 'Yes?'

'This is no hiding place. It is a... a delivery system.'

'Miraculous.' Tasha went so far as to applaud him. 'Once in a while, one sees why he is the Malykant.'

'Once in a while,' murmured Nanda.

Konrad let this pass. 'What is going on in those kitchens, Tasha?'

She grew serious again. 'I cannot tell. I wish I could but it is pitch dark down there, and even I can't see enough to be sure. The serpents helped me a bit with that revolting glowy-thing they do—'

Rude, hissed Eetapi.

Wretch, agreed Ootapi.

'—but there are many rooms down there and it could take us hours to find anything of note.'

'Keep looking,' Konrad ordered, and belatedly remembered to add, 'please.'

Tasha made an ironical little bow.

6

Konrad searched everywhere for Alexander Nuritov, and failed to find him in any of the places the inspector might be supposed to frequent. His room was empty. He was in none of the parlours, or in the dining room. Konrad even put his head around the door of the theatre — cautiously, fearing to openly present himself in case of being lampooned into another rehearsal — but Nuritov was not among those gathered in a knot near the fire.

He began to grow concerned. Adrift as they were inside an unusually deadly house, Alexander's sustained absence did not seem to bode well. Did his status as a police inspector put him in danger? Might those who had killed Alen and Kati decide to remove him, before he could have chance to detect and expose their crimes?

At length, Konrad ran again into Tasha, who brushed past him without acknowledging his presence at all.

'Stop,' he called.

Tasha obeyed, with ill grace.

'Where's Alexander?'

'*Mister* Nuritov is in the theatre.'

'No. I've looked.'

'Did you look on the stage?'

Konrad opened his mouth to protest that of *course* he had — and closed it again. He had barely glanced into the room, not particularly expecting that his search would be rewarded. What would Alexander be doing in there, when there was a pressing case to investigate? He had glanced perfunctorily at the cluster of people — Marko, Eino and Lilli — who were involved, apparently, in some kind of script conference in the warmest part of the room, and finding that it did not include the Inspector, he had moved on.

He hadn't even looked at the stage.

'Why would he—' began Konrad, and abandoned the train of thought. 'Never mind. Thank you. Carry on.'

Tasha carried on, without a backward glance or another word, and Konrad returned to the theatre. Not without a certain reluctance; his notions of surviving the lamentably thespian house party consisted of two policies. One, to keep himself and his friends safe from whoever it was that had taken a fancy to carving people up, at least until the time came to dispose of them. And secondly, to steer well clear of the theatre.

No such luck. Nuritov needed to be apprised of developments, and Konrad wanted to hear his thoughts — and discoveries, if he had any.

So, to the theatre he went, taking a deep, bracing breath along the way.

Alexander was indeed upon the stage, but to say that he merely stood there was to gravely understate the matter. Alexander *dominated* the stage. He was clad in all his nobleman's raiment: draping robes of bronze velvet all a-glitter with burnished embroidery, a soft cap to match, dainty shoes. When Konrad had first seen him thus arrayed, the clothes had undeniably suited him, but there had been an air of mild incongruity about the picture. Not any longer. Inspector Nuritov, every inch his character, was deep in the middle of a monologue.

'My fool sister!' he ranted. 'All soft tenderness of heart, and weakness of the mind! Shall she thus besmirch our family's ancient name? Is it to be borne? It shall not be, not while there is breath left to me!'

Konrad watched, mesmerised, as Alexander went through the scene, acting with lively spirit and — there was no denying it — prodigious skill. And *enthusiasm.* What manner of madness was this?

It only grew worse, for soon Nanda entered, as queenly as the inspector was noble, and on they went together. The chatter around the fireplace ceased; effortlessly the two actors held the attention of the audience. Konrad's included.

When the scene drew to a close, Konrad was left with conflicting feelings. As magnificent a display as they had made, why were they so wasting their time? Two people were dead, and more may yet follow.

He had his answer when Nanda and Alexander descended from the stage, for they were given a rapturous welcome. Konrad stood awkwardly watching as the group fell into animated conversation, Alexander included every bit as much as Nanda. The people who addressed Konrad with wary or distant courtesy treated Alexander as a friend.

He had, in short, made himself one of them. And how better to investigate a difficult case than to make oneself a confidante of the suspects? It was a trick Konrad had never mastered.

He joined the group, attaching himself to its edges, and was gratified by Alexander's immediate attempts to win for him a welcome.

Eino, as ever, dominated the conversation.

'Marvellous progress we make,' he boomed, a wide smile flashing within his voluminous black beard. 'And onward we go! I must have everybody in the theatre this afternoon, every single one of us. And here we will stay until we have rehearsed every act, every scene! We pause only for dinner.' His words were jovial but Konrad detected signs of anxiety: his eyes darted here and there about, too quickly, almost feverish in their activity; he spoke at speed, words falling over words as he gabbled about the play. Konrad suspected him of having another motive for wanting to gather all about him. Was he trying to keep everybody close? Did he seek to protect?

Was he looking particularly at Nanda, as he spoke?

Shortly afterward, Konrad was able to extract Nanda and Alexander from Eino's hold by pleading the need to rehearse. There came a scene, midway through the second act, in which Greta, Vidar and Diederik were all on stage together — Synnove, too, though they were out of luck there, for Tasha did not present herself. Konrad hoped she was busily occupied in searching the lower cellars.

'Holt is uneasy,' Alexander said, the moment he could speak without being overheard. He had led them to the rear of the theatre, where the walls were clad in overstuffed bookcases and lined with tapestried arm chairs, and taken off his cap with apparent relief. 'He makes a good show of cheer, but I think he knows all is not well here.'

'He is downplaying Alen's failure to appear,' Nanda put in. 'I raised the question with him. He mumbled something about Alen's promising only conditionally to come, and perhaps he changed his mind, and then hastily turned the topic. Our Alexander may be a fine actor, but Eino is not.'

Nuritov actually blushed a bit at Nanda's praise, and did not meet her eye. 'Er,' he said with a tiny cough. 'Marko has some manner of secret, which I believe he may be disposed to share with me in the near future. He is furtive and troubled, but I do not think he is afraid. Lilli...'

Nanda broke in upon the inspector's silence. 'Oh, Lilli! What shall we say of her? She despises us all, and for the most part we are delighted to return the sentiment.'

'Why does she hate everybody?' said Konrad.

'I don't know,' replied Nanda with a shrug. 'She confides in no one.'

Konrad looked around. The stage had been taken by Eino and Marko; Lilli had disappeared. 'Where is Denis, today? I have seen nothing of him.'

'I saw him an hour ago. I believe him to be well, but he can be reclusive. Often he hides away in the conservatory.'

'There's a conservatory?'

'A spectacular one. You ought to see it.'

Konrad's gaze strayed back to Eino. The man dominated the stage, too, though in his case it was by sheer advantage of size. He was attacking some scene or another with gusto, but insufficient focus, for he frequently lost his way and had to refer back to the script-pages in his hands.

'Something is definitely bothering him,' Konrad mused.

Tik tik, tik. Nanda tapped her fingernails against the arm of her chair, lips pressed into a thin line. 'There is something much amiss with him, and it's more than whatever is going on in his mind.'

Konrad waited for more, but she paused, seemed undecided how to proceed.

'Whatever it is that's in your mind,' Alexander said in a gentle way, 'Please tell us. We trust your intuition.'

Nanda smiled gratefully at him. 'I hardly know what it is that I suspect, only he... well, I have lately wondered whether it is indeed Eino.'

Whatever Konrad might have expected from her hesitant

preamble, this was not it. 'What? You mean he may be an imposter?'

'I... do not know.' Nanda's brows drew together, and she sighed. 'I knew Eino before, understand, though we were never intimate friends. He was part of my mother's circle when I was... before I left Marja. I shook hands with him, once or twice. The mind and heart I saw into at that time were... well, there is a difference. A subtle one, but it's there. Now, is it merely the passage of time that is responsible? People do change, and some years have passed. Or is it something else? He does not feel quite familiar to me, and he ought to.'

'His appearance is distinctive,' Konrad objected. 'How could anybody pretend to be him and expect to succeed, unless he has a twin?'

'I do not believe him to have any siblings at all.' Nanda shook her head, her frown deepening further. 'Perhaps he has a twin brother I have never heard of, and there is a masquerade afoot. But I cannot see why, and it does not seem likely, for I have tested him repeatedly. He remembers details about our former meetings which would be difficult to impart to another — which I'd hardly expect him to think of, until prompted by me. No, I am convinced that it is Eino — and yet, it is not. It is a puzzle I cannot solve.'

Alexander took out his pipe, from some secret place he had apparently found within his splendid robe. He did not light it, but set it to his lips and disappeared into brief thought. 'I do think that Mr. Holt is the key,' he murmured. 'Somehow, all revolves around him. His is the house to which all are invited; he is our host, and the director of the play. He knows something that disturbs him, either about the house itself or somebody in it. He fears ghosts, though he will not share the reason why. He glosses over the prolonged absence of two of his guests, when the careful and attentive host he is pretending to be ought to show far greater concern. He tries to gather the rest of us close, perhaps to protect us, from some threat he is aware of but cannot or will not counter. And he is afraid.'

'These match my own conclusions,' Konrad agreed. He cast a lingering look at Eino, still holding forth upon the stage, and reached a decision. 'He has confided in neither of you, I take it?'

'To me, but little,' Alexander confirmed.

Nanda sighed. 'He consents to be drawn upon trifling topics, but when I draw near to anything about the house or its guests, he soon finds somewhere else to be.'

'Then we must apply a little pressure.'

'Such as?' Nanda fixed him with a look of deep suspicion. 'Understand, Konrad. He must be brought to confide, but I will not have him harmed. He is a friend, however distant.'

'I won't hurt him, though I do intend to frighten him a little.'

'A little?'

Konrad shrugged. 'Perhaps a lot. I cannot predict his response.'

Nanda looked as though she wanted to object further, but she did not. Perhaps she summoned visions of Alen's dismembered corpse to her mind's eye, or recalled the fate of Kati Vinter. 'Very well,' she allowed, wary. 'What do you have in mind?'

'Oh, a bit of a theatrical.' Konrad smiled. 'What could be more fitting?'

The coming of night brought a fresh wave of cold down upon the house at Divoro. There could be no question of wandering those deepening shadows in the fine costumes of the play's sumptuously-clad characters; the shivering guests arrayed themselves in their warmest layers and thickest furs, and kept as close to the roaring fires of the drawing-room, the dining-room and the parlour as they could.

All except for their host, who was borne off into the oldest parts of the castle by Alexander Nuritov. Courtesy compelled poor Eino to humour the inspector's eager desire for exploration. Time was passing swiftly, Nanda reminded them both; if there was to be time for the thorough investigation of the castle's more ancient features that Alexander desired, then it must be done immediately, and at once. All of Eino's protestations — is it not too cold? Would it not be better to examine those rooms in daylight? — were borne away under the pressure of Nanda's determination, and the exploring party set off directly after dinner. Nanda judged it expedient to wear her outdoor garb: her thick woollen cloak, the hood pulled over her hair; her layered skirts; her padded gloves, and fur muff. Heavy furs adorned the shoulders of Eino Holt and Alexander.

Even these measures were scarce enough to ward off the penetrating chill. The farther they went from the restored, inhabited rooms of the castle, the colder the air became. The soft yellow glow cast by their high-held lanterns illuminated fingers of frost creeping over the damp, half-frozen stone of the walls; their breath misted and froze as it left their lips. Black shadows raced away from them ahead, and crowded in close behind. Corridor after corridor they traversed, peeping into long-abandoned chambers cluttered with decaying furniture, the air thick with dust and neglect.

'I do not know what half of these rooms are,' admitted Eino, casting lamp-glow and a reluctant gaze over a bedchamber. A rotting velvet canopy of indeterminate colour had collapsed over the sagging bed beneath, and threadbare tapestries hung off once-handsome chairs.

'This part of the castle appears long abandoned,' Nanda observed, for the evidence of her eyes suggested a neglect spanning rather further back than the mere decade or so the house was known to have stood empty. 'I wonder how the Vasilescu came to leave so large a space unoccupied? It must be an entire wing like this.'

Eino appeared discomfited by the question. He withdrew smartly from the bedchamber, and closed the door upon it the moment Alexander and Nanda had rejoined him in the corridor outside. 'I do not know.' Indeed, his discomfort had grown steadily, the deeper into the abandoned wing they had wandered, and for some minutes now it had been Nanda more than he who had led the party onward. He now ceded charge of the venture entirely to her, falling into step behind her with visible reluctance. 'Had we not better return to the drawing-room?' he enquired, a plaintive note detectable in his tone. 'It only grows colder.'

'Soon!' sang Nanda, and stepped smartly on.

'But, my dear,' protested Eino, hastening to keep pace, 'I grow concerned for you. Alexander, pray assist me. In her state, she ought not take such frivolous risks! We must persuade her.'

Nanda turned her head to regard Eino steadily for some two or three seconds, one pale brow lifted high. 'What state is that, dear Eino?'

'I... I understand you to be in an uncertain state of health.'

'Hmm.' Nanda walked on, presenting Eino and Alexander both with a vision of straight-backed displeasure. 'You have been in conversation with my mother, I conclude.'

Eino's only response was a deep sigh.

Alexander intervened, observing in his mildest tone: 'If there are ghosts in any part of this castle, I should think they would prefer this very wing. Should not you, Nanda?'

'Of a certainty! It is by far the quietest part of the house, and rarely intruded upon by the living. If I were a ghost, I dare say I would be most content with it.'

'There are no ghosts,' said Eino firmly. 'I have lived here some months, and never seen or heard aught out of place.'

'Ah, but they are not out of place,' Nanda pointed out. 'To them, my dear Eino, the person who is out of his place is *you.*'

Eino had no response to make to this unpromising idea. He raised his lantern a little higher, sending the creeping shadows fleeing up the walls.

Into this silence there came the distant, echoing sound of approaching footsteps: one, two, three slow paces.

Eino's grip upon his lantern turned white-knuckled. 'I am sure of it,' he loudly proclaimed.

'Oh, I am sure they mean no harm,' said Alexander reassuringly.

From some twenty paces to their rear, Konrad watched and listened to all of this with interest. He had cloaked himself in those same shadows that Eino sought to dismiss, and followed along without detection; silence itself, until he permitted those few, eerie footfalls to reach Eino's ears.

Serpents. A little more cold, please.

Eetapi and Ootapi, invisible to all save Konrad himself, obeyed his orders with gratifying promptitude. Ice raced in thin sheets over the smooth tiled walls, frost crept in webs across the floor. Then came those footsteps again, closer now, splitting the heavy silence with sharp, staccato emphasis.

'I believe we have a visitor,' offered Alexander, with smiling affability.

'No, no,' said Eino weakly, casting agitated looks all around himself. 'The others are looking for us, perhaps. It is Marko, or Lilli.'

'Perhaps Kati,' said Nanda, all soft dulcetness of tone.

'I... why, yes, perhaps,' stuttered Eino in reply.

They had walked the length of a long, bare passageway, and now bid fair to turn the corner into some new part of the castle. But a few feet ahead of them, on the left side of the corridor, a heavy door of solid oak and black iron hinges quietly opened itself.

As Eino stared in mesmerised horror, the substantial door swung slowly inward.

'I believe we are invited to go in,' said Alexander, and stepped that way.

'No!' The word emerged at booming volume, echoed off the walls. Eino followed his horrified utterance by hurling himself in Alexander's way. 'On no account go into that room!'

'Why, what is in there?' Nanda, all eager curiosity, darted at once through the doorway.

Despairing, his face as pallid as the snow outside, Eino went after.

Alexander looked in the direction he expected Konrad to be, and mimed a doff of his hat. He, too, went through the mysterious door, and Konrad followed after.

And now a glow, please, Konrad instructed his snakes. *A little, not too much.*

They performed admirably, casting the faintest ghost-light into the corners of the room. It was another bedchamber, as decrepit as every other in this forgotten part of the house. The bed was intact, though so choked with dust as to obscure its coverlets entirely. A series of heavy, dark wooden closets lined one wall, looming out of the darkness like a row of silent giants. Twisted iron sconces hung upon the walls, emptied of light and grace. The dusty tiled floor was partially covered over with a ragged rug, once a magnificent tapestry. The serpents floated through every part of the chamber, tracing their ghost-light over bed-post and sconce, kicking up clouds of choking dust, sending out motes of eerie light to dazzle Eino's eyes.

Silence.

'This chamber must have belonged to someone important,' said Nanda after a moment, her voice an atmospheric whisper. 'Perhaps they linger still.'

Alexander wandered towards the row of closets. Pale light limned the closed doors; something inside was shining. 'I should think it likely.'

Poor Eino stood at the rear of the chamber, as far from those glimmering closets as he could get. 'We must leave. Nanda, please.'

'But what if it is important?' Nanda joined Alexander, and called out: 'We are ready to hear you.'

'No!' cried Eino hoarsely. He tried to back farther away and came up against the wall, shaking. Would he run? He stared ahead, gaze fixed in horror, and seemed unable to move at all.

Konrad chose prudence, and quietly moved to block the exit.

There came a whisper of movement, and a slow *creak*. The doors were opening. Nanda and Alexander stepped back, as one, and the ghost-light blazed, revealing the outline of an ethereal figure traced within its midst.

A piercing scent, sweetly rotten, filled the air.

'*Have you come to visit me?*' The words emerged in a sepulchral whisper, though the tone was light and high: youthful. '*Come closer. I have been so long alone.*'

The spirit drifted forward; frost-flowers blossomed over the floor beneath her incorporeal feet.

Oh, that's lovely. Konrad had given no instructions for decoration; who could have guessed that the serpents possessed an artistic flair?

Thank you, Master. Ootapi sounded pleased.

I believe that was my idea, hissed Eetapi in sniffy irritation.

You are both to be praised, said Konrad soothingly. His peace-keeping efforts were rewarded only with a twin, offended silence.

Tasha may deplore her role as Synnove, but she was doing a fine job of playing the ghost of the house at Divoro. She was sweet and wistful and sad, but as the serpents lowered the brilliance of their magnificent ghost-light she was revealed in all her horrifying glory: a cadaver traced upon the air in threads of shadow and light, hollow eye-sockets gaping, her hair a rotting cloud around a decaying face.

A low moan of pure terror issued from Eino Holt.

The ghost, engaged as she was in inspecting Alexander and Nanda, could not ignore the sound. She looked up, intrigued. '*There is another here?*' And she drifted his way, slow but inexorable.

Eino screamed.

'*But what is the matter?*' Tasha halted, head tilted. '*You do not wish to see me?*'

'Please,' gasped Eino. 'I am sorry for it all, so sorry. Do not hurt me! Do not hurt Nanda!'

'*I will not hurt you.*' The ghost smiled horribly, jaw gaping, and advanced again upon Eino. '*Have you come to talk to me? Shall we play a game?*'

'No!' Eino cringed back, white with fear, then made an abrupt and futile break for the door. Courtesy of the Malykant and his serpents, he found a wall of something icy-cold, invisible but impassable, blocking his way. He screamed, beat his fists uselessly against the obstruction, and finally fell weak-kneed to the floor.

'*Do not run from me?*' Tasha said plaintively. '*What is your name?*'

Eino said nothing, apparently paralysed with fear. So, ever helpful, Nanda spoke up. 'His name is Eino Holt, and he owns this house.'

The ghastly head tilted again. '*Owns it? But it is my father's house.*'

'The Vasilescu are long gone. It is the House of Holt, now.'

'*No.*' Anger vibrated through those sweet, youthful tones. '*My family would never abandon this house! You took it from them.*' She advanced upon Eino, who trembled so hard that his teeth chattered. '*Why?*'

'They... they sold it.' Eino forced out the words, choking. 'I bought it from them.'

'*You should not have bought it.*' The advance slowed not one whit; soon Tasha hovered over the prone shape of Eino, her ethereal form roiling ominously. '*You dare to trespass upon the Halls of the Vasilescu? Did you think that we would permit it?*' Her voice rose to a terrible shriek, and bursts of lightning crackled through the air. '*For this, you will pay.*'

'*No!*' Eino screamed the word, an appalling, tearing sound, and Konrad knew a moment's guilt. He had heard that sound before, once or twice: it was raw despair, and the kind of fear that could break a man's mind. 'It is not my house! It is not mine! I bought it for — for another — but you must not harm her. You must not.'

Konrad blinked. The same surprise registered in Nanda's sudden stillness, in Alexander's swift frown.

Tasha gathered herself. '*To whom have you given my father's house!*' she shrieked. A dry, chill wind blew itself into existence around her, sending choking clouds of dust into Konrad's face. He tried his best not to cough, and thereby reveal his presence.

'Do not ask me!' Eino covered his head with his arms, trying desperately to block out the nightmarish vision of Tasha bending over him.

Tasha, undisturbed, kept up the pressure. '*Why*!' she screamed. '*Why did you give away my house!*'

'Because... because...' Eino failed to finish the sentence; a shudder racked his beleaguered body, so strong as to cut off his words. He gasped, and tried again. 'I had to.'

'*Had to,*' repeated Tasha, in a whisper. The softness of the words fell sweetly upon the air, in stark contrast to the raging fury of a moment before. '*By whose order, Eino Holt? You will tell me!*'

Eino gasped and shuddered, his gaze still averted from the terrible vision of Tasha. 'You must not hurt her,' he babbled. 'You *must not hurt her.*'

Not another word could Tasha induce him to speak. He fell into a stupor, fear-ravaged and exhausted, and lay curled in a protective ball, shaking.

'Enough,' whispered Konrad. Tasha nodded and faded away; the ghost-lights dimmed and winked out, leaving only the guttering glow of the lamps Nanda and Alexander had brought. The sudden silence felt heavy and oppressive.

'We must get him to his room,' Nanda sighed. She regarded the felled form of her terrified friend in thoughtful silence; in her eyes Konrad saw compassion, and the same guilt he felt himself. They had succeeded in their goal: Eino had been frightened enough to talk. But the extent of his terror had not been anticipated. How much harm had they caused?

What's more, his words strongly suggested that he was someone else's tool in this bad business. Whose? How this mystery woman was involved, or what Eino had got himself caught up in, remained unclear; but that he was both reluctant and appalled by it was obvious. He had probably deserved gentler treatment than he had received.

Eino was persuaded to rise, eventually, though he was weak upon his legs and his shaking did not to any degree lessen. The journey back to the habitable parts of the castle was slow; Eino walked, but he was supported on either side by Alexander and Nanda, and he seemed in danger of tumbling to the floor with every step he took.

Konrad went ahead, and entreated the assistance of two of Eino's maids. By the time the forlorn trio reached Eino's chamber, there was a strong fire casting a welcoming heat and a bright glow from the hearth, and his bed had been made up with multiple hot bricks. Once successfully put to bed, he lay there inert, eyes closed, his face as white as death.

They withdrew, and left him to sleep. *Watch over him, please,* Konrad instructed Eetapi, who accepted the task without a murmur of complaint.

Nanda gave a deep, weary sigh as the door shut upon Eino. 'We have used him very ill.'

'It was necessary,' said Konrad.

'Yes. But I regret the necessity. Will he recover, I wonder?'

'The mind is always stronger than it appears,' offered Alexander. 'Stronger than we would like, sometimes. I have seen people far more delicate than he, recover from still greater trauma.'

Nanda's smile was grateful. 'Thank you,' she murmured. 'I hope you are right.'

Konrad's mind turned upon the questions raised by Eino's words. 'We need to reclaim Tasha,' he said. 'And then we need to find those cellar kitchens.'

'She has already found them, has she not?' said Nanda.

'Oh yes, but only in her spirit shape, and she cannot hope to explore every inch of those rooms without aid. We must find a way in. Whatever is going on down there must be the key — to the murders, to the house itself. There is no time to waste.' He thought a moment, and added: 'And I believe I will set one of the serpents to watching the movements of our host.'

7

Konrad wanted to dispense with the pretence, and openly announce that he (and the inspector) were investigating a pair of murders and proceed at all possible speed. He wanted to recruit everyone who was willing to assist and launch a hunt for a way into the secret cellars beneath the house; a hunt that would not cease until access was gained and the cellars were searched, and forced to reveal their secrets. He wanted to employ all possible means to find the murderer and dispose of him or her, before anybody else fell victim to the house's dark mysteries. Above all, he wanted to take Nanda and Alexander and Tasha out of there before they could come to any harm. Would Nanda have felt duty-bound to investigate this strange place, if she had not been acquainted with him this past year or two? He could not shake the feeling that her presence here was, in some indirect way, his doing. His fault.

And two of her mother's friends had already been killed.

He could do none of these things, of course, and his residence in the house — the confined and fixed nature of its proceedings — hampered him severely. Never had his gentlemanly masquerade chafed at him more. Instead of donning his warmest garments and venturing out to investigate the hillside for passages leading below, he was obliged to leave that search in the hands of Tasha and his serpents, and report instead to the theatre. His incorporeal colleagues at least had the advantage of being impervious to the cold; they could search for as long as was necessary. But they were few, and the search could take days.

He waited, and fretted, and took his position in the theatre with very ill grace. The room seemed larger than ever without Eino's giant presence dwarfing various elements of its furniture, and without Kati either. The rest of the guests were there, but there was an air of fatigue, or of lethargy, about the proceedings. Marko sat in a blue velvet chair in one corner, ostensibly going over his lines, though Konrad noticed that he was not turning the pages of his script booklet. Denis stood at one window, staring out at the whirling snow in inflexible silence, his back turned to the room. And Lilli Lahti... she stood upon the stage, which was more enthusiasm than anybody else cared to display. But her mind was clearly far from the play. She picked restlessly at the embroidered front of her golden silk coat, a deep frown furrowing her brow, her gaze fixed upon nothing in particular.

Nanda and Alexander were arrayed in costume once more, though the delight they had formerly taken in their fine garments had dimmed. Both were troubled, no more focused upon the play than Lilli. Konrad had not even tried to affect an interest; he eschewed his thespian trappings, his thoughts too busy and his mind too troubled for theatrical trivialities.

What had Eino meant?

I had to. You must not hurt her!

He was a bundle of fears, Eino, convinced that harm threatened at every moment; not just himself, but his guests, too. Why? He was not wrong, for great harm had already befallen two of the residents of the house. But he did not appear to know about Kati's death; therefore, could Konrad be certain that he knew of Alen's? Perhaps his eagerness to play down the peculiarity of their failure to appear was a product of fear, too. He was petrified to find himself correct to fear trouble, and desperate to convince himself of some other, comfortably mundane explanation for their absence.

Konrad's gaze met Nanda's, and held. He read in her face the same frustration he was feeling himself, and a wordless agreement passed between them. She paused to address a few words to Nuritov in an undertone; Konrad could hear nothing of what she said. Then, quick of step and withan air of purpose, she came to Konrad.

'This is useless,' she said. 'No one here cares a whit for the play, without Eino to chivvy us along. Will anyone note our absence, or care for it if they do? I imagine not.'

Konrad was only too happy to set down his play script. 'You have some other activity in mind?' he enquired.

'I shall go and talk to Eino. He is feeling vulnerable now, and afraid, and perhaps he may confide in me. He may benefit from the presence of a friend, too. Alexander is gone to talk to Lilli. What shall you do?'

Lilli? How curious. But the inspector had indeed approached the sour-faced Marjan woman, and to Konrad's mild surprise, Lilli did not seem to resent the intrusion. In fact, she came close to welcoming it. How *did* Nuritov manage to endear himself to people so well?

'Um,' he said in answer to Nanda's question. His first thought had been to rush outside into the snow and join the search for a way into the cellars. But that was, most likely, futile. What Tasha and his serpents could not discover was unlikely to be revealed by any meagre efforts he could muster; he was but one, and possessed of few abilities which could be of use in a prolonged search. He was, moreover, sadly pervious to the cold.

But there was another prospect.

Konrad bent his head closer to Nanda's. 'Consider what Eino said, to the ghost. *You must not hurt her.*'

'I remember.'

'To fear of this mystery woman's coming to harm at the hands of a resident ghost, Eino must be aware that the lady is within the ghost's reach. Or in other words, somewhere in this house. No?'

'That does make sense.'

'Very well, then. We know of no one else here besides those guests to whom we have been introduced, and the household staff. So who was Eino referring to? It could have been Kati, but that seems unlikely, or surely he would have raised a far greater hue and cry over her apparent disappearance. Lilli seems still more unlikely, for there seems little real friendship between the two of them. That leaves the servants, or—'

'No,' said Nanda. 'He told me that the servants are all recently arrived, many of them hired specifically for this party. And he implied that they were hired by someone else, for he claims to have had little hand in their selection.'

Konrad noted that with interest. 'That rather reinforces my idea: that there may be someone else in this house, a lady, to whom we have *not* been introduced. Who has, in short, been hidden from us. The house is quite large enough for such concealment.'

One of Nanda's brows went up; she was thinking. 'Possible,' she conceded at last. 'I cannot think why Eino might want to hide someone he apparently cares for, but—'

'Because he knew to fear some danger, perhaps?'

'I think not, for why otherwise would he invite his friends here? Why invite me? I think that Eino fears danger *now*, but he did not before.'

'I bow to your superior knowledge of his character.'

Nanda nodded once, satisfied. 'So you will search the house?'

'Yes. Especially those parts into which we have ventured but little before.'

'Be careful, Konrad.' Nan looked at him with an expression uncharacteristically grave, a trace of fear discernible behind her eyes. 'Kati… knew that something was amiss, I think, and she has suffered for it. Take care that the same does not befall you.'

'As must you,' said Konrad softly.

'I shall be well,' she said, rather dismissively, and left the room without another word.

Konrad paused a moment in thought. Nuritov was deep in discussion with Lilli, the latter talking with unusual animation. Marko was nowhere to be seen. Druganin was still at the window — no, he was leaving the window, and approaching Konrad.

'Savast,' said he, with a cool nod.

Konrad did not much like the familiarity of such an address. Nor did he like the way Denis Druganin's eyes travelled to the door through which Nanda had just departed, or the faintly regretful look that crossed his face in the process. The man had not developed an *interest* in Nanda, surely?

'Miss Falenia does not stay for the rehearsal?' Druganin enquired.

'She is feeling a little unwell,' Konrad lied. 'And has gone to her room.' He hoped that this misdirection might prevent Druganin from attempting to follow her.

'A pity,' said Druganin, and surveyed the few who lingered at the theatre, his lips twisting sardonically. 'How pitiful a performance it shall be, with so many absences.'

'You are an enthusiast for theatricals, I collect.'

Druganin regarded Konrad, his expression unreadable. 'I have always loved performing,' he said, which explained his presence at the house, for he did not seem any closer to Eino than Lilli. 'But you are no enthusiast, I think,' Druganin continued. 'Performing holds no appeal for you, if I am not mistaken.'

How true. And how ironic, considering that almost everything about Konrad's life involved some degree of pretence. 'I do not often participate in the performing arts,' Konrad replied.

'I wonder, then,' said Druganin, with a narrow-eyed look. 'Why is it that you are here?'

Konrad had no immediate response to give. He could hardly admit that Nanda had hauled him here expressly to investigate the trouble she had known to expect, and he had no other excuse to hand, for he had not thought that he might be interrogated by his fellow guests. From Druganin's point of view, his presence must seem inexplicable indeed; for he was clearly no friend of Eino's, and he had been so incautious as to make it obvious how little he relished his part in the play.

Before he could think of anything to say, Druganin had made him a tiny bow, his lips twisted into a sardonic smile, and sauntered away again.

Curse it.

Konrad left the room as soon as he felt able, heaping opprobrium upon his own head. If *he* could wonder and doubt and question his fellow guests at the house, small wonder that they could and would do likewise. How was it that he, so well-used to masquerade as he was, had provided himself with no plausible tale?

Konrad soon found that searching the house was only marginally more comfortable than searching the grounds. It had not previously occurred to him to note how very little of the house's available rooms were in use. The kitchens, the scullery, the pantries, a few bedchambers, the theatre and one or two parlours; so few, for so large a building.

The rest were like the wing he had, so reprehensibly, forced Eino to traverse not long since. They looked strongly as though they had not been entered in several years; everywhere lay thick carpets of dust and grime, the windows too besmeared to allow much light to filter through. No fires had been lit since the house had been abandoned, in all likelihood, and the cold had penetrated deep. Walking alone through those deserted halls, his echoing footsteps sending clouds of dust whirling into the air, Konrad shivered and cursed himself, once again, for a fool. He had not even thought to collect his cloak before he ventured forth.

He returned to the room in which Tasha had made of herself a ghost of the Vasilescu, and examined it and its surrounding chambers more closely than he had before. Finding nothing of note, he trod determinedly on, deeper into the dark, draughty old house. It was a sorry vision of decay that met his eyes. In its prime, the house must have been spectacular, richly clad in colour and drenched in light. Would it ever be so again? Konrad had no notion whether Eino's funds extended anywhere near far enough for a total restoration of so large a property, but being by no means ignorant on the topic himself, he tended to doubt it. The house at Divoro was ten times the size of Bakar House, and three times as luxurious. Had any man fortune enough for such a vast task?

Having no map of the property to hand, Konrad's path through the house was winding and haphazard. He covered all of the ground floor fairly swiftly, and some large portion of the floor above. It was not until he had ventured higher still, and begun to find his way into the upper apartments and the towers, that he uncovered something of interest. Not, alas, a hitherto unknown chamber with a mystery guest secreted behind its firmly locked door, but something quite other, the likes of which it had never occurred to Konrad to search for.

He had found his way into a large, strangely empty hall, not far from the long gallery with its eerie, dust-ridden portraits. The chamber was but little decorated, and bore almost no furniture at all. Its floor was covered in a thick, grimy carpet, revoltingly spongy underfoot, and a grand chandelier hung still and dark from the ceiling. That was all, save only for the simple lamps spaced along the walls; these Konrad lit with the torch he held. All of them together threw out a vast deal of light, drowning the room in a bright radiance which seemed starkly at odds with the gloom and the decay they brought into full view.

One wall was covered, end to end, in long drapes of dark blue velvet. And that was odd, because the windows were on the opposite side of the room…

Konrad drew back one long, heavy curtain, touching the aged

fabric as gingerly as he might. The velvet proved sound, however; dust-choked but not decayed. They were relatively new, then, these curtains, and behind them was concealed a sprawling family tree. Painted directly onto the wall, in ornate lettering and with many a flourish, here was an ancestry of which the house's former owners had clearly been proud. Many generations were there recorded, the topmost names undoubtedly dating back hundreds of years. Why had so important a document, and so beautiful a work of art, been hidden behind obscuring curtains?

It was a record of the Vasilescu family, of course; perhaps the concealment had been made shortly before the family's departure from the house. Konrad perused it with great interest, noting in particular those most recent entries upon the tree: Ela Vasilescu and her sisters, Olya and Alina. This third name, Alina, he could barely make out, for someone had all but painted it out. Had she been cast out, this Alina Vasilescu? Why? He could not make out the year of her birth, but if she was approximately of an age with her two sisters, she would now be somewhere in her fifties or sixties.

No children were recorded for any of the three sisters, save only one: a son born to Olya a little over thirty years ago, his name Denis.

... Denis *Druganin.*

Konrad stared at the name in some surprise, and tried to remember if he had ever heard mention of Druganin's connection to the family before. He had not, he was certain. Denis had not been introduced to them as a Vasilescu, nor had he volunteered the information. Yet here was his name, clear as day, and it was too much to imagine that another, unconnected man of the same name — and the right age — had chanced to be invited to this particular house.

The house had been sold when Denis was a very young man, then. By whom? Which of the Vasilescus here recorded had been responsible for the family's downfall? Which of them had sold the house?

Did any of it matter, now? Konrad shook himself out of his absorption, issuing himself a stern reprimand. While the history of the Vasilescu family was interesting, and Denis's concealment of his origins might be considered suspicious, he had no reason to imagine that any of it was connected with the deaths of Kati Vinter and Alen Petranov.

Except, perhaps, for those hidden cellars... if the Vasilescu had lived here for hundreds of years, then surely they had been responsible for building the lowest levels of the house — and for closing them off, later. Why? What was concealed down there? Konrad chafed in impatience, desperate for word from Tasha or his serpents. It had only been a matter of hours since he had last heard from them, but it seemed like days.

He turned his back upon the exquisite family tree, determined upon pressing Denis for information at his next opportunity. Subtly, of course, and discreetly. But he would like very much to know whether Druganin had concealed his connection to the family out of embarrassment or disdain, or… some other reason altogether.

8

On the other side of the house, and up yet another floor, Konrad at last discovered the room he had been looking for all along. It was tucked away into a corner, at the end of an out-of-the-way and disused corridor. It was the footprints upon the floor that alerted him; upon turning down yet another dark, frigid, empty passage his torchlight shone upon disturbances in the thick layer of dust. Someone had walked this way recently — and frequently.

Upon approaching the only door in view, however, Konrad was startled by the sounds of voices talking nearby. Those low-uttered words struck him forcibly, incongruous after so long a time spent among the silence of long decay. He stopped several paces from the door, straining to discern words enough to understand the import of the conversation, or to guess at who was speaking. To no avail; his ears caught only a low babble, incomprehensible except for the fact that at least one of the voices was certainly female.

It seemed more than likely that his theory had been correct: someone lived here in secret. But if so, who else was in the room with her? Was there danger, if he entered? He wished suddenly for his serpents, and regretted that he had not recalled one of them to assist with his search of the house.

Nothing for it, then, but to proceed. He approached, moving as quietly as he could, and laid his ear near to the door…

… and the voices stopped at once, hushed by someone who had, apparently, heard the sounds of his advance. Then came footsteps from the other side, quick and brisk and oddly *familiar* somehow.

The door opened to reveal Nanda.

'Ah!' she said. 'I was hoping you would soon appear. Come in, come in.' She stepped back in invitation and Konrad trailed past her, silenced by surprise.

Explanation enough soon came in the shape of Eino Holt. The big man was seated in a faded tapestry chair near a long window, a great cloak wrapped tightly around him. Nanda's conference with her friend had gone well, then; she had induced him to confide in her, at least to a degree.

Recumbent upon a narrow bed in the far corner of the room lay an elderly woman, dark silken covers drawn up to her chin. She looked frail and tired, her face drawn and sunken with age and too many cares. Konrad made her a polite salutation, biting back all the questions that immediately rose to his lips. 'Ma'am,' he said.

The woman stared at him with wide, suspicious eyes, and made no move to return his greeting.

Konrad paid the same courtesy to Eino, who at least deigned to return it, though his face revealed that he was no more disposed to trust Konrad's sudden and uninvited appearance than the lady.

Nanda bustled to the chair that sat by the side of the bed, and seated herself in it. 'Konrad, this is Eino's mother, Alina Holt. Mrs. Holt, this is a friend of mine, Mr. Konrad Savast. You may trust him, for *I* do, with my life.'

The woman — Mrs. Holt — surveyed Konrad with less suspicion and rather more curiosity, though she did not grow noticeably friendlier towards him.

'Mr. Savast,' said Eino in his deep voice. 'How did you find this room?'

Konrad made him a half-apologetic smile. 'I searched until I discovered it. I knew there must be something like it, you see, after your recent, er, comments.'

By the look on Eino's face, he had not been aware that Konrad had been present to witness his outburst. 'Oh,' he said at last. He looked searchingly at Nanda, and said no more.

Nanda went to him, and took his hand. 'Eino. Mr. Savast has no love for the theatre, as you must have observed. I brought him because he is quite *expert* at dealing with precisely the kind of trouble we have lately experienced — he and the inspector, and the inspector's assistant. I have brought them all to *help*, you see, and you must let us assist you. I could not be more delighted that you have entrusted me with the secret of your mother's residence here, but you must yet trust me with more. Please, will you not explain?'

Eino looked as though he wanted to speak, but knew not where to begin. His lips moved, though nothing emerged, and he cast Nanda a helpless look. 'I—' he began.

His mother interrupted him. 'The theatre,' she whispered, and gave a long sigh. 'Oh, Eino, tell me you have not.'

That galvanised Eino, at last, to speak. 'I— I know I should not have, but… how lonely it has been, since I came here! You must understand, I thought — I thought all would be well. It was only for a few days…'

'No,' said Mrs. Holt fretfully. 'Can you not understand? Have you heard nothing that I have told you? It will *never* be well! This house, this place, is *cursed*, Eino. No one will ever be safe here.' She turned to her son and fixed him with a fierce, anxious stare, saying in an agitated tone: 'Some disaster has come of it, has it not? I knew that it would. You must *tell me!*'

Eino returned her stare, shaking his head with slow incomprehension. '*I* have been safe here, mother. I have lived here almost a year, and you for some months, and we are both unharmed. What, then, should threaten our guests?'

Mrs. Holt gave a short, mirthless laugh, a sound more of despair than of joy. 'My poor, fool boy, you can have no understanding…'

Konrad's attention was diverted by Nanda, who had found something to interest her in Eino's vicinity. She bent over him, intent, her posture suggesting that she was listening for something. But if she was, it was not Eino's words or his mother's that absorbed her. What was she doing? He tried to catch her eye, but she did not notice.

'*Why,* mother?' said Eino, his voice rising. 'Why did you bring us here, if it is "cursed"? Why did you make me buy this place, if it is so unsafe? My *friends!* You cannot imagine what has befallen them!'

'Oh, I can, Eino,' whispered his mother, growing more faded and tired even as Eino grew angry and vehement. 'I can imagine it, all too well. I wish you had listened to me. I wish you had never hosted this ill-advised party.'

Something Konrad had heard nagged at him. Something Eino had said… no, something that Nanda had said. She had not yet said very much; what had it been?

Alina.

Alina Holt, mother of Eino. Where had he lately heard that name? Or seen it, yes, he had *seen* that name, written… written upon the wall, on the other side of the house.

'Alina,' Konrad said abruptly, cutting across Eino's lamentations. 'Alina Holt. Forgive me, ma'am, but are you — were you —'

The lady sighed more deeply than ever, and sank into her pillows as though she would never rise from them again. 'Alina Vasilescu,' she replied. 'So I was, once.' Her lips twisted in brief bitterness as she added, 'My poor husband was not good enough for my father and mother. No money, no status. They threw us off, and little did they know how I blessed them for it.'

'That is how you know so much about this place,' Konrad said, his mind racing.

Her eyes closed. 'I have tried so to forget, but it is of no use. This place haunts me, and shall forever do so.'

'Why,' said Konrad, his mind overflowing with questions. 'Why did you return here, if you despise it so? Why do you hate it? Why do you say that it is cursed?'

'I returned here for my son's sake,' said Mrs. Holt, but she proceeded no further, for Nanda interrupted with a cry of horror which brought Konrad straight to her side.

'Nan, what is it?' He looked her over, heart pounding, appalled to imagine what might have befallen her in this terrible place. But she was whole and hale, no sign upon her of any calamity.

Nanda paid him no attention, for she had none to spare from Eino. She laid a hand against her friend's chest — the left side — and pressed hard against the layers of his cloak, her face ashen. Her other hand gripped one of Eino's, and Konrad knew she was Reading him. 'Eino, what has become of — how is it that you — I knew, I *knew* something was amiss with you, but this! This is unthinkable!'

Eino stared miserably up at her, motionless. 'Dearest Nan,' he whispered. 'If you have come to some conclusion regarding my present state, I beg you will share it, for I have not the least idea how I am altered.' He swallowed, and said: 'I only know that I *am* altered.' He looked to his mother, but she turned away her face and would not meet his eye.

Nanda, at last, remembered Konrad. The look she turned upon

him was heart-rending. 'He is… he is altered somehow *inside,* Konrad. That is, he… I do not think his heart is his own.'

'What,' was all that Konrad could force past his suddenly frozen lips. *Not his own?* His *heart?* The look of sudden, horrified comprehension on Eino's face told a tale; the answering look of apology and entreaty upon his mother's told another.

And a number of things clicked into place in Konrad's mind. The emerging picture left him so sick to his stomach he could not, for one long, terrible instant, breathe at all.

No one spoke.

'You… you were so ill,' said Mrs. Holt at last, and her words fell like stones into the heavy silence. 'You were dying, Eino! How could I let that happen, when I had the means to save you? How could you ask me to lose you, too?'

'But…' said Eino, in a painful whisper. 'How…?'

He did not appear able to finish the question, and Konrad was not at all sure that he wanted to hear the answer, either. But he must.

Mrs. Holt wet her lips, her eyes darting about the room as though she sought in vain for some means of escape. Could she rise from that bed at all? Was she capable, in her frailty? 'I have never told you,' she began at last. 'I have kept from you the truth of your family — of *my* family — for I sought to spare you that pain. How I celebrated, when you were born! That I had found the means to escape from my family, and with their full collaboration! I knew they would never come after *you*, son as you were of so *unworthy* a man. You were safe, and forever.

'But you became ill. The problem was with your heart, they said. It no longer functioned as it ought, and you grew sicker and sicker. Then they began to say that they could no longer treat you; that their medicines and elixirs could no longer affect you. Your heart, they said, would soon stop beating, and forever. You would die. My child, my only son! Your father already gone before you! How could I permit it?

'We had always known what went on below the Vasilescu mansion. My sisters and I *knew*, always — even when we were children. No one concealed it from us, for we were to take our part in it in time. Olya did, of course. She delighted in it, like our mother and father. But I, and Ela — never.'

She lapsed into silence, and did not seem disposed to rouse herself to further speech. 'Is that why Ela sold the house?' he prompted. He was guessing; Ela was the eldest of the three sisters, and most likely to inherit the family property.

Mrs. Holt looked at him as though she had forgotten his presence. 'Oh!' she said. 'Yes, of course it was. The money was gone, that was true, but no Vasilescu would ever have sold this place for so trivial a reason as that.' He could not tell if she spoke sarcastically or not, for her tone was bland. 'When the house came into Ela's possession, she wanted nothing more than to be rid of it. So she sold it, for a mere pittance. Her buyer, she told me, had wanted it for an investment only — had no intention of living here. He or she never set foot in it, that I know of, but the fact that they *could* at any time they wished… well, that did not please Olya.

'I took Eino to her. I begged her to save his life, by *any* means, so long as he lived. And she agreed, but at a price: that Eino should purchase the house, and live here, so that she and her revolting fellows should always be safe. That their *lair* should remain undisturbed.'

'The cellars,' Konrad guessed.

'Caves,' Mrs. Holt corrected. 'They are connected to the cellars, yes, or they used to be.'

'But how…' said Nanda, a deep frown creasing her pale brow. 'Your sister Olya, she… she gave Eino someone else's *heart*?'

'Yes,' whispered Mrs. Holt. 'Do not ask me how, for I do not want to know. But the exchange was made, and my son lived.' She turned her gaze to Eino upon these words, and Konrad read in her face a deep fear of what she had done, and a desperate need for her son's forgiveness. But he, stunned and frightened by her news, could not speak. His chest rose and fell, far too quickly, and his face turned paler than Nanda's.

This was why Alen Petranov's body had been butchered. *This* was why Kati Vinter's organs were missing. They had been slain for their parts — or, perhaps, for their knowledge, at least in Kati's case, and her corpse turned to a grimmer purpose afterwards. They had taken Alen's heart; did they intend it for such another use as in Eino's case? Or did they have other uses for such an organ, taken as it had been from a body that yet breathed? Konrad's imagination quailed, and shied away from the bloody prospects raised by such a train of thought.

But another realisation, equally unpleasant, darted into his mind. 'Druganin,' he gasped. 'Olya married a Druganin — she is the mother of Denis, isn't she? What has he to do with all this?'

Alina Holt looked at Konrad with the wide eyes of pure terror, and she gave a tearing gasp. 'Oh, no. Eino, you did not… you did not extend the welcome of this house to your cousin?'

'I… I did,' whispered Eino. 'He— he is all, nearly all, the family we have left.'

Mrs. Holt erupted into activity, or an attempt at it. She threw off her covers and tottered to her feet, though she had not strength enough to go far. Konrad contrived to catch her just as she fell, and found her far too light in his arms. She was not merely frail; she was wasting away. But why? She was not young, but she was by no means old enough for such decrepitude. Was it care that had worn her away?

'You must help them,' said Alina Holt, her eyes feverish, words tumbling over each other in her haste. 'Denis, he — he is the worst of them all! Far worse even than Olya, than Father — no one here is safe from him, do you understand? *He* is their tool, or so my sister believes. His is the hand that slew your friends, I am sure of it.'

Konrad did understand, at least well enough to feel afraid. Tasha he did not fear for, but Nuritov was somewhere in the house, attempting to coax confidences from Lilli Lahti. Marko Bekk, too, remained, and all the servants…! Poor, foolish Eino had provided his cousin with a veritable buffet of victims.

What if something had already gone awry? What if Lilli — or, Malykt Avert, the inspector — had already been sacrificed to Druganin's predations?

These ruminations were interrupted by the sudden presence of Eetapi in his head. *Master!* she shrieked, at such volume that Konrad jumped. *Master, we have found them! They loiter far below, which is* quite *fitting, dear Master, for they are terrible—*

They are wonderful! Interrupted Ootapi.

—terrible and wonderful, continued Eetapi. *May we have an underground lair, Master? And a coven?*

A coven? Konrad spoke sharply, cutting across his serpents' babble. *A coven of witches!*

They are not witches, Ootapi said crossly.

Then what are they?

I do not know, but—

Enough! Konrad roared the word, and was gratified by the sudden, dead silence that followed. *Witches or not;* who *are these people you have found, and where are they?*

In caves below the house, said Eetapi much more succinctly.

They are the ones who stole the parts, added Ootapi.

Is Denis Druganin among them?

No, Master, said the serpents as one.

Konrad looked at Eino, who remained ashen-faced and sombre. 'Holt. You and your cousin. Would you say that you are friends?'

'Of course, I—' began Eino, but his mother interrupted.

'No!' she said with vehemence, and added with some bitterness towards her son, 'How can you be such a fool as to imagine Druganin *has* friends? If he did, you would be the last to be counted among them, Eino!'

'That is what I was afraid of,' said Konrad grimly. 'Has Druganin any designs upon this house?'

'Of course he does,' said Mrs. Holt. 'They all do.'

9

Upon receiving the serpents' directions into the caves, Konrad's first priority was to establish the whereabouts of Alexander Nuritov. This, to his relief, he accomplished very quickly, for Alexander was where Konrad had left him earlier: in the theatre. Lilli, though, was nowhere to be seen, and neither was Marko.

'Savast,' said the inspector in his friendly way, and smiled as Konrad entered the room. 'I was hoping to speak to you.'

'Can it wait?' said Konrad.

Alexander blinked. 'It— no, I think not. Lilli and Marko have naught to do with this bad business, theirs are personal disputes. But—'

'Such as what?' Konrad interrupted, a little sharply. He knew better than anyone that a mere personal dispute was often considered more than motive enough for murder.

'Poor Lilli has a passion for Marko, but he is, ah... more disposed to favour the maids.'

Konrad thought back to the flicker of some green article of clothing he had caught a glimpse of below-stairs. 'In particular, the kitchen maids?' he guessed. That explained Marko's tendency to loiter around the sculleries.

'Quite so. But Denis—'

'I know all about him,' interrupted Konrad — first checking to ensure that Druganin was not still lingering somewhere in the theatre himself. He was not. The room was empty save only for the inspector.

'Did you know that his room is directly above the pantry?'

'I... no, I did not.'

'*Directly* above, two floors up. The maids say that he requested it especially from Eino.'

Konrad frowned, momentarily confused. Why would Druganin particularly want a room *above* the pantry where— oh. *Oh.*

'That chute,' said Konrad. 'It goes *down* into the cellars — or the caves — but it also goes *up*.'

The inspector nodded. 'It is likely that Alen and Kati were killed below, and... and harvested,' he said softly. 'And their remains passed upwards, to... to Druganin's room.'

'For purposes unknown, I conclude.'

'I have not yet been able to discover what he is doing with them.'

Konrad grimaced. 'I begin to feel that we may wish to be spared the details. Have you been into his room?'

'Briefly. No traces remain of whatever he has been doing with — with the—'

'All right,' Konrad said hastily. 'I must tell you my findings, and then we are to go below. With *all* due haste, for Tasha and the serpents have found the way into the levels below the cellars.'

The inspector gave the matter his immediate attention. Konrad ran through his discoveries as swiftly as he could, and within minutes the two were bundled in cloaks and venturing outside, where Tasha waited. Nanda joined them as they passed the door, wrapped so tightly in her coats and scarves that her face barely showed at all. Konrad ventured a questioning look, which she answered with a low growl of irritation.

'Do not think you can talk me out of going with you,' she hissed, and Konrad stifled the concerns he had been inclined to express. If the truth were told, he was glad to have Nanda's company, for all that he worried for her safety, her health, her well-being, her... well, everything. She was the kind of ally he would keep always at hand, if he could.

'We do not know where Druganin is?' Konrad asked, gritting his teeth against the onslaught of freezing wind that hit the moment he stepped beyond the front door. The promise of further snow hung heavy in the air, and great black clouds massed ominously upon the horizon. There was a blizzard on the approach.

'I have not been able to find him,' shouted Nuritov over the howl of the wind. 'He left the theatre soon after you did, and he has not been seen since.'

That boded ill, and confused Konrad besides. If Denis was not in the caves and he was not in the house, where was he?

Were Eino and Mrs. Holt safe? He and Nanda had wrangled grimly over what was to be done, and had reluctantly trusted to the secrecy of Mrs. Holt's residence in the house for her protection. It would be enough, perhaps; Denis had no reason to suspect Mrs. Holt's presence, or to harm her either (so he hoped). Nor had he any reason to imagine that part of the house to be inhabited.

It was nowhere near enough, but he and Nanda had been able to come up with no better plan. They needed Tasha, the inspector and both the serpents if they were to infiltrate the caves; by the serpents' account, rather more people were to be encountered below than Konrad had expected. *A coven*, Eetapi had said. Olya Druganin, perhaps, and… who else?

Tasha's directions had been specific, and they had *seemed* straightforward. But hearing them and attempting to follow them through a snow-ridden landscape, with the wind shrieking around his ears and his face rapidly turning numb, proved to be markedly different experiences. Konrad, Nanda and Alexander ploughed on into the dark, snowy woods surrounding the house at Divoro, grimly determined in the face of any degree of inclement weather. The black fir trees blurred together after a while, stark as they were against the bleak wooded landscape, and Konrad almost walked straight past the tree he was looking for.

'A twisted fir, its branches resembling corkscrews,' Konrad muttered, recalling Tasha's words. He raised his voice to shout to his companions: 'Do those look like corkscrews to you?'

'Excessively,' Nanda called.

They were close, then. He covered his mouth once again with his thick scarf before his lips could altogether freeze, and cast about for the final signs Tasha had given him in order to... ah, there it was. A little row of fir trees like soldiers stationed upon the watch, and at their farthest end...

'Oh!' shrieked Nanda, and Konrad caught her arm just as she began to topple into the dark hole that yawned in the ground, its mouth half-filled with drifted snow. She steadied herself at once, snatched her arm out of Konrad's grip, and took a determined step forward. 'Let's get this done,' she said.

Konrad would have preferred it if she had permitted him to go first, but he knew better than to try to overturn her decision. So he fell in behind her, while Nuritov brought up the rear.

The roar of the wind cut off abruptly, the moment they were fairly inside the downward-sloping tunnel. Konrad's ears rang in the sudden quiet, and he paused to shake the snow out of his hair and his scarf.

'Finally,' said a voice, and Konrad jumped. Again.

'Tasha,' he growled. 'I *wish* you would stop doing that.'

The inspector's assistant shimmered into view, though her best manifestation still consisted of naught but a ghostly outline etched upon the air. He could still detect her grin, though. 'Sorry,' she said, without a trace of compunction.

'Lead on,' said Konrad, and Tasha shot away at once, soaring forth into the tunnel's depths at such speed he struggled to keep up with her. He made no effort to slow her down, however. She was right to be in a hurry; there was need.

He soon lost track of the route they took, for it was a winding way, past many a branch in the tunnel, down many a fork in the road. It was an inhabited space, that much was evident, for the passage was more than tall enough for even Konrad to walk upright, its walls and floor carefully smoothed. Moreover, there was light: iron torches were embedded into the walls at regular intervals, and though the glow they cast was not strong, it was more than enough to illuminate the way. Konrad spared a thought to wonder by what means the torches remained lit, for the light that burned there was not fire. It did not flicker, the way fire ought; it was steady, serene. Did the torches ever go out?

At last, Tasha slowed and came to a halt. Nanda, dashing along directly in her wake, did not stop in time. Had Tasha been corporeal, the two would have collided; as it was, Nanda and Tasha merged for a moment into a peculiar two-headed creature, half woman and half ghost, until Nanda hurriedly backed up again. Her face suggested that the experience had felt at least as strange as it had looked. 'Sorry,' Nanda said, but Tasha only shrugged, unperturbed.

'Around this next turn,' whispered Tasha, as Nuritov and Konrad caught up. 'We are below the house, though some levels deep. It was empty in there earlier, but let me first make sure we are still alone down here.'

'But the serpents said—' Konrad began, but Tasha ignored this. Before he could finish his sentence, she was gone.

Konrad folded his arms and waited, with poor grace. He shifted on his feet, too restless and uneasy to keep still. 'I do not like this,' he said, very softly. 'Why is it so empty down here?'

'You would think they would post a guard at the tunnel's mouth,' Nuritov agreed.

'Where are your serpents?' Nanda put in, and that was a very good question, too.

Eetapi? he called silently. *Ootapi?*

Their twin voices answered him at once, to his relief. *Master?*

Where are you?

In the caves, said Eetapi helpfully.

Yes, but where in the— He broke off, because Tasha had reappeared and was beckoning furiously. *Never mind.*

He went forward, trying to ignore the sinking feeling of impending doom that uncoiled within. Tasha would not draw them into a trap.

Not knowingly, his mind whispered. Irritably, he shushed it.

'You need to see this first,' Tasha said softly.

Steeling himself, Konrad followed her around a corner. The tunnel opened out into a large chamber — an ancient cave, by the looks of it. The floor, the walls, and the ceiling were all dark, smooth rock, much of it swallowed by deep shadows. The light was concentrated upon the far side, where a dais had been raised. It was a graceless thing, little more than a slab of fallen stone, but its halo of light gave it an air of importance.

Cautiously, Konrad approached. He felt dangerously exposed traversing that wide, open cavern, for there was nothing behind which he could hide if anyone approached, and the only exit he could see was back the way he had come. He crossed in haste, therefore, all his senses alert for signs of danger.

Nothing happened. He made his way to the dais uninterrupted, Nanda and Nuritov but a step behind him.

It was only once he had arrived at the dais, and climbed the rough steps that rose before it, that he could see what it held.

A man lay there, unquestionably dead. His dead skin was drawn tight across the sharp-boned features of his face, yellowish and waxy and traced with fine blue veins. Grey hair swept back from a high, proud forehead. He was dressed in fashions which had vanished centuries before: a sumptuous and ornate velvet coat, deep black, and a fine white shirt, with lace at his cuffs and his throat. Black breeches, pale stockings and elegant silver-buckled shoes completed the ensemble. The effect was sombre, but impressive, and the quantity of silver embroidery declared that here was a man of some wealth and standing.

The silence that accompanied their perusal of this still figure was more confused than anything else. Who was this man, that he was given so hallowed a position in so secret a place? Why was he kept here?

'How is he so... well preserved?' said Nuritov softly.

Konrad had been wondering the same thing. The clothes suggested that he had been dead for a long time, but he looked as though he might have died only yesterday, or perhaps this morning. Was the outfit some kind of costume? He did not think so, though he could not have said what it was that gave him this impression. The man looked like he fitted the clothes, somehow. They suited him.

Nanda spoke, in a whisper. 'It feels wrong in here.'

'Wrong how, Nan?' Konrad asked.

But she shook her head. 'I do not know. I cannot explain.'

A hint of colour caught Konrad's eye, a tiny anomaly in the midst of the stark black and white of the dead, still figure. It was a note of red, dark as wine, smeared upon the elaborate fall of lace at the man's throat. Konrad leaned closer to look.

'How,' he murmured, 'did any blood get there? And recently, too.' For though it was dried, it did not have the black, rusty appearance of old blood. Konrad would guess that it had appeared upon the lace no more than a day ago.

He exchanged a look with Nanda. She swallowed, her face very white and her eyes wide. 'You don't suppose...?' she said.

Konrad just nodded. 'Oh, I do.'

Neither of them moved. It was Nuritov who, with a swift sigh, applied himself to the unhappy task of unfastening the dead man's velvet coat and opening his shirt.

Carved deeply into his torso was a long, straight line, running from his throat to his navel. No old wound, this, inflicted while he lived and duly healed. Someone had cut him open *after* he had died, and carefully stitched the incision closed again afterwards.

Konrad should recognise the signs. It was a duty he was too often called upon to perform himself.

He did not imagine, though, that the motive in this instance bore any resemblance to his own. Why might somebody have wanted to gain access to this man's torso? What had they done to him?

'Alen Petranov's heart,' whispered Nanda.

Oh.

'Kati Vinter's lungs,' said Konrad, with a grimace.

'And who knows what else,' said Nuritov softly. 'Are they trying to — to rebuild him?'

Perhaps. Konrad was more than familiar with the arts necromantic, of course. They were sometimes engaged in by The Malykt's Order, albeit sparingly, and in accordance with their Master's strictures upon such subjects as those.

Dealing with unlicensed, unregulated and unscrupulous necromancers was a duty which sometimes fell to his fellows among the Order. It did not usually form any part of his daily doings, save on rare occasions. Those who turned to necromancy were usually those who had lost a loved one, and could not bear it. They strove to return life to those dead friends, lovers or family members, always unsuccessfully.

Almost always.

Reanimating dead flesh was no simple task, and the longer the person had been dead, the more difficult it became to reinvigorate the body's separate parts into a coherent, living whole. It was virtually impossible, in fact; the only known successes occurred within, perhaps, an hour of the subject's decease.

This did not stop people from trying, of course. Konrad had met a few would-be necromancers in his time with the Order, but *this*... this was something else. He had never heard of anybody trying to bring back someone so very long dead as this man was — if his attire was to be believed. He would have said it was impossible, and it *was*; the man's organs were too long dead, too far deteriorated. They were meat, now, had long since forgotten what it was to know the rush of blood, the energy of life.

But if they were replaced with organs much more recently deceased... would that work? *Could* it work?

Was that what all this was for? Were operations like those upon

Eino Holt merely a sideline, or some kind of test, all intended to aid in bringing this man back to life? For if a heart could be successfully transplanted into a living man and persuaded to function, who was to say that the same could not be true of a dead host? It was the kind of witchery Konrad had rarely heard of, let alone encountered, and his skin crawled at the prospect. Yes, Eino had been given life when he would otherwise have died... but at what cost? Who *else* had died, that Eino might live? For he was under no illusions as to the scruples of those involved.

'Who *is* this man?' Konrad muttered. Someone cared very deeply about bringing him back, and why?

'I have seen him, I think,' murmured Nuritov. 'Not in life,' he hastily added, as Konrad and Nanda both looked sharply at him. 'A portrait. It hangs in the rear hall, in the house.'

Nanda gasped. 'I know the one you mean. Yes, it is very like him.'

Konrad had not noticed any such portrait, but he was oblivious to art at the best of times. 'Did it indicate his identity?'

Nuritov shook his head. 'His name was not marked, but the painting was prominently positioned, and in a most ornate frame. I guessed, at the time, that it depicted a former head of the household, perhaps.'

'Or the head of the family,' Nanda put in.

Was that the way of it? By all accounts, the Vasilescu family's fortunes had deteriorated to nothing over the past century. 'Do they think that bringing the family founder back will somehow reverse their misfortunes?' Konrad mused. 'Not that it matters, for it will never work. They may do what they like to his organs, but the spirit is gone; without it, the body can never revive...'

A terrible thought occurred to him as he spoke. He took a breath, reached for his spirit-vision—

—and Nuritov screamed and sprang back, Nanda with him.

Konrad felt like screaming himself, for the corpse's eyes had snapped open. The man lay there, as dead as ever save for the fact that his eyes looked straight into Konrad's own and *saw* him.

His dead lips stretched into a grotesque semblance of a smile.

Konrad took a prudent step back, moving slowly despite the frightened pounding of his heart. Rarely had he encountered a sight so chilling; the more so once he let his spirit-vision swamp his regular sight, turning the cavern into bright, white light starkly etched over deep shadow. There: a ghost lingered, a pale outline overlaying the dark figure of its once-living body. Much was amiss with that dead presence; its shape writhed and roiled in ceaseless turmoil, laced through with so much darkness Konrad wondered that it could survive at all.

Konrad took another breath, and a second, and gathered himself. *Serpents!* he called. *To me, and at ONCE.*

'Konrad?' Nanda spoke from a little way behind him. 'What is it that you're doing?'

'The spirit is here,' he replied. 'He is, in effect, haunting his own body. Is that not remarkable?'

'Quite impressive,' she agreed, her voice only slightly shaking. 'What do you propose to do about it?'

'Nothing very much,' he murmured, only half his attention upon Nanda's words. The rest focused upon the rapid approach of his serpents. He sensed them, shooting through the winding caverns and growing every moment nearer.

'Specifically?'

Konrad gave a smile to match that of the corpse. 'I believe it is my turn to be terrifying.'

He let his guard fall, releasing all the iron control that hid The Malykt's influence upon him. He shed Konrad Savast like an old coat and became the Malykant, a being neither alive nor undead, but somehow both. The Malykt's terrible power blazed from him, dwarfing the miserable spirit before him.

WHO ARE YOU? he cried, and the ghost shuddered under the impact.

Jakub Vasilescu, whispered the corpse, but the soul was not quiescent; it fought him, desperate to flee, and Konrad welcomed the entrance of his serpents when they came streaming in moments later.

Bind him, he told them, and they fell to the task with a ferocious glee. The spirit's roiling torment stilled, grew quiet at last.

Jakub Vasilescu. Why do you linger?

My family, whispered the corpse, and smiled. *They feed me fresh life, replace my poor, lost body piece by piece... They need me. They say I shall rise, one day, to lead them once again.*

Why do you suppose that they need you?

Look what has become of them! Weaklings! Fools! The Vasilescu has lost its place, and none now live who can restore it.

What place is that?

The place we ought *to hold, in this world and in the next. A place at the forefront of all society! Who is to mend my poor Vasilescu, if not me? There is no one.*

In this world and the next? Konrad frowned, disturbed, but before he could enquire further, Jakub Vasilescu fell into a frenzy. His spirit resumed the tumult in which Konrad had found him, only intensified; he screamed his rage and frustration, and the corpse screamed with him, screamed and thrashed and wept blood. Those anguished howls echoed off the dark cavern walls, growing larger, louder, more piercing, and Konrad winced.

Shut him up, he ordered his serpents. *Quickly.*

They tried, but Vasilescu was strong in all his rage, and he fought violently.

Master, gasped Ootapi. *We weaken.*

'Tash?' said Konrad to the air, for he had long since lost track of where she was. 'Care to help?'

'Gladly,' she replied, and he could hear the grin that accompanied the word.

The fight was over rather quickly after that. If old Vasilescu had ever encountered the lamaeni before, Konrad would be surprised. This first experience was not a pleasant one for him. Tasha-as-spirit leapt upon him with the ferocity of a rabid wolf, and all but tore him to shreds. She took a vicious delight in it, too; Konrad could hear her laughing as Vasilescu tried, without success, to free himself from her inflexible grip.

When she was finished, the corpse lay once more inert, divested even of its withered semblance of life. Vasilescu's ghost hung limp in Tasha's grip, wound tightly about by the serpents. His ghost-light had faded almost to nothing, and he was silent.

'What do you want done with him?' Tasha asked. She had stopped laughing, much to Konrad's relief.

'The serpents will deal with him,' Konrad answered, and silently he ordered: *Take him to The Malykt.*

Yes, Master.

The trio of ghosts faded away, leaving only Tasha behind. She looked strange in his spirit-vision, far more vibrant than a spirit had any right to be. She grinned at him, swept a bow, and vanished.

Konrad let his spirit-sight fade, and stood panting for breath. That kind of work took a heavy toll upon him, and it never really got any easier.

'Right,' he said. 'So that's that. Next problem?'

Nanda and Nuritov stood pale and silent, staring at him with identical expressions of shock. Was there horror layered somewhere in there, too? Yes, there absolutely was. Konrad did not believe in lying to himself (or not too much, at least). Better to face the horrible truth. Was it the screaming corpse that had unsettled them? Undoubtedly, yes, but it was more than that.

His friends were horrified by whatever they had just seen in him.

He tried a smile, but feared that it was about as reassuring a sight as that of the smiling corpse. 'Vasilescu has gone. The serpents took him away. The body shouldn't pose a problem from here on.'

Nanda blinked, and shook herself. 'Good work,' she said, sounding more like her old self. She, at least, had seen such displays from him before.

Nuritov took a little longer to recover his composure. 'Excellent,' he finally said, his smile tremulous. 'Um, next problem. Yes. Druganin?'

'Did we find him yet?

A shake of the head from Nuritov and Nanda. Konrad sighed. Could these murderers never make it easy on him? He was only bringing them exactly what they deserved. They had *earned* his attention.

He did not like to think too hard about where Druganin might have been all this time, or what he might have been doing. Nothing good, he feared.

'It's my belief,' offered Nuritov, 'that when he returns, he will find his way back to the house. To his room, most likely.'

'Excellent,' said Konrad, and checked his pocket-watch. Time marched on, as always, and he was more than ready to be finished with this particular escapade. 'Shall we await him there?'

'Let's,' said Nanda, with an unpleasant smile.

'Tash,' Konrad called.

Let me guess, she replied the silent way. *You have more work for me.*

You are a working woman now, he admonished her. *This is what it means to be an adult.*

I am not an adult! Look at me!

She proved her point by manifesting once again, reminding

Konrad of her youthful appearance.

You might appear *to be about fourteen, but we both know you are not.*

There are all sorts of advantages to looking fourteen.

No doubt, but this is not one of them. Please keep an eye on Eino and Mrs. Holt, until we have taken care of Druganin? I fear for their safety.

Yes, Master. She hissed a bit as she said those words, serpent-like.

That cheek will get you into trouble, someday.

I look forward to it. With which words Tasha took her leave. He wondered briefly where she had left her body throughout all of this chaos, and thought better of asking.

Another two hours passed before Denis Druganin returned to his cousin's house, time which Nanda and Nuritov and Konrad spent in a fever of impatience. The longer Druganin absented himself, the poorer the prospects for whatever he had been doing. It chafed Konrad miserably that they had no means of following him. He could be anywhere within a radius of about twenty miles.

Druganin's room was one of the most comfortable in the house, draped in plush velvets and furnished with soft, deep chairs. Nobody took any pleasure in these delights. However handsome and comfortable his red velvet chair might be, it felt constrictive to Konrad. He wanted nothing more than to be done, and gone.

The serpents returned, and Konrad immediately put them on the watch for Druganin. He felt some compunction upon doing so, for they were weary after their battle with the shade of Jakub Vasilescu. But he needed their assistance.

Inform me the moment he appears, Konrad instructed.

Yes, Master, said Ootapi glumly, and Eetapi only sighed.

I am sorry, he told them. *Soon we will be finished with this bad business.*

Not soon enough, muttered Ootapi, with Konrad's full agreement.

'What of Olya Druganin, and the others?' Nanda asked, somewhere in the middle of the long wait. 'The coven the serpents mentioned? We have seen nothing of them. They must be dealt with, must they not?'

'I imagine that will be a matter for my Order,' Konrad replied. 'Yours, perhaps, as well.'

Nanda nodded slowly. 'They conceal themselves too well. It may take a proper incursion to dig them out.'

'Why, though?' said Nuritov.

Konrad blinked at him. 'Why, what?'

'Why have they concealed themselves? What are they hiding from?'

A fair question. 'Perhaps they became aware of my serpents,' he suggested.

'Or perhaps they are not hiding at all,' Nanda mused. 'The serpents indicated that the cave system is extensive. They may simply be in another, quite different part, one that we have not yet discovered.'

'Either way, I will make sure to send plenty of people after them.' Diana Valentina, head of The Malykt's Order, would want to hear all about this forsaken place, and as soon as possible. Konrad was glad he could hand off the task of dealing with the coven to her; he was heartily sickened by Divoro, and wanted nothing more to do with it.

He was therefore extremely glad when Ootapi finally raised the alarm. *Master, he comes.*

He brings a body with him, added Eetapi.

There were several things wrong with that, but chief amongst them was the absolute absence of Eetapi's customary glee; should not the appearance of another freshly dead corpse please her? Normally it would.

The news that Druganin had been out seeking some new victim could not please Konrad, for it was precisely what he had feared. But it puzzled him, too. Why had he gone so far afield, when there remained plenty of people in the house?

What manner of body is it? he asked.

It is a small one, answered Eetapi.

Konrad's heart stopped, and resumed its beating a moment later with a lurch.

You don't mean—

He got no further, for the door opened to admit Druganin. The man paused on the threshold, taking in his unexpected guests with an air of mild surprise.

'Why, good afternoon,' he said, smiling. 'I had no notion I was to receive the honour of a visit.'

In his arms he held the lifeless body of a child. She was no more than six years old, Konrad judged, and her neck had been broken. Her arms and legs were broken, too, and her sweet, dead face was covered in bruises.

Druganin dropped the child unceremoniously onto the floor, and locked the door behind him. He smiled pleasantly upon them all, his gaze flicking from Nanda to Nuritov to Konrad. 'So you have found me out, have you? I knew that you—' he indicated Konrad with a nod '— were too curious by half. I had a prime spot on my roster reserved.' The smile widened.

Konrad was too appalled to think. He felt frozen.

Nuritov spoke. He had jumped out of his chair the moment Druganin appeared with the child, though he had not advanced. He stood, white-faced and shaking, and somewhere beneath his own disgust Konrad felt a stirring of concern for the inspector. Had he ever encountered such a villain as Druganin? '*Why*,' said Nuritov hoarsely. 'What is any of this *for*?'

Druganin appeared to give the question some thought, for his eyes turned distant. 'You do not know, I suppose, the pleasure of it. The power. The *joy*...' His gaze flicked to Nuritov with something like contempt. 'I do not imagine you ever will.'

Nuritov appeared stunned beyond speech.

'Jakub Vasilescu?' said Konrad, softly. 'What of him?'

'My mother's pet project,' answered Druganin with a shrug. 'There is some little substance to it, I grant that, but it is futile. So they keep the old man alive enough to talk; what of that? All he can do is complain of us, condemn us for wasting his grand legacy. Would he have done any better? Could he, were he to return to life? I think not.' He spoke softly, mildly, but every syllable radiated anger.

'But you might?' Konrad suggested.

'Undoubtedly. I have the resolution, the will, the vigour. I have everything the family needs! They will see it, soon enough.'

'And your cousin?'

'Eino will be dealt with. *After* he has been induced to transfer the house to me.'

Nuritov gestured at the dead child, his face paler than ever. 'But what of... that still does not explain... *why?*'

Denis Druganin smiled gently upon the inspector, and said very softly: 'Because I enjoyed it.'

Nuritov made to speak again; would it be a condemnation, or another ill-fated question? He had heard more than enough, Konrad thought. He spoke, quickly, before the inspector could muster more than a syllable or two. 'Jakub Vasilescu is dead.'

Druganin laughed. 'My good fellow, he has been dead for more than two hundred years. This has not deterred my mother and her friends, as you have perhaps observed.'

Konrad smiled thinly. 'His spirit is now in The Malykt's care, as it ought long ago to have been.'

'Then you have done me a great service, and I thank you.' Druganin bowed gravely to Konrad, then paused, a slight frown crossing his smooth brow. 'Though I should like to know how you contrived it. For curiosity's sake, you understand.'

Konrad stood up, slowly. He was a little taller than Druganin, and he made the most of this advantage. Surreptitiously, he permitted just a *little* of his Malykant's presence to glimmer through, making a more imposing figure of himself.

Well, and why not? Nanda had spent *days* encouraging him to take an interest in the dramatic. Perhaps he was not such a poor student, after all.

But Nanda, who had hitherto stood in a silent stupor of distaste, now recovered herself. She moved, faster than thought, and took hold of one of Druganin's wrists. Her bare fingers to his bare skin; she would Read him. Konrad wanted to stop her, for what could she expect to see in such a mind save the worst, the very *worst,* of which mankind was capable? What could motivate her?

The worst was what she encountered, for she gave a choked gasp, and a rain of sudden tears wet her cheeks. '*How could you,*' she hissed, pain turning to fury in an instant. Her grip tightened upon his arm, her eyes burning with the kind of rage Konrad had never before seen in her.

But Druganin's amusement did not fade. 'Reader, are you?' he said, and only a slight narrowing of his eyes suggested that he found that information at all interesting. He looked at Nuritov again, and at Konrad. 'Which of you would like to be first? Shall it be you?' This last was directed to Nanda, with a smile Konrad could only describe as flirtatious.

Predatory.

Konrad's control melted away for the second time that day, though this was a different thing. Fury swamped his judgement, drowned his better feelings, smothered all rational thought. He heard himself say, with deceptive mildness: 'You realise, I hope, that the man who harms a child places himself forever beyond all possibility of forgiveness?'

Now, at last, he had Druganin's attention. Did the man see his own death approach, when he looked into Konrad's eyes? He should. He *must,* for Konrad was Konrad no longer; he was the Malykant again, resplendent in all his Master's deadly power, burning with the heat of his own rage.

But even this could not long subdue Druganin's infernal confidence. 'I am to receive no mercy, I collect,' he said, with a wry quirk of his lips. And he was fool enough to grab for Nanda — with what purpose in mind, Konrad could not imagine, for what could he now hope to achieve?

'None whatsoever,' said Konrad.

10

Konrad was not proud, later, of what he did to Druganin that day. Justice was his job, vengeance both his duty and his pride. But the revenge he enacted upon Denis Druganin was a particularly terrible one. He shuddered, later, to remember with what delight he had inflicted pain upon the shrinking murderer; with what unholy joy he had listened to the man's screams.

He tried not to think of it very often.

He could not feel, though, that the punishment had been unwarranted. Nor could Nanda, for in her deathly white face he had read a deep-seated approval for what he had done. Tasha had been furious at being left out, once she had heard of the full extent of Druganin's depravity. She had not yet forgiven Konrad for leaving her on Boredom Duty, as she put it, when she might have joined with him in punishing Druganin. As they made their slow, shiversome way back to Ekamet through the drifts of snow, their carriage's wheels groaning in protest, Tasha spent the entire journey staring out of the window, her face turned away from Konrad.

Nuritov... was a different matter altogether. The inspector was quiet on the journey home, deeply subdued. But then, so were they all. Even Konrad himself had rarely encountered so deeply unpleasant a case as that of the house at Divoro; poor Alexander had probably never experienced its like. Nanda regretted having forcibly dragged him along, but Konrad knew that the fault was his own. Had he never befriended Nuritov, the inspector would now be comfortably ensconced in his office in Ekamet, intent upon some important but less horrific case.

He must be deeply regretting the day he ever became acquainted with the Malykant.

Eino and Mrs. Holt, and Lilli and Marko, had been escorted to the village prior to their departure, and put into a passing stage-coach. Nanda would not even think of leaving until they were made safe, and tired though he was, Konrad would not argue. Eino dismissed all the servants, too, and the house was empty and silent when Konrad, Nanda and Nuritov finally took their leave.

But there had been the problem of the nameless child. She could not be abandoned, for all that they had been too late to help her. That fact alone tormented Konrad almost more than he could bear, for it could have turned out differently. Couldn't it? If he had realised Druganin's involvement sooner, kept a watch on him, set one of the serpents to tail him... the man would never have been able to slip away from them, to disappear so completely into the snow that there was no following him.

The child, whoever she was, might not have died.

The very least that they could do was ensure that she was returned home — if they *could*. Konrad flatly refused to make any attempt at reviving her departed spirit, not even for long enough to draw from her an idea of where her home lay. If he succeeded then she would, for a few moments, live again. She would remember Druganin, and everything he had done... no. Konrad could not, would not, risk that.

It fell to Nuritov's well-honed detective's instincts to come up with an alternative plan. 'There cannot be too many possibilities,' he observed. 'She must have come from somewhere nearby, for Druganin must have walked there on foot, and in deep snow. There is, I suspect, only the village of Divoro within that range, but I will enquire of Eino.'

Which he did, and soon confirmed his theory. After that, it did not take them so very long to discover which house the child had come from, for her absence had been noted in the village, and a search sent out for her.

Nuritov took it upon himself to manage the difficult task of returning the tiny, inert form to her parents.

'I do not think it wise,' Nanda had said, laying a hand upon his arm. Konrad agreed, for though the inspector had adopted a credible facade, it was clear that his true emotional state was still disordered.

'It is my duty,' he had said. 'I am the police.'

He had suffered Nan to go with him, in the end, but had rejected everybody else. Especially Konrad. When the two of them returned, they were both silent, pale and weary, and Konrad knew not what to say.

Druganin's corpse they left where it fell, alone in the room he had made into a place of nightmares. Konrad would leave word with Diana, and his body would be suitably disposed of. He would receive no burial. The bodies of murderers were typically burned by the Order, their ashes scattered upon a designated site sacred to The Malykt. It was no honour; rather, it was part of their torment. The Malykt ensured that the fate of their physical remains was as much a torment to their spirit as the rest of the... consequences... that He enacted upon them.

Konrad felt that even this would not be enough for Druganin.

The journey home passed in almost unbroken silence, their minds too busy and their spirits too low for conversation. Upon their eventual arrival in Ekamet, very late at night, Nuritov and Tasha were set down directly outside the inspector's house. Nuritov departed the coach with a polite nod of his head to both Konrad and Nanda, and a few murmured words of farewell; Tasha merely gave an ironic salute.

Then they were gone. Konrad closed up the door and signalled to the coachman, suffering a mixed array of feelings. Alexander was just tired, most likely, and emotionally wearied by everything that had passed. He would be all right.

Wouldn't he?

'A night's rest or two will set him to rights,' said Nanda, as sensitive to his thoughts as ever. Sometimes, she did not need to touch a person to understand their feelings with startling accuracy.

'I am sure you're right,' Konrad replied, with an attempt at a smile. He hesitated before adding: 'And... and you? Will a night's rest set you to rights?'

Nanda looked away. They had not discussed the details of what she had seen in Druganin's mind, and Konrad did not wish to. But if it were to trouble Nanda, he knew he must do what he could for her. And he would, gladly, even if it meant sharing in that terrible vision with which she had burdened herself.

'I will be all right,' she said, after a longer silence than Konrad was comfortable with.

'Nan... if you need me—'

'I will be all right,' she repeated, more firmly, and Konrad subsided into silence.

'But,' she said sometime later. 'Thank you.'

Konrad nodded.

'I am here if you need me, too.'

He managed a smile. It was a poor one, but it was enough, for Nanda smiled back. But the smile quickly faded. 'I have been thinking,' she said.

'That is sometimes unwise.'

She acknowledged this point with a slight inclination of her head, but continued: 'About Eino, and his terrible fear. Do you think... do you think that a person's organs retain any trace of their personality? Their spirit?'

Konrad blinked, confused by the apparent randomness of the question. 'I do not know. I have never had cause to give the matter any thought. Why do you ask?'

She took a deep breath, her mouth set in a grim line. 'The Eino I used to know was never so helplessly fearful as we found him. If the heart he received was torn from a living body, if it was taken in a moment of terrible agony and fear... would Eino feel some echo of that? Is that why he was so prone to fits of terror?'

This was a disturbing thought, and one which Konrad did not wish to dwell upon too long. 'Perhaps,' he allowed. 'But. His fears manifested the most around the subject of ghosts, did they not? And then we discovered the ghost of Jakub Vasilescu, a malevolent figure if ever there was one. His mother must have known all about him. She was probably terrified of that particular ghost herself, and may have imparted some of that to her son — knowingly, or otherwise.'

'Perhaps that's it,' said Nanda, sounding relieved. But she frowned, and he saw in her face that she was troubled still. 'I had better keep an eye on him,' she decided. 'He and Alina. They live within reach of my mother's house, I understand. It will not be too difficult to visit, from time to time.'

Konrad smiled, touched by her endless capacity to care. 'I am sure they will both appreciate that.'

Nanda nodded, and managed another smile in return. This one held, just about, and he decided to capitalise upon it if he could.

'How about a midnight banquet?' he ventured. He was unwilling to leave Nanda at her own house alone, and equally unwilling — though he would never acknowledge as much — to be left at *his* house alone.

'I do not think I could eat,' said Nanda.

'A small one? Light on the viands, heavy on the tea?'

Nanda thought that over, and rewarded him at last with another smile — a real one, this time. 'That would be delightful.'

'Then, madam, my kitchen and dining room are at your disposal.'

Her smile turned into an echo of her usual, impish grin as she said: 'Your poor cook will positively detest us.'

'Undying hatred,' Konrad agreed.

SNOWBOUND

1

The proud city of Ekamet, jewel of the realm of Assevan, wears the pale, icy verdure of the Bone Forest like a mantle, shrouded as it is on all sides by miles of contorted, thick-clustering trees — except, of course, for where its ancient buildings give way to the sea. Out beyond the confines of the Bones, the plains stretch for many miles farther north. Drowned in snow for much of the year, they are loosely scattered with knots of haggard evergreens, and an occasional stout little town braving all the worst that winds and storms can throw at it. Some of these are built from brick and wood and stone, and endure; others are just for the winter, the walls of their dwellings wrought from stacked blocks of snow and translucent ice.

They are not always rude, primitive structures. Houses of extraordinary grace rise from the blanketing snows, thriving upon the bone-deep chill of the Assevan winter. Just such a one has lately sprung up unusually close to the city — only three miles north of its gates.

It had not been there for long before it began to attract notice, for even in a realm of wonders it must excite remark. A castle in miniature, its jumble of turrets and towers glint, clear and cold, under the wan winter sun; its grand doors, exquisitely carved, stand open, an invitation to all; it even possesses a semblance of windows, each pane cut from translucent ice. Word of the marvel spread from town to town, and at last to Ekamet itself, whereupon it caused an instant sensation — for two things about the ice castle excite comment. One, its extraordinary beauty; for its ice mosaics, its snow sculptures, and carved furniture of snow-dusted ice make a fairy palace fit for kings and queens.

The other, the elaborate designs built into its soaring walls. Wrought with splendid skill, they depict vast summer trees, their leaf-laden branches spreading in icy pallor across the walls; bears and birds, fish and flowers darting from room to room; and in the great hall, a collection of human figures, arms spread wide, suspended a few feet from the floor, their snow-white faces staring sightlessly down upon those whose footsteps and wondering chatter disturb their icy slumber.

These number five, extraordinarily detailed. Lifelike, if such still, silent figures could ever be called such. Days passed before anyone grew bold enough to touch the sculptures upon the walls, to brush at the snow that formed the feet and legs of the five watchers.

Then, a shoe was revealed.

It was not, like its many counterparts, carved from glittering snow. A mere ordinary boot, of old black-dyed leather frozen stiff, it belonged to a giant of a man, his broad, bear-like form swathed in a heavy cloak of snow, his thick hair a halo of pallid ice around his head. His eyes were closed, his face still beneath its layer of enshrouding snow.

These were no sculptures.

Five dead faces stared, glassy-eyed, from the walls of the ice palace, ringing the great hall in macabre splendour. Five glacial figures hung in forlorn companionship, but one was given a prominence not shared by his fellows: a youngish man, slender of figure and well-dressed, set higher than the rest, and positioned directly opposite the grand, wide-flung doors.

Rumour claimed that, alone of the five, he was not wholly encased in ice; for he (it was said by some of those who had passed that way) had more than once been observed to open his eyes.

And while no one could be found to confirm the rumour, this report, too, winged its way back to Ekamet.

***

Konrad Savast sat at the table in his breakfast-parlour. His cook had provided a sumptuous array of breakfast dishes for his delectation; a fire blazed merrily in the hearth; and he sat at his ease in his favourite morning coat, surrounded by comforts yet feeling anything but serene.

For on this frigid morning — unlike nearly all the preceding mornings, for more years than Konrad cared to think of — he was not alone.

'I do so enjoy toast,' Nanda commented, spreading a thick layer of butter upon her third slice. 'And this is the very best, Konrad. I do not often envy you the luxury you wallow in, but I believe I shall make an exception of your breakfast table.'

'Wallow?' he echoed. 'Do I?'

Nanda cast a considering eye over the figure Konrad made, lounging in an upholstered chair before the fire, a cup of steaming chocolate before him and a plate laden with perfectly cooked delicacies. 'Is this in any way unusual for you?'

'No.'

Nanda inclined her head, gracious in victory. 'Precisely.'

Konrad grunted something inaudible in reply. Even he could not have said what it was.

Her eyes twinkling, Nanda consumed her toast with leisurely relish, and moved on to coffee and eggs. Unlike Konrad, she was fully dressed for the day, clad in a garnet-coloured gown with white frills at the collar and cuffs. A thick shawl draped over her shoulders and arms, but despite this and the blaze roaring away not four feet from her chair, she did not appear warm. No roses flourished in her pale cheeks; she looked white, even more so than usual, and despite her obvious determination to appear lively, Konrad detected more than one sign of weariness in her.

'Are you warm enough?' he said.

'Perfectly, thank you.'

'Your chair could perhaps edge just a bit nearer to the fire, if you wanted.'

'Doubtless, but I should be sorry to set my boots alight. I am especially fond of this pair.'

'Another shawl? I'll send a maid to fetch one from your room—'

Nanda set down her porcelain cup with a ringing snap. 'I am well,' she informed him, in a crisp tone which brooked no argument. 'Please don't fuss.'

'I'm concerned for you.' Unsure what to do with his hands, Konrad picked up his own cup and gulped chocolate.

She softened, slightly. 'You need not be.'

He had no response to make to that, for how could he argue? Nanda had never voluntarily taken him into her confidence. He had learned by accident that she was, in some way, ill; she had never chosen to elaborate as to how, or what it meant for her.

So he sat and drank, burning his mouth on the sweet, scalding beverage, and wracked his brains for some way of supporting her, but without seeming to do so.

He came up with nothing. Nan was far too clever for such subterfuge. She would catch him at it in no time, and he knew better than to imagine that she would appreciate what she persisted in terming his "fussing".

But he had no cause for complaint, for Nanda had been a guest at Bakar House for over a week. Never had he ever thought she would consent to stay so long. Upon their return from the town of Divoro, and the house party they had unwisely attended there, Nanda had accepted his offer of accommodation at once and gone, subdued, to bed. She had not emerged from her chamber until two days later, whereupon she avoided discussing any of the events of those few, harrowing days with Konrad.

He knew better than to force the issue. She grieved for Kati Vinter, her mother's friend; for Alen Petranov, an old acquaintance of hers; and for the smallest, most heart-breaking victim of all, a child carelessly slain by the would-be heir of the house. Konrad could not cease to think of these things himself, nor of the dark secrets the house held — chief among them the coven of necromantic sorcerers that lurked among the shadows and the depths of the grand old house. He wanted to talk of these things, but Nanda did not; so he brooded over them alone.

He had, upon returning home, met speedily with Diana Valentina, head of The Malykt's Order. Troubled by his news, she had dispatched several excellent men and women of the Order to investigate the house at Divoro right away.

They had found… nothing. No coven; not even the slain bodies of their victims. The house possessed the eerie, silent air of a building long abandoned, and not the smallest signs of life, or of recent habitation, had been discovered.

It was as though the party and its horrific events had never happened at all.

If only that were true.

Inspector Nuritov — no, Konrad corrected himself; *Alexander* — had come three times to dine with them. Konrad read in the detective's mild eyes a sense of deep-seated trouble, and suspected that he came to air his distress among those who had endured those terrible days with him. But he, too, bowed to Nanda's obvious disinclination and held his peace.

And so the deaths of two guests, the slaughter of the child, and the predations of some of the house's most depraved inhabitants went unmentioned — until later that same morning, when Konrad had but just set aside (with customary regret) his comfortable morning-coat in favour of more correct attire. Nanda, full of toast and brittle cheer, had taken herself away to her favourite parlour, the small, snug one with the green silk furnishings and large, bright windows, to while away the morning with a book. For all her apparent disdain for Konrad's luxuries, she clearly took great pleasure in the sharing of them, at least at present. Or was it the company she sought? Tough as she was, she was not impervious to horror. If she was minded to cling to Konrad for a little while, Konrad was in no way disposed to discourage it.

The doorbell rang. Ensconced in the library with a newspaper, Konrad paid no heed to the low, murmured tones of his butler, Gorev, as he intercepted and interrogated the visitor. But the footsteps which shortly afterwards approached the library door struck him as familiar, and as he formed that thought, there came a tap upon the door and Alexander Nuritov's face appeared, peeking apologetically around the door.

'Your butler said I might find you here,' he remarked.

'He has instructions to admit you whenever I am at home.' Konrad put aside his paper, and remembered to smile a welcome. The inspector had become something of a friend in recent weeks, but Konrad — so long devoid of friends, save perhaps for Nanda — had forgotten how such a relationship worked.

Thankfully, Alexander did not seem minded to take umbrage when Konrad frequently forgot the pleasantries. A mild-mannered man, he made no objection to the long silences when Konrad forgot to talk, nor was he offended by Konrad's lack of confidences when he did not. Today, though, he was different. The passage of a week and more had slightly dulled the impressions of Divoro, so Konrad had previously judged, for the distress had faded somewhat from his face, and he had stopped fidgeting with his pipe. But now it was all come back. Alexander's favourite pipe was in his hand, unlit; as he stood, apparently unsure how to begin, he raised it to his lips and held it there, though there was nothing to smoke. His eyes searched Konrad's face, and then travelled restlessly around the crammed bookshelves of the library.

'What is it?' Konrad said, when still the inspector did not speak.

Alexander sighed, and half-sat, half-fell into the nearest chair. 'Have you heard the news?'

Konrad glanced, puzzled, at the paper he had just set down. 'Which particular piece of it?'

'Oh, it is not in the newspaper. Not yet. Word of mouth only. I had it from two of my constables this morning, who cite two separate sources, both street-folk.'

Konrad waited.

'There is a new ice-house,' Alexander said, too heavily for the banality of the subject matter, and Konrad frowned. 'A ways north. Splendid place, apparently, like a castle, only much smaller. Turrets, that sort of thing. Sculptures. No word as to who might have had the time, the money and the motive to build such a place in the middle of nowhere.'

'You did not come here just to tell me about a minor architectural wonder,' Konrad said.

'Ah — no, I did not.' Alexander lit his pipe, and inhaled. 'The story is so absurd I hardly know whether to imagine it the truth, but it could be. It could be.'

'What story?' Konrad concealed his impatience as best he could. It was not like the inspector to ramble so.

'They say that some of the sculptures are not sculptures at all.' Alexander puffed twice upon the pipe, exhaling fragrant smoke. 'They are… people. Too convincing to be mere carvings. There are five of them, up on the walls.'

Konrad stilled. 'People?' he repeated.

'Stone dead. Packed up there in snow.'

Picturing this, Konrad was briefly bereft of words. So macabre a display was… unheard of, even in his long experience as the Malykant. Who would go to such trouble? What could possibly be the reason for it? 'Are you sure?' he said at last.

'No,' said Alexander. 'Because it's also said that… well, that with one of them, the eyes sometimes open. That cannot be, of course, so it is likely that the whole report is mere rumour, or superstition—' he stopped, for Konrad had rocketed out of his chair. 'What is it?'

Konrad could not say what it was in the inspector's words that had so electrified him. He only knew that he was gripped by a fierce urgency. 'My carriage, five minutes,' he informed an astonished Alexander. 'I'll fetch Nanda.'

2

The pale, winter-bare trees of the Bone Forest sailed by beyond the windows as Konrad's carriage made its way, at inadvisable speed, due north. He'd told his coachman to hurry, and the man had taken the order seriously. Wheels spun and slid on the snowy road and the three occupants endured the journey with white-knuckled grip upon their seats.

Konrad sat in grim silence. He knew he was disturbing Nanda and alarming Alexander, but he could find nothing to say to reassure them. A knot of steel had his stomach in a vice, and breathing had become challenge enough. If his fears were correct, nothing he could say could prepare Nanda for what lay ahead.

The moment the coach slowed, Konrad flung the door open and jumped out. He sank up to his ankles in powdery snow, and spared a moment's futile wish that he had thought to change his attire before barrelling out of the city. Nothing for it but to ignore the slow seep of melting snow inside his city shoes—

He stopped dead, eight or nine paces into the trees. A clearing opened up ahead, a wide space hosting one of the most elaborate and exquisite snow structures Konrad had ever beheld. The sheer grace of its turrets stole his breath; the glitter of wan sunlight on icy, perfect windows mesmerised him.

When recognition hit, it hit hard.

'That's the…' he began as Nanda came up next to him. 'The—the house at Divoro.' It was; he did not imagine it. The house was a perfect replica in every feature of the near-palatial mansion he and

Nanda had recently attended as guests, only this version was far smaller.

'Gods,' whispered Nanda.

Konrad ran. His long legs devoured the distance between the road and the pair of great, ice-carved doors which graced the front of the house. They stood half-open; Konrad darted inside and came to a skidding stop in the centre of the great hall.

Suspended before him, halfway up the opposing wall, hung the frozen shape of a slender man, arms outspread. Two figures flanked him on either side: to his left was a bear of a man with broad shoulders and a mane of ice-crusted hair, a young woman with wide, snowy skirts his next neighbour. On the other wall hung a second woman and another man. Few identifying characteristics marked these snowbound sculptures; identical in posture, each with out-flung arms and raised chins, they stared sightlessly at the domed ceiling of their ice prison.

Konrad turned in a slow circle, and then again, his mind blank with horror. Despite their uniform presentation, despite the featureless, pristine snow which blanketed their faces, their limbs and their clothes, he knew who they were. He knew who all of them were.

He did not realise Nanda had caught up with him until he heard her choke. 'Eino,' she gasped in a terrible, hoarse voice. 'Lilli? Marko? It... this cannot be.'

'Eino Holt,' said Konrad bleakly. 'Alina Holt. Marko Bekk. Lilli Lahti. And— and Denis Druganin.' Their host at last week's house party at Divoro; his mother; their fellow guests.

Nanda stood like a statue, barely breathing. Alexander came up on Konrad's other side and stood in a like silence, and for some moments no one spoke.

'I thought they were safe,' Nanda finally said, and her voice broke on the final word. 'We put them on the stage — they should have reached home days ago.'

They had gone to some trouble to ensure that the house was empty before they'd departed themselves, and so it had seemed. Except for the body of Denis Druganin. Konrad had killed the man himself, and left his misshapen remains splendidly alone in his own chamber of horrors. He'd thought the Order would have cleaned it up.

Apparently not.

Konrad took a slow breath, mentally kicking himself. Time enough for self-reproach later; he had to focus. If only the fist of steel in his belly would let up, let him breathe—

'Savast,' said Alexander, gripping his arm. 'Steady.'

Konrad did not want to imagine what the good inspector had seen in his face just then. He swallowed down his horror and regret, thrust away fear, retained only the slow, simmering burn of anger that warmed his chilled limbs and fired his heart. Fury: that he would keep.

'I am well,' he said, his words ringing with a strength he was yet only halfway to feeling. He went to Nanda, steadied her with a light touch to her hair and a reassuring grip of her fingers. She barely seemed to feel it. Her pale eyes turned up to his with an expression of heart-breaking sadness — and a rage to match his own. 'That damned coven,' she hissed. 'We should have stayed, Konrad, until we'd found them. Until we'd wiped them out.'

'I know.' He kissed her forehead. 'This time, we will.'

He moved a few paces away, seeking a moment's quiet reflection. There were messages here, and he needed to read them clearly. The coven of Divoro must be behind this grisly display, but Konrad struggled to guess at their motivation. Yes, he had deprived them of Druganin; by the man's own account, he had been their tool, one who arranged for them to receive a regular supply of dead (or, still worse, living) organs for their twisted purposes. The inclusion of Druganin's corpse in this little pageant might be best taken as a declaration of war; simple enough there.

But Eino Holt? Alina, his mother? She was a Vasilescu by birth, one of their own, and that made a blood relative of Eino, too — even if the pair had been disowned years before. What's more, Eino had only recently received the benefit of their questionable assistance: the substitution of a healthy heart for his own, faulty one had saved his life. Why had they taken that trouble, only to slay him anyway?

And what of Lilli and Marko? They had, to Konrad's knowledge, no connection with the Vasilescu family or the house at Divoro at all. They had been invited as Eino's friends. That was all.

'Why this, then?' Konrad said aloud. 'What is this for?' In truth, he knew, and that knowledge sickened him too much to say it aloud.

'Revenge,' said Alexander quietly. 'For Druganin.' He pointed at the still forms of Lilli Lahti and Marko Bekk. Pointing next at Eino and his mother, he added, 'And revenge for their betrayal.'

'That is half of it,' Konrad agreed.

Alexander shot him a questioning look, but before Konrad could elaborate, Nanda spoke.

'It's a challenge,' she whispered.

'A challenge,' Konrad agreed. 'And a trap.'

'They know that one of us killed Druganin,' she went on. 'Perhaps not which. But have they guessed why?'

In other words, had the coven at Divoro realised that the Malykant had been a guest at Eino Holt's party? That The Malykt's foremost servant had delivered the brutal justice Druganin had received? Perhaps. Konrad had dispatched Druganin according to his custom: a sharp, sturdy bone from each of his slain victims, delivered through the heart. But — he blanched to recall — he had not been finished with Druganin's corpse with that alone. He had... gone further. Done worse.

Well, the man had shown up with the body of a six-year-old child in his hands. He'd shown not the smallest flicker of remorse for stealing her life. Konrad had been forced to open the torso of a dead little girl and mutilate her small, delicate bones; her infant blood still stained the cuffs of the shirt he'd worn that day.

Her rib bone had gone through Druganin's eye.

His mind shied away from a clear recollection of the state he'd left the body in at last, but he could not think that the presence of three extra rib bones in strategic places had been particularly obvious anymore.

He drifted nearer to the inert form of Druganin, straining to discern detail through the thick layer of snow that packed his corpse. Were the weapons he'd made of Kati and Alen and the little girl's bones still there? He could not tell.

Druganin's eyes snapped open.

Konrad stumbled back, colliding with the inspector.

Dark, frozen eyes regarded Konrad with icy indifference. Then, slowly, the snow-crusted lids lowered again.

There had been not a trace of recognition in those dead eyes, but Konrad's heart had taken off at a gallop and would not be soothed. He was alive. 'How can he be *alive*?' Konrad gasped.

'Is he, though?' said Nanda, and it was her turn to steady Konrad.

He felt her hand at the small of his back and took a breath, grateful for the comforting touch. 'He has more animation than is typical for a corpse, but that is not necessarily the same thing.'

Serpents, Konrad called, and flung the thought far and wide. He had not heard from them for some days; were they near?

He waited.

At length, the thin, ear-splitting tones of Ootapi answered him. *Master.*

I need you. Immediately.

We are at a party, Ootapi informed him. *There is fresh meat, blood—*

Konrad hastened to cut off any further enumeration of the party's delights. His mind shied away from envisioning what kind of a "party" might impress a pair of bloodthirsty ghost snakes. *This is better,* he informed the serpent.

It cannot be. Pure disbelief rang through every word.

Come and see. Bring Eetapi.

They arrived moments later, invisible to all but Konrad, a pair of chill presences drifting silently at ceiling height.

Eetapi spoke first. *You forgot both of our deathdays,* she hissed. *Again. But… now we forgive you.*

This is ten deathdays all at once, Ootapi agreed.

These are not gifts, Konrad said sternly. *These are victims and we are here to help them.*

Oh. The serpents spoke together, equally disappointed.

Tell me. Are these people dead?

Oh, yes! Eetapi all but sang the words. *Stone dead.*

But?

But what?

That one— Konrad pointed *—retains some muscle function.*

He watched as his serpents sailed towards Druganin and conducted a thorough — he hoped — investigation of the circumstances. Nanda and Alexander waited, watchful; they could not see the snakes as he could, but they knew by now how he worked.

His spirit remains, Ootapi at length announced.

'No.' Konrad, forgetting himself, spoke the word aloud. 'It cannot be.' He'd dispatched Druganin himself, by the most final, irreversible means at his disposal. Nobody came back from that.

Ootapi's response radiated irritation. *I say that it is.*

He is right, Master, said Eetapi. *They are all still here.*

What?

All their spirits linger, she repeated, patiently. *But, they are… asleep.*

Asleep?

I do not know how else to call it. They are here, but they are not alert.

That, too, was bizarre. Ghosts did not really sleep. Why would they need to?

What were these five doing lingering over their corpses? What held them here, if they were not conscious enough to make that decision for themselves? *Serpents,* he said. *How are they here?*

They are bound to their bodies. As we are, Master.

Konrad let out a slow breath, his heart sinking. He'd been afraid to hear that answer.

A week ago, or a little more, he had encountered the long-dead body of a man called Jakub Vasilescu. Despite the many, many years which must have passed since his death, the man had been, to some degree, aware. His ghost had never passed on; somehow, it had retained residence of its own body, but not to the extent of being either fully alive or fully undead. He was, in effect, haunting his own corpse.

Not, Konrad knew, without considerable help from the coven — his own descendants.

The effect was not unfamiliar to Konrad. It was much the same thing he achieved himself, with his serpents' assistance, whenever he encountered a freshly-slain corpse. For a limited time after the unfortunate victim's expiration, the serpents could bind up what remained of his or her soul and force it back into the body, permitting the corpse to speak of what had happened. Konrad had solved many a murder that way. It was simple, direct, efficient — and difficult to achieve. Even the serpents could not hold a spirit that way for long.

How, then, had the coven kept Vasilescu in an essentially similar state, and for so long?

Was that what they were now doing to the Holts, and Marko Bekk, and Lilli Lahti?

Was that what afflicted Druganin?

'We need to find out more about this coven,' he said grimly. 'But carefully. I fear they're more dangerous than we imagine.'

Alexander nodded. He had his pipe in one hand; the other fumbled for a match. Both were shaking. 'Shall I send my men to fetch down these poor souls, or shall your Order handle it?'

'Neither.'

Alexander glanced, questioningly, Konrad's way.

'Leave them there.'

'Konrad—' Nanda began.

'I know,' he said. 'But something is badly wrong here, and until we find out what's afoot, they stay up there.' It cost him to utter such words, and when the look Nanda turned on him proved to be both pleading and disgusted he almost gave in.

But he could not. Not yet.

Alexander lit his pipe, and puffed in silence.

'We cannot leave them here alone,' Nanda said at last.

'They won't be alone. I am sending Diana out here.'

3

From the moment he had seen the dead face of Denis Druganin suspended above the icy hall of the snow castle, Konrad had known that his return to the house at Divoro was inevitable. Few prospects could be less welcome to him. He had driven away from the dismal place with a feeling of profound thankfulness that he need never go there again; fool of a hope. Eino Holt had called the house cursed. Absurd superstition, Konrad had thought then. But Holt was right to a degree: a dark past and darker future hung around the house like a suffocating shroud, stifling everything that ought to have been good and beautiful about it.

At least he need not go back alone, and unprepared.

'Olya Vasilescu,' he said to Alexander later that morning. 'The second of three sisters. Ela was the eldest, Alina the youngest. Alina is — was — Eino's mother. Olya is — *was* — Denis's.'

They had adjourned to the inspector's office at the police headquarters, there to raid the records for any information about the family that had built, and subsequently corrupted, the house. The room was a monument to the inspector's habits: no fewer than three pipes littered the desk, amid stacks of books and papers Alexander had, presumably, employed for the solving of a case in the near or distant past, and never restored to whatever had been their original position. More such piles occupied two of four chairs; these were slightly shabby, like the coat that Alexander always wore. It was not, Konrad thought, that the inspector was either poor or mean; he simply grew attached to things and remained so, however threadbare they became.

It struck Konrad for the first time how little he knew of the inspector's private life. They had been at least friendly acquaintances for years, and had often worked together. Yet, Alexander never mentioned a family, or a wife, or anything outside of his job as detective.

Neither, of course, did Konrad.

'So Ela inherited the house?' Alexander scrawled notes in a worn old notebook, its binding coming loose.

'Yes. According to Alina, she hated the place and was so desperate to be rid of it, she sold it for a song. Much to the fury of Olya, who had other ideas.'

'Hence the plot to put it into Eino's hands.'

'Which cannot have been much to her taste. I wonder why they did not engineer its passing into Denis's hands to begin with?'

'How might they have achieved that? Once Ela had sold the house, I suppose it was no longer possible to get it back except by purchasing it.'

'The Vasilescus must be poor,' Konrad mused. 'And the Druganins likewise. I wonder what has become of their fortune? They must once have been richer than kings, to build such a mansion.'

Alexander nodded, and made another note. 'A cruel piece of irony, isn't it? That the despised youngest sister and her son, expelled from the family in disgrace, should be the ones with the power to retrieve their house.'

'But not the inclination. They used Eino's heart to force the issue.'

'I wonder,' said Alexander, still writing, 'where Ela Vasilescu is.'

A good point. 'And Olya,' Konrad said. 'Though I imagine she is with her coven.'

'Wherever they are.'

'At Divoro. I am convinced of it. Diana found nothing there, but I am more inclined to think that they were successfully hiding than that they were gone.'

'Why?' The inspector set down his notebook and took up his pipe, puffing upon it as he gazed at Konrad with keen attention.

Konrad took a moment to sort through his thoughts. 'Perhaps because they have shown so much attachment to the house. Such lengths they went to, to get it back! That place is steeped in their family's history — and until recently, it was still the residence of their star ancestor, Jakub Vasilescu. Everything they have, everything they care about, is there. Would they leave it, unless forced?'

'I think you are right,' said Alexander slowly. 'But, recall. They left it for long enough to build that snow palace.'

'And to… decorate it. Yes.' Was that why Diana had not found them, when she had searched? The Vasilescu coven *had* been gone — albeit, Konrad was still convinced, temporarily.

'I think they would go back.'

'I think so, too. But whether or not they have just yet, is a different question. What do you suppose was the primary point of the snow palace, and all those murders? Do you think it was aimed at you?'

Konrad was pleased to note that the inspector could now speak of it without his hands shaking. He looked his usual calm self once more, though his composure did not necessarily reflect the state of his thoughts. 'Yes,' he said simply. 'But, I am not yet sure why. Is it only revenge? That seems… insufficient. Too petty, perhaps. Druganin alone was proof of the resolve and the ruthlessness this family is capable of. Eino was proof of how little they are affected by sentiment, or even family loyalty. Are they so consumed with grief — or anger — at the death of Denis as to go to so much trouble just for vengeance?'

'He was Olya's son. Perhaps she was fond of him.'

'Perhaps she was. Then again, she and her coven were more than happy to use him as a tool, as long as it suited them. Their behaviour thus far has indicated a coolness, a total lack of emotion, which is incompatible with a display of enraged passion now. I think that the snow replica of the house and its contents are of a piece with the rest: carefully thought out. Calculated. Aimed at eliciting a certain, desired response. Only I cannot guess what response they are hoping for.' Except to lure him back to Divoro, but even then: why?

Alexander set down his pipe. 'I will see what I can find out about the family.'

'Thank you.' Konrad rose from his chair. 'Oh. May I borrow Tasha from you?'

'I'll see if I can find her.'

'Thanks. She saw a lot more of those cellars under the house than the rest of us did. I want to ask her some questions.' And, when he went back to Divoro, he wanted her with him. If he was going to face the coven again, he wanted as many supernatural allies at his back as he could command.

Back in his own library at Bakar House, he sat at his desk with a sheet of paper before him and a pencil in hand. *Serpents*, he called. *I require assistance.*

Yes, Master, came both voices at once, chiming discordantly in his head.

Must you do that?

Yes. The disharmony was different this time, but still repulsive.

Konrad sighed, and rested his forehead in one cool hand. *The cellars at Divoro. You explored them thoroughly, did you not?*

Yes, Master.

I want you to describe them to me. What's there, how they are laid out. Everything.

He ought to have known better.

They go on for miles, said Eetapi, and began to sing in haunting tones, *miles and miles and miles and miles…*

All right, Konrad interrupted. *They are extensive. And?*

Cold, chimed in Ootapi. *Frost on the walls, and the water all frozen.*

Water? Where?

A lake, deep below.

Konrad adjusted his ideas. He ceased to think in terms of cellars, and pictured instead a network of subterranean caves. It was not unheard of for lakes to form, far below the surface of the earth. Though for one to freeze there was, perhaps, less usual.

Good, he said, encouraged. He set pencil to paper and began to draw. He had walked some little way into those caves himself; that was how he had encountered the unusually talkative body of Jakub Vasilescu. He drew, as near as he could remember, the passages he had walked down, and added the large chamber in which Jakub's bier had lain. Now that he came to think of it, those passages had not had the appearance of naturally-formed structures; someone had dug their way into the caves. How long ago?

What lies beyond these areas? He asked of his serpents, indicating the blank expanse of paper with a sweep of his hand. *I would fill this space with a map of your making.*

Many passages, said Eetapi.

Excellent. In which direction do they tend?

All directions.

Konrad massaged the space between his eyes. *Ootapi?*

Yes, Master?

Do you have better information?

No, Master.

Konrad went to screw up the paper in sheer frustration, but thought better of it. Perhaps Tasha would prove more useful. *Very well,* he said, as calmly as he could. *Tell me, then, everything you do remember. There were people in some places?*

Oh, yes! Said Eetapi, energised. *A great many!*

Alarmed, Konrad sat up. A great many? Just how big was this coven? If they were as numerous as all that, he would need more than Tasha and the serpents when he went after them. He should take Diana, half the Order—

He remembered who he was talking to.

Define "a great many", Eetapi.

She thought. *As many people as there are eggs in a clutch.*

Not helpful. Konrad's knowledge of the breeding habits of snakes was not profound, but he did know that, depending upon the breed, a typical clutch of eggs could contain anything from half a dozen to over a hundred. *How many is that?*

I have just told you.

The snakes, and perhaps Konrad's sanity, were saved by the arrival of Tasha.

Not that Konrad knew anything about this until her voice spoke from a mere six inches distant. 'Are you *that* bored?'

'I don't draw for my own amusement. I want your help with this.' The room being, ostensibly, empty, he added, 'Where have you left your body?'

'None of your business.'

'For that matter, why have you left your body?'

'That's none of your business either. What do you want me to do?'

Konrad spent a few minutes apprising the little *lamaeni* of the day's events. He expected some form of sarcastic commentary, but she listened in silence.

When he had finished, she said: 'I believe they understand you perfectly.'

'What do you mean?'

'It's the perfect way to get your attention. Pique your interest, make you angry, add a few layers of guilt, and you will go chasing down there at your earliest convenience.'

'All right. Yes. I had worked that out for myself. But why do you imagine they want me to go chasing down there?'

'If Druganin's been blinking, he's probably been talking, too.'

'So?'

'They know who killed him, and they can probably work out why.'

'So they know who I am.'

'Undoubtedly.'

'What could they want with the Malykant?'

'I don't know,' said Tasha, and added cheerily, 'but you're about to find out.'

'How exciting.'

'Do you know, I think it just might be.'

'In all the wrong ways. Why don't you help me not get myself killed, and fill in this map for me?'

'Killed? I doubt that's the plan.' But she took up the pencil — which, to Konrad's eyes, whirled by itself into the empty air — and began to sketch out an extensive network of passages, chambers and caves. The way she drew them, some appeared naturally formed while others had the neat proportions and squared corners of man-made rooms and corridors. The caves had probably been inhabited for generations. 'It would be such a waste.'

'Fitting retribution, however.'

'Maybe. But you don't believe that's the reason either.'

Konrad wondered how she could tell. 'I do not. I wonder if it has anything to do with Jakub Vasilescu?'

'The corpse? But you dispatched him to your Master's tender care, did not you?'

'I did. Perhaps they want him back.'

'Plausible. They aren't to know you have no such power.'

'I wonder what they think I can do.'

Tasha actually giggled. 'You have heard the stories, I'm sure.'

'The Malykant striding through the dark of the night, striking down wrongdoers with malevolent glee? Dark cloak billowing in an eerie wind, eyes aglow with fire and ice, The Malykt's will blazing from every pore?'

'All of which, you'll allow, is the truth.'

'If I had fire and ice in my eyes I think I would feel it.'

'Maybe not that part.'

'And as for malevolent glee—'

'Don't even try to deny it.'

Konrad fell into a slightly injured silence.

The door quietly opened as he was thus engaged, and Gorev, his butler, appeared. 'A young gentleman to see you, sir,' he said. 'I understand it is a matter of some urgency.'

'Show him in.'

Moments later, Konrad's visitor all but ran into the room. His lanky frame, flyaway dark hair and prominent cheekbones looked familiar, though Konrad could not put a name to the face; an initiate of the Order, he thought. 'My lord,' gasped the boy, out of breath — from what, running?

'I am no lord,' said Konrad. 'Sir will suffice.'

'Sir,' said the boy. 'Miss Valentina requests your presence at the castle, right away.'

'Which castle? The snowy one?'

'Yes, sir. They're talking. She said you would understand.'

'*Talk*— right.' Konrad was out of his chair and at the door in a matter of seconds, almost mowing the poor boy down in his haste. 'Tash,' he called over his shoulder. 'You're with me.'

'Yes, *sir,*' came Tasha's disembodied voice.

The initiate's eyes widened, though whether it was the lack of visible company that troubled him, or the sarcasm Tasha imbued into the honorific, Konrad did not wait to find out.

4

Diana Valentina stood in the great hall of the macabre snow castle, surrounded by underlings. Her relative youth — she was, Konrad thought, barely thirty — had not prevented her from rising to the very top of The Malykt's Order, and no wonder. She was shrewd, highly intelligent, and had a razor-sharp focus Konrad envied. When she was around, things simply got done. Obstacles were of no moment whatsoever.

She did not turn to look as Konrad approached, but began speaking the moment he was within hearing. 'We've been trying to draw them out,' she told him. 'I've brought all our best ghostspeakers down here, and they — well, for a while it seemed that nothing could do it. But then one of them spoke. That one.' She pointed to Eino's corpse.

'What did he say?'

'Nothing very coherent. Mostly apologies, though to whom I couldn't say. He seemed upset. And that set the others off. For a while, they were all babbling at once.'

Babbling. The word was dismissive, and Konrad wanted to object. But he held his peace. These particular people were real to him because he had known them all in life, albeit briefly; to Diana, they were another day's work. 'Nobody said anything significant, or useful?'

'It was hard to distinguish much in the hubbub. I don't think they imparted any real information. Most of it was, I think, pleading or screaming or abject apologies. Except for this one.' She pointed out

Denis. 'He spoke so low that I couldn't discern a single word, but his manner was… different. He was in no way upset. I didn't like his composure. It seemed wrong.'

It would at that. Konrad had cut down Denis at the height of the man's powers, single-handedly destroying all his carefully-laid plans for the future. And he hadn't been kind. He had made Denis Druganin suffer. Why wasn't the severed spirit more disturbed? He'd been a man of near unnatural composure in life, this was true, but for him to carry that all the way to the grave and beyond was… chilling.

'They're silent now,' Konrad pointed out. 'What stopped them?'

Diana shrugged, and pushed a stray, dark curl out of her eyes. 'I don't know. Eino stopped talking, and one by one the rest of them did, too. Denis was the last one to speak, but even in the relative quiet we still couldn't hear what he was saying. And though he seemed to be staring at us, I don't think he was seeing us. I don't know what he was seeing.'

Konrad stared upwards. If Druganin's eyes had been open before, they were tight shut again now. All five corpses appeared to be, once again, thoroughly dead.

'They are not asleep,' came Tasha's voice. 'I think they can hear us. But they won't talk to me.'

Diana looked about, brows raised. 'Who is that?'

'Tasha, this is Diana Valentina, head of His Lordship's Order. Say hello.'

'Ma'am,' said Tasha, with, for her, a relative lack of irony.

'Diana, Tasha's attached to the Ekamet police. Inspector Nuritov lends her to me sometimes.'

'*Lends,*' said Tasha in disgust. 'Like I'm an old coat or something.'

'Ghost?' said Diana.

'Lamaeni,' Konrad supplied.

'Ah. A pleasure, Tasha. It had not occurred to me to bring one of your kind along. What else can you discern about them?'

'Little else. They—'

She was interrupted by a throaty whisper from Eino. It sounded, to Konrad's horror, like his own name.

Eino spoke again, louder this time. *Konrad. Konrad Savast.*

Konrad took several steps nearer to the big man's suspended corpse. 'Yes, it is Konrad Savast. I am so sorry, Eino. I never thought you might still be in danger or I would have—'

Malykant, said Eino.

Konrad stared.

Konrad Savast, the Malykant. Malykant. Malykant. Malykant, said Eino, over and over, louder and louder.

The word was taken up by Lilli, then by Alina, and finally by Marko. Their eyes opened and they stared down at Konrad with glassy eyes, repeating his title in a susurrant wave of sound. Alina began to scream.

Some instinct turned Konrad in Denis Druganin's direction. That man alone of the five remained silent, but he, too, stared at Konrad, with a more focused stare than the rest; he saw him.

Konrad did not at all like the smile that curved those cold, dead lips, nor the glow of smug satisfaction in his frozen stare.

'Chilling,' remarked Tasha from the empty air. 'I would not like to be in your shoes today.'

'I begin to wish I wasn't, either,' Konrad agreed, speaking lightly to disguise the feeling of chill apprehension turning his guts to ice. 'They are far too excited to see me.'

'At least someone's excited to see you. So what if they are dead? You can't have everything.'

'How lucky I have you at hand to puncture my ego.'

'Free of charge. Hang on. I shall go and question them.'

Konrad waited, eyes averted from the malevolent Druganin. The knowledge that his identity had somehow made a corpse's day was bad enough; worse when it was *that* corpse. What might the child-murdering monster have in mind to do with the information?

Diana joined him. 'Not good,' she said laconically.

'I'd say very bad.'

'Any idea what they might want with you?'

'None whatsoever. I am fairly sure none of them learned who I was when they were alive. Whether they had reason to suspect the Malykant was among the house guests… I cannot say, but I don't think so. Denis Druganin, of course, learned my identity the painful way.' I pointed him out to Diana.

'Mr. Pride-of-Place. I'd think he would look a bit less happy about it.'

'A horrible thought occurs to me.'

'Let's hear it.'

'I was there because Nanda — you remember Irinanda Falenia?

The Shandrigal's servant?'

Diana rolled her eyes. 'We've been acquainted for years, Konrad.'

'I— oh. Yes, of course you would be.' It had not occurred to Konrad that the higher-ups among both Orders might be in regular contact, but it made sense. They might be in service to the Great Spirits of opposing ideals, but that didn't make them opposed to one another. 'Her mother's an Oracle — I am sure you know that, too — and warned Nanda not to go to Divoro. Apparently she foresaw some part of the disasters that duly unfolded. Well, I wonder. Oracles are rare, but not that rare. What if Druganin consulted one, too? Or the coven?'

'You mean what if they knew the Malykant was going to be there?'

'That is my thought.'

'Mm. But they did not know which guest it was.'

'Perhaps those murders were committed to draw me out.'

'So you duly killed Druganin, and now he knows who you are. They all do. And the coven?'

'I can only assume he has told them. *They* strung him up here, after all. They probably got some words out of him first.' Konrad sighed, and shoved his chilled hands into the pockets of his overcoat. 'I should not have left his body there unattended. I don't know why it didn't occur to me that the coven might retrieve it.'

'Probably it did,' said Diana kindly. 'But what of that? You couldn't anticipate that they could make him talk.'

'But I should have. I'd seen Jakub Vasilescu, after all. The truth is, I was… disordered.' Upset, would be a fitter word. Not just by what Denis Druganin had done — the child's dead, bruised face still haunted his thoughts sometimes — but by what he himself had done to Denis Druganin afterwards. All he'd wanted was to get away from Divoro, without delay.

He would pay for that, he feared.

Diana patted his arm. 'Are you well, Konrad?'

'Perfectly.'

She looked up into his face, a slight frown creasing her brow. He read concern, doubt and a faint irritation in her gaze. 'That is a lie, is it not? You are not perfectly well. Konrad, if you need assistance you must tell me.'

'I will.'

'Your well-being is of paramount importance to the Order, and it is among my duties to take care of you.'

Only Diana could manage to make such a statement sound so impersonal. 'I know I'm a prized asset,' he said, rather sourly.

'You are, and difficult to replace. I don't want to have to train a new Malykant anytime soon, Konrad. I am not ready for that.'

'I will be all right.' He believed those words as he said them, but he did not add that it had become harder to do so. He missed the years of relative peace, when The Malykt had kept his heart frozen in ice. He'd felt so little. No torment, no guilt, no horror, no fear — save when his Master appeared. No joy or passion either, but the trade was a fair one. Damn Nanda's meddling. Why could he not return to that blessed state?

He said none of this, only returning Diana's searching look with a bland stare. 'Very well,' she said. 'But I am coming with you to Divoro.'

'I would be glad of your company.'

Her brows shot up at that. 'Stubbornly independent Konrad would be glad of my company? What fresh hell is this?'

That drew from him a reluctant smile. 'Blame Nanda, perhaps. And the inspector, and even Tasha. I am growing positively sociable.'

He'd spoken in jest, but Diana did not smile. 'I see that,' she said. Mercifully, she abandoned her scrutiny of his face and returned her attention to the five inert forms packed into the snowy walls. They were silent again now, eyes closed, as though they had never spoken at all; but Konrad could almost fancy he still heard the word *Malykant, Malykant* echoed upon the wind. 'We'll bring them down this afternoon and take them for burial. Igor will collate whatever we've managed to get by way of transcripts, though I don't hold out much hope that they'll be any good. We go to Divoro in the morning.'

'Diana.' Konrad pointed, once again, to Druganin. 'Cremation for that one, and be careful with him.'

Diana nodded. 'Right.'

Divoro in the morning. Konrad left the snow castle with Tasha trailing somewhere behind, consumed with a sense of dread for what lay ahead. Foolish, he scolded himself. Was he not the Malykant, indeed? He was far from helpless. Had he not, with his serpents' assistance, dispatched Jakub Vasilescu with consummate ease? Had he not disposed of Denis Druganin?

Only, he was beginning to feel a sense of growing unease about those two events, as well. Should it have been so easy to dismiss Jakub to his Master's care? Where had the coven been then? Why had they not guarded their precious ancestor? Was it enough to assume that they'd had no idea he might be in danger? That explanation no longer seemed quite sufficient.

And if Druganin had known that the Malykant would be present at the house party, and had sought to attract his notice… all the worse. Konrad had been manipulated throughout — but to what end?

Foolish! Konrad cursed himself for an idiot, for what was he doing but indulging in useless fears? Paranoia, even! All was mere speculation; he had no concrete grounds to justify such imaginings.

Except only for the way those five slain corpses had whispered his title, over and over again, and the gleam of satisfaction in Denis's dead eyes as he heard it.

Konrad shook his head to clear away such reflections. The carriage sailed smoothly back to Ekamet, a light-falling snow blurring the pale shapes of the trees that lined the road. He forced his thoughts into another train, and called up Nanda's face for his mental perusal. If he must worry about anybody, he would worry instead about her. Not that she would thank him for it.

He wondered what had become of her these past hours, but was not left to wonder long. His driver brought him smartly to the door of the police headquarters of Ekamet, and upon making his way directly to Inspector Nuritov's office he found Nanda inside, deep in conversation with Alexander. They both looked up as he went in.

'Good to find you both here,' he said with a smile of greeting.

If he had hoped that Nanda might be moved to reveal her purpose in haunting Inspector Nuritov's office, he was, as always, destined for disappointment. But the smile Nanda directed at him was almost as good as a confidence.

He noticed a dark, dead shape lying against the rear wall, directly behind Alexander's desk: Tasha's body. She lay in sweet repose, her arms folded over her chest, her young face pale and tragic.

'Hamming it up a bit, Tasha?' he said.

The corpse grinned, and stood up. 'No harm in having a little fun.'

Konrad related the recent developments at the snow castle,

couching the news in the gentlest possible terms for Nanda's sake. She did not appear unduly disturbed, though he detected a suppressed wince when he spoke of Eino's apologies. 'We go to Divoro in the morning,' he finished.

'I will be ready at seven,' said Nanda.

Konrad opened his mouth.

'Do not even think about arguing,' she said, and he closed it again.

'I, too, will come along,' said Alexander.

Here at least Konrad could be permitted to argue. 'It is out of your way, isn't it? Surely the local police of the region can be prevailed upon to assist us.'

'Would you rather have them along?'

'No, I would far rather have you. But…'

Alexander waited, his pipe at his lips.

'Enough friends have died,' said Konrad.

'I am not planning to make myself part of their number.'

'Do you think the coven cares what your plans are?'

Alexander set down his pipe, and fixed Konrad with an uncharacteristically steely look. 'I feel obliged to point out that I have been a police inspector for several years without yet coming to grief.'

'Nuri— Alexander, I am not questioning your capability. But these are not your usual criminals. They are… something else. You have no defences against their brand of magic.'

'And yet, I am still alive.'

The inspector's calm logic rather defeated Konrad. Importunities he could withstand; the cool presentation of irrefutable facts posed more of a problem. As he strove to muster another argument, he became aware that Nanda was laughing at him.

'Something amuses you?' he said with dignity.

'Poor Konrad,' she said, her eyes sparkling with amusement. 'I know it is out of the way of your regular experience, but is it so very, very difficult to have friends?'

Konrad struggled with himself, but the word 'Yes,' popped out anyway.

Nanda patted his hand. 'We probably won't die.'

'Probably?'

'You probably won't die either.' If she recalled that Konrad had died twice already in the past year, she wisely kept those reflections to herself.

'I will be ready at seven,' said Alexander firmly, and Konrad capitulated.

'I'll be along,' said Tasha, and patted his hand just as Nanda had done. Somehow she managed to turn a comforting and only mildly satirical gesture into pure mockery. 'I won't let those nasty necromancers eat the inspector.'

'Thanks,' said Konrad.

'You're welcome.'

You have us, Master, said Ootapi and Eetapi together. He had not known they were near; the sudden intrusion of their icy, discordant voices into his already roiling thoughts made him jump.

Tasha grinned.

'Anyway,' said Konrad, taking a chair with what he hoped was casual insouciance. 'Have you found out anything about the family?'

'Oh — yes, actually, a few things.' Alexander began riffling through the stacks of newspapers, notebooks and folders on his desk, disordering them further. He extracted a newspaper and waved it at Konrad. 'I found a death notice for Zoran Vasilescu, father of Olya, Alina and Ela. He died quite young, nearly ten years ago. The house passed to the eldest daughter, Ela, though without much money to go with it. I haven't found any clues as to where the family fortune went, yet.'

'Considering the state of the house, I'd say they spent it long before Zoran died,' said Konrad. 'The house has not received much maintenance in many years. It has the dilapidation belonging to a property uninhabited for at least a few decades, not a mere ten years.'

'Very true,' murmured Alexander, and scrawled a note for himself. 'I'll look further back. I found an advertisement offering the house for sale. It was posted only a few months after Zoran's death.'

'Who bought it?' Konrad asked.

'That I do not yet know. I have sent a couple of men out to Divoro to talk to the locals, on that and other points. A prominent family like that attracts notice, there must be a lot of gossip circulating about them.'

'I am curious about Ela,' said Nanda. 'She sold the house at the first opportunity, and then vanished? Where is she?'

'If I had family like that, I, too, would run far, far away,' said Alexander.

'Well, yes,' said Nanda with a small smile. 'It is not to be wondered at. Still, her absolute disappearance and subsequent silence seem odd. Even Alina did not so irrevocably cut ties, and she was disowned.'

'Perhaps she followed her younger sister's example and left Assevan altogether,' Konrad suggested. But he was disturbed by her mention of Alina, the youngest sister, whom Olya had killed. Had she murdered her elder sister as well? Perhaps in hope of being the next to inherit the house — only to find that Ela had already sold it.

'Perhaps,' said Nanda, and he saw the same disquiet on her face.

5

At seven o'clock the following morning, Bakar House was unusually bustling. Dawn was some time away, and the night's frosts had yet to clear from the windows. Nonetheless, Konrad himself was awake, fed and dressed, choosing his stout wilderness layers instead of his city attire. Nanda and Alexander stood together in the hall, both shrouded in similarly thick, snow-proof articles of clothing. Tasha eschewed such practicality in favour of her usual dark coat and cap, though being undead Konrad supposed her relationship with the cold did not much resemble his.

Diana Valentina stood impassively in a corner. She had brought her own spirit familiar, an arctic fox, whose incorporeal form Konrad could dimly perceive hobnobbing with his serpents. Much sibilant hissing and muttering was underway, though Konrad could not decide whether the sounds denoted friendly or hostile relations between the three of them. Two further members of the Order had come with Diana: a man whose iron-grey hair proclaimed his age to be ten or fifteen years in excess of Konrad's own, with a bristling beard and a steely-eyed glare to rival Nanda's; and a woman about Nanda's age, unassuming in appearance, her brown hair neatly bound and her thin frame swathed in a plain, dark blue cloak. These were Lev Antonov and Anichka Zima, two of the Order's best necromancers. Konrad had no idea what their duties to the Order consisted of, and was in no way disposed to ask; but their presence on this unwelcome expedition was a boon and he was grateful.

The numbers gathered looked promising, when collected into the relatively confined space that made up Konrad's front hall. Nonetheless, he eyed them with misgivings. They did not know how many they would face at Divoro; would these several people be enough?

No way of knowing.

Two coaches waited outside the house: his own, which was designated to carry himself, Nanda, Alexander and Tasha, and a handsome equipage belonging to the Order, which would convey Diana, Lev and Anichka. Konrad took Nanda's arm and escorted her to his carriage, seating her beside him. When the vehicle rolled into motion only a few minutes past the seventh hour, he watched the familiar contours of Bakar House fade into the night with mixed feelings. On the one hand, the coven at Divoro had to be disposed of. Even a moment's reflection upon their various misdeeds brought a burning anger to his heart; not the least of which was the ruthless killing of Nanda's friends, and the encouragement they had given to the depredations of Denis Druganin. They had earned a vicious retribution, and he would be delighted to visit a world of pain upon them.

On the other hand, nothing short of such strong inducements could have persuaded him to go back to Divoro. Especially not with Nanda along.

A few short hours — too short — brought them to the gates of the doomed house. Konrad watched the dark shapes of its towers draw nearer and nearer with a growing sense of foreboding. A feeling of dread uncurled in his stomach and his heart quickened its pace.

He spoke sternly to himself. How foolish he was being. Just because horrors had occurred in that house, and recently too, did not mean anything of a similar character was guaranteed to occur again. No doubt everything would be—

'Curse it,' said Tasha. She was staring out of the carriage window.

Konrad sat up, his heart pounding. 'What? What is it?'

She did not reply. The moment the coach came to a stop outside the house's gates, she threw open the door and jumped down into the blanketing snow. A gust of chill, snowy wind blew through the gaping door.

Konrad exchanged a dark look with Nanda, then darted after Tasha.

The gates of Eino's cursed mansion had always struck Konrad as especially handsome. Wrought iron, twice as tall as Konrad and ornate in design, they offered an elegant first impression which perfectly augured the grandeur to come.

Today, they'd received an augmentation. Two men hung from the intricate, coiled iron, one to each gate. Their purple faces and bulging eyes heralded the manner of their deaths: they had been strangled. As a further indignity, they had been stripped naked and haphazardly mutilated. Their dead, marble-white flesh gaped here and there with red, glistening wounds.

Behind Konrad, Alexander choked.

'Your men, I assume?' Konrad said.

'Pyotr and Yevgeni.'

Konrad stood immobile, frozen with indecision. What to do? Ordinarily, his duty would be clear. He would task his serpents with gathering whatever tattered shreds of the two men's departing spirits they could find; these he would interrogate for information. After that, he'd take the usual bones from each and set about finding their killers, with the usual result.

But these were Alexander's men — his friends, perhaps — and he was standing three inches away from Konrad's elbow.

Diana came up and stood a moment in thoughtful silence, taking in the sight of the two strung-up bodies. Whatever her thoughts were, she did not share them.

'Are you going to do it?' she said at last.

'No.'

'Lev and Anichka will talk to them. Come back for the bones.'

He tipped his hat to her, too relieved at not having to question the traumatised ghosts of Nuritov's friends to mind the order which followed.

He collected Nanda, but she was not disposed to be ushered past the slain policemen just yet. Instead, to Konrad's surprise and mild horror, she reached out both hands — her gloves removed, despite the numbing chill to the air — and pressed her fingers to the dead flesh of each corpse. She stood motionless for a full minute, her eyes closed, face grimly composed. Konrad watched as a tremor ran through her, and she coughed.

When she opened her eyes, he detected a sheen of suppressed tears there, but otherwise she was calm. 'I can sometimes glean a glimpse of their last thoughts, if they are not long dead,' she said in answer to Konrad's unspoken question. 'I do not like to do it, as I am sure you can imagine.' She withdrew her hands from the bodies and drew on her gloves. 'Their tongues are cut out,' she said.

'We'll use Martita, then,' said Diana, unruffled. Konrad sensed a flicker of wild joy from the little arctic fox as her mistress spoke her name, and she rushed to coil herself about the dangling feet of the nearest corpse.

Konrad was both relieved and horrified to learn that a bloodthirsty joy in death was not quite unique to his serpents. He could not decide which feeling was predominant.

'They died in the caverns,' Nanda added. 'The wounds were inflicted prior to death, not after. Their bodies must have been moved out here later, for our benefit.' With these words she unlatched the gate, pushed it open and sailed through it, her chin high, no signs of distress about her save, perhaps, for a slightly greater pallor than usual.

Konrad followed.

Nanda's dauntless stride carried her to the enormous, heavy front doors in no time, despite the depth of the snow crunching underfoot. But there she stopped, for the doors were not only closed but soundly locked.

Nanda demonstrated this fact beyond all doubt by thumping a hand against the thick, carved wood, and then kicking it for good measure. 'Konrad?' she said crisply.

'Ah… yes?'

'Could you…?' said Nanda, and wiggled her fingers in the direction of the wrought iron lock.

An unwelcome, and increasingly familiar, sensation of nausea gripped Konrad's unhappy stomach, and he swallowed. 'Um, do we not have a key?'

'We do not need a key, not with your magic fingers to hand.'

Konrad stared down at the fingers in question, his mouth set in a hard line. He ought, he knew, to have confided in Nanda sooner. If he had, he would not be obliged to humiliate himself right here, in this moment of tension, in front of Alexander and Tasha and three prominent members of his Order. Could he bluff his way out of it somehow?

He had hesitated too long. Nanda was growing impatient; her brows had gone up, and she stared at him. 'It is rather cold,' she pointed out, as though he might not have noticed the bone-deep chill for himself.

Konrad sighed, removed the glove from his right hand, and touched his fingertips to the lock.

What ought to have happened: the encouraging *creak* and *groan* of ancient tumblers rolling back as the lock opened in response to Konrad's "magic" fingers.

What actually happened: Nothing. Nothing at all.

Konrad silently replaced his glove.

Nanda stared. 'How long…?'

'A few weeks.'

'You didn't say anything?'

'I didn't even want to think about it.'

'Why not?'

'Because it petrifies me.' These words emerged testily, harshly, and he sighed. It was not Nanda's fault, he ought not to bite at her. 'Would it not you?' he said in a softer tone.

Nanda just nodded, slowly, her eyes thoughtful.

It was the first time in Konrad's years as the Malykant that any part of his Malykt-given powers had failed him. Never before had he reached for any ability only to find it gone, unresponsive. Now, the repeated failure of this trick. Though it was among the simplest of his skills, and not absolutely vital to the performance of his duties — locks might be opened by other means, after all — it raised unpleasant prospects for the future. If this power could fail, then… then any of them could.

And then there was the little matter of *why* it was failing. Konrad could not guess at a reason: he only knew that there could be no good one.

'Right,' said Nanda, and gripped Konrad's hand briefly. He appreciated that little, swift gesture of comfort, and returned the pressure of her fingers before she withdrew her hand. 'Anybody with a key?' she called, turning back to the group of people waiting in the courtyard.

Diana's eyes fastened at once upon Konrad, her look searching. She, of course, knew full well that he ought not to need one.

He returned her questioning stare with a bland smile, and looked away. He would have to deal with Diana later.

When nobody spoke, Tasha rolled her eyes and marched up to the door. She shook a sleeve, and something metallic fell into the palm of her hand. She went to work on the lock without a word.

'I observe there is no end to Tasha's questionable talents,' Konrad said to Alexander, who had come up to stand with him.

'She is useful to have around,' he agreed. He waited a moment in silence, giving Konrad room to talk. Ever perceptive, he'd have noticed the odd series of reactions to the mundane problem of a locked door.

Konrad toyed, briefly, with the idea of confiding in the inspector. But he could not force the words to his lips. Was this what friendship was? Making a display of one's weaknesses, darknesses and failures, and hoping to be loved anyway? He was not equal to it.

The silence stretched.

'Good,' said Tasha, as the door swung ponderously open with an unpromising squeal of its hinges. She disappeared inside, and Konrad hurried to push past Nanda and Alexander. He would not choose to send them in ahead of him. Anything could be awaiting them inside, all of it dangerous.

But when he stepped into the darkened hall, he found it echoingly empty. No coven waited in the shadows, and — to his relief — no more corpses decorated the interior. The great chamber was unchanged from his previous visit, save for the hollow, still quality so quickly developed by an unoccupied house.

Serpents, he called. *Survey the house, please. If there is another soul here, living or dead, I must know of it at once.*

Master, said the snakes together, and streamed silently away, Eetapi into the east wing and Ootapi to the west.

Tasha had already disappeared. Konrad hoped she, too, had gone to search the apparently deserted house, and had not already fallen victim to some fiendish trap.

He pushed the thought aside.

Konrad kept everyone standing in the hall until the snakes returned — and Martita, who joined the hunt with enthusiasm. *Empty,* hissed Eetapi, a cold wind brushing his ear.

Not a soul left alive, Ootapi added.

Konrad felt a flicker of alarm. *Left alive? Have others been slain?*

No, said the serpents together, identically mournful. *Not dead. Only gone.*

'Alexander,' Konrad said aloud. 'Did you happen to discover who now owns this house?'

The inspector shook his head. 'If Eino left a will, I have yet to hear of it.'

'What if he had no will?'

'Then... the house must go to his nearest living relative. If he had no children, and there is as yet no reason to imagine that he did, then — then with his mother being dead, and his cousin Druganin...' Alexander frowned. 'There is no sign that he had any siblings either, or any other cousins.'

'Is his father still alive?'

'A good question.'

Denis Druganin's mother, Olya, would be after the house. That much Konrad could guess. It had been she, and her repulsive son, who had pressured Eino into purchasing the house from its former owner in the first place — apparently because he alone among their diminished family had the means to meet what must have been a steep asking price. Eino's acquisition brought the house back into the ownership of the family, rather than some wholly unconnected person. But Eino and his mother had been disowned and reviled. She would want to have the place secure in her own hands, and now that Eino was dead — had his death been part of the plan all along? — what next? How would Olya Vasilescu now ensure that she became the next heir?

'Eino's father died years ago,' said Nanda.

'If Ela, the eldest sister, had any children,' put in Konrad, 'they are not recorded on the family tree. Nor is any marriage of hers.'

'In that case,' mused Alexander, 'who would qualify as Eino's nearest living relative? Olya or Ela?'

'All other things being equal, the law usually favours the elder party,' said Nanda.

'So Ela inherits the house.' Konrad thought about that. 'She could not wait to rid herself of it in the first place.'

'I imagine it would not please,' Nanda said.

Diana approached, and with a sharp look at Konrad, said: 'I would not wish to remain here beyond today, so I trust we have a plan?'

'Since the house is deserted,' said Konrad, 'we must go below. We have already discovered a way into the cellars — or caves, in fact — that lie beneath the surface. We must begin again there, and this time explore much farther. Tasha, the serpents and Martita will, I hope, guide our steps.'

Diana accepted this with a nod, though her eyes were troubled. 'They wait for us down there like cats at mouseholes and you want to just… walk in?'

'What else can we do?' Konrad had turned that question over and over in his mind all the way to Divoro, and had come up with no better plan. Yes, they were stepping into an obvious trap, but he could see no other way to proceed. They would have to spring the trap, and hope that their disparate skills would be sufficient to win through.

'Very well,' said Diana, apparently as devoid of cleverer notions as he. The fact that she did not like it was clearly written across her usually serene face.

Well, he did not like it either. He liked very little about his daily obligations, as it happened. When had that ever mattered?

'A moment,' he murmured, a thought occurring to him. He spun and made for a door at the back of the hall, which hung half-open. Beyond was another hall, slightly smaller, rather more private, and prominently placed upon the walls there was the portrait of Jakub Vasilescu.

Konrad could not have said what impulse had brought him to study it. He knew what the man looked like, having seen him in the flesh — even if it had been dead, only partially reanimated flesh at the time. But he stood before the painting anyway, and gazed long at it.

It was a handsome piece, and large; it took up several square feet in space. The frame was ornate, heavy and gilded, and the painting itself scarcely less grand. Jakub Vasilescu was depicted in a noble pose, his chin high, hair elaborately coiffed. He wore the garments of centuries past: a long velvet coat, a braided waistcoat with many polished buttons, stockings and buckled shoes. The living man, captured in oils, had a vibrancy and energy about him that had been absent from his wasted, preserved corpse, but the eyes were the same: penetrating, dark and merciless.

Here was a man to unite a family. Everything about him spoke of a strong will, a ruthless nature and a relentless ambition. You would follow such a man, die for such a man.

Having hardly glanced at the painting before, Konrad now began to see why the Vasilescu might be so desirous of bringing this man back. One only had to make the most cursory inspection of their empty, cobweb-ridden house to see how their fortunes had faded. And who among the living could take this man's place? Not Ela Vasilescu, who despised everything about her family. Not Olya, who for all her determination was only the second of three daughters. Not Denis Druganin, a man too distracted by his repulsive predilections to excel at, or even care for, leadership. If the Vasilescu fortunes were to be revived, they needed this man.

Or someone like him.

Konrad went back to the main hall, thoughtful.

'Come, Konrad,' said Diana, with a touch of impatience, as he reappeared. 'Please call your serpents to order.'

'Why, what are they doing?'

For answer, Diana merely pointed a single finger upwards.

Konrad raised his eyes to the ceiling.

The many, ancient cobwebs that drifted from corner to corner had caught his serpents' attention. Seemingly they had grown bored, as Eetapi had wreathed herself in puffs of spider's webs and now sailed from wall to wall, swaying dreamily from side to side. She herself might be invisible but the cobwebs were not; the effect was, even to Konrad's informed eye, disturbing. Ootapi had chosen to decorate the walls rather than himself, and was halfway through arranging a mass of tattered, silvery spider-silks into a design no doubt macabre.

Konrad chose to speak aloud, for the benefit of Alexander and Nanda. 'Stop that, Eetapi. Ootapi, leave it alone.'

But, Master, hissed Ootapi. *It is almost finished!*

'It would be better for everyone if your masterpiece remained incomplete, I have no doubt.'

Moments later, Konrad felt something airy brush past his ears, and settle in his hair. Eetapi had chosen to express her disdain by shedding her cloak of cobwebs upon his head.

He brushed them away, trying to keep a grip upon his temper. 'Diana,' he growled. 'If I were to apply for new help, what are the chances that you might oblige me?'

'Fairly high.'

Chastened, the serpents drifted sulkily after Konrad as he stepped back out into the dull grey light of midday, drawing his coat tighter around himself.

You would not truly replace us, Master? whispered Eetapi dolefully.

Konrad felt a twinge of remorse. *No,* he answered. *Though there are times when I am sorely tempted.*

6

The walk through the snow-laden pines surrounding the house, culminating as it did in the descent into the darkness of the caves, struck Konrad as eerily familiar. Everything was too much the same: the sounds of his companions' passage through the blanketing snow, muffled by ongoing snowfall; the dark shapes of the fir trees, stark against the prevailing white; the sudden cessation of daylight as he followed Tasha into the narrow passage that led into the depths, and the flicker of wan torchlight upon the rock walls. Had it only been a week since he had last made this journey? Less? It could have been the same day, the same hour, save that this new incursion comprised greater numbers, greater strength.

He hoped it would be enough.

Tasha led the way. She walked with a reassuring confidence, as though she knew exactly where she was and where she was going. She had explored extensively only a handful of days ago, though not in her corporeal form. Some part of the caves had eluded even her reach, however, and those must be the areas inhabited by the coven. Somehow, they would have to do better today.

Serpents, Konrad said, once every member of their group had passed into the dark silence of the caves. *We rely on you to discover the coven. Find them, please, and take note of their location.*

That could take days, Master, said Ootapi. *You do not know how extensive these passageways are?*

Consult with Tasha. She has searched many of them already, and knows where it is futile to look.

He detected a hint of disdain, or perhaps it was merely dissatisfaction, in the words, *Yes, Master,* uttered by Ootapi in long-suffering tones. But away sailed the serpents, Diana's fox chasing at their tails.

The route Tasha followed was familiar to Konrad: she was retracing their earlier steps into the large cave where they had, not long ago, encountered Jakub Vasilescu, a man not nearly as dead as he should have been. As the walls of the passage fell away and the confined space opened up into the wide, high-ceilinged cave Konrad remembered, he noticed at once a difference. Whereas before, the chamber had been largely sunk in darkness, now it was brightly lit. Torches set into the walls at regular intervals gave off a bright, cheery glow, though for whose benefit Konrad could not have said, for the cave was empty.

The dais upon which Jakub Vasilescu had lain was still there, ringed in a halo of light. To his surprise, a body lay there.

He paused. Diana walked directly behind him; he waited for her to join him, and whispered: 'Did you not remove the corpse that lay here?'

'I did.' She frowned, gestured to Lev and Anichka, and advanced upon the dais, Konrad at her side. They prepared for trouble, alert and ready to counter any threat that may emerge.

None did. Alexander and Nanda consented to fall a little behind the Malykt's Order as they advanced, though Tasha, with her usual insouciance, beat them all to the dais. 'Different body, methinks,' she offered.

It was indeed. Different in form, feature, and… freshness. Konrad's mind formed the latter word with distaste. Whereas Jakub's body had been marked by the yellowed, withered skin and waxy demeanour of the long, long dead, the woman that lay in his former place looked as though she might have died only this morning. Her pale skin had not yet lost the vitality of life and health, and her slightly greying dark hair was full and glossy, spread over the dark rock of the bier. She was as richly clad as her predecessor, though in more recent fashions: a gown of dark purple silk, buttoned up to the throat and ornamented with lace; polished black boots; jewels of gleaming jet. She looked so healthy, in fact, that Konrad doubted her condition. Was she dead?

Yes. He watched closely, but failed to discern any movements of her torso, however slight. She was as still as a marble statue, not breathing.

Konrad briefly regretted having dispensed with his serpents, however urgent their errand.

'She looks familiar,' said Nanda softly.

Alexander nodded. 'There is a resemblance to… to Eino's mother.'

He was right. Konrad, too, had noticed it, though his mind had not been so quick to make the connection with the living as the inspector's. The woman had the same hair as Alina Holt, nee Vasilescu, and her features were similar.

'Ela?' suggested Nanda.

'Or Olya,' said Alexander grimly. 'I believe it to be one of the sisters, certainly.'

Three sisters Vasilescu, at least two of them dead. Alina, the youngest, had been slain by her own family… or had she? They had not yet determined exactly who had carried out the macabre massacre of Alina and Eino Holt and their erstwhile guests. Had Olya Vasilescu been responsible? Konrad had assumed, perhaps unfairly, that she led the coven that hid itself away beneath her family's ancestral home. Was he correct, or had she been supplanted? Was it she who lay here, slain by her own fellows? Or had they somehow discovered the whereabouts of the eldest sister, Ela, and tracked her down?

Tasha spoke, a warning note in her low voice. 'There's something odd about her. I cannot say what, but I would… step back.' Tasha retreated a little from the dais as she spoke, which was sufficient to alarm Konrad. Tasha feared nothing, and hardly knew the meaning of the word "caution".

Nanda threw her a startled look and followed suit, as did the inspector. Konrad, however, stood his ground, as did Diana and her necromancers. He reached for his spirit vision, and sight faded; instead of rock and skin and cloth he saw searing white light and deep black shadow, his eyes looking now into the spirit world.

No shades lingered near the dais. The corpse, traced now in shadows and lights, lay alone and unattended.

This ought to have reassured Konrad, but he felt a moment's disquiet. It made no sense. Why was this woman here, if her soul had passed already into The Malykt's hands? If she had lately died — or been, by some means, slain — and merely awaited burial, why had she been left in this spot? It was as though she had been placed there deliberately, in expectation of discovery. Konrad knew that he was meant to find her, meant to examine her — meet her? He could not have said. The coven's motives remained impenetrably obscure.

Still, if he could neither see nor sense a shade attached to this particular corpse, then it was probably all it appeared to be: nothing but dead flesh. He permitted his spirit-sight to fade once more, and stood blinking in the aftermath, an unpleasant thought worming its way through his attempts at tranquillity.

If his fingers had ceased to obey him as they should… could he rely on his spirit-sight? What if that, too, had weakened? Just because he had not detected a spirit adrift, did that absolutely mean that there was not one?

He was relieved to note, when he had wrested his mind away from such unhelpful reflections, that this particular corpse had not yet turned talkative.

Diana looked hard at him. 'All is well?'

Konrad could only shrug. 'I think so.'

Tasha's voice split the air, sharp and penetrating. 'This way.' The words came from some little distance away, echoing down dark passages. How far had she gone? Konrad hastened to reach her, for her tone clearly announced that she had found something. The coven? Some danger?

No. Another bier, and another body. He hurried down two winding passageways, each torchlit like the cavern, and emerged into a second cave-chamber, rather smaller than the first. A low dais dominated the centre of the room, and upon it lay a second dead woman. Konrad recognised the coarse, dark blue dress and white cap that she wore: she'd been a maid at the great house until, perhaps, two days ago. His experienced gaze detected the signs of a day's decay and more; dark bruising around her throat proclaimed the manner of her death. She was young, perhaps not even twenty years old.

Konrad took in the scene in grim silence.

'There will be more,' said Alexander quietly.

'Many more, I fear,' Konrad agreed, for what the two corpses represented was the beginnings of a trail.

No; more than two. The mutilated bodies at the gates had been the start. Now they were being led, body by body, deeper into the depths of the caves. Straight into the clutches of the coven.

Serpents? Konrad called, but though he sent the word as far and wide as he could, no reply came.

Tasha had hardly waited for her companions to catch up before she had dashed away again. Soon her voice came echoing back, much as before. Diana, Lev and Anichka went on, but Nanda and Alexander remained with Konrad.

He'd paused to look for the maid's spirit, should it happen to linger still. But of her ghost there was no sign.

He hesitated.

'What's the matter?' Nanda asked, with a narrow look at him.

Konrad glanced at the inspector. 'I… do not know what to do. I need…' He gestured at the unlucky maid's torso, trying to indicate his duty to wrest a bone from her without having to say the words.

Alexander smiled faintly. 'You need not tiptoe around me.'

True. It was too late to hide any part of himself from Inspector Nuritov. 'She is clearly murdered, and I ought to take a bone. As I ought from Olya, or Ela, whichever she is. But—'

'There isn't time for that,' Nanda said, already walking away from him, in the direction that Tasha had gone.

'It is my duty to deliver justice.'

'So you will. Later.' She did not slow down.

Konrad answered Alexander's bland look with a small sigh, and followed Nanda.

They traversed many more winding passages and three more expansive cave-chambers in similar fashion. Each cavern held a bier with a newly-dead corpse, most of them erstwhile staff at the house. Sickened by the extent of the carnage, and deeply disturbed at what it might betoken, Konrad maintained an increasingly grim silence. Nowhere could he discern any trace of a lingering spirit, which began to trouble him as well. Murder led to unquiet spirits, and they often tarried at the site of their death, unable to understand or accept what had happened to them. It was part of the reason for Konrad's existence: his task was to shepherd such agitated spirits upon their way, in part by granting them the justice they so badly needed.

So many corpses and yet no attendant ghosts made him uneasy. Either his worst fears were true, and his spirit-sight was failing him; or something else was at work, something he had never before encountered.

Perhaps an hour had passed since they had entered the caves, and their route — guided, in such macabre fashion, by their quarry — had taken them along a winding trail, ever deeper down. Konrad did not think he imagined that they were journeying in a loose spiral, aiming, perhaps, for some dark heart at the centre of the caves.

'*Konrad.*' Tasha's voice again, emanating from the depths of the shadows wreathing the mouth of the next dimly torchlit passage.

He broke into a run, pushing past Diana and Lev, and arrived, breathless with exertion and cold and alarm, in yet another cave. But this one was the size of his own parlour at home, and fitted up in similar fashion. Its occupant corpse lay not upon a cold stone bier but upon a silk-upholstered divan, and it was handsomely dressed.

'Did we not earmark this gentleman for a good, solid burning?' Tasha demanded.

Konrad swallowed. 'I… thought we did.' For it was Jakub Vasilescu lying there.

Diana looked thunderous — and disquieted. 'I gave orders for him to be taken out of here.'

Konrad thought he could read her thoughts. Had something befallen the men and women she had sent in to remove the erstwhile head of the Vasilescu family? Would she soon be forced to stare into their dead eyes, and wish she had taken more care?

His own thoughts wandered down a slightly different road. *Serpents,* he called, sharply, but still no reply came.

He drifted nearer to Diana. 'Have you been hearing from Martita?'

'Not for the past hour.' She did not ask after his serpents; his tone, and his subsequent silence, told her enough. She straightened from her scrutiny of Jakub's corpse — mercifully inert, this time — and said crisply: 'Lev, Anichka. I need you to reanimate this one.'

'Surely they cannot,' said Konrad. 'I sent his spirit into The Master's care myself.'

Diana made to speak, but Konrad held up a hand, for a slithering voice that moment sounded in his mind. *Master, something is gravely amiss.*

You think so? Konrad returned, more tartly than he ought.

We have found no one alive, Ootapi continued, ignoring Konrad with admirable grace. *But we have found many, many that are dead. They are everywhere.*

I know, we have encountered a few of them ourselves.

You do not understand. That was Eetapi, in a splintering tone that set his teeth on edge. *Come deeper down, Master, into the darkest places. Then you will see.*

Konrad relayed this. Something flickered across Diana's face — recognition? Dread? But she said only: 'We go on. Quickly.'

Tasha sped on, and Konrad fell in behind. Despite his serpents' assurance that nothing was left alive, he felt a sense of impending danger that grew with every step he took. As he strode deeper into the caverns, passing several more silent corpses stretched upon cold funeral biers, he let his Malykant's powers ripple to the fore. His stride lengthened and ate up the ground; strength washed through his wearied limbs; his mind cleared, focused, and his fears melted away.

Then Eetapi appeared, shimmering sickly white in his mind's eye. *In here, Master.* She streamed through one of three yawning arches, and Konrad followed.

The chamber beyond shone with warm, welcoming light, and unlike the rest of the labyrinth it was comfortably warm. The source of the heat was a series of fireplaces dug at regular intervals into the walls, each roaring with a cosy blaze. That alone was odd, for if nobody was alive down there, who was tending the fires?

'Mercy,' gasped Nanda, and stopped upon the threshold.

The floor was covered with corpses. They were neatly arranged, evenly spaced, and all in the same posture: supine, their eyes closed, legs outstretched and their arms lying by their sides. It was less as though someone had placed each body in that pose; more as though they had arranged themselves, all lain down together and… and died.

You are sure they are all dead? Konrad asked of his serpents. The display reminded him of another, earlier case: when he had first encountered the *lamaeni* people. He'd found a room not unlike this, filled with apparently deceased bodies — only they had not been. They had merely done as Tasha so often did: separated their spirit-selves from their physical selves, and wandered off in the former state, leaving their bodies temporarily behind. Perhaps such was the case here.

Stone dead, said Ootapi, dashing that idea. *Are they not lovely? It is like a field of flowers.*

Bind some of them, he snapped. *I would have speech with a few.*

We cannot, said the serpents together. *They are all empty.*

Empty. Empty of life, in any conceivable form. 'Tash,' he said aloud. 'I have to be sure. These are not your people, are they?'

'No.'

'You're sure? You can tell?'

'I can tell, and I am sure. These are nothing but dead meat.'

Diana had said nothing. Neither had Lev or Anichka, Konrad realised; not in all the time they had wandered down here. The two of them were impassive, absolutely focused upon whatever duty Diana had laid upon them when she had brought them with her.

Konrad felt they had been silent for long enough. 'Mr. Antonov,' he said. 'Miss Zima. Considering that we seek a group said to practice the same arts as your own: what does this look like to you?'

They both looked at Diana, who looked sideways at Konrad. 'You can tell them,' she said, after a moment's thought.

Lev Antonov nodded. 'There is more than one possibility. Some of our people envy the lamaeni, and try to emulate them. It is rarely productive of very much. Usually they fail to return to their physical forms. Or, in other words, they die.'

'Sometimes they are subsequently reanimated,' put in Anichka. 'Instead of being able to choose between a physical form and a spirit form at will, they become simply undead.'

'Why would anybody make such an attempt?' asked Alexander, his eyes wide and a bit wild as he took in the sheer quantity of inanimate bodies littering the room. There must have been at least twenty. 'If it always fails?'

Anichka hesitated. It was Lev who said: 'There is a myth about the lamaeni. Some say that the state is not a curse, as some believe. It is said that the first of them were necromancers, able to manipulate not only the bodies and souls of others after death, but their own as well. Some still believe that a necromancer of sufficient talent and vision can achieve the same.'

Konrad suspected all such necromancers of incurable stupidity, but kept the thought to himself. 'It seems unlikely that so many would make any such attempt all together like this, surely?'

'Most unlikely,' Lev agreed. 'The second possibility…' He looked, again, at Diana.

She gave him a nod. 'Go on.'

'There have been some troubling rumours circulating in the past month,' said Lev. 'There have been… incidents. Of possession.'

Konrad blinked. 'How many incidents?'

'Too many. You'll know, Malykant, how important it is to the Order to stamp out this practice. It is among your own sacred duties to rid the world of those spirits, wraiths and ghosts who fail to find their way into The Master's care. Sometimes, should they linger too long and grow too unquiet, they… cling to anything they can find that is alive. Usually to another person. In some cases, a powerful and unhappy ghost has succeeded in pushing aside the consciousness of a living person and taking control of their body, at least intermittently. Several such cases have been reported across Ekamet in the last few weeks. This is almost unheard of. Something has changed, and we have been seeking the source.'

That was why Diana had brought these two, then. Had she hoped to find the source down here?

But this train of thought unravelled, swept away by another burgeoning idea. One which took hold with frightening rapidity, and he felt a growing horror as it unfolded, for everything fit. Everything fit far too neatly.

'Diana,' he said softly. 'I think I know why neither Tasha nor my serpents ever found anybody alive down here — not now, not when they searched before. It isn't because the coven is gone, or hiding somewhere we have yet to find. It is because they are dead. All of them. They have been dead for years.'

7

Konrad gestured at the neat rows of bodies lying, waiting, upon their slabs of stone. 'These are vehicles. Ready to be taken up at need, and used as necessary to commit whatever deeds they see fit.' Like murdering all the residents of the Vasilescu family mansion; building its replica in snow; and hanging Eino Holt and his mother from the walls.

'I agree with your first surmise,' said Diana slowly. 'But not, I think, your second.'

Anichka was shaking her head. 'Dead flesh makes a poor vehicle for possession. It fails to respond the way it needs to, because it's — well, because it is dead. Only live flesh can think and move and react. Ask the lamaeni.'

'Correct,' said Tasha. 'If a lamaeni is separated from his or her body for too long, the flesh will deteriorate and die and they will no longer be able to return to it. Many of us have been… stranded, that way. If that happens, an alternative vehicle — as you put it — must be found, and a nice, live body is preferred. Or a *really* fresh corpse.'

These, Konrad saw at a glance, were not very fresh. Nor were they much decayed. He walked down a row or two, examining them more closely. They were varied; a mix of men and women, ranging from early youth to advanced age. Their garments proclaimed their backgrounds to be equally varied: some wore the silks and lace of gentry, others wore the coarser, plainer garb of labourers or tradesmen. There was no consistency to their styles of clothing; if their funeral attire was to be believed, they had all died at different times over the past century at least.

'They're preserved,' Konrad said thoughtfully. 'Somehow. They look recently deceased, but they are not.'

'A coven of dead necromancers,' said Diana. 'I have never heard of such a thing, but…' She lifted a brow in Lev's direction.

'I have,' he said. 'Though not recently. There is an old Marjan tale of such a coven.'

'I've heard it,' murmured Nanda.

Lev nodded. 'They were said to be more powerful dead than alive, given to possessing the minds and bodies of small children.'

'And lo, many a night's sleep has been ruined by these stories,' said Nanda, with a tiny quirk of a smile. 'It has been my lifetime's mission to believe them just that: stories.'

'Some part of the tales are likely exaggerated,' said Lev. 'But there is much truth to it.'

Konrad was only half listening, his mind busy. 'Why preserve their bodies, if they are more powerful dead than alive, and they cannot go back to their corpses anyway?' he said. 'And for that matter, where are they now? If their ghosts were here, the serpents would have seen or sensed them by now.'

'I wonder,' said Alexander, 'whether they intended to die.'

Konrad looked sharply at the inspector. 'Go on.'

'Well.' Alexander stood with his hands in his pockets, staring out over the small sea of corpses with a bleak expression on his mild face. 'How do you suppose Jakub Vasilescu died?'

'Yes,' said Konrad. 'He was not young, but nor was he elderly and frail.'

'Absolutely neither. If he died before his time, perhaps that explains the urgency of his descendants to keep him, in some sense, around. Well, what if it was not just him? What if the whole coven was cut down, years ago?'

Nanda said, 'That would go some way to explaining why they used Denis Druganin to bring them bodies. If they are both dead and barred from returning to their own forms, however well-preserved these are…' She stopped, frowning at the nearest example — a stout, middle-aged woman in a worn wool dress.

'It might,' Konrad agreed. 'But you are also right to doubt. The explanation is too simple. If preserving their erstwhile physical forms is of no use to them, why are they doing it?'

'And how are they performing their organ-replacing procedures?' said Diana. 'As they did on Eino. There must be some left alive.'

Konrad thought back to his encounter with Jakub Vasilescu. If Alexander was right, and he and several of his fellows had been prematurely swept away, then perhaps it was not just Jakub upon whom the living coven members were practicing their questionable arts. Near to hand lay the body of a man in, perhaps, his sixties, his grey hair fanned around his serene face. Konrad quickly opened the well-cut black coat he wore, and the white linen shirt underneath.

Like Jakub, this man had an incision from throat to navel. It looked fairly fresh, and newly stitched up again. Had something been removed from his torso? No. Judging from the state poor Kati Vinter and Alen Petranov had been left in, no one would trouble to sew closed the wound if he had merely been harvested of parts. No, something had been put *in.* This man, like Jakub, had been the recipient of fresh, living organs — and recently.

But that did not make sense either. For one thing, replacing a few dead organs with equally dead — if more recently deceased — examples could hardly achieve much. It did not make the corpse any less dead. For another, at least Jakub's spirit had still been demonstrably present; there was no sign of a resident ghost haunting any of these corpses. Were their spirits only temporarily absent, or had they passed on into The Malykt's care? If the latter, no amount of tinkering with their physical forms could possibly bring them back.

'What is all this *for,*' said Konrad in frustration. 'The signs suggest someone wants to bring all these people back, but that is impossible. It cannot be done. Is that not true?' He looked for confirmation to Lev and Anichka.

'I have never heard of any such thing,' said Lev.

'Nor I,' Anichka added. 'Dead necromancers retaining some portion of their powers even after severance from their physical forms, yes. Even tales, reasonably credible ones, of their being still more empowered in that state. But of reversing death completely, even long after life has faded? It is one of the biggest, and most tragic, misconceptions about necromancy: that the art can restore true life to the dead. It cannot. A reanimated corpse might move and speak and act, but it is not alive.'

'How does that work?' said Konrad. 'Does it move and speak at the pleasure of the necromancer — like a puppet — or is the original spirit in some fashion restored to reanimate the husk?'

'Both are possible. The former is more common, the latter more difficult — and transitory. Undeath is a fragile, unpleasant state and it does not last. The lamaeni being the only known exception.' Anichka nodded her respect to Tasha.

Tasha, however, was characteristically ungracious. 'You are all being dense,' she said. 'It is completely impossible to bring the dead back to life, yes — except when it isn't.'

Konrad blinked. 'What?'

She sighed. 'More specifically: it is impossible for you or me to restore life, but there is more in the world than living people and undead lamaeni.'

'Oh,' Nanda breathed, and turned horrified eyes upon Konrad.

'Exactly,' said Tasha. She folded her arms, and said with a glower: 'Who do we know who's been dead once or twice before?'

Konrad swallowed.

'Mm. And look how alive you are.'

That, Konrad thought, had proved to be a matter for some debate, in the past. There had been one or two lamaeni who had called his precise state of being into question — implied, horrifyingly, that he was *not* quite alive anymore, though he had not passed into a state of undeath either. What that meant, he had decided not to think about.

Nonetheless, Tasha was right.

He had wondered why the coven of Divoro had so obviously wanted to lure the Malykant back to their caves. Was this his answer?

'We must leave,' said Diana crisply. 'You were right, Konrad. This is a trap, but a far worse one than we imagined possible. Lev, Anichka. Get Konrad out of here.' She was moving as she spoke, alert for trouble, her keen eyes scanning the low-lit chamber.

'No,' said Konrad. 'We came here to get to the bottom of this, and to dispense with the coven once and for all. I will not leave until we have accomplished that.'

'*We* will accomplish that,' said Diana. 'You are not only in a great deal of personal danger, you are likely to become a danger yourself if we let them get hold of you.'

'Why? What can they possibly do to me?'

But as he spoke, the word *possession* floated through his memory, and he blanched.

Suddenly, the long silence of his serpents began to seem sinister.

Eetapi, he called, sending the word as far and as fast as he was able. *Ootapi!*

He thought he heard a call in reply, a thin, distant sound that vibrated with distress.

'Martita?' he said to Diana.

She shook her head, mouth set in a grim line. 'Something is wrong.'

'I'll find them.' Tasha did not waste time lying down. She keeled over backwards, apparently stone dead, as her shade separated from her body and sped away in pursuit of the absent spirit-familiars. It was a trick she had pulled on Konrad before, but only in jest. The sight was much more horrific now.

Be careful— he called after her, but too late. She was already gone.

For his own part, he shed his habitual caution and reached for the strength, speed and resilience that was his due as the Malykant. *Please, do not let these fail me too,* he prayed, thinking of locks no longer responding to the touch of his fingers.

To his relief, they came. He stood taller, radiating dark magic, his vision sharpened and his resolve strengthened. When he moved, he knew he would move at three, four times his usual pace, his long strides eating up the ground.

It was not enough. When the strike came, it came without warning, and hit him with the colossal power of a united coven behind it.

It felt, he thought later, as though a hammer had been applied with skull-splitting force, felling him in a single blow. Only the effect was spiritual, not physical; it was not his body, but his mind, that fell. A searing pain lanced through his head, stealing his breath, drawing from him a bellow of agony — and then he was shunted aside, packed into a too-small space inside his own skull, and his thoughts were no longer his own.

A presence invaded his mind, a presence too powerful to resist. That intruder harvested Konrad's thoughts, harnessed his will, and took control of his limbs, leaving Konrad's own consciousness an enervated, emaciated shadow. He could only scream, wordless, useless frustration, as his stolen body surged into motion and he was helpless to stop it. What had he done but put his Malykant's powers at the disposal of his attackers? He, Konrad, was the Malykant no longer. Someone else had taken possession of his role.

8

Konrad's body began to move, though it was not he who had bid it do so. The motions were not his own, either; an odd sway to his hips suggested that his captor was a woman, or had been in life.

He could see, but his vision was distorted — doubled. A glance at Nanda showed him two women: the Nan he knew, familiar and loved, beautiful in every feature; and a second Irinanda, tall, icy and haughty, the planes of her face angular and unpleasing. His possessor's view of Nanda was quite different from his own.

'Konrad?' she said, watching him warily. 'Where are you going?'

He tried to answer, but she who had taken control of his limbs kept his lips pressed tightly together, and no words emerged. He fought, and for a time, sight and sound faded altogether as he threw everything he had at the interloper. For a moment he thought he might succeed; she stopped, and staggered, her concentration broken.

Yes! Konrad exulted, and surged up in triumph. He would reclaim himself, and then he would wipe every last one of the ghosts of Divoro off the face of the—

Iron bands clamped around his skull, or so it felt. They tightened, and squeezed; something splintered, and he screamed.

Do not fight me, said a low, female voice, echoing through his thoughts like a sharp sound in an empty room. *Our alliance is temporary.*

Olya, he spat. *It is Olya Vasilescu, is it not?*

Who else could have power enough?

Why then do you need mine?

Because I cannot do all that I would wish.

Vision returned, and hearing. He had passed out of the cavern of corpses and proceeded some way back along the passage, wending steadily upwards. What had become of Nanda, Alexander and the others? Distantly, he heard a pounding, as of someone hammering upon a locked door.

They need not be killed, Olya remarked conversationally, as Konrad's body proceeded onward at a measured pace.

Konrad needed no assistance to read the implied threat in her words. *You could not have asked for our aid?*

You would not have given it.

She was right, for another few steps brought Konrad in his usurped body back into the little room in which Jakub lay. Konrad — Olya — knelt by the divan upon which he reclined, and took his hand. 'Dedushka,' said Konrad's voice, with a timbre and inflection not his own. 'Today you rise.'

He cannot rise, Konrad snapped. *He is gone.*

Thanks to you, so he is. But what you have done, you will undo.

I cannot. His soul lies in The Master's care now.

He felt his lips curve in a smile. 'Bring the serpents here,' said he/Olya aloud.

What. Muffled as his senses were, Konrad became belatedly aware that they were not alone in the room. Lev and Anichka came into view, both walking with odd, slightly stiff movements, as though they, too, were directed by others. Each bore one of his serpents wrapped around one arm. The tight embrace might have looked affectionate, except that Konrad could feel rage and agony radiating from them both. They were bound there.

Konrad felt his lips move again; Olya was speaking. 'It was you who carried away this man's spirit. You will fetch it back.' She pointed at Jakub; Konrad's arm rose and fell.

We cannot, gasped Ootapi. *The Master will never permit it.*

'You will have to find a way to do it without his knowledge.'

You cannot compel us, spat Eetapi. *We do not obey!*

Olya said, with chilling calm, 'Then your Malykant will never be restored to you.'

Konrad made another futile attempt at escape. But wrest though he might, every struggle only entangled him more thoroughly; with every straining effort, his bindings tightened. *Diana will deal with you,* he informed Olya.

She ignored this. 'Well?' she said to his serpents. 'What shall it be?'

Konrad tried to resign himself to disaster. Try though she might, she could not hold him forever. It must tire her to keep him bound this way, and sooner or later he would wrest himself free. He only hoped she would not do too much damage in the interval.

But to his immense surprise, Eetapi said, in a shivery whisper, *Very well.*

He was, for an instant, surprised into silence. Loyalty? From the *serpents*? Did they not rebel against his every order? Had they not argued with every syllable he had ever uttered, mocked him for his every mistake and delighted in his every failure? If one Malykant came to grief, The Malykt would soon install another. That was the way of it.

Eetapi, he said. *Ootapi, you must not.*

They did not hear him, trapped as he was behind the curtain of Olya's iron will. That, or they chose to ignore him. They heaved a twin sigh, their pale, half-manifested forms flickering.

Quite what they did, Konrad was in no position to detect. That it cost them greatly, he could well imagine; time passed, and shadows began to roil about their coiled forms.

Eetapi screamed something in a tongue Konrad had never known.

Then a third ghostly presence materialised by slow degrees: male, aged and furious. Cold radiated off the spirit of Jakub Vasilescu, turning the stone floor to ice at his feet.

'Dedushka,' breathed Olya. 'How I have missed you.'

The wraith that was Jakub stared down at Konrad, his expression more malevolent than pleased. It was not his many-times-removed great granddaughter he saw kneeling at his feet, but the dispossessed Malykant. 'It is fit,' he said in a wintry voice.

Then Olya addressed Konrad again, silently this time, and the bands of pain tightened around him. *Malykant, you will raise him.*

I cannot, gasped Konrad.

These words brought instant punishment: agony wracked his tortured spirit. He screamed, and for a few blissful moments lost consciousness.

He was brutally shaken awake. *A lie,* hissed Olya. *Have you not, alone among all mankind, died and risen and died and risen again?*

Distantly, Konrad wondered how she knew anything about it. How long had these abominable cultists been researching his doings, spying upon his escapades, and laying their revolting plans?

That is the truth, he admitted. *But it is not by my own will that I am raised. It is no power granted to me, or to any woman or man. Only the Great Spirits can restore true life.*

Still you lie, she snapped. *This cannot be the truth.* She spoke, then, aloud, lifting Konrad's arm to point at grey-faced Lev and wan Anichka. 'One of them shall raise him, then. Are not the very best practitioners admitted into The Malykt's Order?'

Lev and Anichka stared back at her, glassy-eyed. Konrad could imagine a similar battle going on in each of their minds with those who held them in thrall. For a moment Anichka looked likely to break free; her eyes narrowed, she gave a tearing gasp, and her possessed body broke for the door.

It did not last long. Her growl of rage became a scream of torment, and she collapsed.

All this Jakub beheld with the air of a disdainful lord. *And is this the best that you have to offer? My descendants' wits have weakened along with our blood.*

'Why!' screamed Olya with Konrad's voice. *Why,* she snarled again inside his mind. *Why will none of you aid me?*

Another wave of shattering pain accompanied these words, and Konrad's senses deserted him again. *Because,* he gasped, *because we cannot. What manner of necromancer are you, that you believe the fundamental laws may be so easily broken? It is given to none of us to restore anything but a semblance of life to dead flesh. Replacing parts of the body with living tissue is of no use whatsoever. Nature cannot be tricked. Your plan has failed.*

The solution, said Jakub silkily, *is obvious.*

Konrad did not at all like the satisfied smile that wreathed the wraith's ethereal face.

'What solution?' whispered Olya.

If it must be living flesh, there is plenty of that to hand.

He looked right into Konrad's stolen eyes as he spoke.

Abandon this old shell of mine, he ordered Olya. *What use is it to me, when I might have a younger, stronger frame instead? I shall have this one.* His smile widened.

Konrad had no time to prepare himself. Jakub struck at once, and after a brief, surprised interval, his granddaughter joined him.

And it was done, with extraordinary ease. In the same way that one might, with clever timing, send a tumbler spinning to the ground with a very little pressure, so Konrad's consciousness was somersaulted out of his own body. A push from the one; a tug from the other; and Konrad was bodiless, shivering near the ceiling, made a wraith in Jakub's place.

He watched, helpless, as Konrad-that-was rose to his feet. The erstwhile wraith's repulsive smile was translated to Konrad's own face; he hated the way that grin stretched his familiar lips, hated the way his own dark eyes burned with a monstrous glee he had never been guilty of himself — not even at his very worst moments.

Jakub stretched, rolled the shoulders of his fine new body, and nodded his satisfaction. 'It shall suit me admirably,' he said, and even Konrad's voice sounded different; lighter, darker, deeper, anything but his own.

His head tilted to look up, up at the ceiling, where Konrad's shocked spirit clung. 'Enjoyable, is it not?' he said, the smile fading. 'A century or two in that state and you, too, will trade anything at all to reverse the events of this day.'

It would not take anywhere near so long as a century. Konrad screamed his frustration and dove, intent upon thrusting Jakub out of his stolen limbs and reclaiming his own self without an instant's delay.

To his humiliation, Jakub fended off this ill-judged attack with ease. And laughter. 'You forget!' he called, with offensive joviality. 'I have a great deal of experience at the incorporeal state, while you have none at all.'

This was inarguable. Konrad had enough to do to keep himself together; what was left of his being sought to dissolve into tatters and stream away, leaving him blessedly insensate. He recalled how often he had instructed his serpents to collect and bind just such a beleaguered spirit, a soul too shocked, appalled and frightened to manage the process for itself.

What was worse, an insistent part of himself fought the necessity, for the prospect of oblivion interested him more than he could ever have expected.

Jakub walked away. 'Come, Olya,' he called, and to Konrad's horror it was Anichka who answered the summons, falling into step behind her grandfather with none of the awkward gait of before. She walked fluidly, confidently, her carriage different from the Anichka he knew.

He cast around blindly, and soon saw her: another recently dispossessed ghost like himself, curled into a tight ball in a corner of the ceiling. She was doing better work than he: her spirit-self shone brightly, subject to none of the deterioration he fought in himself.

This was what it meant to be among the greatest living necromancers, he supposed. Her talents far exceeded his own there.

Master, hissed Eetapi from somewhere far too close by. *What are you doing on the ceiling?*

9

Bind me up, Konrad ordered his serpents. *I cannot do this alone.*

But, Master—

No questions! I will fray to ribbons before I can answer them.

Yes, Master.

Konrad's relief was short-lived. He discovered, by the most unpleasant means imaginable, how repulsive a process it was to be bound back to wholeness and coherence by his serpents.

I find that I have had enough of pain for the present, he said tightly as the wretches brutalised his fragile shade. It is not possible to be fractionally more gentle, I suppose?

How full of complaints you are, Master, Eetapi returned with a depressing lack of sympathy. *Had you rather be ribbons?*

Yes. Forget it, let me have oblivion—

No. That was Ootapi, cold as winter and approximately as comforting.

Konrad resigned himself, once again, to suffering.

But when the process was complete, it brought a cessation of the struggle which had, in so short a space of time, already threatened to overwhelm him. There was peace enough in that, and he felt able to relax.

A little.

Anichka uncurled herself and hung for a moment, emanating a peaceful white light. Serenity itself. Lev, she said, and streamed away floorwards.

The body of Lev Antonov had not been claimed. He lay

insensible, his face an unhealthy shade of grey. Was he breathing? Konrad trailed down after Anichka, his wits distracted and disordered by the very strangeness of his predicament. To move in so many directions at once was disorienting; no more mere forward or backward, left or right. He might now go anywhere he pleased, but could not immediately master the means.

At length, after only a little embarrassing error, he contrived to arrive at Anichka's elbow. So to speak.

You are not very good at this, are you? said Eetapi.

It is my first time as a ghost.

That is patently obvious.

Whatever Anichka was doing to Lev did not look pleasant either. His big body shuddered and convulsed, his eyes bulging from his grey face, his mouth stretching in a silent scream. But he breathed; and when, after a minute or two of this treatment, he struggled to a sitting posture and bellowed, 'Enough!' Anichka retreated with a glow of satisfaction.

His attempts to stand did not fare so well. He made it halfway, then staggered and abruptly sat back down again, shaking his head. 'I see we are vanquished.'

No! said Konrad. *This is a setback, nothing more.*

Lev looked dubiously Konrad's way. 'Have you been ghosted before?'

Never.

'Well, I have. It is no easy matter to reverse it.'

Easy. Konrad paused a moment to reflect. *I distantly remember the days when things were occasionally easy.*

Lev nodded acceptance of this unanswerable point, and regarded Anichka instead. 'What has become of the others?'

I do not know, she answered.

I think they were locked in, Konrad said. *With the buffet of bodies.*

Eetapi glowed with approval at Konrad's choice of words, which caused him instantly to regret them. You proceed apace, Master.

He did. Was it the state of having passed beyond death that dulled a person's reason and sensitivity? Then again, Konrad had not died, precisely. What was he now? Neither living nor dead nor undead? An uncomfortable state.

Anichka bore it with serenity, however, and therefore so must he.

Lev forced himself to his feet, successfully this time, and managed a creditable stagger in the direction of the door. His entourage of spirits, Konrad included, followed.

How frustrating, Konrad soon saw, to be a ghost. He outstripped Lev's pace with ease and went sailing ahead; but when he reached the threshold of the cavern in which Nanda was in all probability imprisoned, he found a closed door impeding his progress.

As a man (at the height of his powers), he need only have reached out and touched the lock, then turned the handle, and in they would go.

As a shade, he was forced to wait for Lev to perform all the action for him. Had such impotence driven Jakub mad? Then again, that man bore all the signs of having been plenty mad enough already.

You can go through it, Master, said Ootapi, demonstrating this point. *You do know that?*

Yes, he said testily, though in fact the idea had not occurred to him. *But Nanda cannot.*

Oh.

You see the difficulty.

It is an obstacle.

The locked door gave Lev pause, but only for a moment. Just as Konrad was reflecting on where Tasha, with her lockpicking skills, might have got to, Lev lifted a booted foot and delivered a shattering kick to the door. Three more achieved the objective: the wood, solid oak, held, but the hinges did not. The door fell inwards.

Several faces stared back at them from the other side. Nanda was ashen, but resolved; Alexander wore a puzzled, troubled look; Diana looked enraged.

Tasha was nowhere in evidence.

'Where is he?' said Nanda, upon beholding (as far as she could see) only Lev. 'Where's Konrad?'

'Dead,' said Lev brutally. At Nanda's appalled expression, he amended the statement to: 'In a manner of speaking.'

'Anichka?' said Diana.

'The same.'

Never had Konrad endured a greater sense of frustration than to see Nanda so distressed, and be unable even to speak to her. He tried. *Nan, I am here! Not dead. Lev exaggerates, the brute. It is true that I no longer live either, precisely, but the matter is by no means as serious as all that. Can you hear me? Nan?*

She could not, nor could she see him. Her eyes remained fixed upon Lev's face as he delivered a brief account of all that had happened since Konrad, Anichka and Lev had left the chamber. Nothing that he said appeared to ease Nanda's distress, though it did incite her fury.

Diana simmered with such anger, he could almost see it radiating from her. 'Right,' she said, tight-lipped, once Lev's account was complete. 'I have had enough of this coven.'

As had Konrad.

He lost track of the conversation thereafter, for something odd caught his eye. A flicker of movement, perhaps? Something pale, barely visible, on the far side of the room. He drifted that way to investigate.

Whatever it was whisked out of sight as he approached. Something in the movement struck him as furtive.

Come out, he said. *There is no danger here.*

No one answered, and nothing moved.

At length Konrad drifted away again, thoughtful. To Anichka he said: *I begin to think the people here are not—*

'Konrad!' yelled Tasha, rising from her recumbent posture in a single bound. 'Please explain why your miserable corpse is walking about up there without you in it.'

'He's here?' Nanda began looking about the chamber, as though she might see Konrad's dispossessed shade hovering nearby if only she tried.

'About two and a half feet from your left elbow.' Tasha favoured Konrad with a look of utter contempt. 'You're the Malykant. You're supposed to be better at this kind of thing.'

In my defence, it is an event without precedent.

'So what?'

Konrad could think of no argument to offer in reply, so he made none.

'Konrad?' said Nanda, staring nearly enough at the spot he more-or-less occupied. 'You are not dead?'

'He is not,' said Tasha. 'Though lacking a living body amounts to the same thing after a while. Take it from me, I should know.'

I intend to retrieve my miserable corpse, as you put it, said Konrad to Tasha.

'And you're making an excellent start so far — no, hang on. What are you doing floating about down here?'

Regrouping. Forming up the troops. Working out what is going on down here that makes the return of Jakub Vasilescu so important.

'And how is that going for you?'

Why don't you tell me what you discovered while you were gone?

Tasha rolled her eyes at Diana, whose mouth — to Konrad's indignation — twitched in response. 'Yes, Master. You were right about the coven. They are, for the most part, thoroughly dead. They've moved into the house.'

'What are they doing in there?' said Diana.

'As far as I can tell, they are planning a mass resurrection.'

'Of whom?' Diana's eyes narrowed.

Tasha shrugged. 'Nobody went out of their way to explain that part.'

Konrad took a look around at the bodies neatly laid out, slab by slab. *These?*

'It would appear likely,' said Tasha.

But who are they? We thought they were the coven's mortal shells but I think perhaps they are not.

Tasha surveyed the room. 'They could be. Why do you think they aren't the coven?'

The Vasilescus are highly elitist, are they not? So attached to the ancient honour and status of their family as to be urgently desirous of restoring it. And they ejected Eino's mother from the family for marrying someone they considered inferior. Look, then, at some of these bodies. They are dressed like farmers and servants. Do you think such people would be admitted to a coven led by Olya Vasilescu?

'You make some good points.' Tasha relayed the salient points of the argument to Nanda and Alexander.

'They are not victims,' said Alexander. Konrad noticed that the inspector was keeping his eyes carefully averted from the area Konrad occupied. 'They are too… intact.'

That is true, Konrad agreed. *Remember the state poor Kati Vinter was left in, and Alen Petranov?* They had both been hacked to pieces, their bodies discarded with missing limbs, heads… it had not been pretty.

'And I do not see why they would so carefully preserve the bodies of people they had slain purely to harvest… parts,' said Alexander.

Nanda said, 'If they are not coven and not the coven's victims, then… are they vassals? If they are servants, perhaps they served the

Vasilescu family in life.'

'And in death,' Diana agreed. 'But what service are they expected to perform next?'

Konrad drifted back to the spot where he had, shortly before, witnessed some kind of movement. *Will you not come out? he entreated. As you may observe, we are inclined to take your side. And we have not been well-treated by your former masters ourselves.*

It was a gamble. Konrad's ideas had run along similar lines to Nanda's; he was inclined to conclude that a lifetime of service had not been sufficient for the arrogant family that had once ruled Divoro. Servants across Assevan were often tied to the area of their birth, condemned to labour all their lives for whoever owned those lands. They could not leave. Had even death failed to release the labourers of Divoro from their toil?

A thin voice answered. *The Master says as we're to live again.*

The Master? Konrad prompted.

Some time passed, enough that Konrad thought he had lost his conversationalist again.

Then he heard, distantly: *I've to answer! What harm can it do us now? Ain't we fallen as low as can be already?*

We would like to help, Konrad offered.

After that, silence.

Then the thin voice said: *The Master, that be the old one. They say as he's ruled down here for hundreds of years.*

Jakub Vasilescu, said Konrad.

That's him. He says he and his folk will put us back into our bodies and we'll go back to the house and after that we're to set it to rights.

Konrad judged he was talking to a former housemaid, perhaps. *Are all of you to be put to this task?*

No. Some are to work the land—

As if there's much left of it, put in another, sour voice.

Aye. And there's some as never was bound in service in the first place. Them in the fine clothes. You'd think a person as has money and freedom would find something better to do with it than swear theirselves in loyalty to the likes of our lot.

Sycophants. Minor gentry or wealthy tradesmen, blinded by the apparent glamour of the grand house at Divoro and its elegant, superior, sophisticated inhabitants. What might such men and women pledge themselves to do, in return for… what? Connections, money, a place at some future table?

They mean to reign over this neighbourhood again, do they? Konrad guessed.

That and more. They say as how the Master had great plans, when he was alive, only he died before he could carry them out.

What kind of plans?

You know what gentry does.

Gentry tended to engage, primarily, in alliances — judicious intermarriages with other wealthy families could bring huge increases in wealth, land and power as the generations passed. But was that all?

'Konrad,' said Nanda, from some distance away. 'You should see this.'

A moment, Konrad excused himself, and went at once to Nanda's side. Lev, Diana, Alexander and Tasha had already gathered there when he arrived.

'He's here,' said Diana.

Nanda nodded. 'Look at this lot. What do you make of them?'

She indicated a few rows of biers with a sweep of her arm. Konrad had not inspected this particular group before, and upon doing so he found they displayed marked differences to the rest. They were all men, for one thing, and they looked to have been powerful men at that. They wore largely identical clothing: dark red coats with polished buttons, tall, sturdy boots, and square hats.

Soldiers? Konrad guessed.

'Military men,' said Tasha, both translation and confirmation.

'This is perhaps not the only such chamber down here,' said Nanda. 'There are likely more.'

'All full of soldiers?' Diana guessed.

Tasha, tell them that Jakub had major expansion plans when he was alive, and the family's lands are diminished. He might have meant to expand their territory by force.

'Army of undead soldiers,' said Tasha, having relayed this. 'Nice. They don't even need to be reanimated for all that long.'

'Few would oppose such a force,' said Alexander. 'Easy victories. But it must take a great deal to raise so many undead, no?'

'Oh, yes,' said Diana grimly. 'And now they've got themselves a Malykant's stolen shell, and the best living necromancer besides.'

Burn them, said Konrad.

Diana, Lev and even Tasha regarded him with something akin to horror. 'What?' said Diana.

Burn all these bodies. It is the quickest way to prevent their being used by the coven.

Tasha saluted him. 'I like you more and more all the time.'

Diana and Lev were not nearly so happy with him, but — having exchanged a long, speaking look between themselves — they nodded. 'You're right,' Diana said to him. 'But—'

Anichka interrupted her. *But their ghosts. They are bound to their physical forms in some way. What will become of them? Will they be destroyed?*

They must be sent on, said Konrad. *They are overdue at The Master's door as it is.*

No! The thin little voice had followed Konrad.

It is the preservation of your bodies that keeps you here, Konrad said, as soothingly as he could. Their destruction will weaken those ties, and we will do the rest.

It is not that, said the voice. *I have not breathed for fifty years. What use is dead flesh to me? But we would not be sent meekly on without our chance at revenge!*

'Interesting,' said Tasha.

How many are there who agree with you? Konrad demanded of the voice. *Show yourselves.*

There are many.

If you would oppose the coven, there can be no more hiding. Show yourselves.

The owner of the thin voice was the first to materialise. She was, at best, sixteen, Konrad judged, a spindly girl with her lank hair haphazardly bound up. Her manifestation was thin, too, and weak; so pale and translucent, Konrad could barely make out her features. But it was a brave gesture, and he applauded her in his heart. *Come on, then!* she called. *Here's our chance!*

'They will not all answer,' Lev warned. 'Some will still feel loyalty to the family.'

Largely the ones in the finer clothing, Konrad judged. Had Jakub promised them some kind of reward for their aid? *Serpents,* he called. *Where is the fox? Is she well?*

She is spying on the coven, said Eetapi.

You left her there alone?

You needed us.

Inarguable.

Watch for the rebels, please, he told them. *Those must be caught up and dispatched to The Master the moment they emerge.*

Mere moments passed before the first fell victim to the serpents, judging from the exhilarated shriek Eetapi uttered, and the strangled cry that followed from some hapless soul.

All around Konrad, the wavering shades of long-dead servants and soldiers came flickering into view. None were much stronger in appearance than the little housemaid; was this what long severance from their bodies did to a ghost? Konrad pushed away the feeling of disquiet this idea produced. The numbers were considerable, but he was not much reassured. They were weak, and had been under the coven's control for many years. What could they now do to oppose their erstwhile masters, even as a mustered force?

Alexander and Nanda might not have the eyes to see the growing army of spirits, but the inspector certainly felt them. He inched closer to Nanda, his eyes wide, visibly repressing the impulse to glance over his shoulder.

If only it had been possible to dissuade he and Nanda from coming at all. It was certainly not the inspector's field.

Right, he said to Tasha. *We burn everything.*

'And if that helpfully dispatches half our force on the spot?'

So be it. We cannot risk their being raised and turned against us — or the neighbourhood.

'Fair enough.'

'One problem,' said Lev. 'I do not like that we have been permitted to wander down here at our leisure, while the family are engaged in such important endeavours above. Why are we not considered a threat?'

I will investigate, said Anichka, breaking off her conversation with one of the many shades.

'They are planning to do something nefarious and painful to us all,' offered Tasha with a beaming smile. 'Something best carried out while we are nicely boxed up down here.'

'At the very least, they'll have stopped up the exit,' Nanda agreed.

I imagine we are supposed to be done in by the first wave of soldiers, once they begin to stir, Konrad said. *All the more reason to burn them first.*

'And how are we to get out, if the exit is blocked?' demanded Lev.

Tasha grinned. 'Methinks our glorious leader has a plan.'

Don't call me that.

'You're right, you are not at all glorious.'

Anichka returned. *The way out is filled in with rocks and snow,* she reported. *It does not look as though they expect ever to use it again.*

That gave Konrad pause. What would be the use of raising an army of undead servants and soldiers if they could not get out of the caves?

Nanda thought the same. 'I think we have missed something. Their plans cannot be so simple. Did — was it said that these spirits were promised life?'

Tasha pointed a finger at the housemaid. 'So she said.'

Nanda frowned. 'Did they mean a state of undeath, and merely applied a simpler word to the concept? Or did they mean something more akin to true life?'

Whatever they might have meant before, Konrad said slowly, *Might they not alter their ideas based on what has happened since?*

It was Diana who conveyed that thought, and added her own: 'Divoro is remote, but not that remote. And there are many houses within a radius of, say, a few miles.'

Anichka said: *How many people live hereabouts?*

Diana looked around at the litter of bodies. 'Enough. More than enough, even if there are other chambers like this one. What they have just done with Jakub, they can do with their servants, too.'

'You mean bind them into living bodies?' Alexander looked ill at the prospect.

'Exactly,' said Diana. 'How are these spirits supposed to restore the house and work the land efficiently as undead puppets? Surely they cannot. Better to grant them healthy, living bodies, even if the procedure proves only temporary. And now that they have proof such a thing can be done…'

It still does not make sense to trap us down here and stop up the exit, said Anichka. *They would need access to the spirits they wish to raise—*

They can summon us, put in the little housemaid.

Anichka stopped. How?

The housemaid's ghost flickered unhappily. *Don't you have servants? We was born here, every one of us. We served them all our lives long. We're bound here, living or dead, and if they call us, we must go.*

Alexander went suddenly rigid, his nose lifted to the air. He inhaled deeply, and began to look wildly about. 'We are a bit late, with the burning,' he said, almost conversationally. 'They have started without us.'

Nanda sniffed the air. 'Smoke. That's why we are down here. They mean to burn the lot of us.'

10

'Anichka,' said Diana. 'Did you see signs of another way out?'

None, said Anichka.

'Tasha?' Diana said crisply (did nothing rattle the woman?) 'Serpents. You've wandered these caves more than the rest of us. There must be another way out.'

There is, said Konrad.

Tasha nodded. 'It's not a good way out, but it works.'

'Get us there,' ordered Diana.

I hope you know how to find it, Konrad said to Tasha.

'Of course I do.' Tasha set off — not in the direction of the door through which they had entered, but the other way. An arch loomed in a dark corner of the cave, so well tucked away Konrad had failed to notice it.

Less promisingly, wisps of smoke drifted through it.

Tasha, the fire seems to be that way.

'The fire is all ways. This one also leads to an exit. What more do you want?'

I want my body back.

'Next on the agenda. Everybody with me?' She did not pause to check, but ducked through the low archway and disappeared into the dark passage beyond.

Konrad waited while Nanda, Alexander, Diana and Lev followed, and then trailed after them, a stream of agitated ghosts drifting in his wake. He felt numbed. He could see smoke but could not smell it; he could feel neither heat nor cold. Some help that made him.

He wondered if the spirits who had so long dwelled down here felt any regret at the imminent loss of their wasted physical forms. Probably not. How many years of severance would it take before one's own body began to seem like nothing more than an old hat or glove, once a favourite but since forgotten?

The route Tasha took was winding, and far longer than Konrad could accept with equanimity. Small comfort to him that his own body was out of the way of the fire; all the people he cared about in the world were down in these wretched caves, and it was his fault that they were here. He could not feel the gathering heat, nor could the thickening smoke clog his lungs. But he saw the smoky haze well enough, could imagine its choking effects. Nanda wrapped a length of her shawl over her face, her breathing growing shallow, and Alexander began to cough.

Tash, is it much farther?

If I could fly everybody there in an instant I would, she snapped. *Stop fussing.*

But she hastened, and said a moment later, out loud: 'Almost there.'

Another turn brought them into a different space: a rectangle of a room with squared-off walls and a floor of laid stones. A cellar. They had once speculated that another, older layer of cellars and storerooms lay beneath the sculleries and pantries of the house, and here was the proof.

Tasha marched to the back of the room, and began clawing at the wall with her nails. A block came loose; she dragged it out and hurled it to the floor, where it fell with a rumbling clatter. Nanda fell to work beside her, and soon they had made a hole large enough for a body to pass through.

'What is this place?' said Diana, muffled behind a scarf.

'Denis Druganin's cupboard of horrors,' said Tasha as she crawled inside the hole. Her voice echoed back to them. 'Complete with removable panels and all such good things. It is actually several cupboards built on top of one another, and properly arranged they make a nice chute up or down which a body might be passed. The problem is—' her voice grew fainter —'it is meant for hauling dead weights, not climbing, so I'll have to go up and pull the rest of you after. Give me a moment.'

Konrad tried not to notice the thickness of the smoke, or to reflect on its probable meaning.

He failed. *Half the passages we have just gone down must be full of fire by now. How far behind us is it?*

He checked on Nanda. She looked pale but resolute, and not at all frightened, which made him feel both proud of her and ashamed of himself. If she was afraid — and she would be mad not to be — she hid it well.

Diana, of course, looked like granite.

There came some clanking and grinding sounds from somewhere above; Tasha clambering up, he supposed, and removing obstructions. This theory was borne out by the sudden appearance of a large plank of wood that came hurtling down, and smashed upon the floor. 'Ready,' came Tasha's voice, distant and echoing weirdly. 'Somebody take the rope.'

Nanda goes first, Konrad said, *and Alexander.* He need not have. Diana spared him a faintly withering look, already pushing Nanda forward. Nan grasped the rope without hesitation, and braced her feet against the stone walls. She soon disappeared from view, hauled up by slow degrees; Konrad heard a faint squeak and a small *thud* as she hit a wall on the way up, then nothing.

'Next,' Tasha yelled.

Alexander followed, then Diana. By the time Lev's turn came, bright licks of flame were curling around the cellar door, and the smoke was so thick that Lev's breathing came in harsh gasps. Konrad gave a small, ethereal sigh of relief as the necromancer's feet vanished up the chute — much more quickly than the others had. He supposed they had all joined in with the hauling.

Only then did he realise that the room was empty save for himself, and his serpents. The shade of Anichka had wafted away up the chute some time before; but what had become of the other ghosts?

What's happened to the rest? he asked of his serpents.

They surged off, while you were clucking over Irinanda, said Eetapi.

Surged off where?

Eetapi gave the snaky equivalent of a shrug. *Up.*

Konrad surged *up* as well, just as fire erupted into the cellar room with a roar.

Get away from here, he snapped, upon finding Lev and Nanda lingering still near the cupboard. *The fire will be up here in no time.* Tasha had brought them back into the pantry in the servants' quarters —

the same room in which he had discovered the bodies of Druganin's first victims, only the week before. It was empty, dark and cold, but would not remain so for long.

'Diana's found the rest of the coven,' said Lev, striding for the door. 'They have been busy, while we were down there. What was left of the servants have been put to use. We have several new possessions in progress, courtesy of the coven, and they are being used to bring villagers in. Up in the hall.'

'Are you all right, Konrad?' said Nanda, looking about in a futile attempt to see him.

No, said Konrad. *Yes.*

Of course, she could not hear him. Nor could she feel him, not even when he wrapped his ghostly self around her and tried his best to hold tight. She sighed and walked away, following Lev into the kitchens. Konrad could only drift after.

The great hall was a scene of chaos; the more so to Konrad's eyes, for every dispossessed spirit was as clearly visible to him as their living counterparts. Jakub stood in Konrad's stolen body in the centre of the hall, Olya-as-Anichka at his side. Five others stood with them, all youngish men and women wearing the plain, uniform attire of the house's servants: these must be coven-possessed. They stood waiting, for… what?

Gathered at their backs were a host of wavering ghost-forms. These, too, had an air of expectancy. The family's former sycophants, Konrad supposed. His serpents had thinned their numbers, but not much; there were too many. Clustered in knots in the corners and strewn across the ceiling were the rest of the haunters of Divoro: the erstwhile servants, retainers and labourers so long bound to the house. Wan and weak, they were numerous but feeble; what manner of force could they muster against the might of the coven? Very little. As Konrad watched, one or two of those pallid shades flickered out altogether as their bodies burned below.

And what did Konrad have with which to oppose the coven? Himself: already bested, divested of his physical form and with it, much of the strength of his powers. Nanda and Alexander, bright minds and brave souls but poorly equipped to fight in this particular arena. Anichka and Lev and Diana: more than a match for a few of their peers, but what could they hope to achieve against so many necromancers — all far older and, in all probability, more powerful than they?

This is hopeless, he said.

Lev stood with Diana a ways back from the hall, staring in some dismay at the vision before them. 'We are not prepared for this.'

'Should have brought the whole Order,' muttered Diana.

Nanda and Alexander stood slightly to one side, conferring. 'Konrad,' she hissed softly. 'The fire. They will not expect it to spread up here. The stone walls of the cellars should have confined it. They did not think we knew of the chute, nor that we would use it.'

Good point, he said uselessly. It would take a little time for the lower levels of the house to burn through, but once that happened the fire would spread up to ground level — including the hall. It would be too late, then, to extinguish it; the whole house would likely burn.

That would damage their plans. But what to do until then? The fire would spread slowly through the stone-built and sparsely furnished kitchens and pantries. Meanwhile, Jakub and Olya Vasilescu were free to proceed.

And proceed they did. A roar of protest interrupted whatever Nanda was trying to say next. Two young men dressed in the livery of grooms marched into the hall, bearing between them a struggling youth. Their faces were hard, merciless; whatever souls powered their muscular limbs were not their own. They threw the youth down upon the cold stone floor before Jakub Vasilescu and kicked him into submission.

It happened quickly after that. A moment, no more, and the youth collapsed, boneless, like a marionette with cut strings. A fresh, screaming ghost rose from the prone corpse; the waiting host fell upon it with a cry, and tore the spirit to shreds.

Konrad swallowed.

Then the young man rose, wobbling, to his feet, his face set in the same grimly exultant lines as the two grooms. Another dead necromancer given borrowed limbs; or was it one of the waiting flunkies who had received the fresh, new body as his reward? It hardly mattered which. Jakub issued crisp orders to the youth, who received them with a nod, and went out with the two grooms.

This process was to be repeated many times over the next quarter of an hour. Konrad tried not to look too hard at his own, stolen face. He could not bear the malice, the cruelty and the obscene jubilation that he saw there. Had he ever worn those expressions?

He forced himself to think. *We have not the numbers for this,* he said.

'You think not?' muttered Lev sourly.

Where is Tasha? And Anichka?

'Tasha is somewhere in there.' Lev tilted his head in the direction of the furore in the great hall.

I am here, said Anichka from close by, making Konrad jump. She had mastered the art of near invisibility remarkably quickly. Had she taken spirit-form before? Quite possible.

If we cannot win by force we must win by trickery, Konrad said.

'Trickery.' Lev said the word in a flat, unimpressed tone.

But Anichka said, *I am listening. Have you an idea?*

I do. But we are going to need Tasha. Serpents, find her and bring her here.

He asked a great deal of them, he knew. They had fled the hall already, outnumbered and endangered by the mass of wraiths there gathered. Konrad dimly sensed them some way above, coiled into a cowed, protective knot.

Master, whined Ootapi. *They will tear us apart.*

And they might. Had Konrad not witnessed just such an occurrence moments before? *You are capable of great stealth, when you need it,* he reminded them. *Tasha is out there somewhere alone. She needs you and we need her.*

Why then do you not go, Master? hissed Eetapi.

A fair question, and Konrad had not time to argue with them about it. Perhaps he had expected enough of them already.

Steeling himself, he took a deep breath — cursing himself for a fool, upon remembering that he need not breathe anymore — and did his best to suppress the glow of his soul that must give away his presence among so many spectres.

I will go, said Anichka.

'Go where?' said Tasha, coming up behind Konrad.

Where have you been? Fear and frustration made Konrad shout. He had just been about to plunge himself into great danger on her behalf.

'In there.' Tasha nodded her head at the hall. 'And other places. What, were you about to go after me? I am flattered.' She grinned, her usual cheeky expression, but the salute she gave him was a shade less ironic than usual.

All right, Konrad said ungraciously. *What did you find out?*

'They are a lot stronger than we are.'

You think?

Tasha nodded gravely. 'I am glad you didn't go in. They would rip you to pieces in seconds.'

Encouraging.

'So! I recommend we don't fight them.'

I had a mind to indulge in a spot of fakery.

'You have my attention.'

Konrad outlined his plan.

To his dismay, Tasha laughed. 'But you hate pageantry.'

Yes.

'Right.' She relayed his ideas to Nanda and Alexander, both of whom, he was gratified to see, fell in with the plan at once.

'A little blasphemy never hurt anybody,' said Nanda.

Alexander developed a pained look. 'What would you say are the chances of my being smited from on high?'

'Acceptable,' said Tasha.

'Acceptable for whom, you or me?'

Diana gave a wintry smile. 'Let it be known that our Malykant is fully deranged and his word ought not to be trusted.'

Alexander blinked. 'I see.'

'Are you still prepared to go ahead with it?' She fixed the inspector with a gimlet eye.

'For some reason, I am.'

'Excellent. I shall bear any unfavourable consequences that might arise from… certain quarters.'

'Good of you,' said Alexander faintly.

Nan? said Konrad. He was asking a great deal of her, too.

'I am with you,' she said. 'As always.'

Konrad permitted himself a moment's heartglow.

'Right,' said Diana. 'Tasha, you and I and Martita are with Konrad and the inspector. Anichka, Lev and the serpents, with Nanda. That ought to be sufficient?'

I think so, said Konrad.

'Then we go.' Diana stepped farther away from the door, tucking herself into a shadowed corner.

Then, to Konrad's utter astonishment, she collapsed. Not gracefully, in an elegant swoon. She fell like a tree, and her spirit rose, shimmering, into the air.

Tasha whistled. 'Not even I saw that one coming.'

You are lamaeni?! Konrad's mind reeled.

The shade of Diana chuckled. *Who better to lead The Malykt's Order? Or did you think it was because of my good looks and ineffable charm?*

Konrad, perhaps wisely, made no response.

11

It began as a glittering black forest, creeping in icy fingers across the ceiling of the great hall. Scarcely noticeable; just a deepening chill and a darkening of the gloom. A slow blossoming at first, soon pitch hoarfrost raced down the walls and carpeted the stone floor, spreading in eerie fractals radiating an otherworldly cold.

Then the voices began. A babble of distant distress, they grew nearer, louder and more insistent. Frigid whispers emerged, the sort that echo through the bones and set the teeth on edge.

If the hoarfrost escaped the notice of the coven and its followers, the voices did not — especially when they began, as one, to scream. Jakub Vasilescu, barking orders to his coven and gesturing with Konrad's expressive hands, broke off.

Olya, in Anichka's form, paled and stared, aghast, at the frost-blackened ceiling. 'This — this is not — who is that? This is unnecessary! Be still at once.'

Her words were barely audible in the tumult.

Jakub interjected with a roar. 'SILENCE!' He stood tall, wreathed in power and dark magic, radiating authority. If ever there was a vision of man who expected obedience without question, here was he.

The screaming only intensified. The cacophony had abandoned words, and exhibited their distress in a stream of incomprehensible babble, at piercing volume. The wordless tumult emanated from the walls, from the stones set into the floor, from the air itself. The shades of the coven and their followers, so confident moments before, faltered now, and shrank closer to one another.

The servant-wraiths vanished altogether.

Just when Konrad judged the senseless howls had done their work, came then a radiant light streaming through the wide-open double doors. No mere daylight, this, as of a pale sun rising; white, clear light blazed, intense as core-fire, setting the carpet of hoarfrost sparkling with a scintillating light to dazzle the eyes.

Jakub faltered, and took a step back.

In the midst of that light appeared a figure in silhouette. A woman, impossibly tall, statuesque, wreathed in an effulgence too bright to look into. She paused there some time, as her light filtered into every corner of the dark hallway.

When she spoke, the cacophony of voices fell silent in respect.

What manner of desecration is this? whispered she, and her voice echoed.

Jakub drew himself up, though it cost him a visible effort. 'Eject this woman,' he barked.

His host of ghostly followers gathered themselves up, and... hesitated.

For the lady was attended not only by a bright, cleansing light, but by warmth and vibrancy as well. A greenish glow threaded its way into the clear white light; not the sickly green of ill-health but the vivid hue of fresh, new growth. Frost melted under its onslaught, replaced by unfurling tendrils and budding leaves.

Beautiful, Nan, Konrad breathed.

Around him he heard hushed whispers building: once someone had uttered that one, crucial word, *Shandrigal,* it was taken up and repeated all over the hall. *The Shandrigal. It cannot be? The Shandrigal!*

Right, then, Konrad murmured. *Time to terrify the life out of them.*

When the attention of everyone in the hall was fixed upon the vision of The Shandrigal descended upon Divoro, a blast of freezing air emanated from somewhere above, driving back all the gentle warmth Nanda had (somehow) brought with her. The wraiths fell back as one. This time, the babble of distressed voices were theirs.

The cold intensified. Jakub and Olya began to shiver, teeth gritted, baleful gaze turned upwards.

Down came The Malykt.

He manifested as little more than a shadow, barely man-shaped, His frame wreathed in roiling darkness. The killing cold of deep winter radiated from His form; a dark sound, like a mirthless laugh, made the walls shake and sent ice dripping down the walls.

What desecration is this? He said, a low, dire rumble; with every syllable, fresh frost bloomed. Ice crept up the feet and legs of those left alive, and blossomed across their faces.

Jakub's nerve fractured. He stared up at the descending vision with fear in Konrad's stolen eyes, shivering so violently in the wintry cold that his teeth chattered. 'My Lord,' gasped he. 'We — I — I am Your servant!'

You are no servant of Mine. You have wrested my true servant from Me. Dare you stand before Me in his stolen form, and call yourself My own?

Konrad could just detect the inspector's intonation in the words, cloaked though his every utterance was in eerie echo, and impossibly amplified. Tasha and Diana, bodiless and hidden, held him aloft. The serpents wreathed Nanda's form in radiance; Diana's arctic fox melded herself with the inspector, lending him all her ethereal powers.

The effect, Konrad felt, was impressive.

The Malykt spoke again. *You have displeased Me, and shall suffer My wrath.* The shadows around Alexander deepened as he began, inexorably, to descend, Jakub Vasilescu his target.

From the doorway, Nanda said, in her Shandrigal's whisper, *So too shall I express My displeasure.* She took a step forward, and another, and the light moved with her, keeping her an indistinct silhouette.

Olya stared from one to the other, her face a rictus of fear.

But something… something happened. Her eyes narrowed; she looked, again, from The Malykt to The Shandrigal, and her fear faded. 'Remember!' she barked. 'They do not manifest. Not ever. Is it not known that They do not?'

Damnit, Konrad muttered. She was right: no credible tale of a manifestation by either Great Spirit had ever been reported. Why should such powers condescend to show Themselves? He had been counting on the coven's being too disturbed for such clear reflection.

But Olya's words had their effect. The coven members flanking Jakub, gathered for a little while into a frightened knot, now separated, and drew themselves up. A few converged upon Nanda.

'Who, then, are you?' hissed Jakub, glowering upon the suspended form of Alexander some several feet above his head.

Emboldened, the swarm of wraiths closed in upon the inspector.

NO! shouted Konrad. *Stand firm, Alexander!*

They must not be permitted to reach the inspector, or Nanda. Desperate, Konrad reached for his Malykant's powers — something he had not dared do since the loss of his body. Those powers were woven into his being, body and soul. Well, body and soul were parted, fracturing his identity as the Malykant. If he called, would anything answer?

No. He reached and strained and nothing came. He was a mere ghost after all, divested of everything that had ever made him the Malykant. As feeble as those pallid shades who had, so easily, fallen victim to the machinations of the Divoro coven. Ineffectual. Helpless.

Nanda stood tall and unafraid, and her light brightened to the eye-watering radiance of a small sun. *Do you dare approach Me?* She uttered, unfazed.

Her assailants barely hesitated. Two reached for her; Nanda flowed away, evading their grip with ease.

But in so doing, she gave herself away. What need would The Shandrigal have to dodge? Several more converged upon her; she could not evade them all.

'Bring that one down here,' barked Jakub, and the host of wraiths swooped upon Alexander.

Konrad! Diana's voice lanced through his mind. *He will not answer me.*

He? Did she mean Alexander, Lev, or… or The Malykt?

Ah.

Konrad gathered himself, and screamed his frustration. He put every shred of his severed soul into the cry, sent it soaring into the aether, into the spirit planes and beyond.

It cost him dearly. He had not the might for such a gambit, not now, nor had the serpents the strength to hold him bound under it. His spirit weakened, fractured and split; shards of himself broke into ribbons and flowed away. He would break up entirely, dissolve into nothing but whispers and memories, and nothing would or could bring him back.

So be it. He screamed and screamed—

—and, abruptly, stopped, the sound cut off as sharply as a door closing.

Fear swamped him, a bone-deep terror that bereft him of words, of thoughts, of everything. He cowered, mindless with dread. Bodiless, it was so much worse…

Time slowed.

Yes, said a freezing, and too familiar, voice. *Done.* The words scattered his wits anew. He waited, trembling, for the end; his last thought was for Nanda. *Take care of her.* He knew no one would hear him, not now.

The light vanished, sounds faded, and Konrad's wandering shade uttered one last sigh.

Then came the cold.

'Konrad.'

Some indecipherable amount of time later, consciousness dawned. Slowly. Painfully.

Painfully.

Konrad permitted one eye to open a crack.

'Alive,' Tasha reported. Restored to her physical body, she was leaning over him. He appeared to be occupying a recumbent posture upon the floor, for hers was not the only anxious face looking down upon his. Nanda was there, too, and Alexander, and Diana. Above them hovered a distant ceiling, still dark with black ice.

He croaked something incoherent.

'Yes, we are happy too,' said Tasha, and patted him on the shoulder.

He felt it.

'Good,' said Diana, and withdrew. He heard her say something to someone else a moment later, and Lev's voice answered. Then Anichka's.

Konrad lifted his hands and stared at them in wonder. There they were, both of them, in the flesh: his own fingers, all ten of them. His own, brown skin, hale and healthy.

He reached out to Nanda's face, and felt soft skin under his fingertips.

'But,' he said after a while. 'Why am I alive?'

'Diana,' said Nanda, with a faint smile. 'Did… something, to Jakub. He is gone.'

'Vapour,' said Tasha, waving her fingers expressively to indicate dispersal.

'Olya, too,' Nanda went on. 'And, apparently, the rest of them.'

She pointed.

Konrad turned his head, wincing as his neck muscles cramped. Still bodies lay across the floor like a litter of discarded coats, emptied of the shades that had possessed them. Whatever had become of their own souls, Konrad could not determine. It did not seem fair or just that he had been restored to his own limbs, and they had not.

Done, had said the Master. Some kind of deal was struck upon that syllable. What had it been? Konrad had offered himself in exchange for the safety of Nanda and Alexander. He had gone gladly into the cold. Why, then, was he alive?

He did not think it fit to correct Nanda's mistake. Let her attribute the vanquishing of the Vasilescus to Diana, if she would. It was a less… difficult explanation.

Then again, was it a mistake? Nanda's eyes held his, and he fathomed a number of unfathomable things from their expression. He thought of the warmth and the growth Nanda had summoned into the hall not long before. The Shandrigal's handmaiden she was; how far was she permitted to borrow her Mistress's power? She knew full well what was possible for a woman in Diana's position, and what ought not to be.

Konrad looked at Alexander. 'You were magnificent.'

The inspector actually blushed. 'A pity it could not quite carry the day.'

'Came damned close, though.' Konrad sat up, and gave an involuntary squawk of pain as every muscle he possessed went into revolt. What had Jakub done? It was like lending out a hat and getting it back, battered and broken and barely fitting anymore.

Well, not lending out. Losing a hat to a thieving devil of a man. Ordinarily, one did not expect to get the hat back.

Konrad began to shiver.

'Everything is… well?' he said, glancing about. Were the wraiths gone, or was he simply unable to see them anymore?

'Largely,' said Diana, reappearing.

'Oh,' said Konrad, as his eye fell upon the far door. 'Not quite.' Smoke poured in from the corridor beyond, his nostrils suddenly full of the acrid scent of burning wood. A flame darted over the threshold, then another.

'Time to go.' Tasha hauled him ruthlessly to his feet. He swayed, gritting his teeth against a strong desire to vomit.

Nanda ducked under his shoulder, holding him up. 'Do *not* throw up,' she ordered him. 'This is my favourite gown.'

'No, ma'am,' he agreed.

12

Konrad had not expected to feel regret, upon driving away from the beleaguered house at Divoro. He had felt nothing but dread at the prospect of returning to it. Why, then, should he deplore the fire that tore through its ancient halls, and would, soon enough, reduce it to naught but a blackened shell?

Perhaps it was the tragedy of it. It had been a place of haunting, if slightly mad, beauty, a unique structure whose potential had been corrupted and destroyed. The house itself could not help its inhabitants.

The same could be said for some of its scions. Had Denis Druganin been born elsewhere, to another family, would even he have been so much a monster? Perhaps, perhaps not. Evil so often begat still more depravity.

Or was it merely that it destroyed whatever least resembled itself?

Konrad enjoyed a day's rest upon his return to Ekamet, time of which he made the fullest use by remaining in bed. The choice was not absolutely his own. As grateful as he was to be restored to the full use of his own, familiar limbs, the severance was not so easily reversible as he had hoped. Every time he attempted to rise from his bed, he was instantly assailed with a sense of ill-fitting wrongness, as though he had put his coat on backwards. Had The Malykt stuffed his soul back in inside out, or upside down? The possibility appalled him. Better to sleep it off.

The day following demanded much more of him, for it was the designated day of Eino Holt's funeral — and that of his mother and closest friends. Had it been only his own convenience to consider, he might have been tempted to stay away. Had he not paid his respects already, in more direct fashion than attending their farewell rites?

But Nanda would be there, of course. He would not leave her to bear so melancholy an event unattended. So, come the first light of morning, he grimly hauled himself from the warmth of his blankets and endeavoured to dress.

Serpents, he said after a while. *I may need your help.*

Eetapi uncoiled herself from the light fitting and drifted down. *Yes, Master?*

The problem is… Konrad clung to the door of his closet, his head spinning. *I cannot seem quite to remain upright.*

He felt Eetapi's scrutiny as a feather-light touch, whisking through whatever passed for his thoughts that morning. *What do you wish me to do?*

Can you… I hardly know. Hold me together? It is like being drunk, only without the pleasant aspects.

Poor Master, you are soul-drunk. It is an affliction that can be remedied.

Konrad rejoiced to hear that. *And how is it—*

Words dissolved in a sharp cry of pain, for Eetapi's idea of medicine turned out to be characteristically brutal. With the sensation of a coach, say, or perhaps a small house, slamming full-tilt into Konrad's cringing psyche, his obliging serpent forcibly knocked his spirit into shape.

He stood, head reeling, for about three seconds before he slowly sank to the floor.

Thank you, I think.

I am here to serve. With which words, Eetapi returned to hanging from the lights.

Slowly, painfully, Konrad dressed himself.

The coven of Divoro's victims were to be cremated. Those whose remains had been salvageable, that was; many had burned with the house. Konrad thanked his stars that he had not had to witness the bringing-down of the Holts, and Lilli Lahti, and Marko Bekk, from their ice-palace of a mausoleum. The indignity of their treatment still rankled. What a pity that he had already delivered retribution to Denis Druganin, and that the coven's leaders had been dealt with by a higher power. For such brutality, somebody ought to pay. He hoped that his Master was making their after-lives duly miserable.

Of course He was.

Druganin's cremation had already occurred; Diana had personally overseen the burning herself. Whatever weird power had led the corpse to open and shut his eyes… well, it was no more. A mystery Konrad was happy to leave behind.

He arrived at The Malykt's temple unattended, save by his serpents. Eetapi and Ootapi had flatly refused to be left behind, a funeral being their idea of a carnival. *Behave yourselves,* he ordered, and suffered the instant mortification of seeing Eetapi go sailing loop-the-loop over the heads of the gathered mourners, cackling with glee.

Fortunate that few would witness these antics beside himself.

One of those few was Diana, who intercepted him the moment he stepped into the funeral hall. 'Konrad,' she murmured. 'Feeling restored?'

'Somewhat.' He tried not to grimace as he spoke, with only modest success.

She nodded. 'Good. I would have words with you, after.'

Words. He studied her face, in hopes of receiving some clue as to the extent of the disaster, but she was impassive as always. 'Very well,' he said neutrally.

Diana patted him on the shoulder, an oddly motherly gesture, and departed. It was not at all like Diana Valentina to be motherly. His apprehension grew.

Nanda and Alexander were seated together, at the front of the assembly. To his pleasure, they separated upon his approach, leaving a seat free between them. Nanda awarded him a smile, and laid a hand briefly against his forehead. 'Functional, I see.'

'Mostly, thanks to my miserable minions. Actually, just Eetapi. Ootapi must have drawn the short straw, and had only to watch while his sister did the brutalising.'

Nanda smirked. 'If it worked, then today I am in favour of your being knocked about.'

'Thank you.' Konrad looked with some interest at Alexander. He had suffered some disquiet on the inspector's account, during the hours he had spent prone in bed. Nanda he worried about as a matter of course, but only up to a point. Had she not proved and proved herself more than equal to anything? But Alexander was more used to quieter, less horrific doings. Detective he was, and no stranger to murder, but his investigations were more usually conducted from the relative safety of his offices, or the wide streets of Ekamet, and he typically dealt with lesser horrors. Poor fortune, that his growing friendship with Konrad should put him in the way of the very worst that life — or death — had to offer.

'Savast,' said Alexander, eyeing him back. 'Is there something on your mind? Besides, that is, all of this.' He indicated the assembled mourners, the four coffins, and the ceremonial servants of The Malykt with a flick of a finger.

Konrad dispensed with polite caution in favour of truth. 'I am wondering how much damage our escapades have done to your poor soul.'

Alexander's lips twitched. 'Some. Certainly a little, possibly a lot.'

'I am sorry for it.'

'I believe I chose to attend you.'

'You could not have known what it would entail.'

'No.' Alexander retrieved his pipe from a pocket of his coat and sat turning it about in his hands. 'But is that not essentially true of all choices, even familiar ones?'

'So it is.'

'Stop fussing,' murmured Nanda. 'Or clucking, as your charming serpents put it. You are not responsible for every bad thing that happens, Konrad.'

In a way, he was. It was his job; if not to prevent terrible events, then to — to settle their accounts, to balance for them. He opened his mouth to say some of this.

'No,' said Nanda, cutting him off. 'It is a form of egotism, you know, to take responsibility for too much. I am sorry to tell you, but you are not that special.'

Konrad had to smile. Typical Nanda-style comfort; why did such barbed words soothe him so well? Perhaps because she was right.

Diana led the ceremony herself, an unusual choice. Did Eino and Alina, Lilli and Marko know, wherever they were, what honour was afforded them by The Malykt's Order? He supposed not, but it comforted him and it comforted Nanda. At least now, he could attend the burning of their vacated bodies with a sense of peace. Justice had been delivered for them — in slightly unusual ways, perhaps, but justice nonetheless. Their tormentors had been bested, dismantled and destroyed, and the ancestral house Alina had so despised was gone, and all its history of horrors with it. They could rest easy.

As for him…

The ceremony over, he excused himself immediately to go in search of Diana.

'Is something wrong?' Nanda asked, alerted by some small sign, though he had thought himself tolerably composed.

'Audience with Diana,' he murmured. 'I fear it will not be a pleasant one.'

'We'll wait for you.' That was Alexander. Nanda nodded her agreement.

He wanted to wave them on, to tell them it was nothing, let them go about their business. But that they would stay, and wait, and be here when he was finished, was… comforting. 'Thank you,' he said.

Nanda gave him a shove. 'Time to be brave.'

He found Diana in her private room, two levels beneath the main temple floor. It had none of the grandeur one might expect of a chamber set aside for the sole, personal use of the Order's supreme head. Barely six feet square, it possessed a desk, an upholstered arm chair, a thick, dark red rug, and an array of lamps throwing out a bright, steady light. Upon opening the door, he found Diana ensconced in the chair. No, ensconced sounded too regal. *Sagged* would better describe her weary posture. When she beheld Konrad, the predominant impression he received from her was one of infinite tiredness.

'You are not going to enjoy this conversation,' she told him, gesturing for him to close the door.

'I know.'

'Neither am I.'

He nodded, uncertain, and remained standing near the door.

Diana passed a hand across her face, and sighed. 'You have lately struggled with your role, I think.'

'I…' Konrad wet his lips, and swallowed. 'I have performed my duties as normal, I think? I have… there have been no significant failures.'

'I do not criticise the performance of your duties. You are an effective and efficient Malykant. I merely observe that it has been noticeably harder for you to do so. The strain of the role is taking its toll, as it must upon all who take up this particular mantle. It is a cruel duty.'

Konrad, unsure how to respond, remained silent.

'You have lasted as our Malykant for rather longer than is the average,' she said. 'And that is so much to your credit. You have also retained a strong sense of duty throughout, and — still more to your credit — kept a hold of your wits, too. I do not know if you are aware how rare that is.'

'I… know little about my predecessors,' Konrad admitted. 'For some reason, nobody wants to talk to me about them.'

'Because it is a dark and difficult history. Fully half the Malykants of the last century have gone mad. Did you know of that? To behave, day in, day out, with such ruthlessness, such violence… it changes a person, whatever the motive. You are unusual in having so balanced and healthy a perspective, even after years in the role.' So complimentary were her words; why then were her eyes so cold? 'Nonetheless, I believe the time has come for you to relinquish these duties.'

'I… w-what?'

Her expression, at last, softened. Fractionally. 'I like you, Konrad. I do not wish to see you go the way of… of so many of the others. I do not wish to watch you break.'

'I am not broken!' His fists clenched; he leaned back against the door, for fear that his knees might give out. Shock weakened every muscle. 'You cannot retire me. Please.'

'You are not broken. Not yet. But you will be, if you go on for much longer. And I like you too much to permit it, Konrad.'

Bitterly, he shook his head. 'Like me. Well, thank you. That means a lot.'

Diana sighed, and dismissed him with a wave of her hand. 'I am sorry. I know that this will look different to you.'

About to stagger out into the cold, Konrad hesitated. 'Have you… have you already recommended my retirement to The Master?'

Diana met his gaze squarely. 'Yes. I have.'

It was over, then. Konrad bowed his head, unwilling to let her witness his sense of utter defeat. He fumbled with the door handle, got the door open somehow, and all but fell into the corridor beyond.

'Take care, Konrad,' said Diana.

He did not trouble to muster a reply.

'I do not understand,' said Alexander a little later. 'If she is so happy with your work, why retire you?'

'Who knows,' Konrad sighed. 'I am, perhaps, an anomaly. They do not know what to make of me, so fall back upon — statistics. I have already lasted longer than almost any other Malykant before me, therefore: I must be nearing the end of my usefulness.'

They had retired to Bakar House, and Konrad's cosiest parlour. A fire roared in the grate; a sad necessity, since the ordinarily comforting flames brought to mind the devastation at the Vasilescu House. Still, at least it was warm. Nanda occupied her favourite chair, her hands wrapped around a cup of chocolate. Alexander sat, rather less at his ease, near the fire, looking not so much out of place in so luxurious an apartment as a man who felt out of place. Konrad hoped he might come to get over that feeling, given time.

'If she is concerned for you,' Nanda said, 'I can well understand that.'

Naturally she could, for had her own mistress, The Shandrigal, not sent her into Konrad's life in the first place for similar reasons? Nan had arrived as his personal anchor to humanity (though unbeknownst to him at the time). And she had served that role admirably. If he was saner than the average Malykant at this stage of his career, much of that must be attributable to Nanda's presence. Surrounded as he was by death, Nan reminded him what life was like. What love was for.

Apparently, it had not been enough.

'Unfortunately,' he said, with another sigh, 'I could not fairly tell her that she was wrong. I have been… struggling. Ever since I was restored to full feeling.' He often missed those days when he had felt so little. Everything had been simpler, easier, less painful.

But that, of course, was the problem. Killing should never be easy, or painless. That was how monsters were made. Had he been muted for too long? Was the fact that he had needed such intervention part of the reason for his retirement now? A Malykant who felt too little was a liability; so was a Malykant who felt too much.

Nanda laid a hand on his arm. 'Shall you mind so much? It has been clear to me for some time that you have not relished the role.'

'You could join me,' suggested Alexander, with a half-apologetic smile. 'The life of a police detective is nowhere near so dramatic or prestigious, of course, and it does not come with half so many perks.' He glanced about at the expensively furnished parlour as he spoke. 'But you are an excellent detective, and in joining us you can retain some semblance of your present life.'

Konrad looked from Alexander to Nanda. 'Have I been unclear? I will have no opportunity to join you, Alexander, though I thank you for the offer.'

Nanda frowned. 'I do not understand.'

'No one simply resigns as the Malykant. One does not so much retire, as one *is retired*.'

Nanda's face darkened. 'You cannot mean…'

'I do. It would be dangerous and troublesome to have former Malykants littered about the city, bereft of a job, wits gone begging, possibly as monstrous as those they used to prey upon. They must be cleared away. The role of Malykant is only passed on when the current incumbent dies.' He knew this, because it had been made clear to him when he had accepted the role himself. At the time, the prospect of his eventual death had been distant enough not to unduly worry him.

Things were different now.

'They would not… she would not…' Nanda stared at him, white-faced.

'Kill me? No, no. They are not so ruthless as all that. But when next I am killed, I will not be coming back.'

Supposing, of course, that The Malykt accepted Diana's recommendation to retire him. The final decision naturally lay with The Master. But Konrad could not shake a settled sense of disquiet about the business. He recalled, with cruel clarity, the single word his Master had spoken: *Done*. What had been done? What had he offered? Had Diana already broached the subject of his retirement by then? Had The Malykt, in essence, accepted Konrad's soon-to-be-delivered death in exchange for immediate assistance? He feared so. He had, half voluntarily and half otherwise, promised soon to die, and The Malykt had granted the idea His approval.

Nanda was silent for some time. He was encouraged to see the horror drain out of her face; but it was replaced with that stern resolve she displayed whenever she set out to do something bordering upon the impossible. 'Then we shall have to look after you,' she said.

'Indeed,' said Alexander. 'The best way to avoid a permanent demise is not to die at all, no?'

'Easier said than done,' Konrad murmured, thinking back, with a strong shudder, over the several deaths he had suffered over the course of his career.

'Nothing worth fighting for was ever easy,' said Nanda firmly. 'We will keep you alive, if you promise to be less reckless.'

'I can try. It is a dangerous job—'

'*Promise*, Konrad,' said Nanda fiercely. 'I don't care what Diana says, I absolutely refuse to let you die.'

'But.' Konrad paused, struggling to force the terrible words past his lips. 'What if she is right? What if I will… break? Go mad? Become a monster?'

'I refuse to let you break either. You have something those other Malykants probably did not, Konrad. We love you too much to let you fall apart.' Nanda gripped his hand. It hurt, but it was a small, welcome pain.

Konrad swallowed something that absolutely was not a lump in his throat. 'Thank you.'

ALSO BY CHARLOTTE E. ENGLISH:

THE MALYKANT MYSTERIES:

Death's Detective (Volume 1)
Death's Avenger (Volume 2)

THE DRAYKON SERIES:

Draykon
Lokant
Orlind
Llandry
Evastany

THE LOKANT LIBRARIES:

Seven Dreams

THE DRIFTING ISLE CHRONICLES:

Black Mercury

Printed in Great Britain
by Amazon

76185315R00234